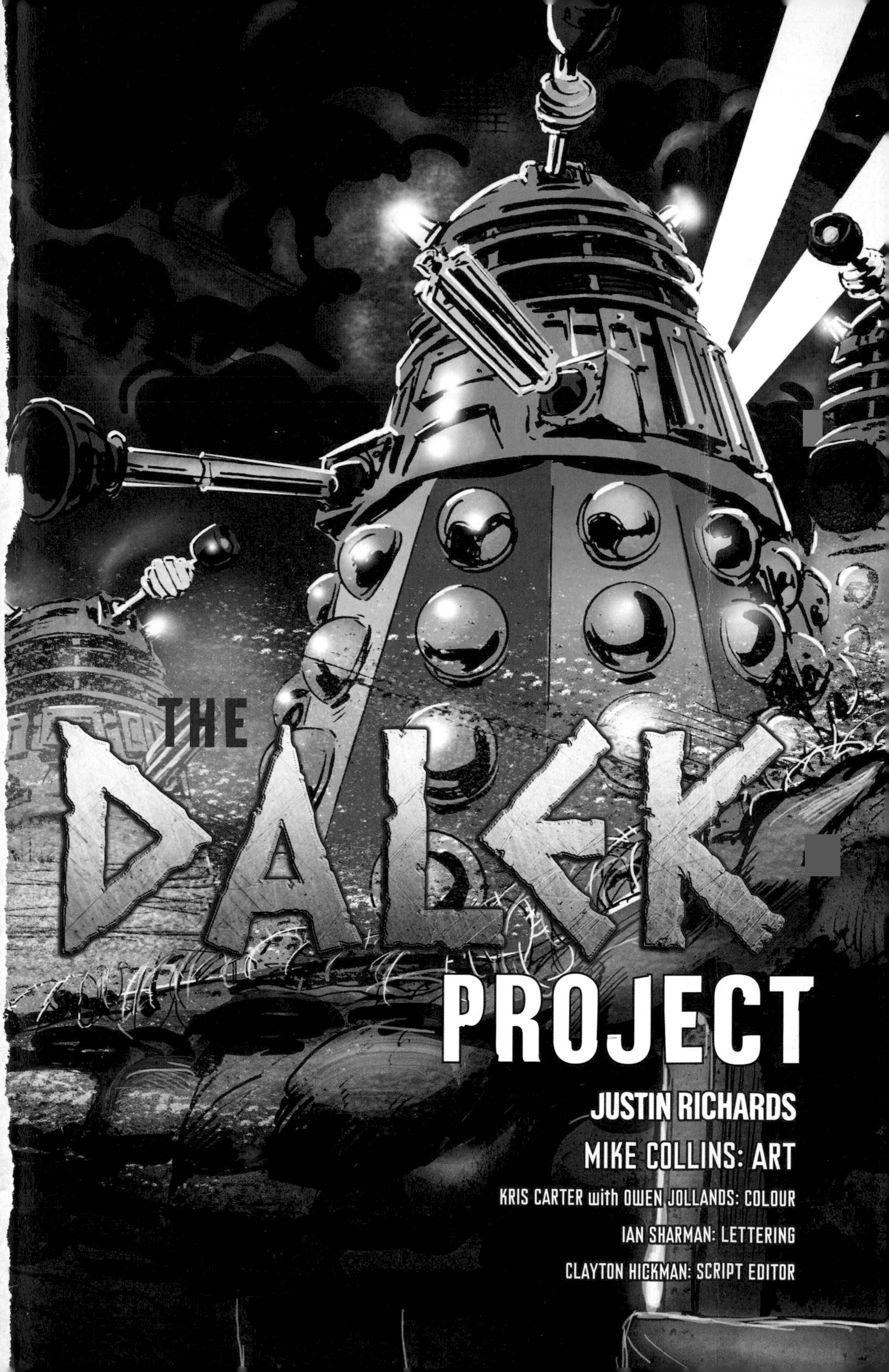
THE
DALEK
PROJECT
JUSTIN RICHARDS
MIKE COLLINS: ART
KRIS CARTER with OWEN JOLLANDS: COLOUR
IAN SHARMAN: LETTERING
CLAYTON HICKMAN: SCRIPT EDITOR

PROJECT

1 3 5 7 9 10 8 6 4 2

Published in 2012 by BBC Books, an imprint of Ebury Publishing.
A Random House Group Company

The Random House Group Limited Reg. No. 954009
Addresses for companies within the Random House Group
can be found at www.randomhouse.co.uk

A CIP catalogue record for this book is available from the
British Library.

ISBN 978 1846077555

Commissioning editor: Albert DePetrillo
Editorial manager: Nicholas Payne
Series consultant: Justin Richards
Cover design: Mike Collins & Two Associates © Woodlands
Books Ltd, 2012
Design: Lee Binding @ tea-lady.co.uk
Production: Phil Spencer

Printed and bound by Firmengruppe APPL, aprinta druck,
Wemding, Germany.

To buy books by your favourite authors and register for offers,
visit www.randomhouse.co.uk

For Julian and Chris - both huge graphic novel fans. Sorry, guys,
but Batman isn't in this one.

And for Gary Russell - colleague, advocate, and friend.

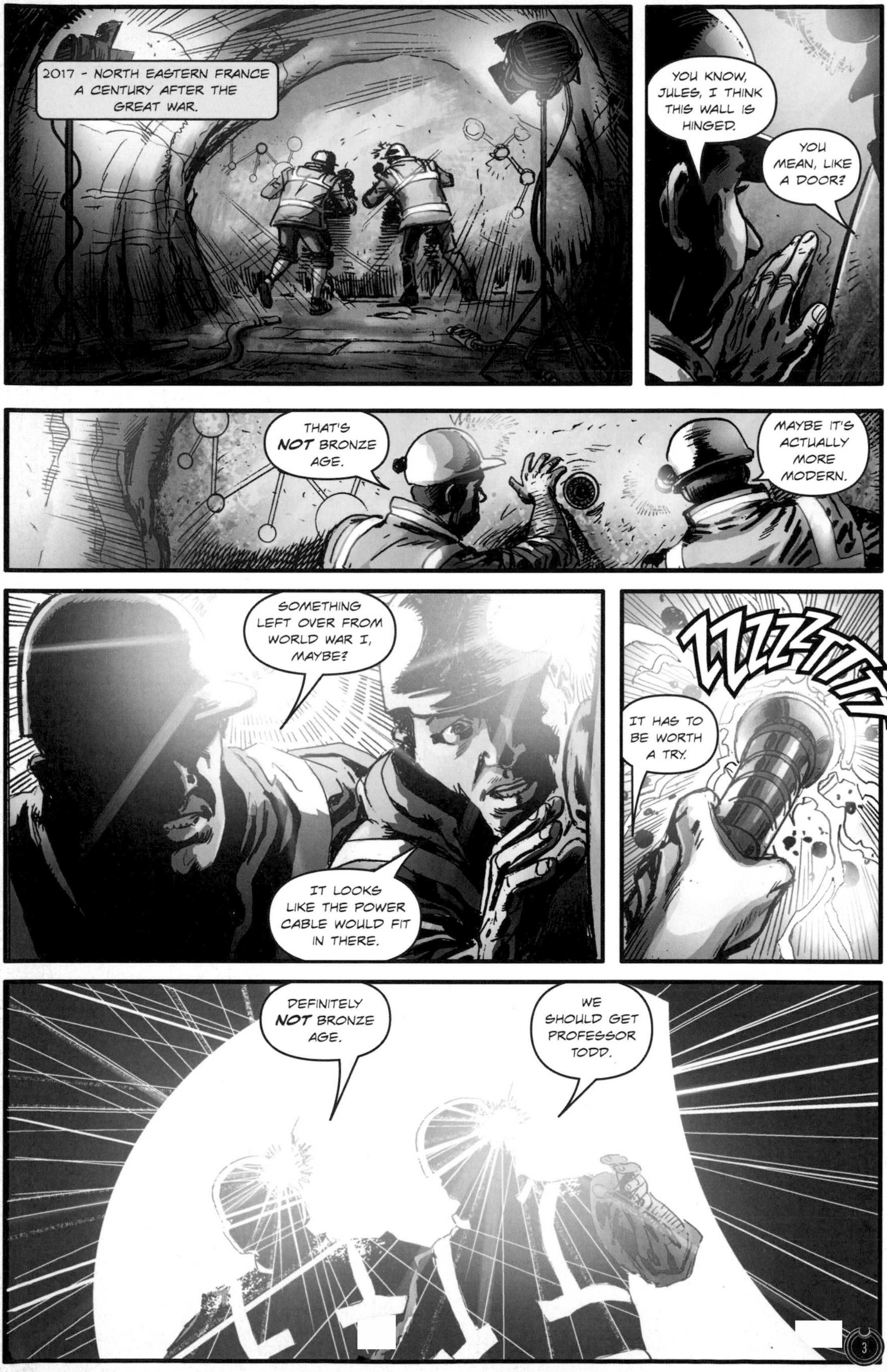
2017 - NORTH EASTERN FRANCE
A CENTURY AFTER THE
GREAT WAR.
YOU KNOW, JULES, I THINK THIS WALL IS HINGED.
YOU MEAN, LIKE A DOOR?
THAT'S **NOT** BRONZE AGE.
MAYBE IT'S ACTUALLY MORE MODERN.
SOMETHING LEFT OVER FROM WORLD WAR I, MAYBE?
IT LOOKS LIKE THE POWER CABLE WOULD FIT IN THERE.
IT HAS TO BE WORTH A TRY.
ZZZZZTTTT
DEFINITELY **NOT** BRONZE AGE.
WE SHOULD GET PROFESSOR TODD.

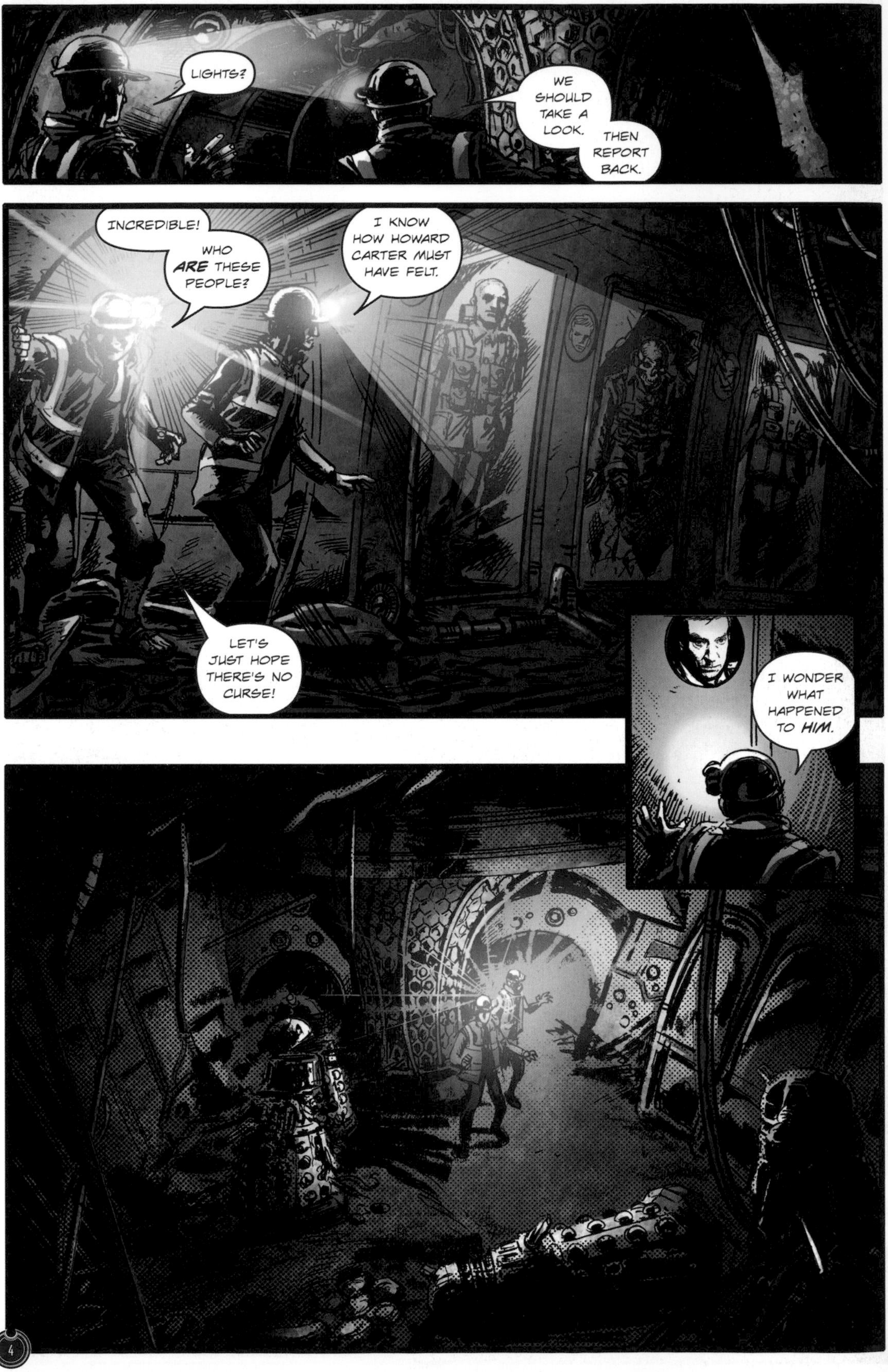
LIGHTS?
WE SHOULD TAKE A LOOK.
THEN REPORT BACK.
INCREDIBLE!
WHO **ARE** THESE PEOPLE?
I KNOW HOW HOWARD CARTER MUST HAVE FELT.
LET'S JUST HOPE THERE'S NO CURSE!
I WONDER WHAT HAPPENED TO **HIM**.

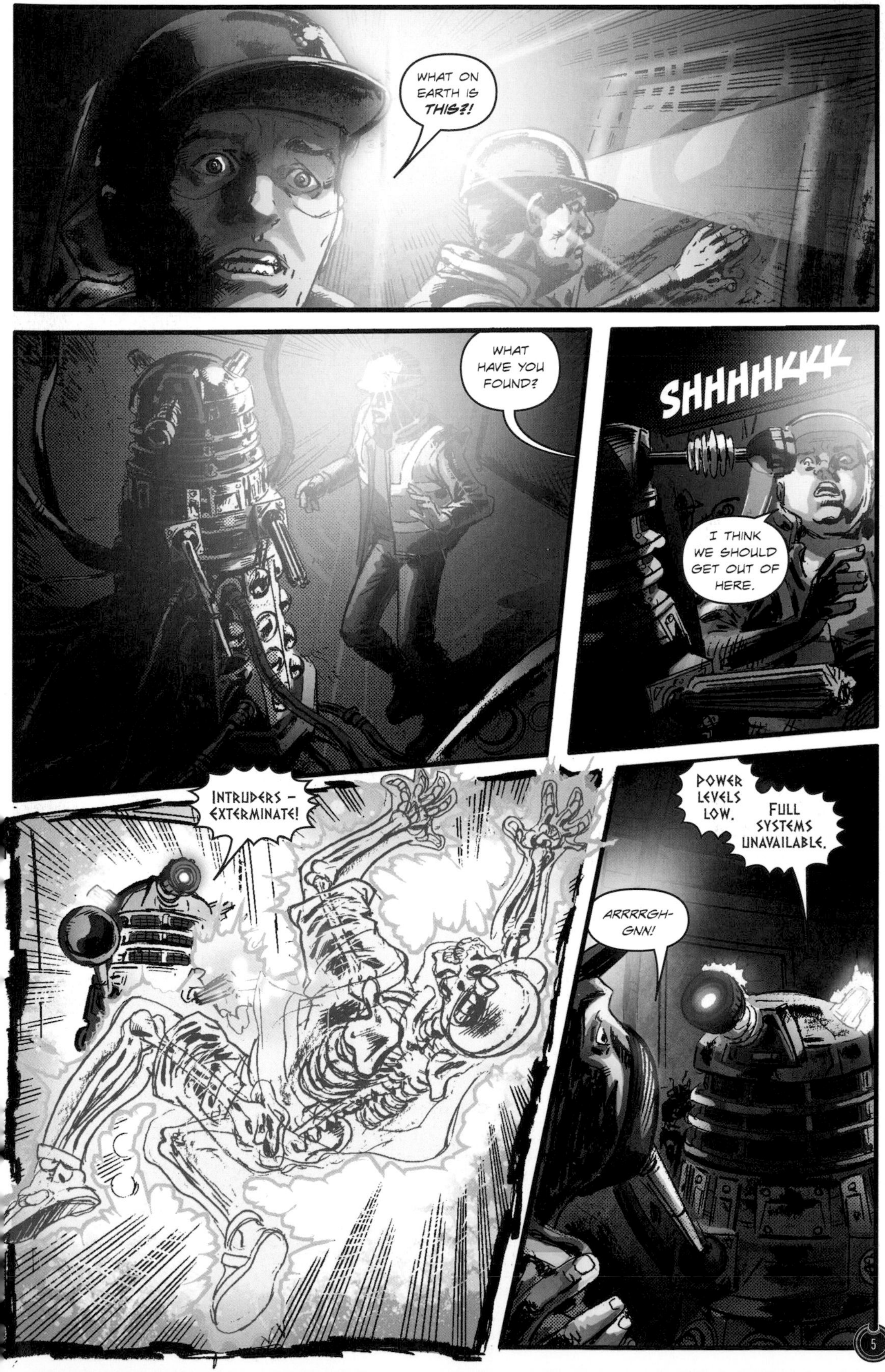
WHAT ON EARTH IS THIS?!
WHAT HAVE YOU FOUND?
SHHHHKKK
I THINK WE SHOULD GET OUT OF HERE.
INTRUDERS – EXTERMINATE!
POWER LEVELS LOW.
FULL SYSTEMS UNAVAILABLE.
ARRRRGH-GNN!

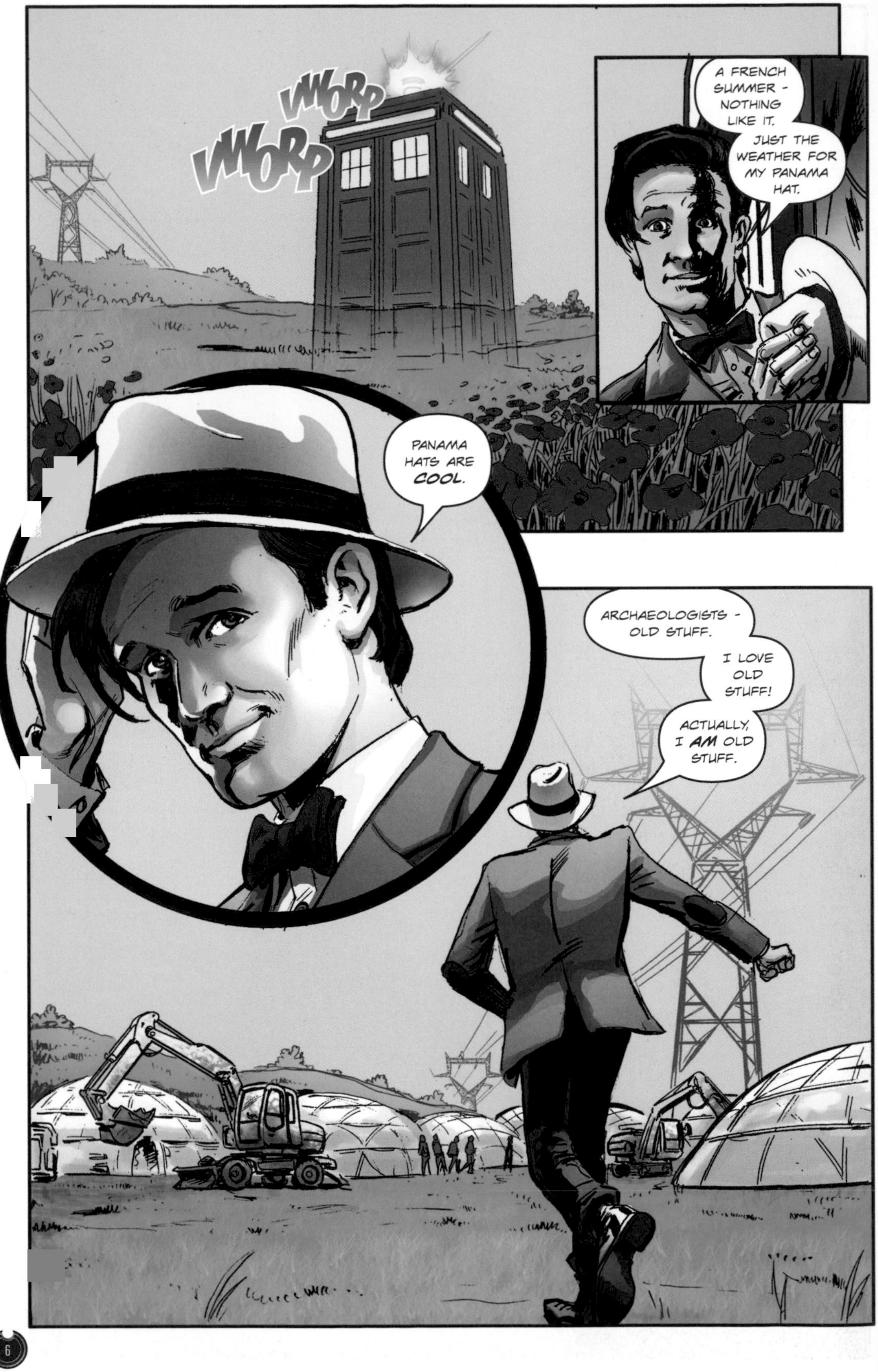
VWORP
VWORP
A FRENCH SUMMER - NOTHING LIKE IT.
JUST THE WEATHER FOR MY PANAMA HAT.
PANAMA HATS ARE **COOL**.
ARCHAEOLOGISTS - OLD STUFF.
I LOVE OLD STUFF!
ACTUALLY, I **AM** OLD STUFF.

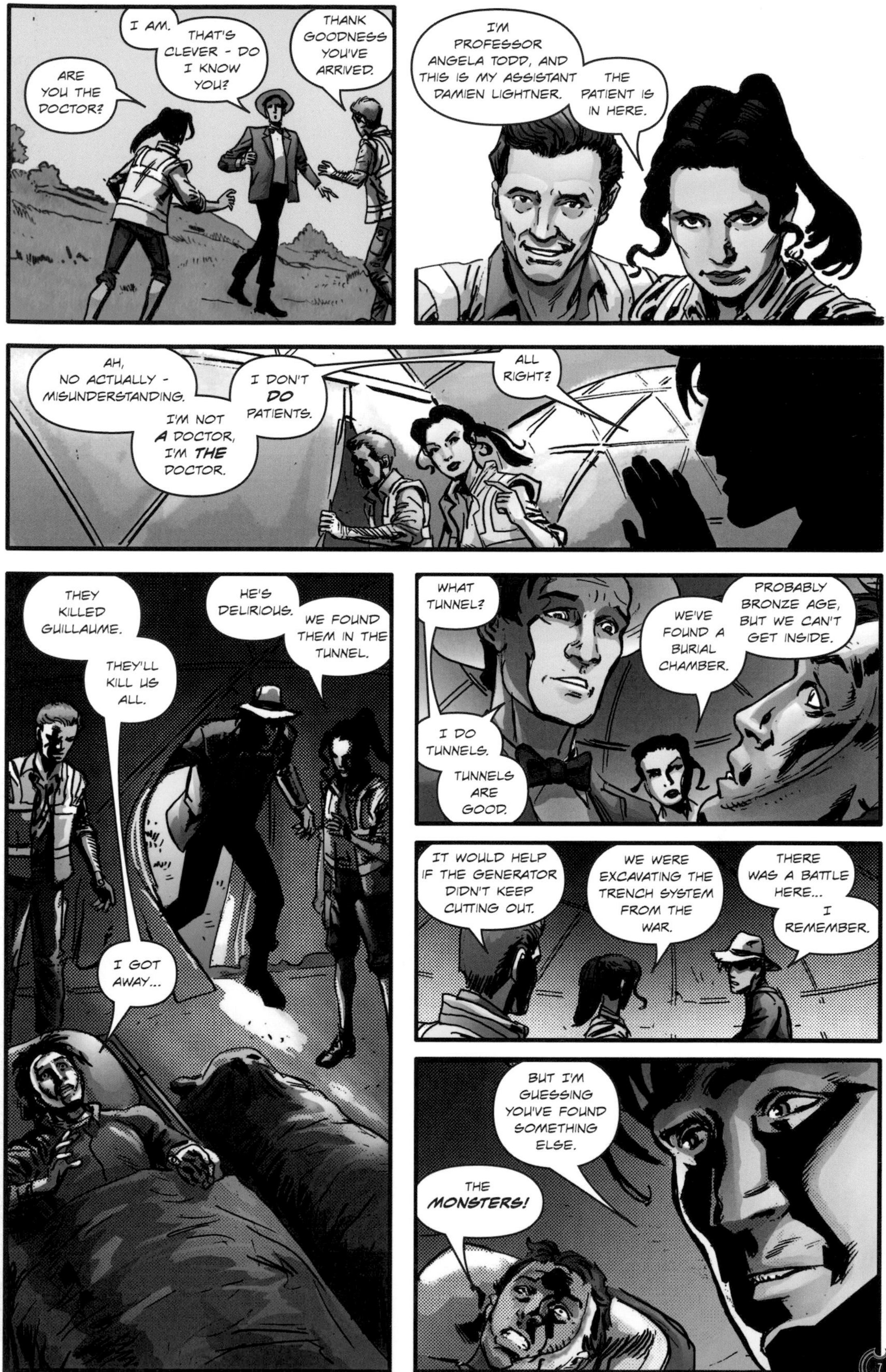
ARE YOU THE DOCTOR?
I AM.
THAT'S CLEVER - DO I KNOW YOU?
THANK GOODNESS YOU'VE ARRIVED.
I'M PROFESSOR ANGELA TODD, AND THIS IS MY ASSISTANT DAMIEN LIGHTNER.
THE PATIENT IS IN HERE.
AH, NO ACTUALLY - MISUNDERSTANDING.
I'M NOT A DOCTOR, I'M THE DOCTOR.
I DON'T DO PATIENTS.
ALL RIGHT?
THEY KILLED GUILLAUME.
THEY'LL KILL US ALL.
HE'S DELIRIOUS.
WE FOUND THEM IN THE TUNNEL.
I GOT AWAY...
WHAT TUNNEL?
I DO TUNNELS.
TUNNELS ARE GOOD.
WE'VE FOUND A BURIAL CHAMBER.
PROBABLY BRONZE AGE, BUT WE CAN'T GET INSIDE.
IT WOULD HELP IF THE GENERATOR DIDN'T KEEP CUTTING OUT.
WE WERE EXCAVATING THE TRENCH SYSTEM FROM THE WAR.
THERE WAS A BATTLE HERE...
I REMEMBER.
BUT I'M GUESSING YOU'VE FOUND SOMETHING ELSE.
THE MONSTERS!

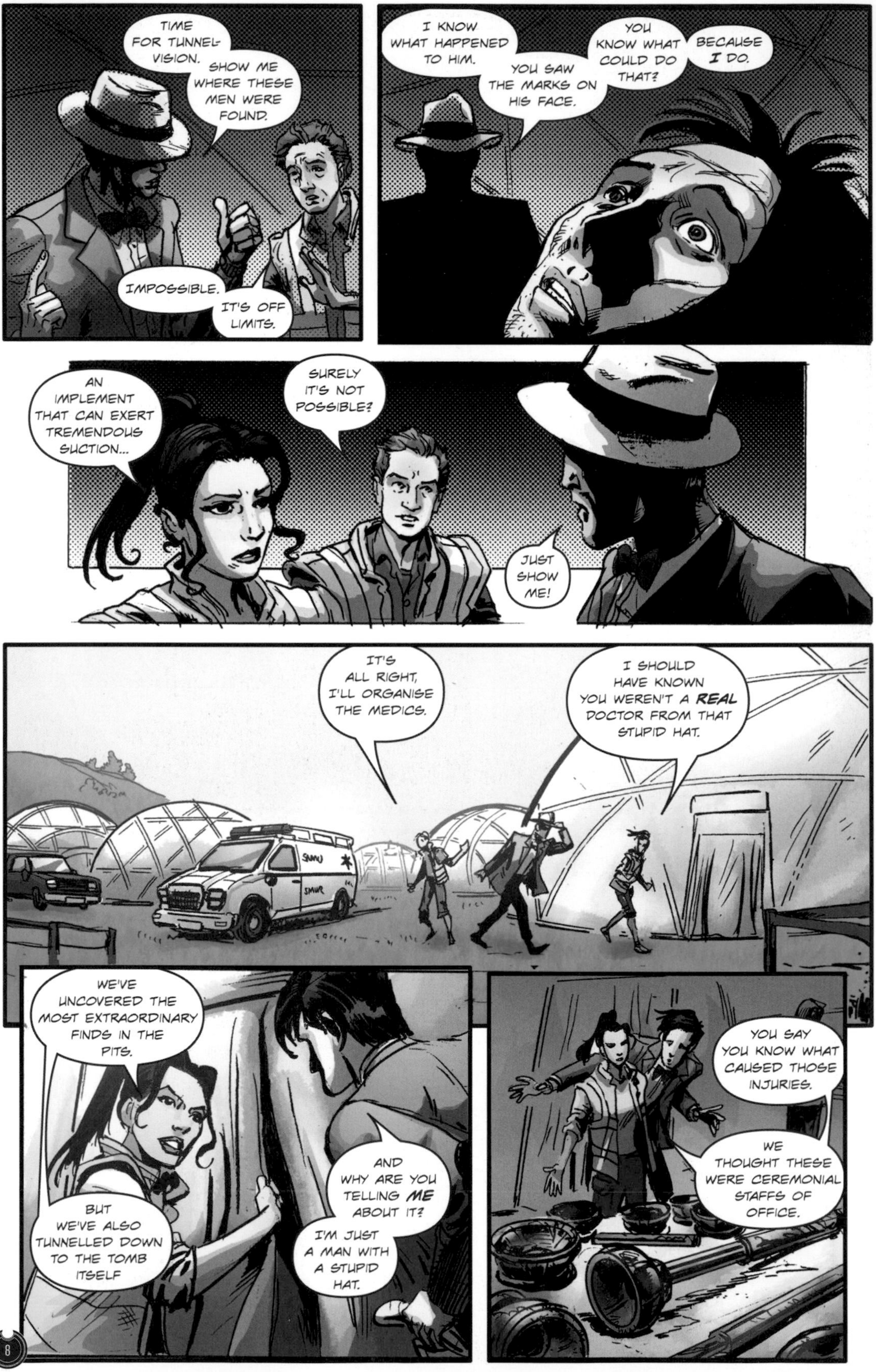
TIME FOR TUNNEL-VISION.
SHOW ME WHERE THESE MEN WERE FOUND.
IMPOSSIBLE.
IT'S OFF LIMITS.
I KNOW WHAT HAPPENED TO HIM.
YOU SAW THE MARKS ON HIS FACE.
YOU KNOW WHAT COULD DO THAT?
BECAUSE I DO.
AN IMPLEMENT THAT CAN EXERT TREMENDOUS SUCTION...
SURELY IT'S NOT POSSIBLE?
JUST SHOW ME!
IT'S ALL RIGHT, I'LL ORGANISE THE MEDICS.
I SHOULD HAVE KNOWN YOU WEREN'T A REAL DOCTOR FROM THAT STUPID HAT.
WE'VE UNCOVERED THE MOST EXTRAORDINARY FINDS IN THE PITS.
BUT WE'VE ALSO TUNNELLED DOWN TO THE TOMB ITSELF
AND WHY ARE YOU TELLING ME ABOUT IT?
I'M JUST A MAN WITH A STUPID HAT.
YOU SAY YOU KNOW WHAT CAUSED THOSE INJURIES.
WE THOUGHT THESE WERE CEREMONIAL STAFFS OF OFFICE.

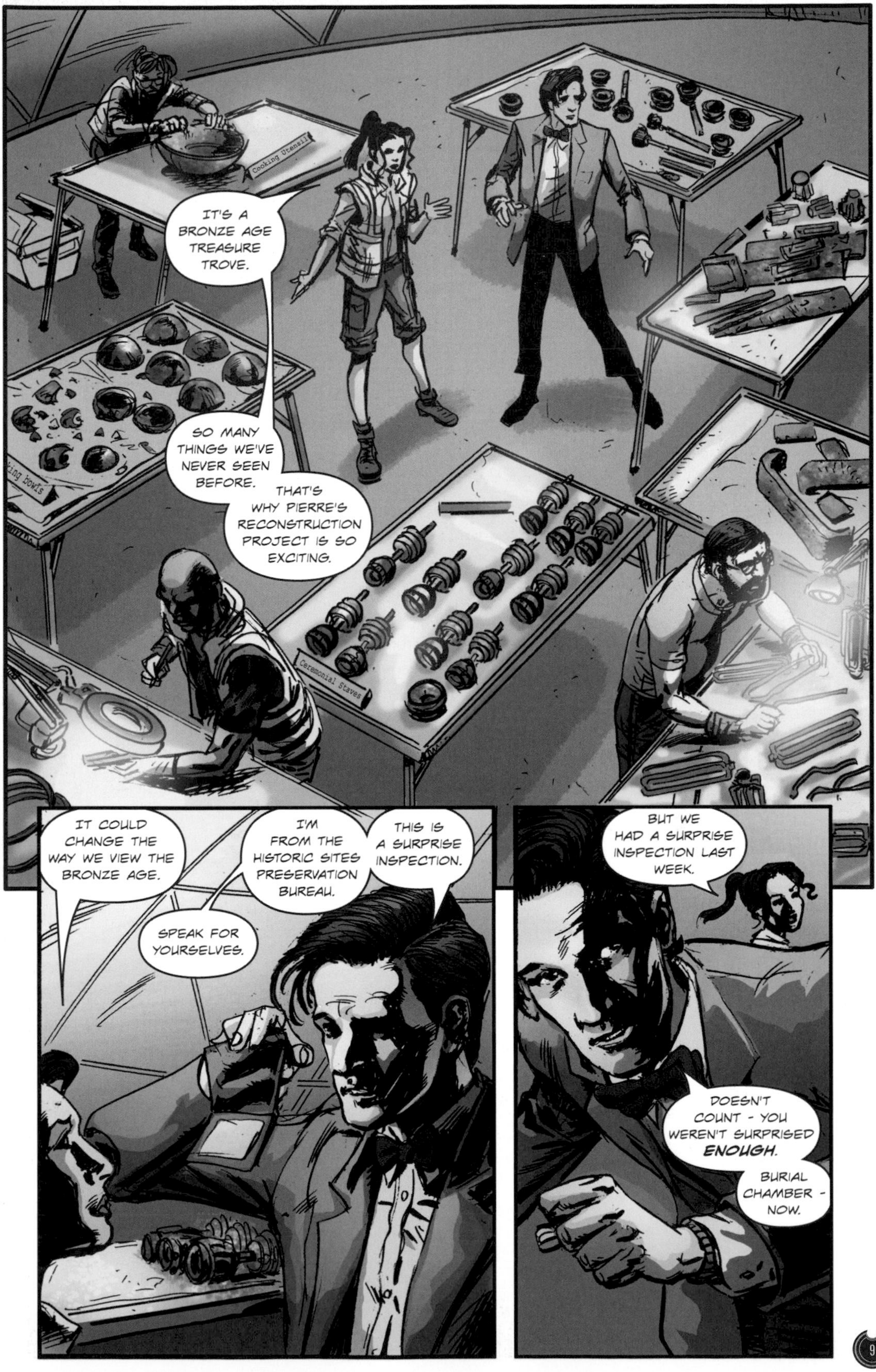
IT'S A BRONZE AGE TREASURE TROVE.
SO MANY THINGS WE'VE NEVER SEEN BEFORE.
THAT'S WHY PIERRE'S RECONSTRUCTION PROJECT IS SO EXCITING.
Ceremonial Staves
IT COULD CHANGE THE WAY WE VIEW THE BRONZE AGE.
SPEAK FOR YOURSELVES.
I'M FROM THE HISTORIC SITES PRESERVATION BUREAU.
THIS IS A SURPRISE INSPECTION.
BUT WE HAD A SURPRISE INSPECTION LAST WEEK.
DOESN'T COUNT - YOU WEREN'T SURPRISED **ENOUGH**.
BURIAL CHAMBER - NOW.

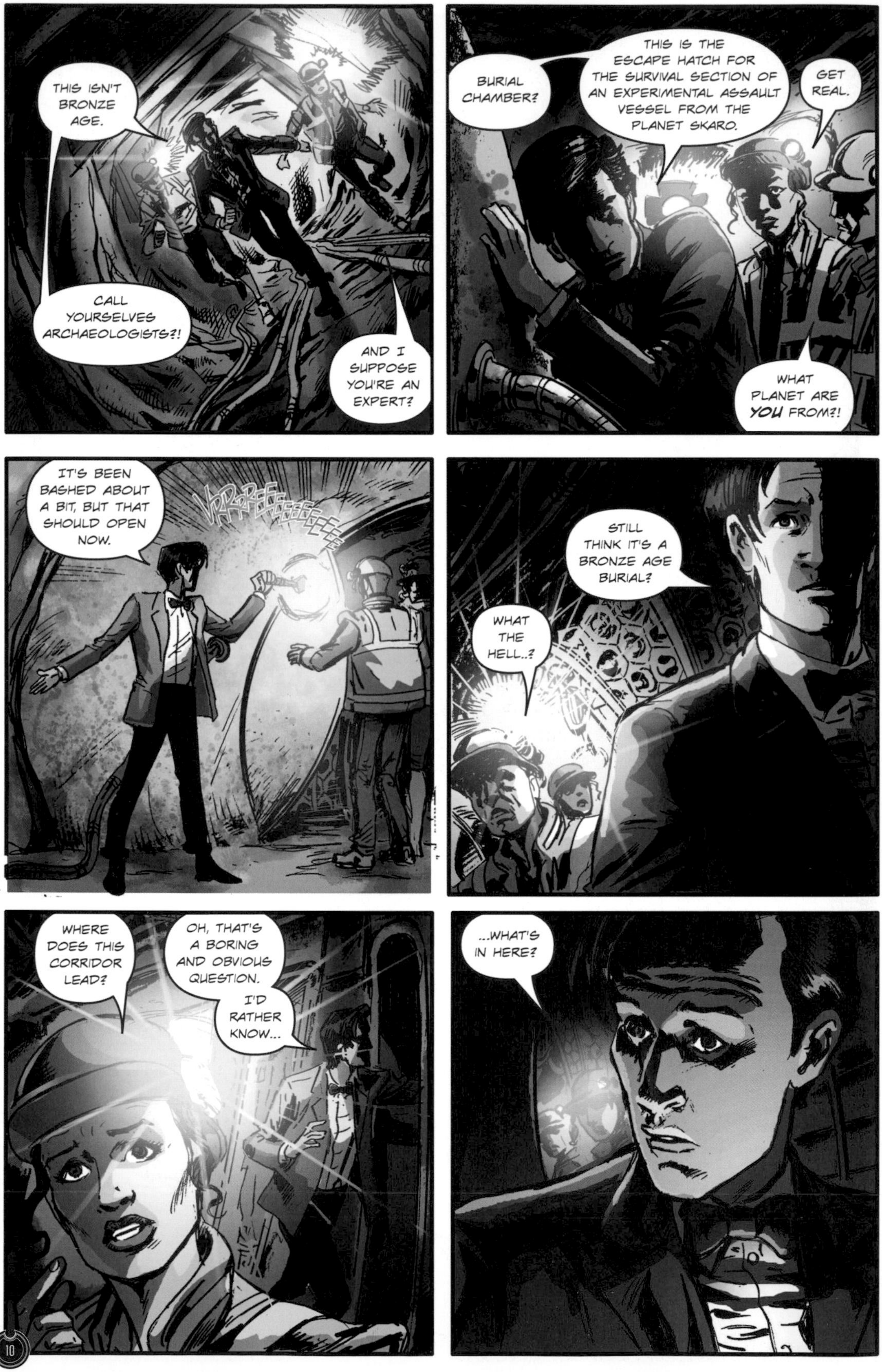
THIS ISN'T BRONZE AGE.
CALL YOURSELVES ARCHAEOLOGISTS?!
AND I SUPPOSE YOU'RE AN EXPERT?
BURIAL CHAMBER?
THIS IS THE ESCAPE HATCH FOR THE SURVIVAL SECTION OF AN EXPERIMENTAL ASSAULT VESSEL FROM THE PLANET SKARO.
GET REAL.
WHAT PLANET ARE **YOU** FROM?!
IT'S BEEN BASHED ABOUT A BIT, BUT THAT SHOULD OPEN NOW.
VRRREEEEEEEEEEEEE
STILL THINK IT'S A BRONZE AGE BURIAL?
WHAT THE HELL..?
WHERE DOES THIS CORRIDOR LEAD?
OH, THAT'S A BORING AND OBVIOUS QUESTION.
I'D RATHER KNOW...
...WHAT'S IN HERE?

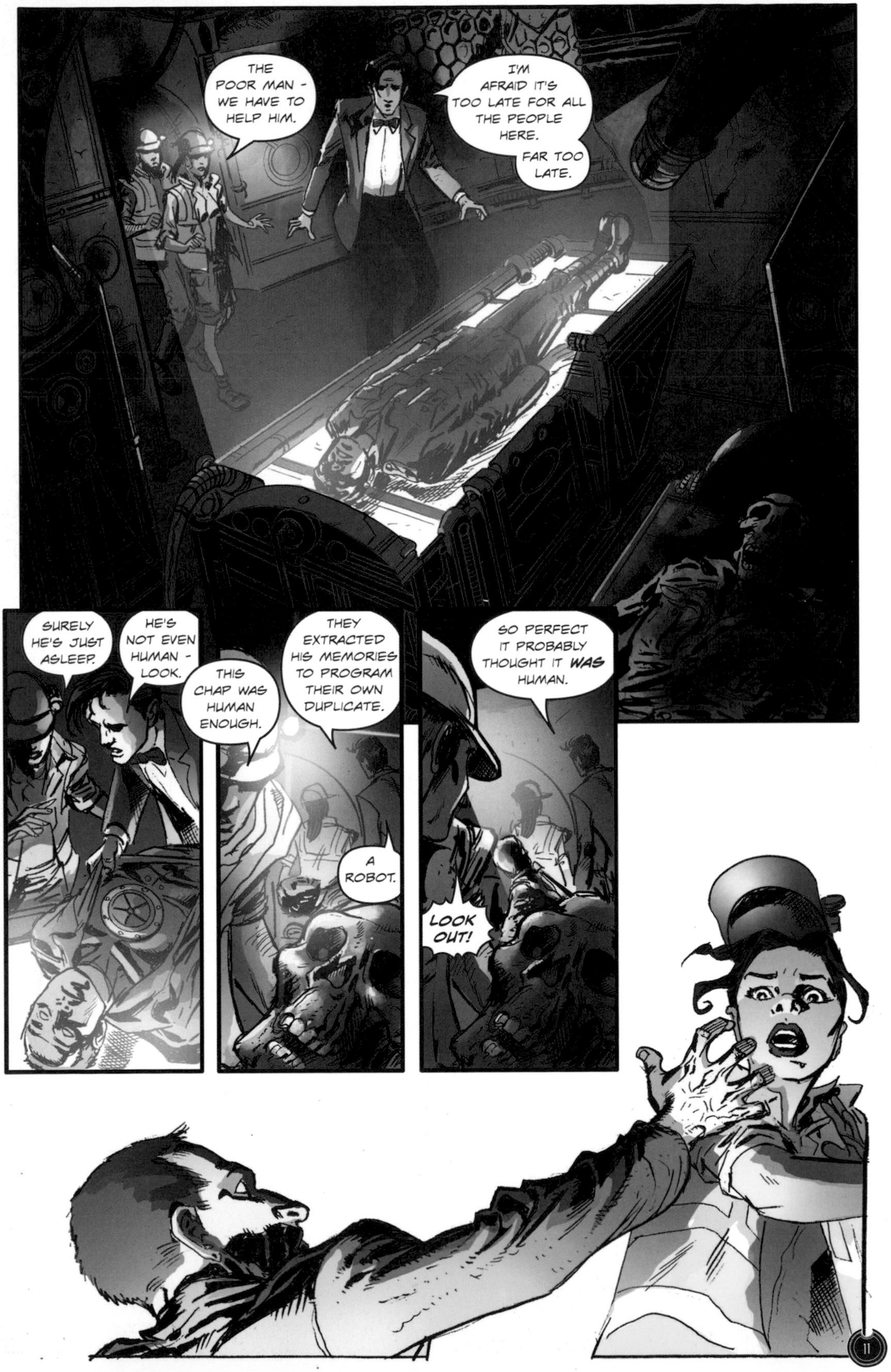
THE POOR MAN - WE HAVE TO HELP HIM.
I'M AFRAID IT'S TOO LATE FOR ALL THE PEOPLE HERE.
FAR TOO LATE.
SURELY HE'S JUST ASLEEP.
HE'S NOT EVEN HUMAN - LOOK.
THIS CHAP WAS HUMAN ENOUGH.
THEY EXTRACTED HIS MEMORIES TO PROGRAM THEIR OWN DUPLICATE.
A ROBOT.
SO PERFECT IT PROBABLY THOUGHT IT WAS HUMAN.
LOOK OUT!

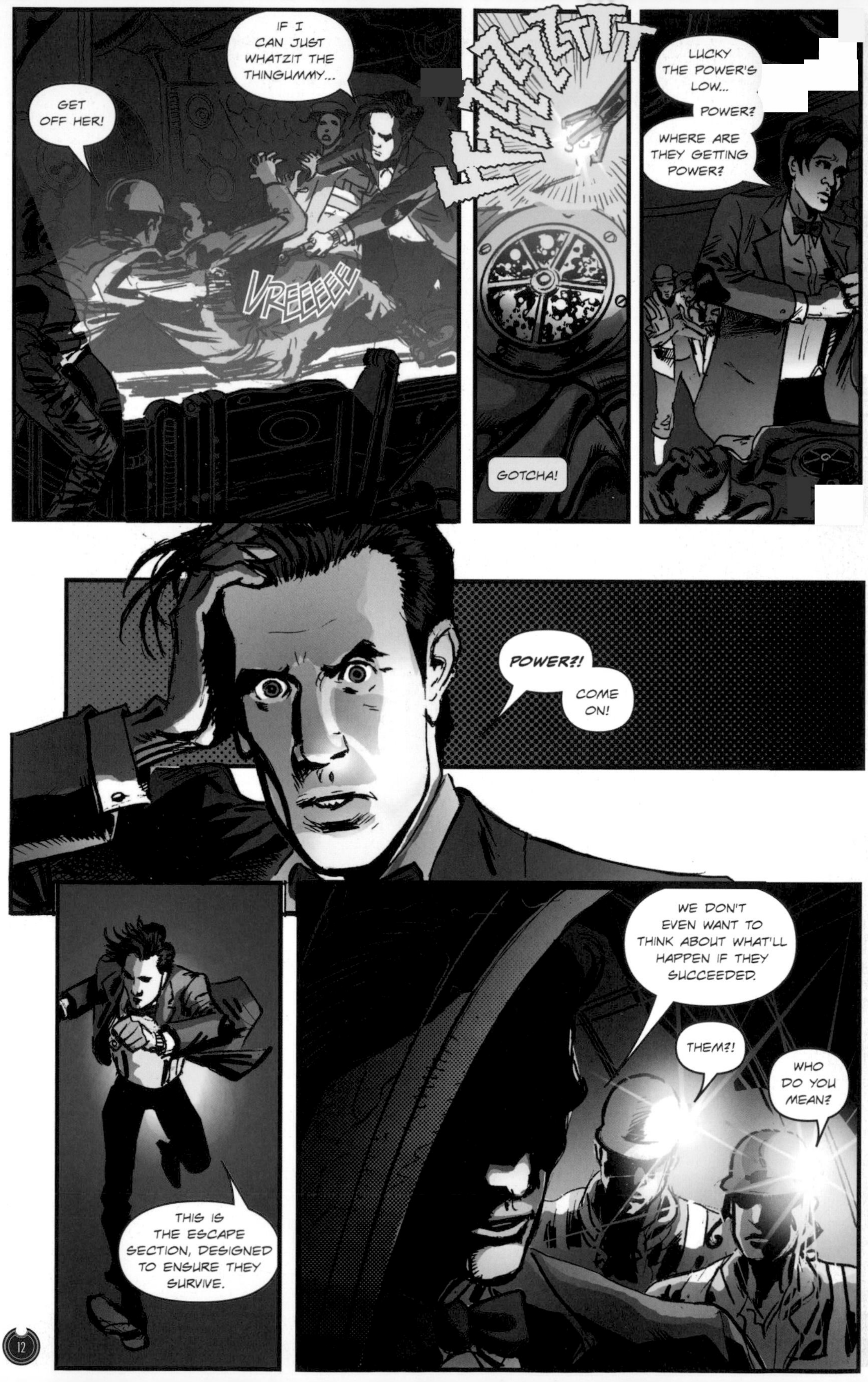
GET OFF HER!
IF I CAN JUST WHATZIT THE THINGUMMY...
VREEEEEE
FZZZZTTT
GOTCHA!
LUCKY THE POWER'S LOW...
POWER?
WHERE ARE THEY GETTING POWER?
POWER?!
COME ON!
THIS IS THE ESCAPE SECTION, DESIGNED TO ENSURE THEY SURVIVE.
WE DON'T EVEN WANT TO THINK ABOUT WHAT'LL HAPPEN IF THEY SUCCEEDED.
THEM?!
WHO DO YOU MEAN?

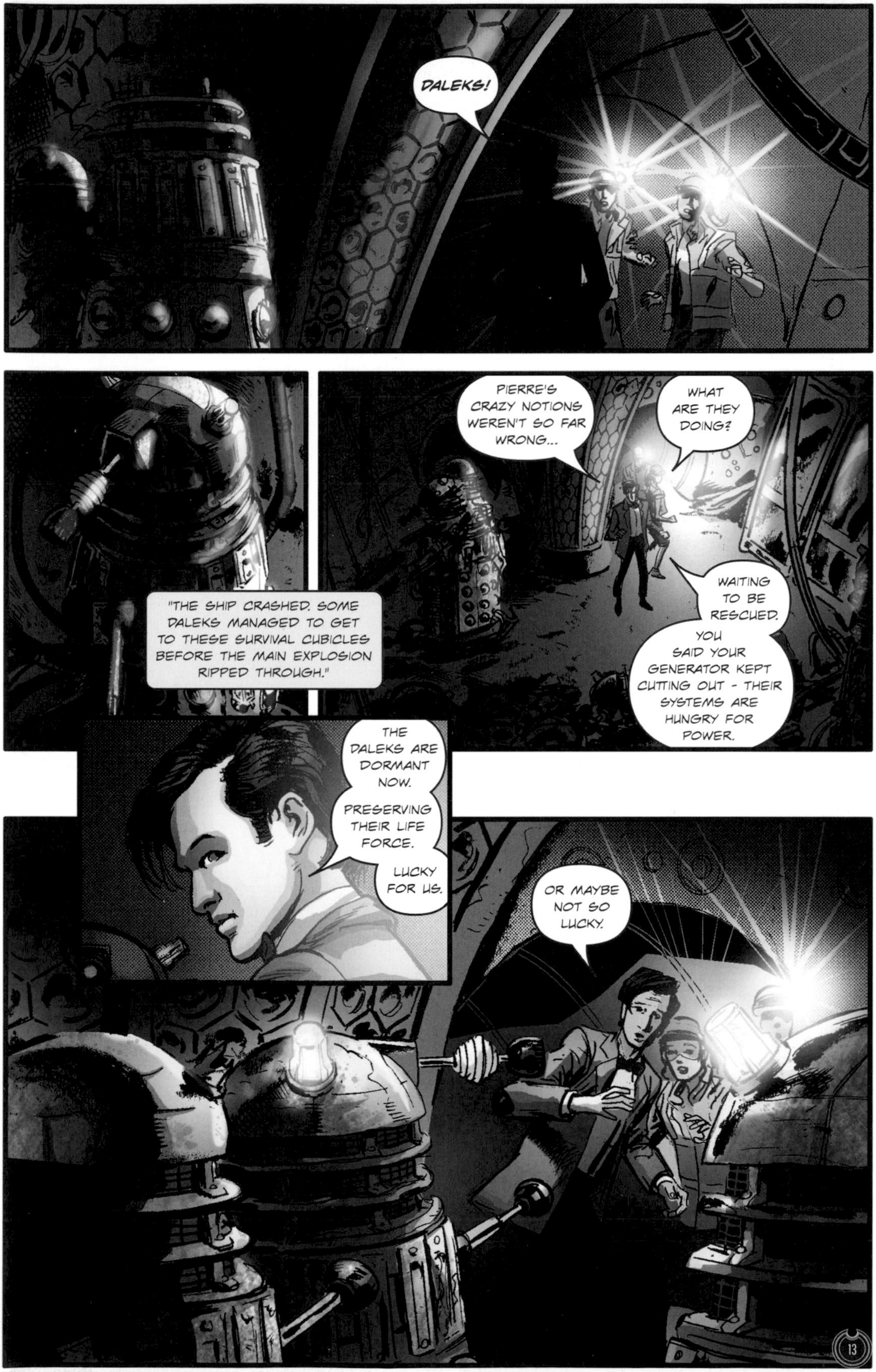
DALEKS!
PIERRE'S CRAZY NOTIONS WEREN'T SO FAR WRONG...
WHAT ARE THEY DOING?
"THE SHIP CRASHED. SOME DALEKS MANAGED TO GET TO THESE SURVIVAL CUBICLES BEFORE THE MAIN EXPLOSION RIPPED THROUGH."
WAITING TO BE RESCUED.
YOU SAID YOUR GENERATOR KEPT CUTTING OUT - THEIR SYSTEMS ARE HUNGRY FOR POWER.
THE DALEKS ARE DORMANT NOW.
PRESERVING THEIR LIFE FORCE.
LUCKY FOR US.
OR MAYBE NOT SO LUCKY.

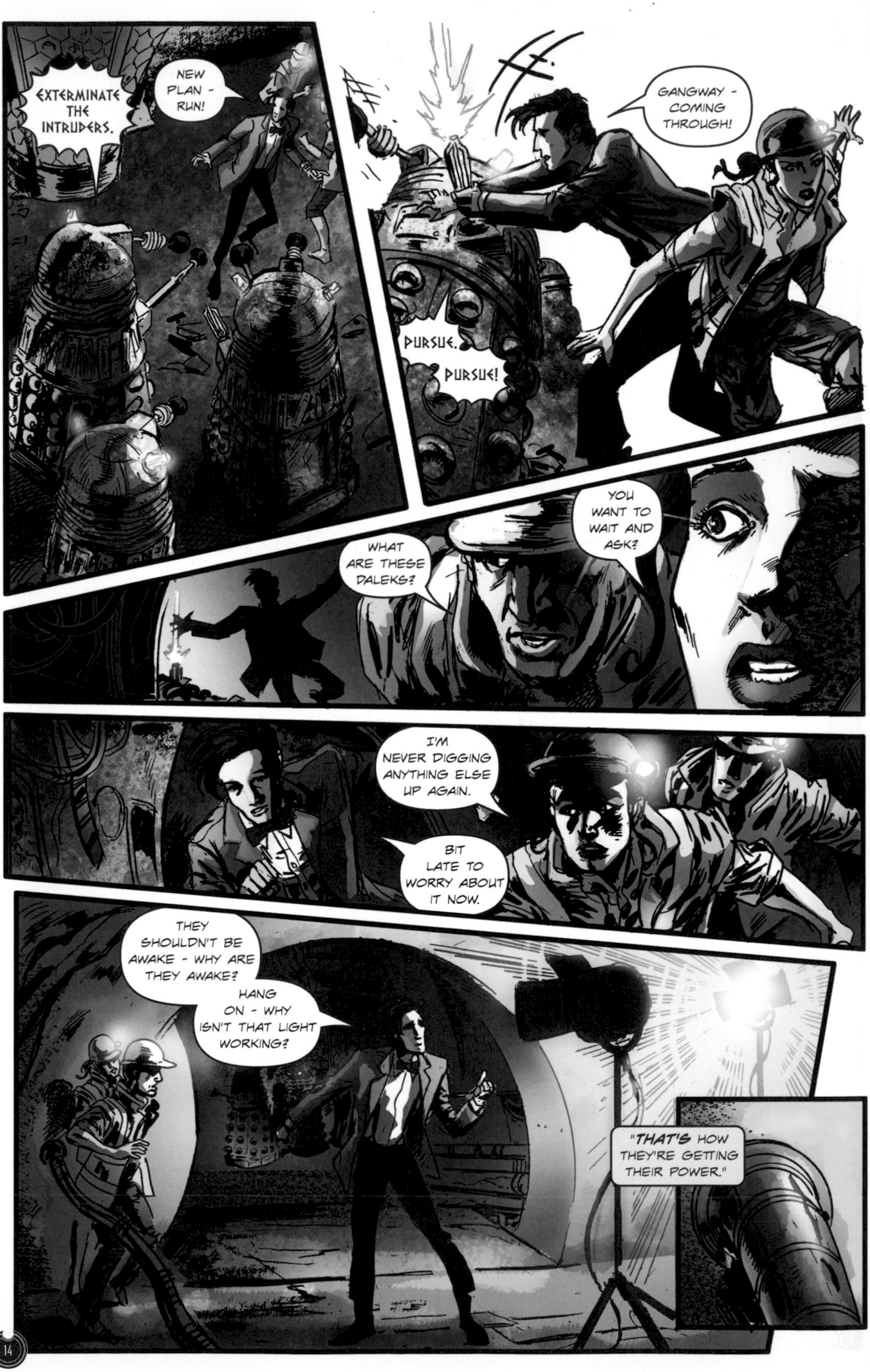
EXTERMINATE THE INTRUDERS.
NEW PLAN - RUN!
GANGWAY - COMING THROUGH!
PURSUE.
PURSUE!
WHAT ARE THESE DALEKS?
YOU WANT TO WAIT AND ASK?
I'M NEVER DIGGING ANYTHING ELSE UP AGAIN.
BIT LATE TO WORRY ABOUT IT NOW.
THEY SHOULDN'T BE AWAKE - WHY ARE THEY AWAKE?
HANG ON - WHY ISN'T THAT LIGHT WORKING?
"THAT'S HOW THEY'RE GETTING THEIR POWER."

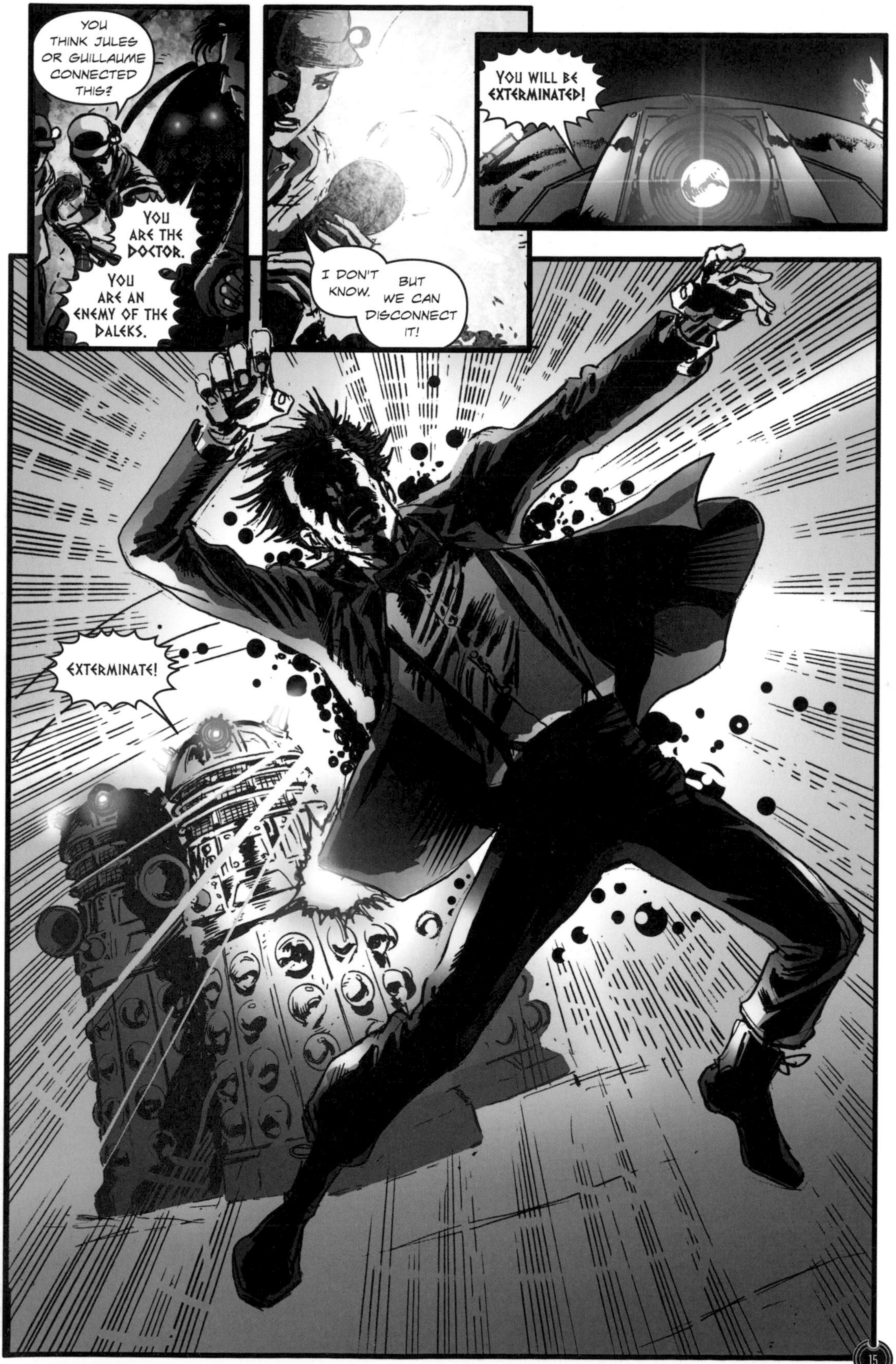

YOU THINK JULES OR GUILLAUME CONNECTED THIS?
YOU ARE THE DOCTOR.
YOU ARE AN ENEMY OF THE DALEKS.
I DON'T KNOW.
BUT WE CAN DISCONNECT IT!
YOU WILL BE EXTERMINATED!
EXTERMINATE!

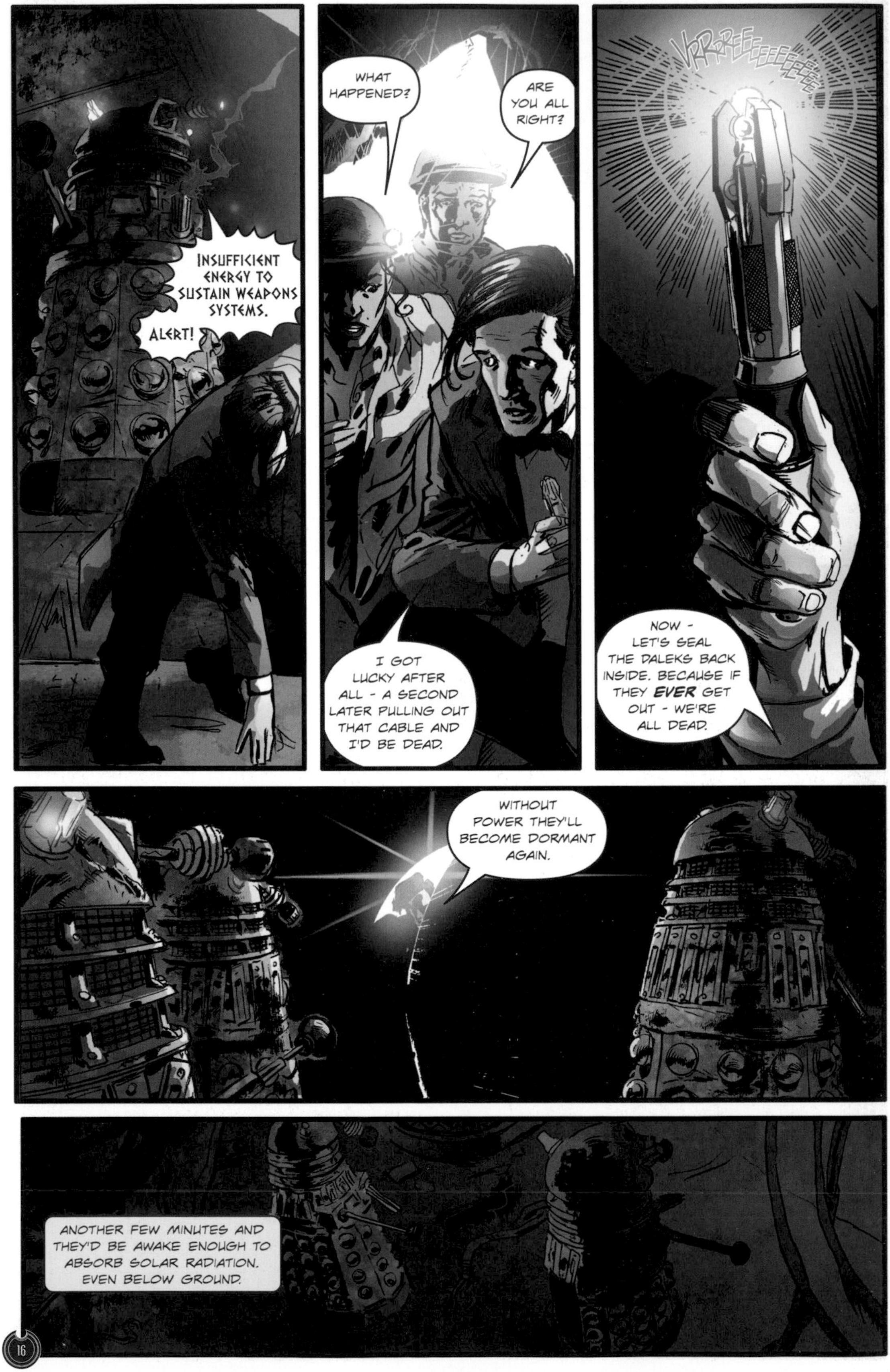
INSUFFICIENT ENERGY TO SUSTAIN WEAPONS SYSTEMS.
ALERT!
WHAT HAPPENED?
ARE YOU ALL RIGHT?
I GOT LUCKY AFTER ALL - A SECOND LATER PULLING OUT THAT CABLE AND I'D BE DEAD.
VRRRREEEEEEEEEEEEE
NOW - LET'S SEAL THE DALEKS BACK INSIDE. BECAUSE IF THEY **EVER** GET OUT - WE'RE ALL DEAD.
WITHOUT POWER THEY'LL BECOME DORMANT AGAIN.
ANOTHER FEW MINUTES AND THEY'D BE AWAKE ENOUGH TO ABSORB SOLAR RADIATION. EVEN BELOW GROUND.

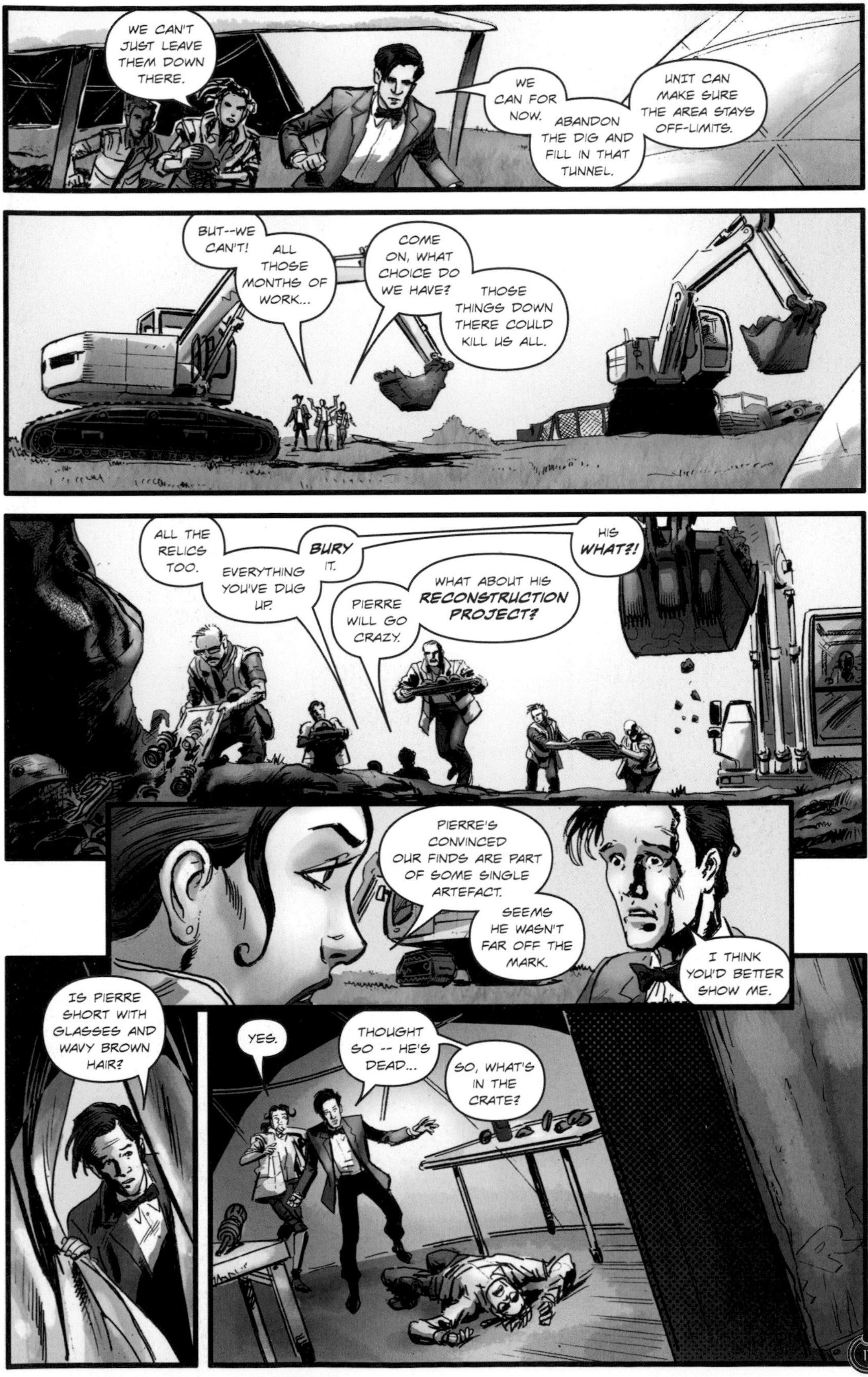

WE CAN'T JUST LEAVE THEM DOWN THERE.
WE CAN FOR NOW.
ABANDON THE DIG AND FILL IN THAT TUNNEL.
UNIT CAN MAKE SURE THE AREA STAYS OFF-LIMITS.
BUT--WE CAN'T!
ALL THOSE MONTHS OF WORK...
COME ON, WHAT CHOICE DO WE HAVE?
THOSE THINGS DOWN THERE COULD KILL US ALL.
ALL THE RELICS TOO.
EVERYTHING YOU'VE DUG UP.
BURY IT.
HIS WHAT?!
PIERRE WILL GO CRAZY.
WHAT ABOUT HIS RECONSTRUCTION PROJECT?
PIERRE'S CONVINCED OUR FINDS ARE PART OF SOME SINGLE ARTEFACT.
SEEMS HE WASN'T FAR OFF THE MARK.
I THINK YOU'D BETTER SHOW ME.
IS PIERRE SHORT WITH GLASSES AND WAVY BROWN HAIR?
YES.
THOUGHT SO -- HE'S DEAD...
SO, WHAT'S IN THE CRATE?

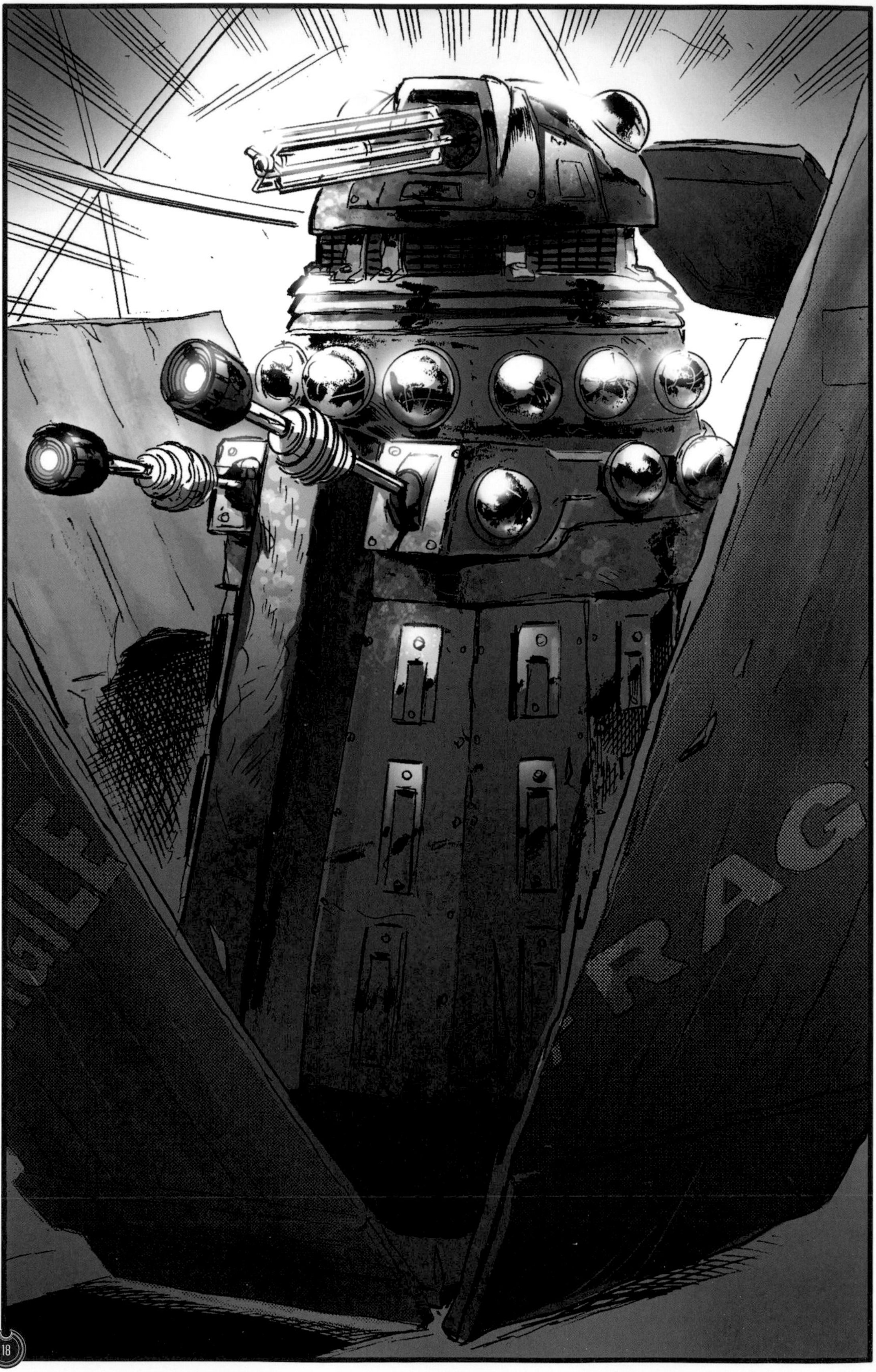

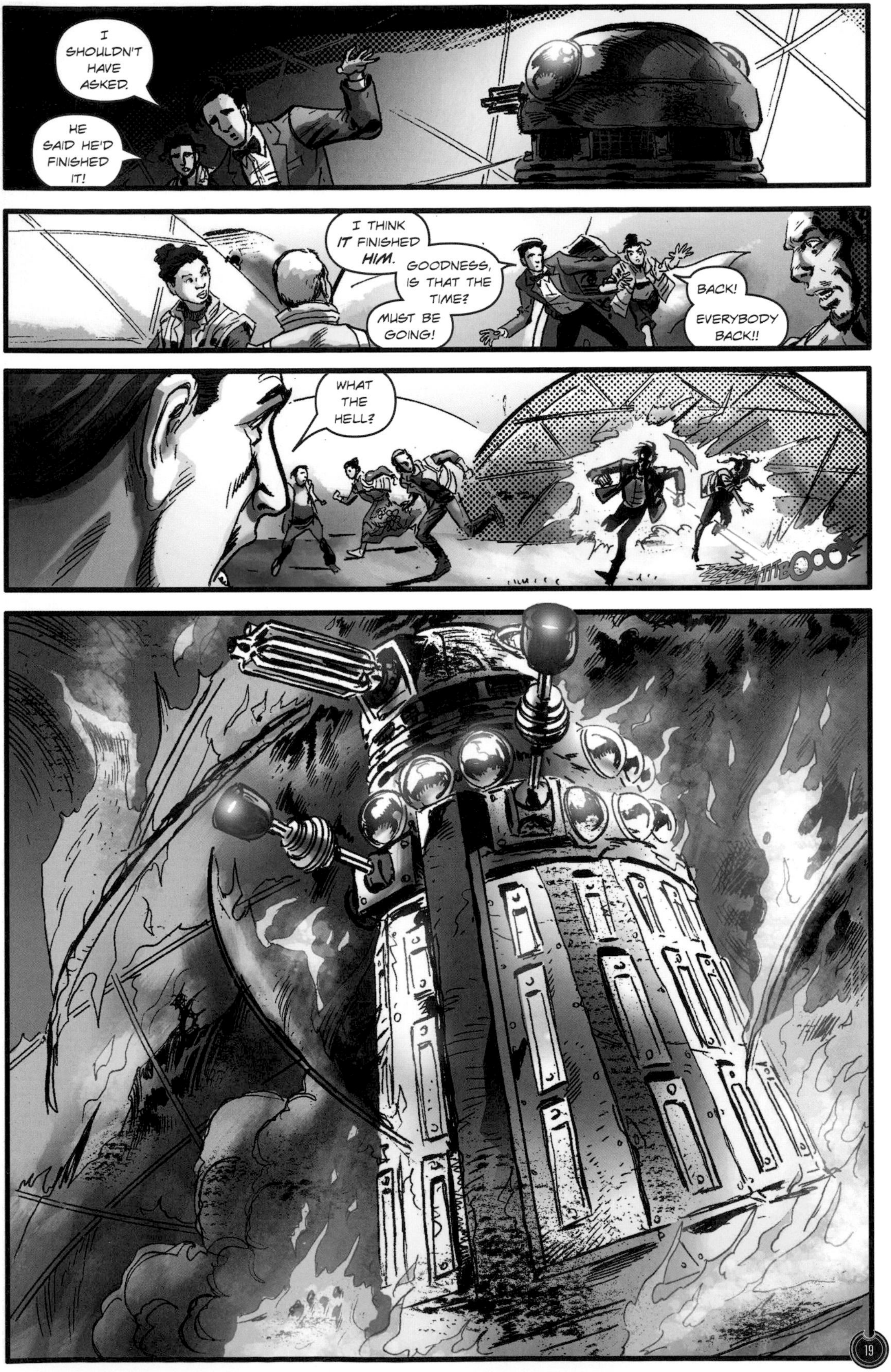
I SHOULDN'T HAVE ASKED.
HE SAID HE'D FINISHED IT!
I THINK *IT* FINISHED **HIM**.
GOODNESS, IS THAT THE TIME?
MUST BE GOING!
BACK!
EVERYBODY BACK!!
WHAT THE HELL?
ZZZZZTTTBOOOM

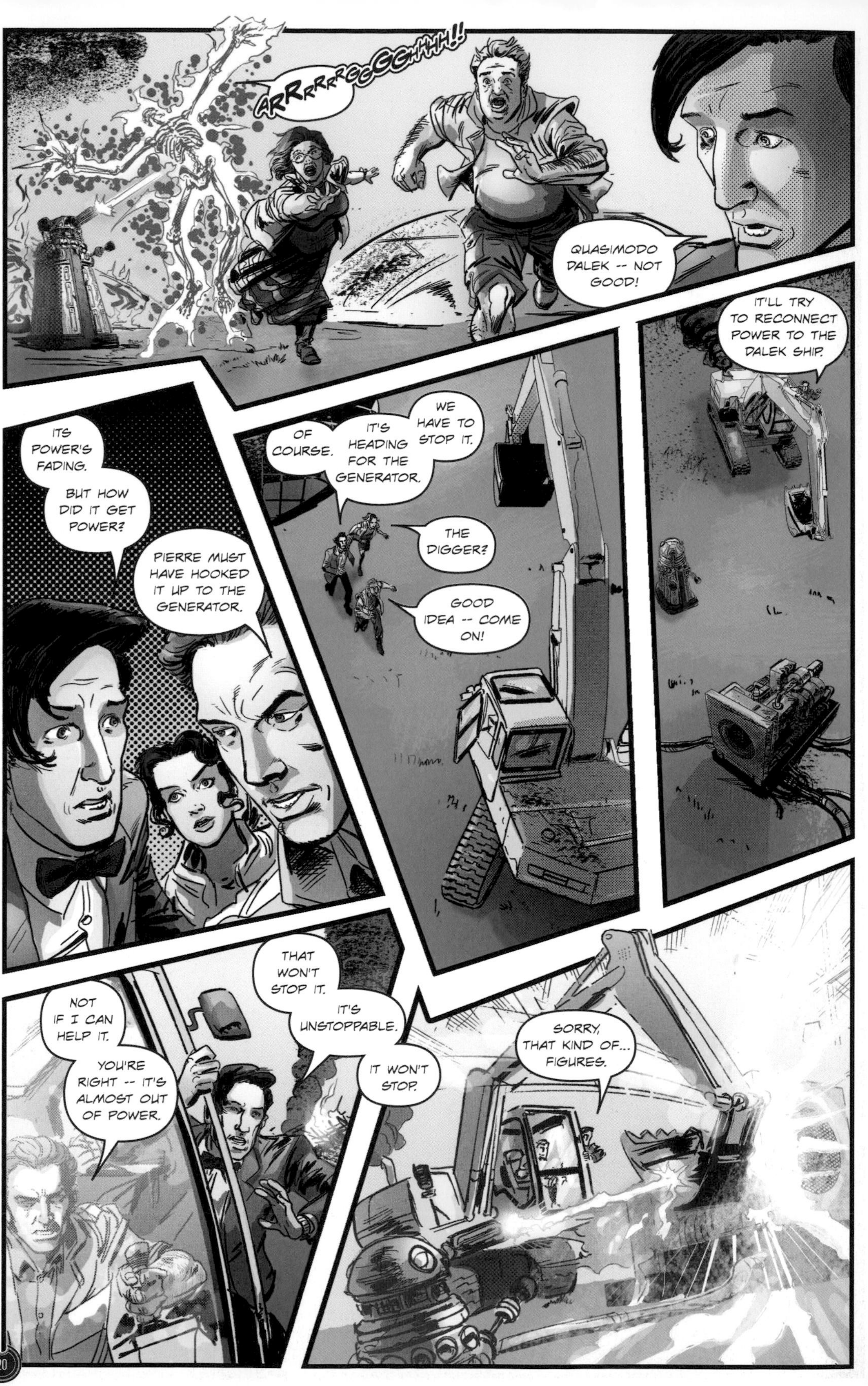
ARRRRRRGGGGHHHH!!
QUASIMODO DALEK -- NOT GOOD!
IT'LL TRY TO RECONNECT POWER TO THE DALEK SHIP.
ITS POWER'S FADING.
BUT HOW DID IT GET POWER?
PIERRE MUST HAVE HOOKED IT UP TO THE GENERATOR.
OF COURSE.
IT'S HEADING FOR THE GENERATOR.
WE HAVE TO STOP IT.
THE DIGGER?
GOOD IDEA -- COME ON!
NOT IF I CAN HELP IT.
YOU'RE RIGHT -- IT'S ALMOST OUT OF POWER.
THAT WON'T STOP IT.
IT'S UNSTOPPABLE.
IT WON'T STOP.
SORRY, THAT KIND OF... FIGURES.

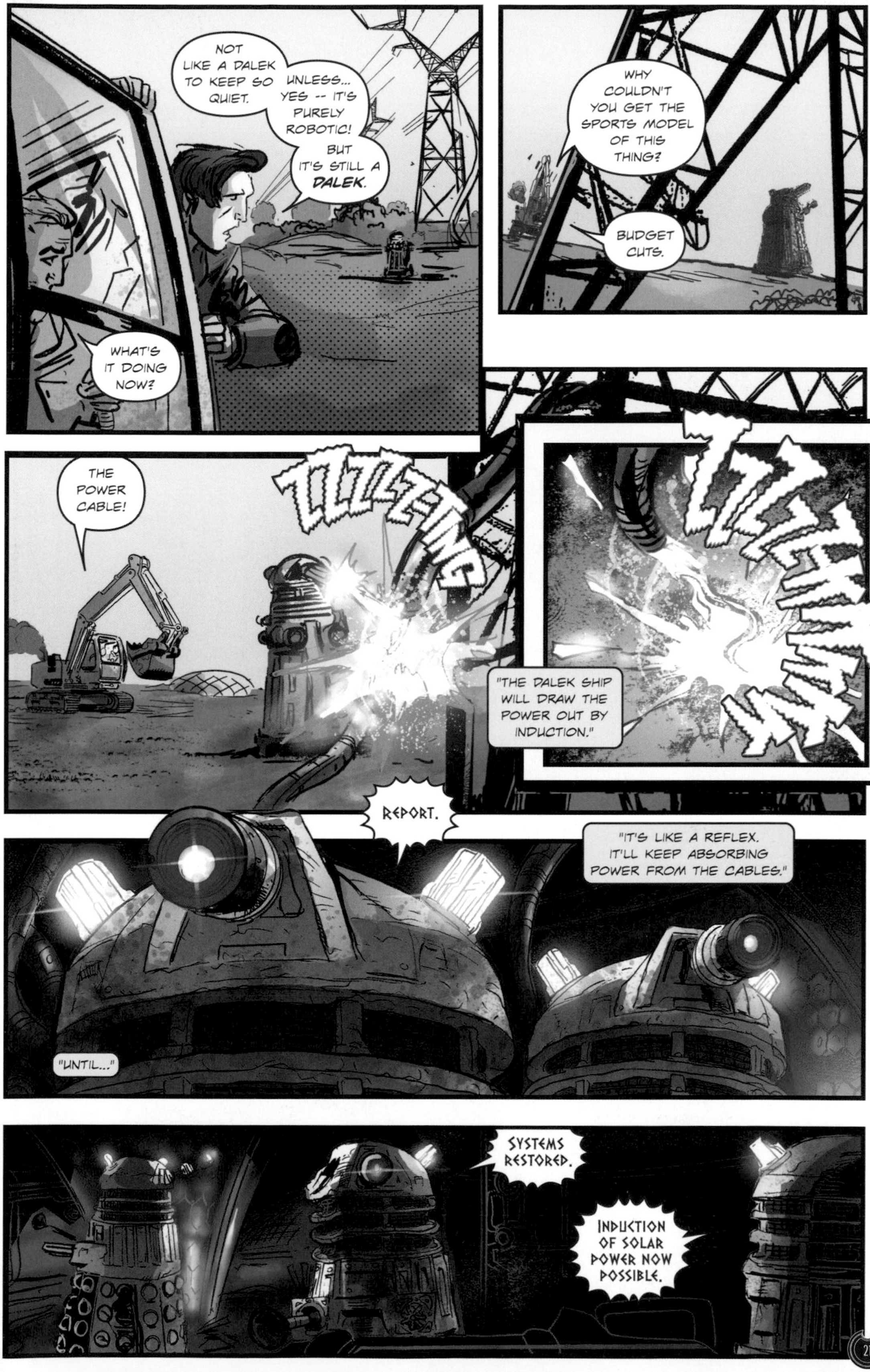
NOT LIKE A DALEK TO KEEP SO QUIET.
UNLESS... YES -- IT'S PURELY ROBOTIC!
BUT IT'S STILL A DALEK.
WHAT'S IT DOING NOW?
WHY COULDN'T YOU GET THE SPORTS MODEL OF THIS THING?
BUDGET CUTS.
THE POWER CABLE!
TZZZZ-TING
TZZZAHMMMM
"THE DALEK SHIP WILL DRAW THE POWER OUT BY INDUCTION."
REPORT.
"IT'S LIKE A REFLEX. IT'LL KEEP ABSORBING POWER FROM THE CABLES."
"UNTIL..."
SYSTEMS RESTORED.
INDUCTION OF SOLAR POWER NOW POSSIBLE.

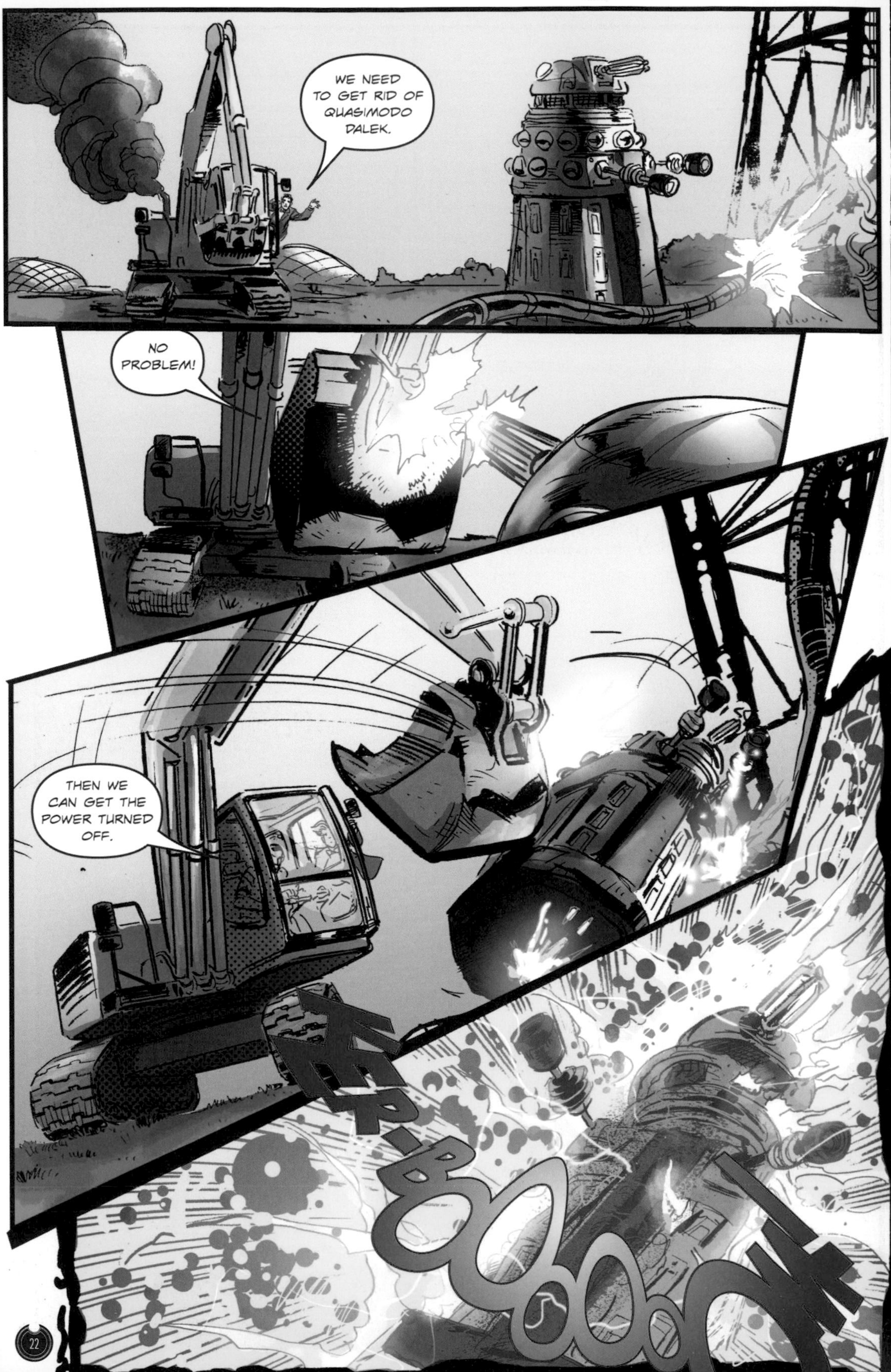
WE NEED TO GET RID OF QUASIMODO DALEK.
NO PROBLEM!
THEN WE CAN GET THE POWER TURNED OFF.
KER-BOOOOOM!

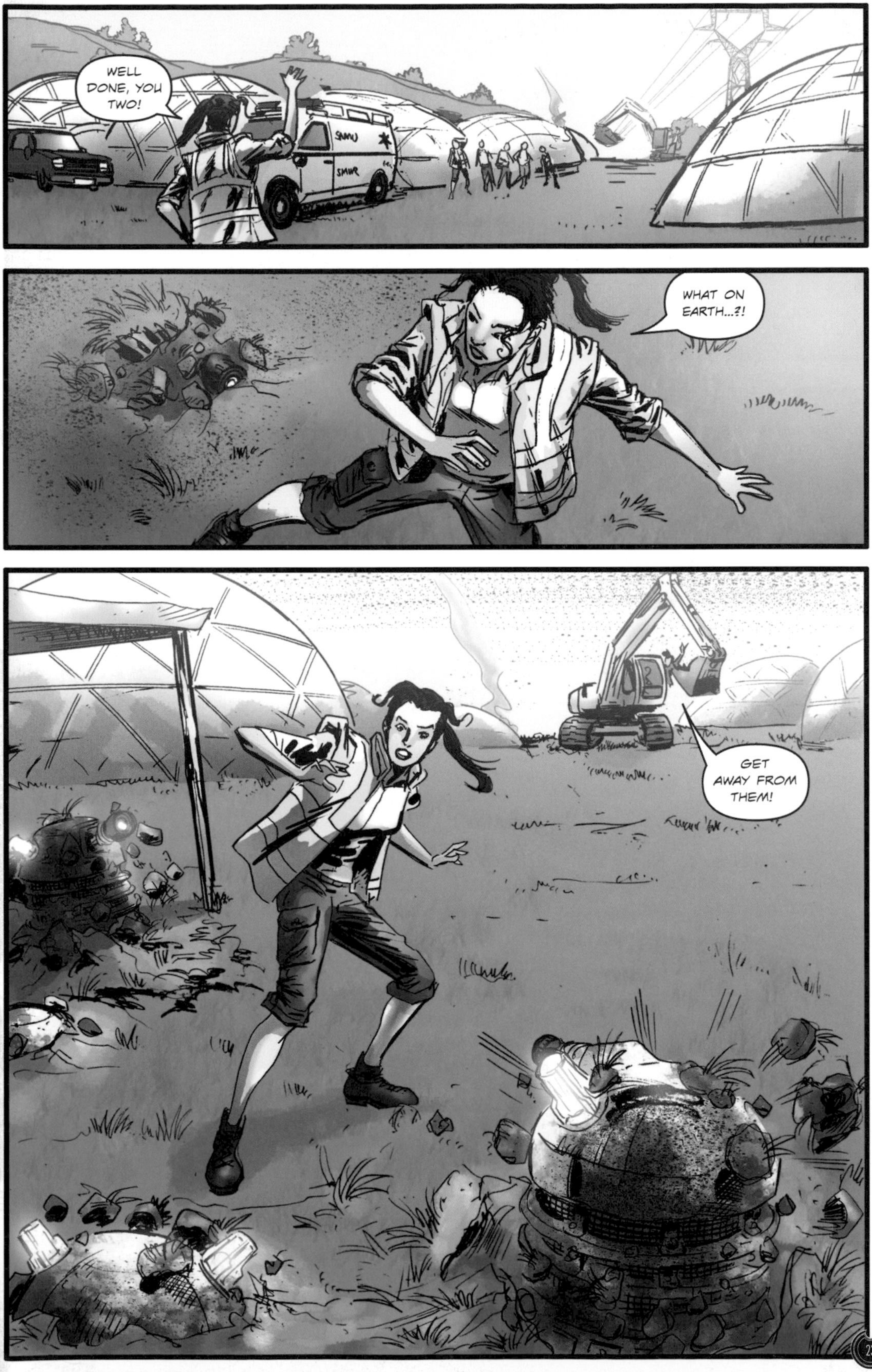
WELL DONE, YOU TWO!
WHAT ON EARTH...?!
GET AWAY FROM THEM!

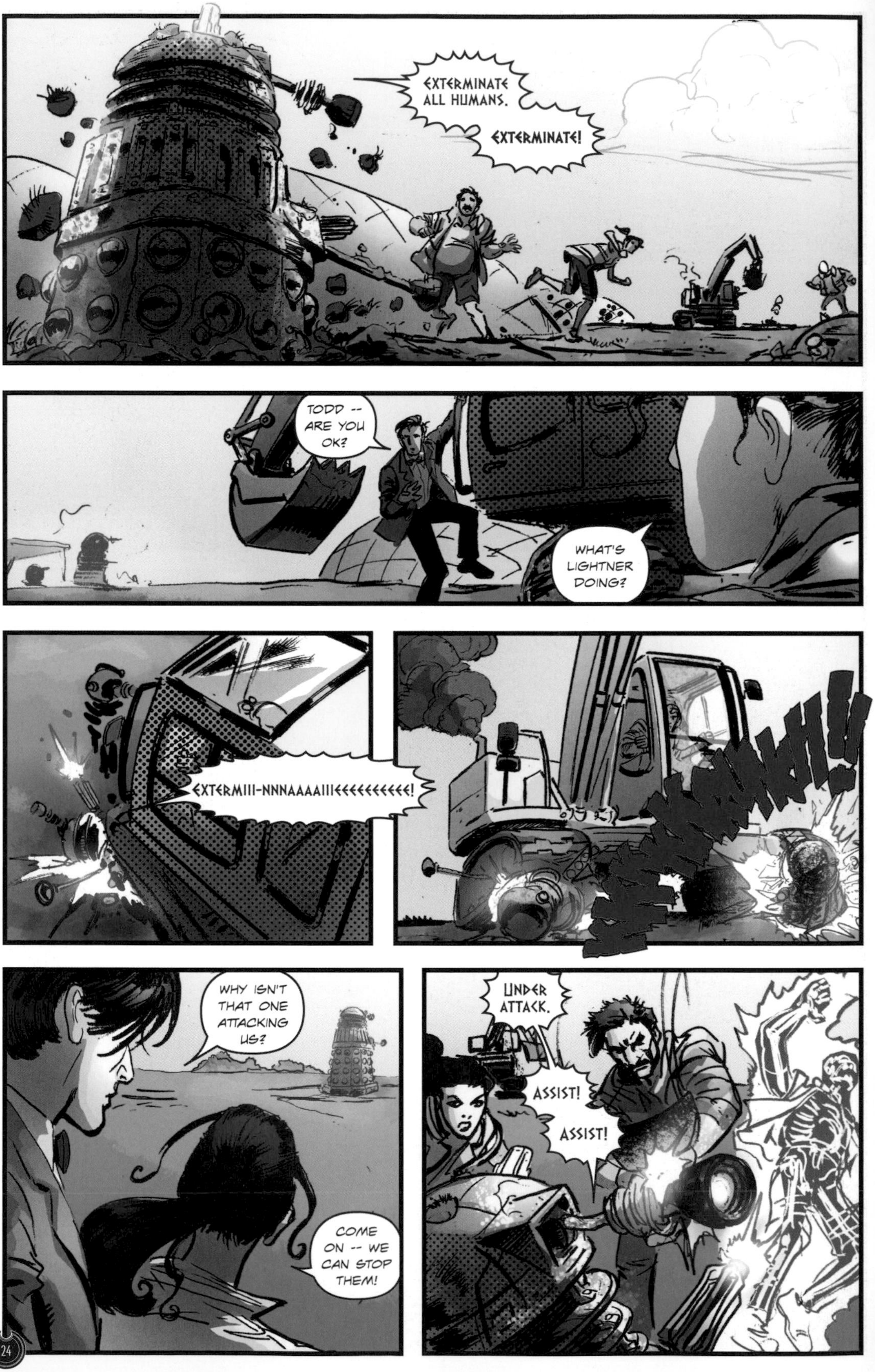
EXTERMINATE ALL HUMANS.
EXTERMINATE!
TODD -- ARE YOU OK?
WHAT'S LIGHTNER DOING?
EXTERMIII-NNNAAAAIIIEEEEEEEEEEE!
WHY ISN'T THAT ONE ATTACKING US?
COME ON -- WE CAN STOP THEM!
UNDER ATTACK.
ASSIST!
ASSIST!

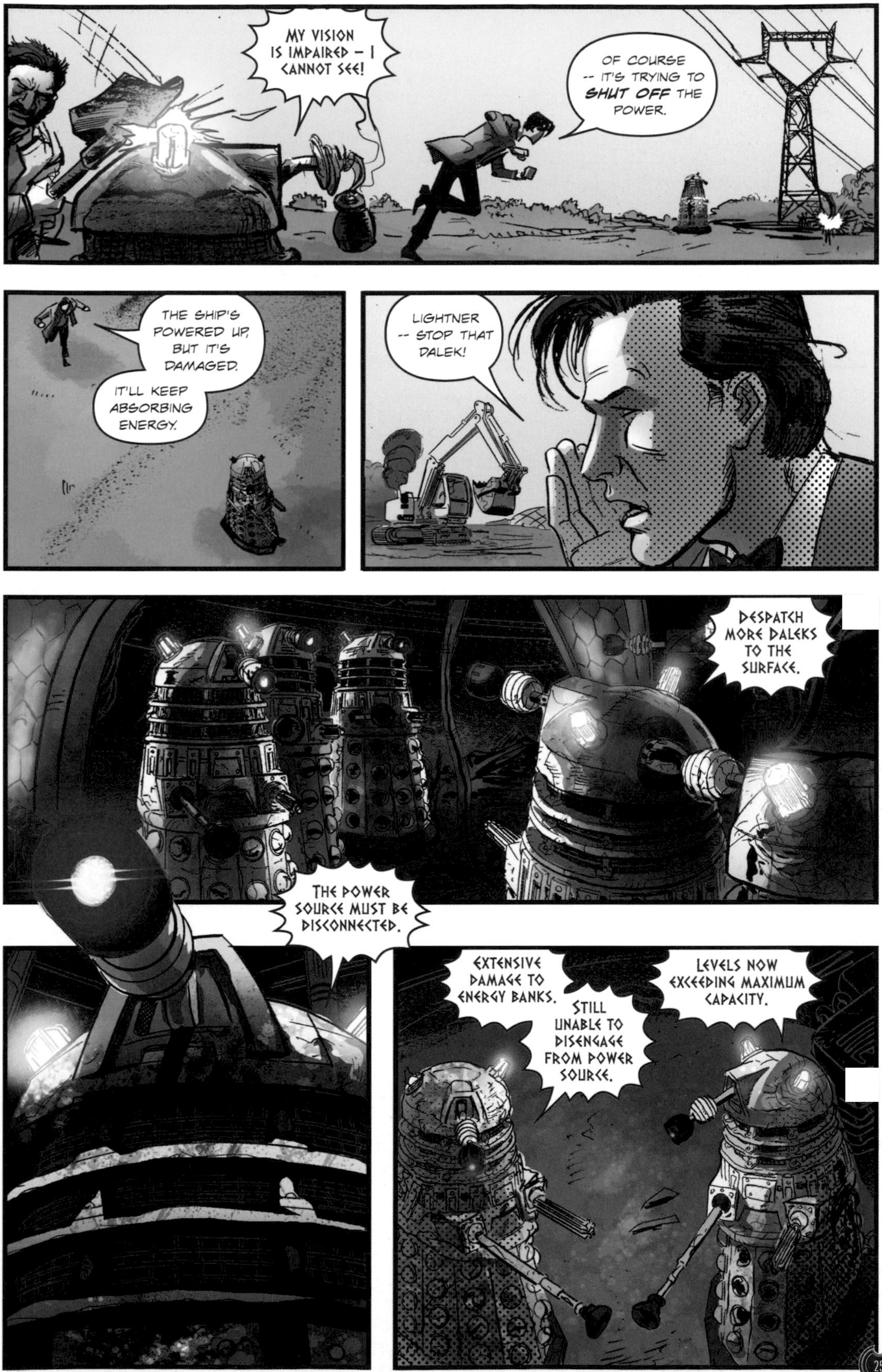
MY VISION IS IMPAIRED — I CANNOT SEE!
OF COURSE -- IT'S TRYING TO SHUT OFF THE POWER.
THE SHIP'S POWERED UP, BUT IT'S DAMAGED.
IT'LL KEEP ABSORBING ENERGY.
LIGHTNER -- STOP THAT DALEK!
DESPATCH MORE DALEKS TO THE SURFACE.
THE POWER SOURCE MUST BE DISCONNECTED.
EXTENSIVE DAMAGE TO ENERGY BANKS.
STILL UNABLE TO DISENGAGE FROM POWER SOURCE.
LEVELS NOW EXCEEDING MAXIMUM CAPACITY.

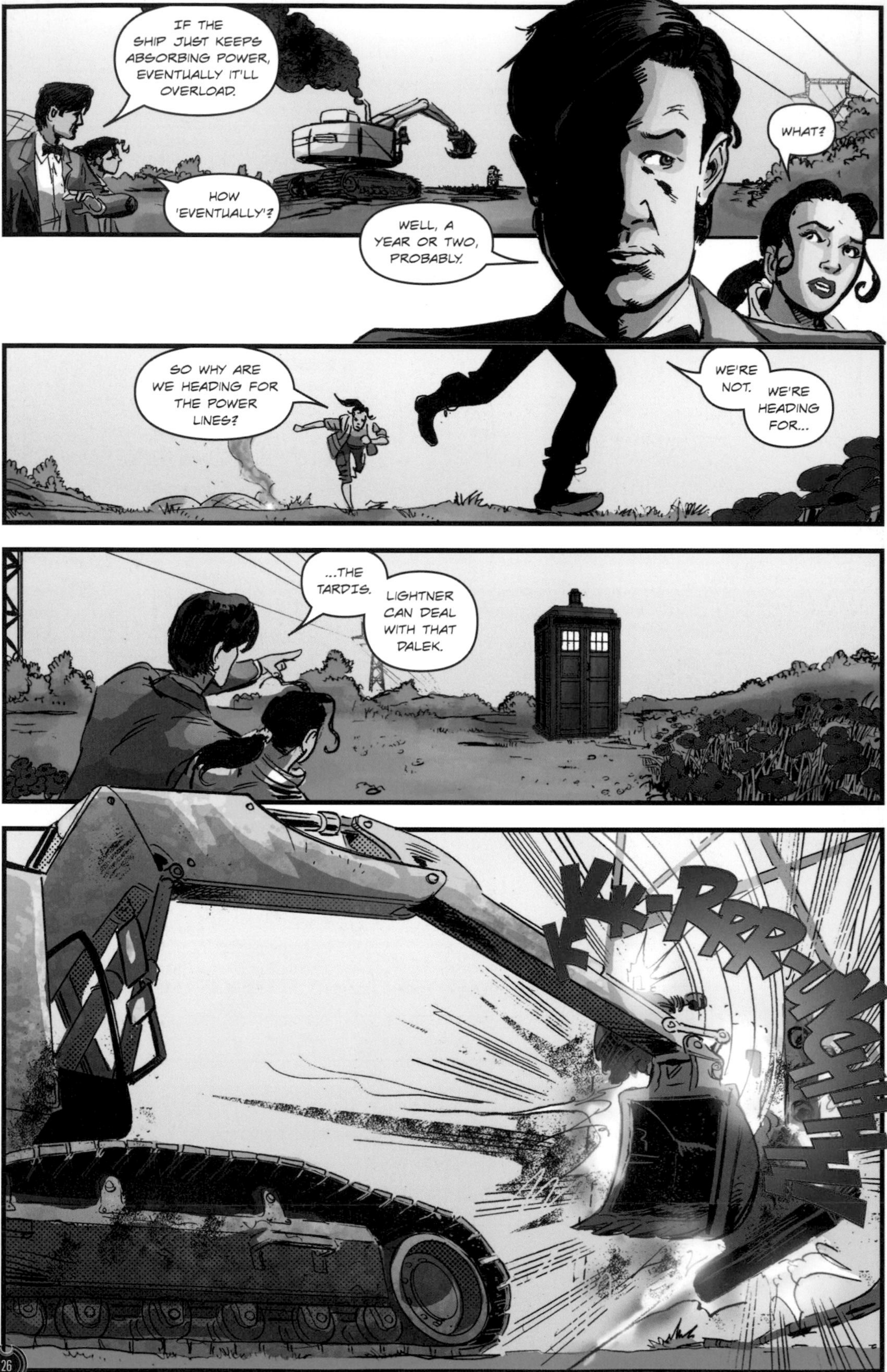
IF THE SHIP JUST KEEPS ABSORBING POWER, EVENTUALLY IT'LL OVERLOAD.
HOW 'EVENTUALLY'?
WHAT?
WELL, A YEAR OR TWO, PROBABLY.
SO WHY ARE WE HEADING FOR THE POWER LINES?
WE'RE NOT.
WE'RE HEADING FOR...
...THE TARDIS.
LIGHTNER CAN DEAL WITH THAT DALEK.
KK-RRR-UNCHHHH!

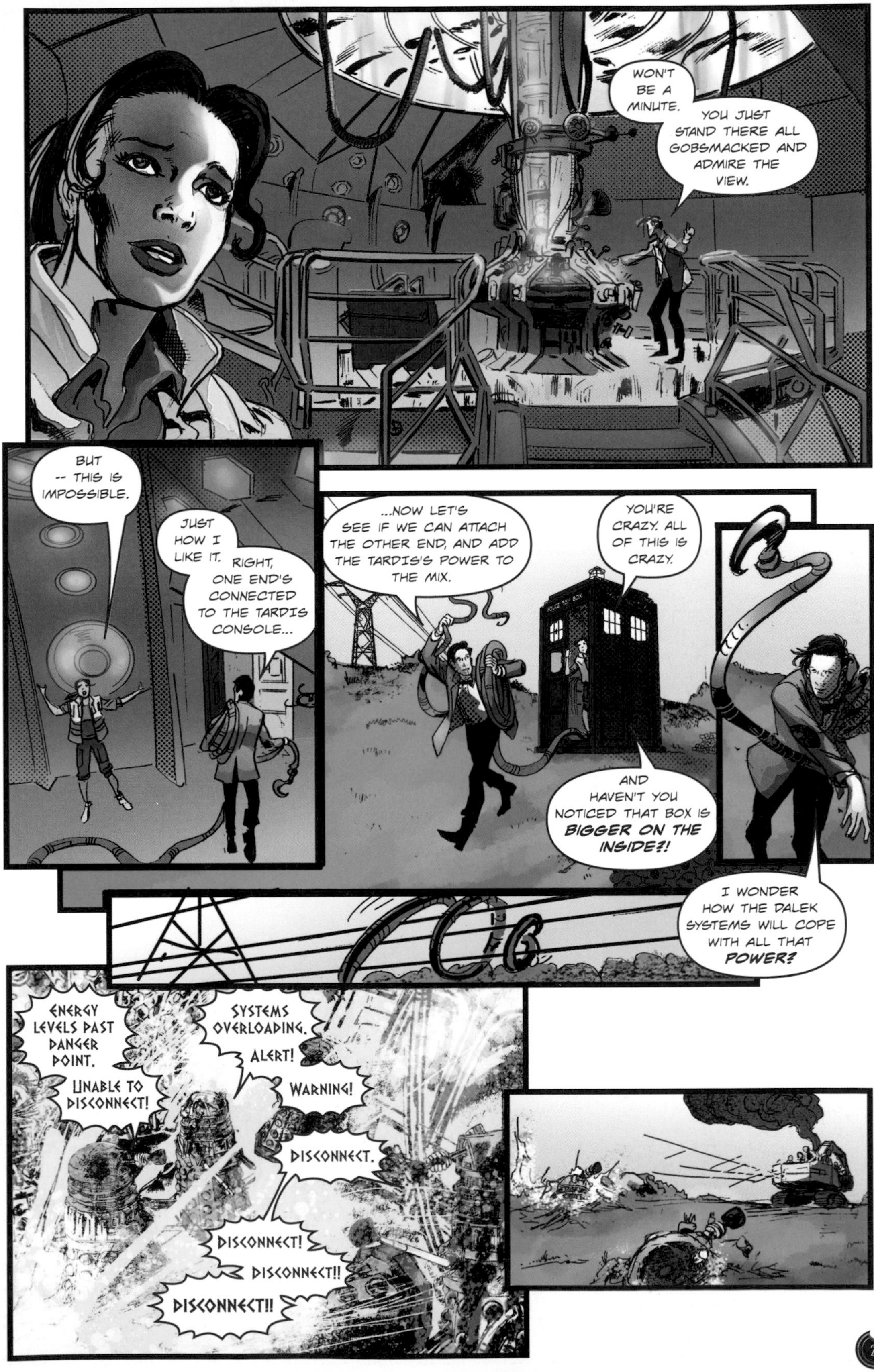
WON'T BE A MINUTE.
YOU JUST STAND THERE ALL GOBSMACKED AND ADMIRE THE VIEW.
BUT -- THIS IS IMPOSSIBLE.
JUST HOW I LIKE IT.
RIGHT, ONE END'S CONNECTED TO THE TARDIS CONSOLE...
...NOW LET'S SEE IF WE CAN ATTACH THE OTHER END, AND ADD THE TARDIS'S POWER TO THE MIX.
YOU'RE CRAZY. ALL OF THIS IS CRAZY.
AND HAVEN'T YOU NOTICED THAT BOX IS BIGGER ON THE INSIDE?!
I WONDER HOW THE DALEK SYSTEMS WILL COPE WITH ALL THAT POWER?
ENERGY LEVELS PAST DANGER POINT.
UNABLE TO DISCONNECT!
SYSTEMS OVERLOADING.
ALERT!
WARNING!
DISCONNECT.
DISCONNECT!
DISCONNECT!!
DISCONNECT!!

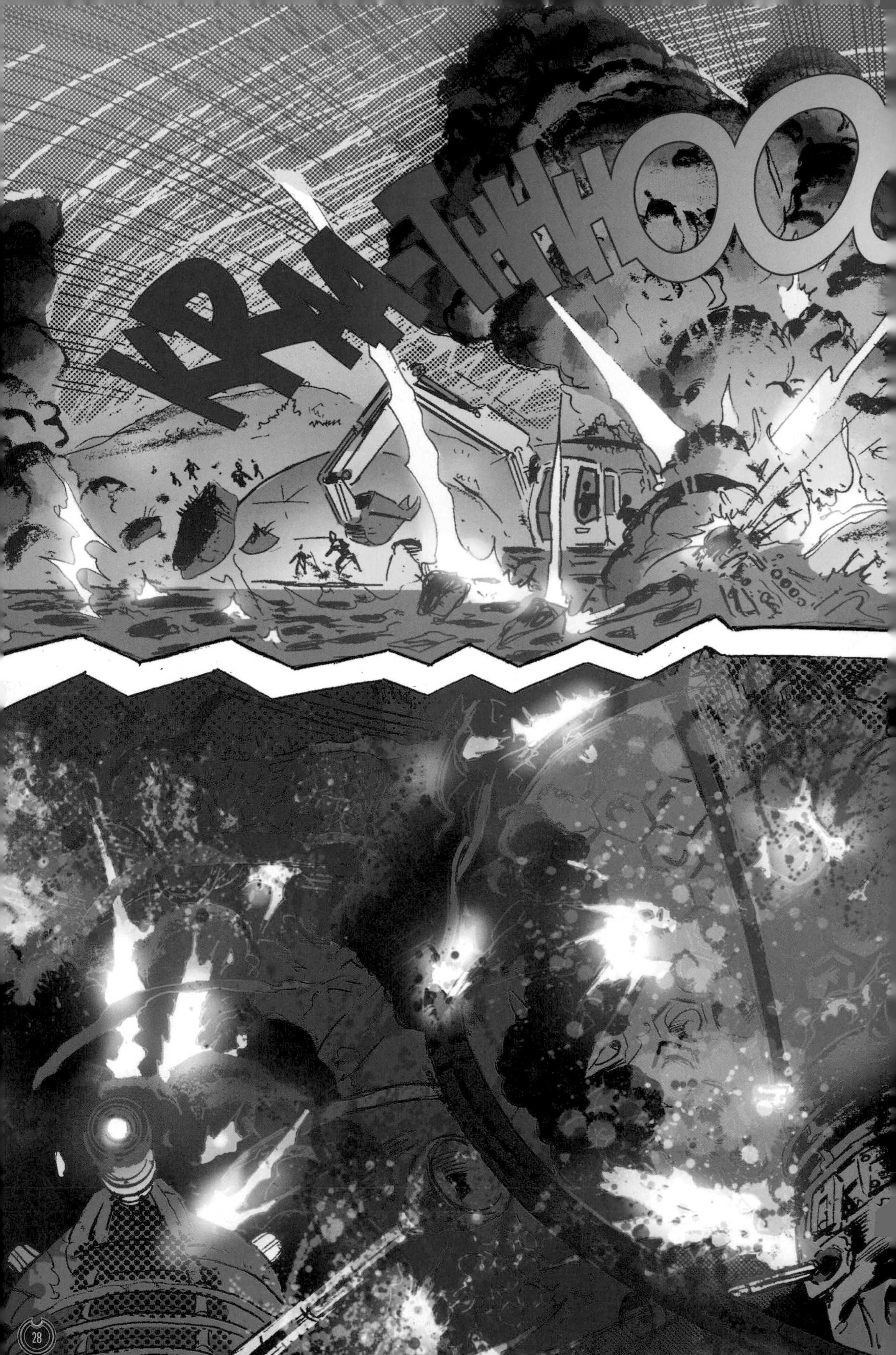
VRAA-THHOOO

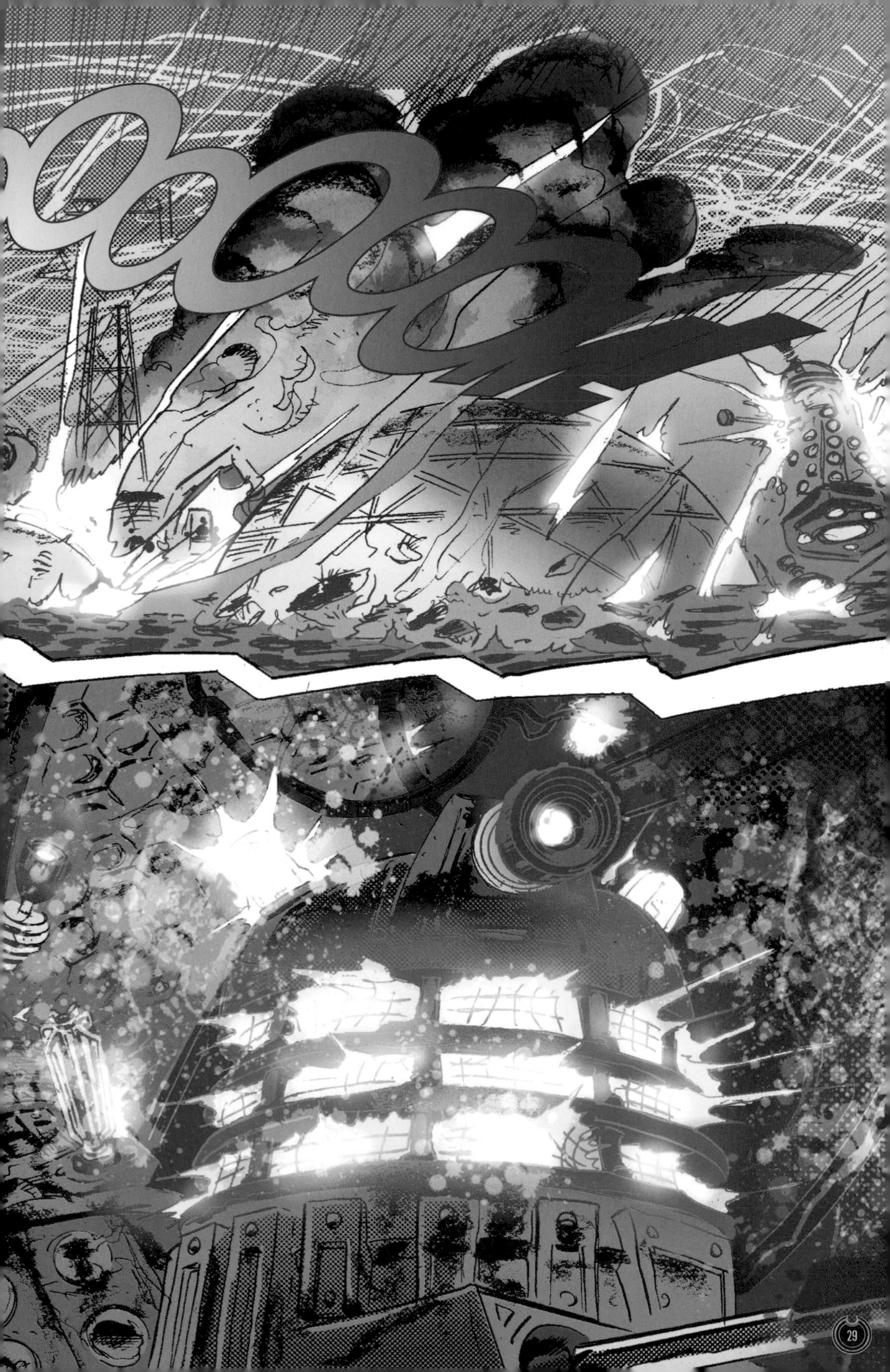

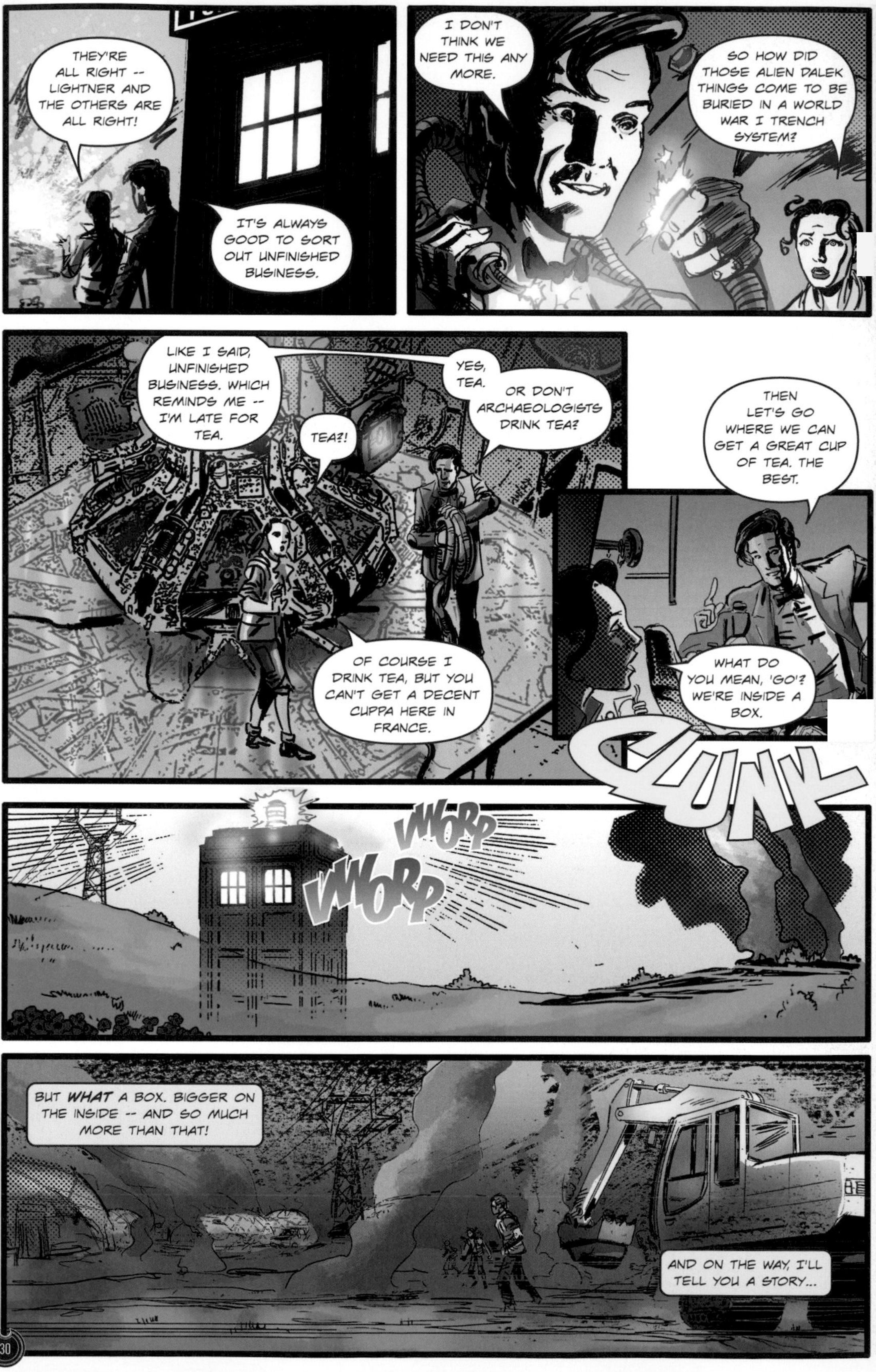
THEY'RE ALL RIGHT -- LIGHTNER AND THE OTHERS ARE ALL RIGHT!
IT'S ALWAYS GOOD TO SORT OUT UNFINISHED BUSINESS.
I DON'T THINK WE NEED THIS ANY MORE.
SO HOW DID THOSE ALIEN DALEK THINGS COME TO BE BURIED IN A WORLD WAR I TRENCH SYSTEM?
LIKE I SAID, UNFINISHED BUSINESS. WHICH REMINDS ME -- I'M LATE FOR TEA.
TEA?!
YES, TEA.
OR DON'T ARCHAEOLOGISTS DRINK TEA?
OF COURSE I DRINK TEA, BUT YOU CAN'T GET A DECENT CUPPA HERE IN FRANCE.
THEN LET'S GO WHERE WE CAN GET A GREAT CUP OF TEA. THE BEST.
WHAT DO YOU MEAN, 'GO'? WE'RE INSIDE A BOX.
CLUNK
VWORP
VWORP
BUT *WHAT* A BOX. BIGGER ON THE INSIDE -- AND SO MUCH MORE THAN THAT!
AND ON THE WAY, I'LL TELL YOU A STORY...

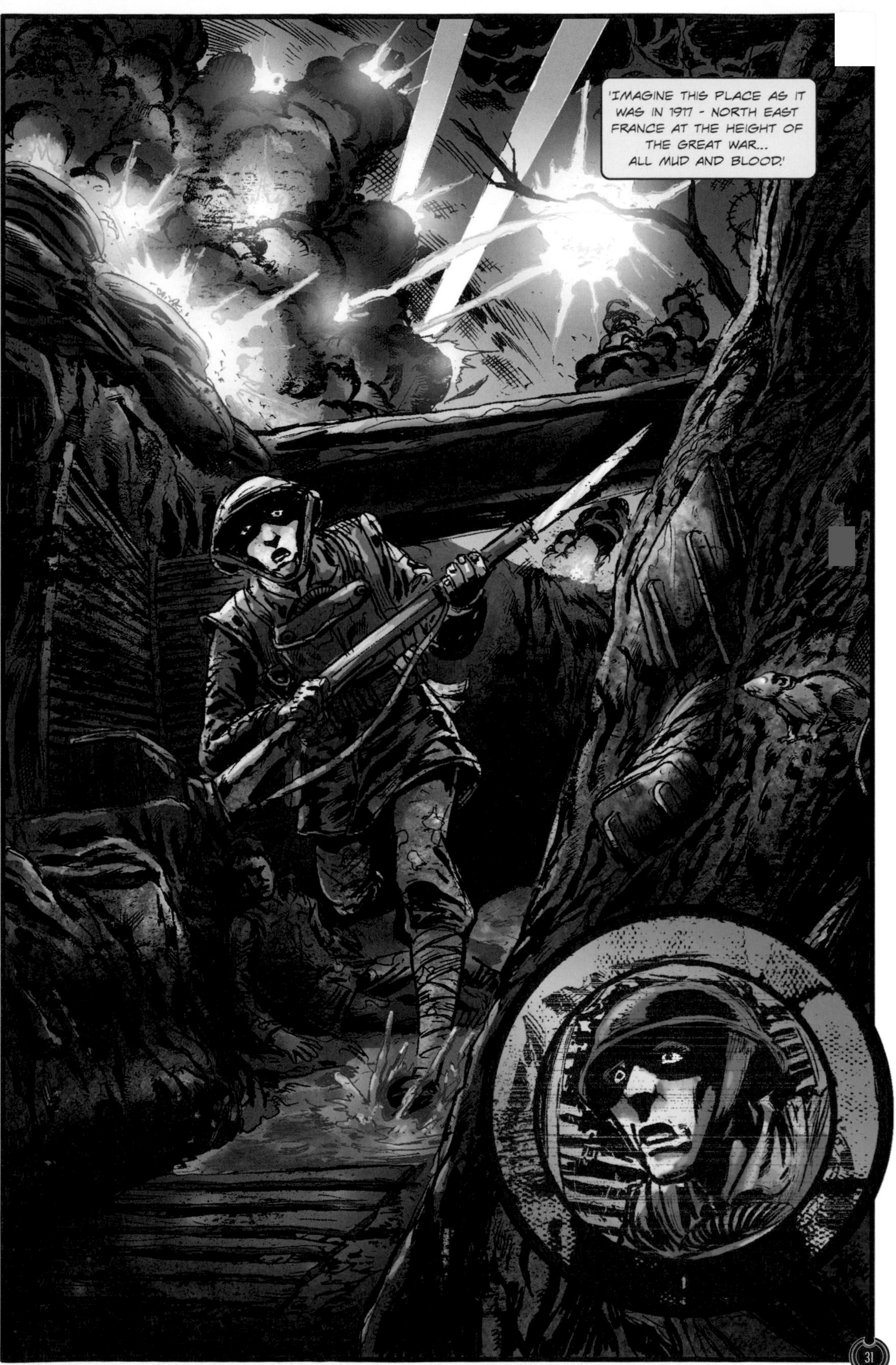
'IMAGINE THIS PLACE AS IT WAS IN 1917 - NORTH EAST FRANCE AT THE HEIGHT OF THE GREAT WAR... ALL MUD AND BLOOD.'

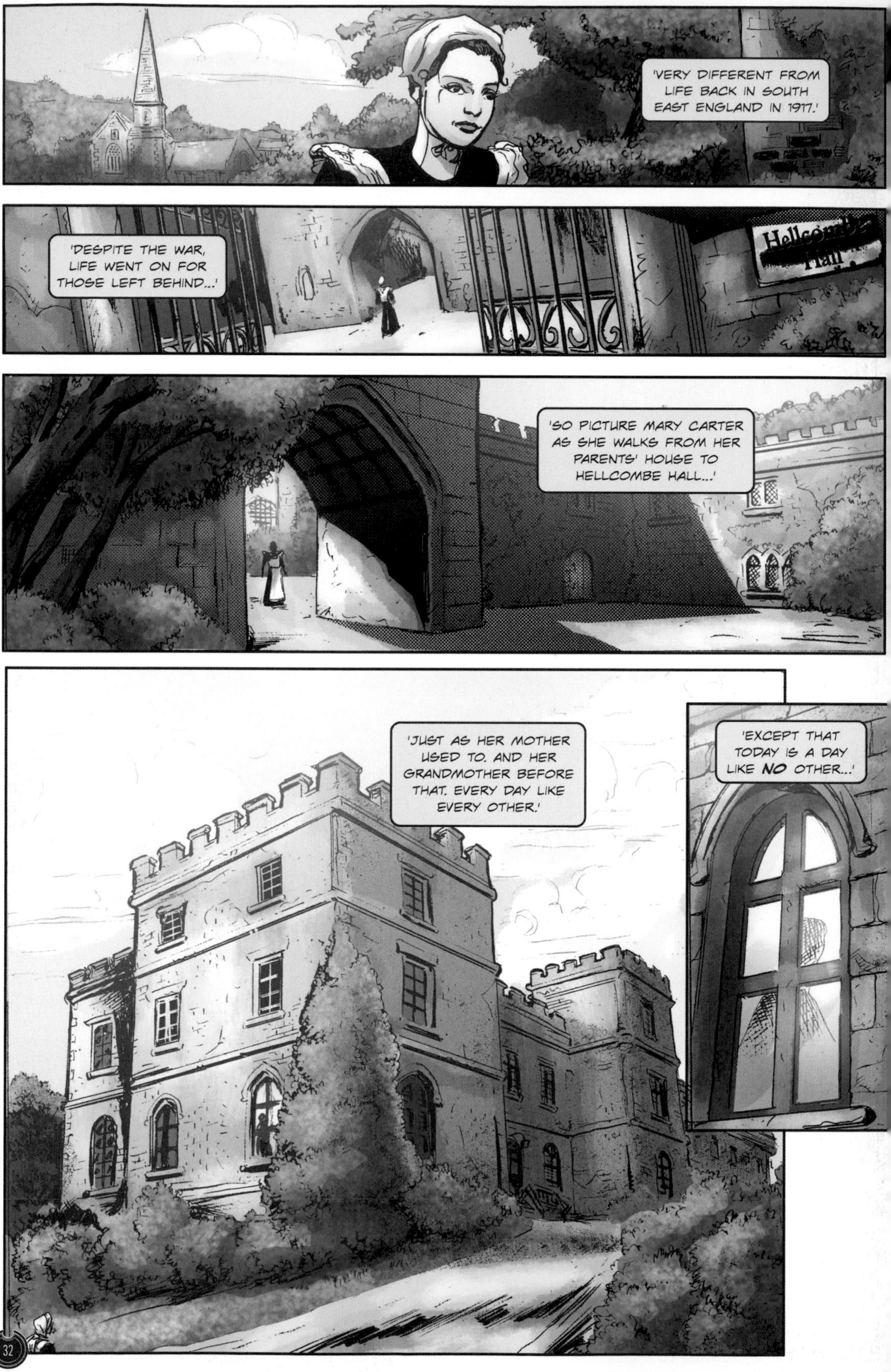
'VERY DIFFERENT FROM LIFE BACK IN SOUTH EAST ENGLAND IN 1917.'
'DESPITE THE WAR, LIFE WENT ON FOR THOSE LEFT BEHIND...'
Hellcombe Hall
'SO PICTURE MARY CARTER AS SHE WALKS FROM HER PARENTS' HOUSE TO HELLCOMBE HALL...'
'JUST AS HER MOTHER USED TO. AND HER GRANDMOTHER BEFORE THAT. EVERY DAY LIKE EVERY OTHER.'
'EXCEPT THAT TODAY IS A DAY LIKE NO OTHER...'

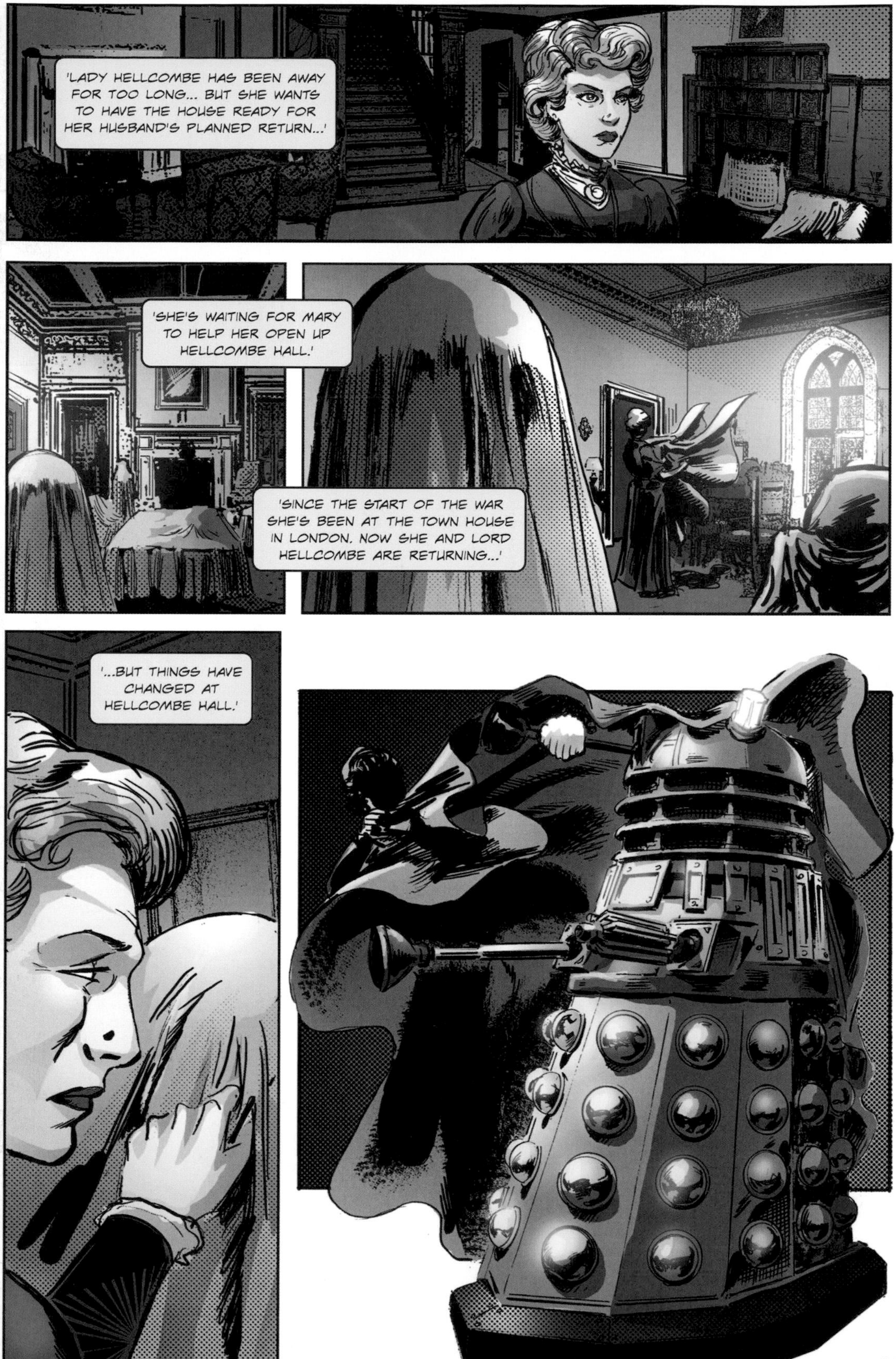
'LADY HELLCOMBE HAS BEEN AWAY FOR TOO LONG... BUT SHE WANTS TO HAVE THE HOUSE READY FOR HER HUSBAND'S PLANNED RETURN...'
'SHE'S WAITING FOR MARY TO HELP HER OPEN UP HELLCOMBE HALL.'
'SINCE THE START OF THE WAR SHE'S BEEN AT THE TOWN HOUSE IN LONDON. NOW SHE AND LORD HELLCOMBE ARE RETURNING...'
'...BUT THINGS HAVE CHANGED AT HELLCOMBE HALL.'

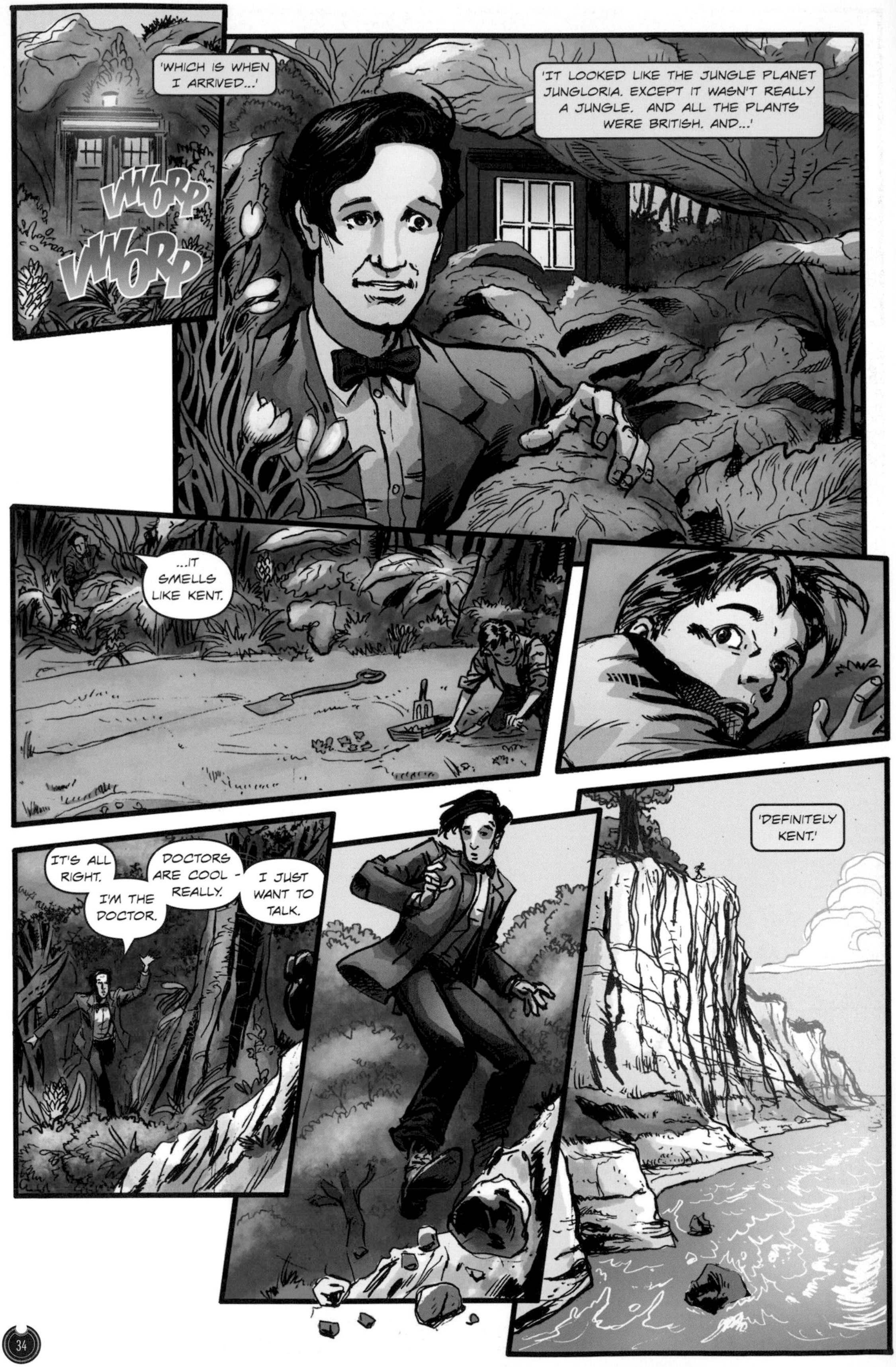

'WHICH IS WHEN I ARRIVED...'
VWORP VWORP
'IT LOOKED LIKE THE JUNGLE PLANET JUNGLORIA. EXCEPT IT WASN'T REALLY A JUNGLE. AND ALL THE PLANTS WERE BRITISH. AND...'
...IT SMELLS LIKE KENT.
IT'S ALL RIGHT.
I'M THE DOCTOR.
DOCTORS ARE COOL - REALLY.
I JUST WANT TO TALK.
'DEFINITELY KENT.'

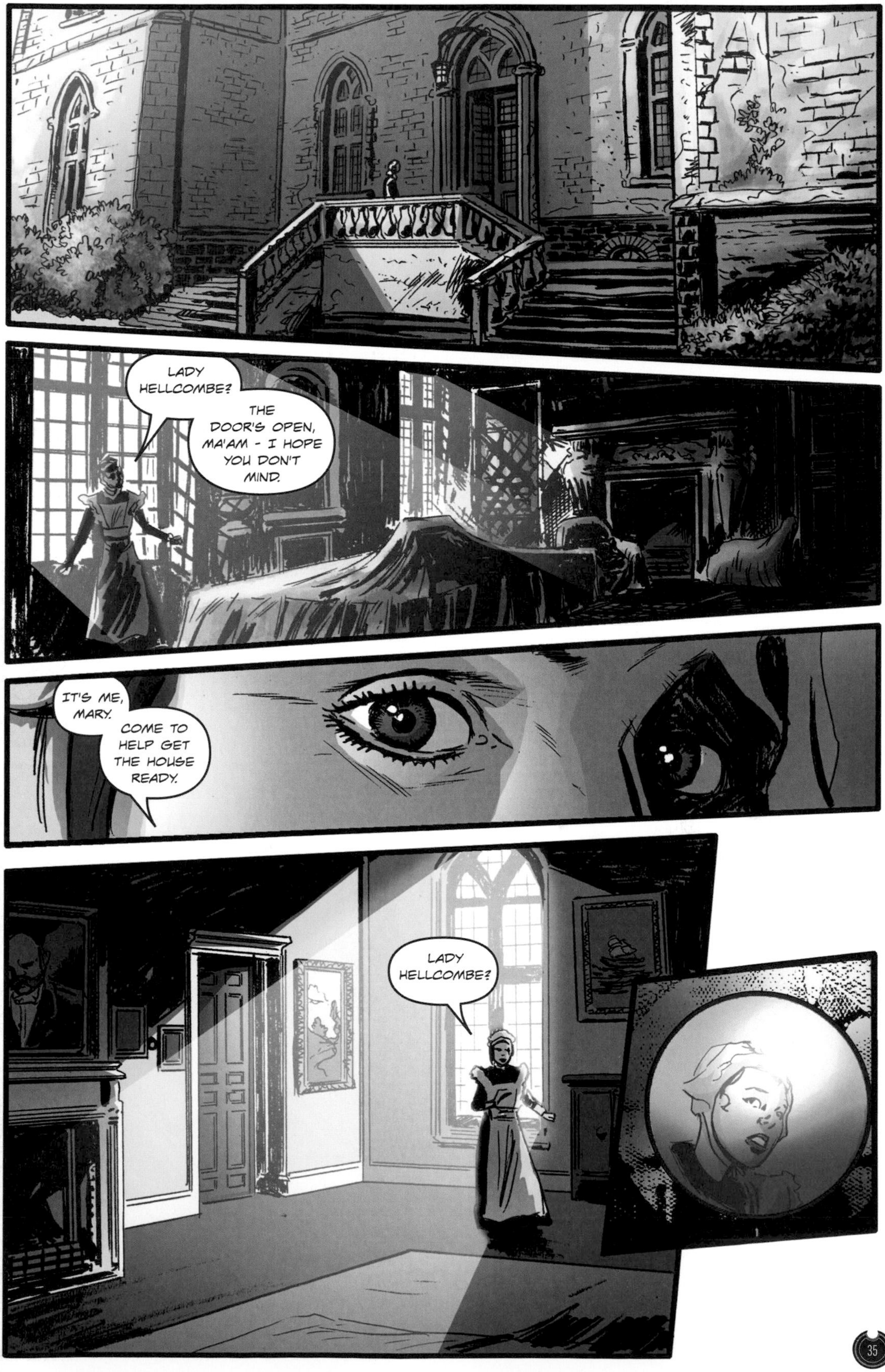
LADY HELLCOMBE?
THE DOOR'S OPEN, MA'AM - I HOPE YOU DON'T MIND.
IT'S ME, MARY.
COME TO HELP GET THE HOUSE READY.
LADY HELLCOMBE?

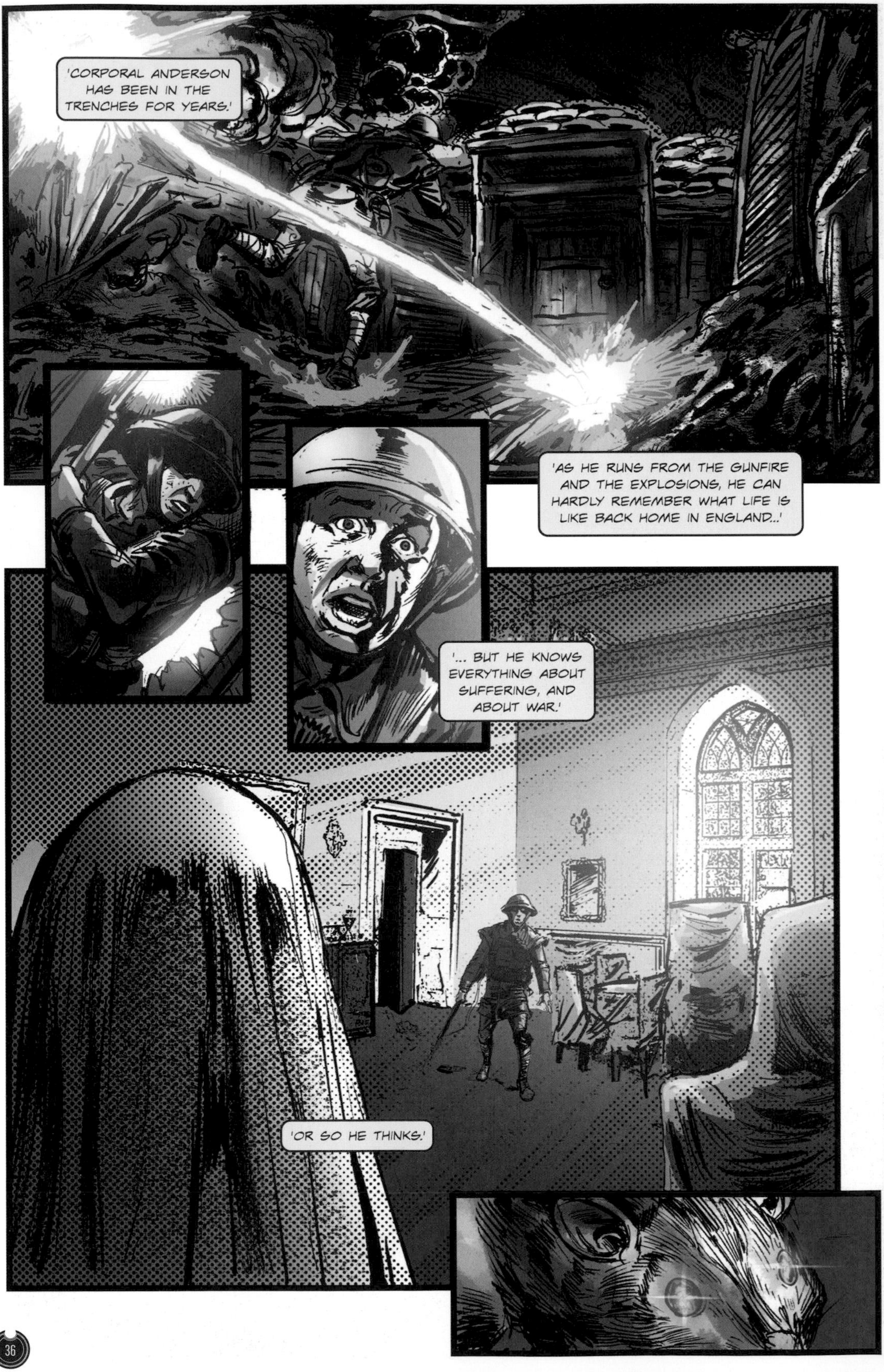
'CORPORAL ANDERSON HAS BEEN IN THE TRENCHES FOR YEARS.'
'AS HE RUNS FROM THE GUNFIRE AND THE EXPLOSIONS, HE CAN HARDLY REMEMBER WHAT LIFE IS LIKE BACK HOME IN ENGLAND...'
'... BUT HE KNOWS EVERYTHING ABOUT SUFFERING, AND ABOUT WAR.'
'OR SO HE THINKS.'

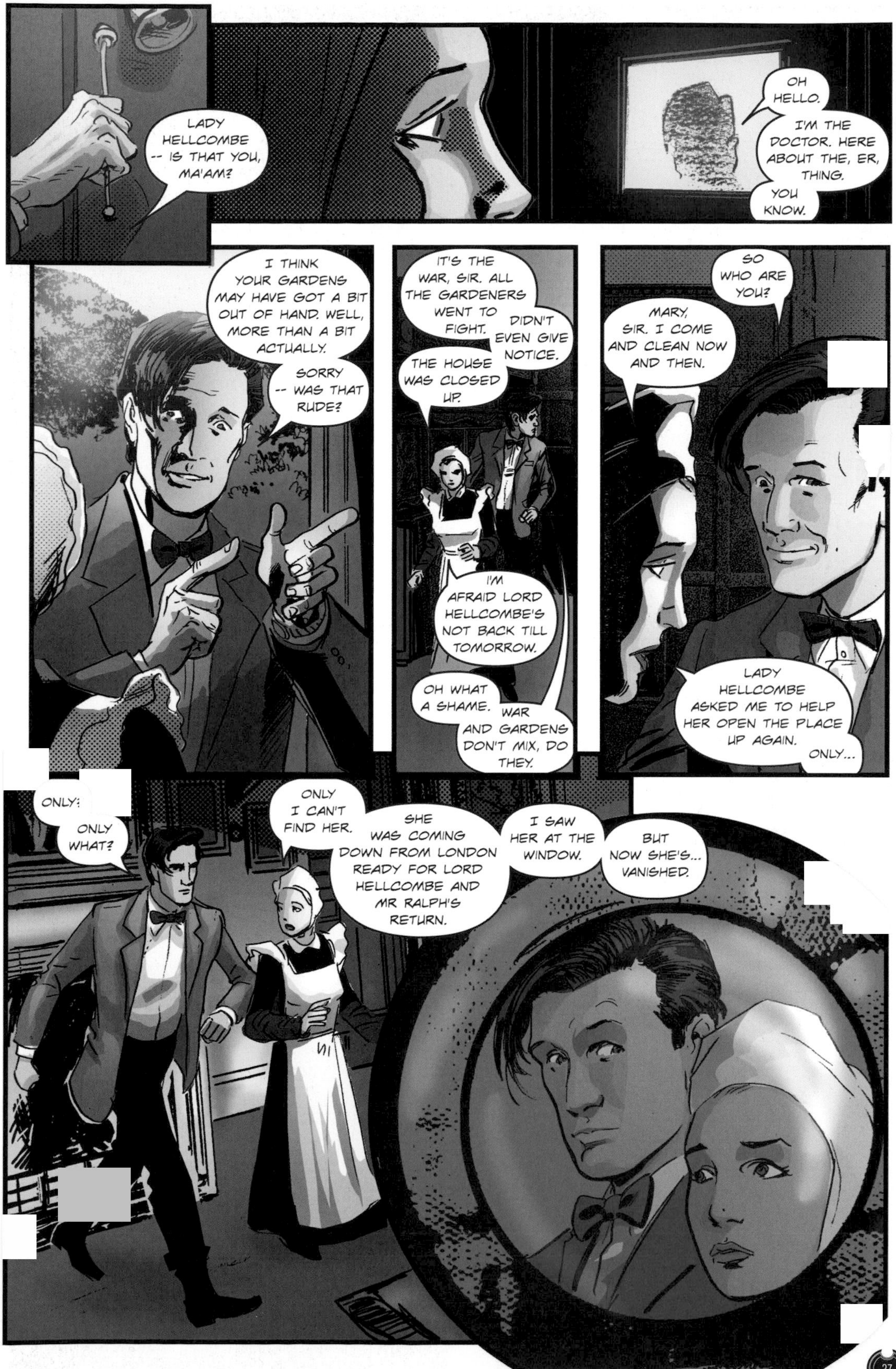
LADY HELLCOMBE -- IS THAT YOU, MA'AM?
OH HELLO.
I'M THE DOCTOR. HERE ABOUT THE, ER, THING.
YOU KNOW.
I THINK YOUR GARDENS MAY HAVE GOT A BIT OUT OF HAND. WELL, MORE THAN A BIT ACTUALLY.
SORRY -- WAS THAT RUDE?
IT'S THE WAR, SIR. ALL THE GARDENERS WENT TO FIGHT.
DIDN'T EVEN GIVE NOTICE.
THE HOUSE WAS CLOSED UP.
I'M AFRAID LORD HELLCOMBE'S NOT BACK TILL TOMORROW.
OH WHAT A SHAME.
WAR AND GARDENS DON'T MIX, DO THEY.
SO WHO ARE YOU?
MARY, SIR. I COME AND CLEAN NOW AND THEN.
LADY HELLCOMBE ASKED ME TO HELP HER OPEN THE PLACE UP AGAIN.
ONLY...
ONLY?
ONLY WHAT?
ONLY I CAN'T FIND HER.
SHE WAS COMING DOWN FROM LONDON READY FOR LORD HELLCOMBE AND MR RALPH'S RETURN.
I SAW HER AT THE WINDOW.
BUT NOW SHE'S... VANISHED.

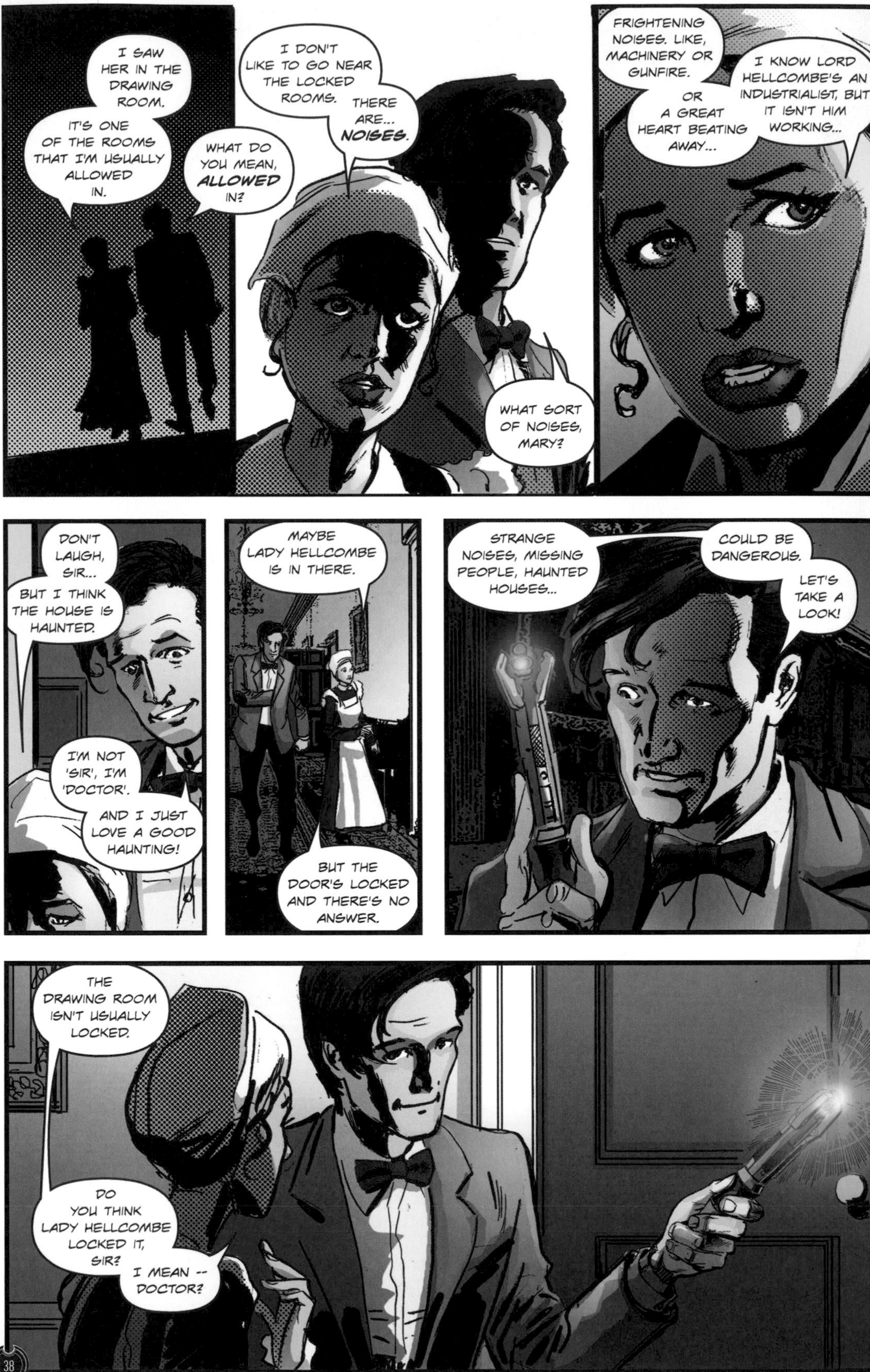

I SAW HER IN THE DRAWING ROOM.
IT'S ONE OF THE ROOMS THAT I'M USUALLY ALLOWED IN.
WHAT DO YOU MEAN, ALLOWED IN?
I DON'T LIKE TO GO NEAR THE LOCKED ROOMS.
THERE ARE... NOISES.
WHAT SORT OF NOISES, MARY?
FRIGHTENING NOISES. LIKE, MACHINERY OR GUNFIRE.
OR A GREAT HEART BEATING AWAY...
I KNOW LORD HELLCOMBE'S AN INDUSTRIALIST, BUT IT ISN'T HIM WORKING...
DON'T LAUGH, SIR...
BUT I THINK THE HOUSE IS HAUNTED.
I'M NOT 'SIR', I'M 'DOCTOR'.
AND I JUST LOVE A GOOD HAUNTING!
MAYBE LADY HELLCOMBE IS IN THERE.
BUT THE DOOR'S LOCKED AND THERE'S NO ANSWER.
STRANGE NOISES, MISSING PEOPLE, HAUNTED HOUSES...
COULD BE DANGEROUS.
LET'S TAKE A LOOK!
THE DRAWING ROOM ISN'T USUALLY LOCKED.
DO YOU THINK LADY HELLCOMBE LOCKED IT, SIR?
I MEAN -- DOCTOR?

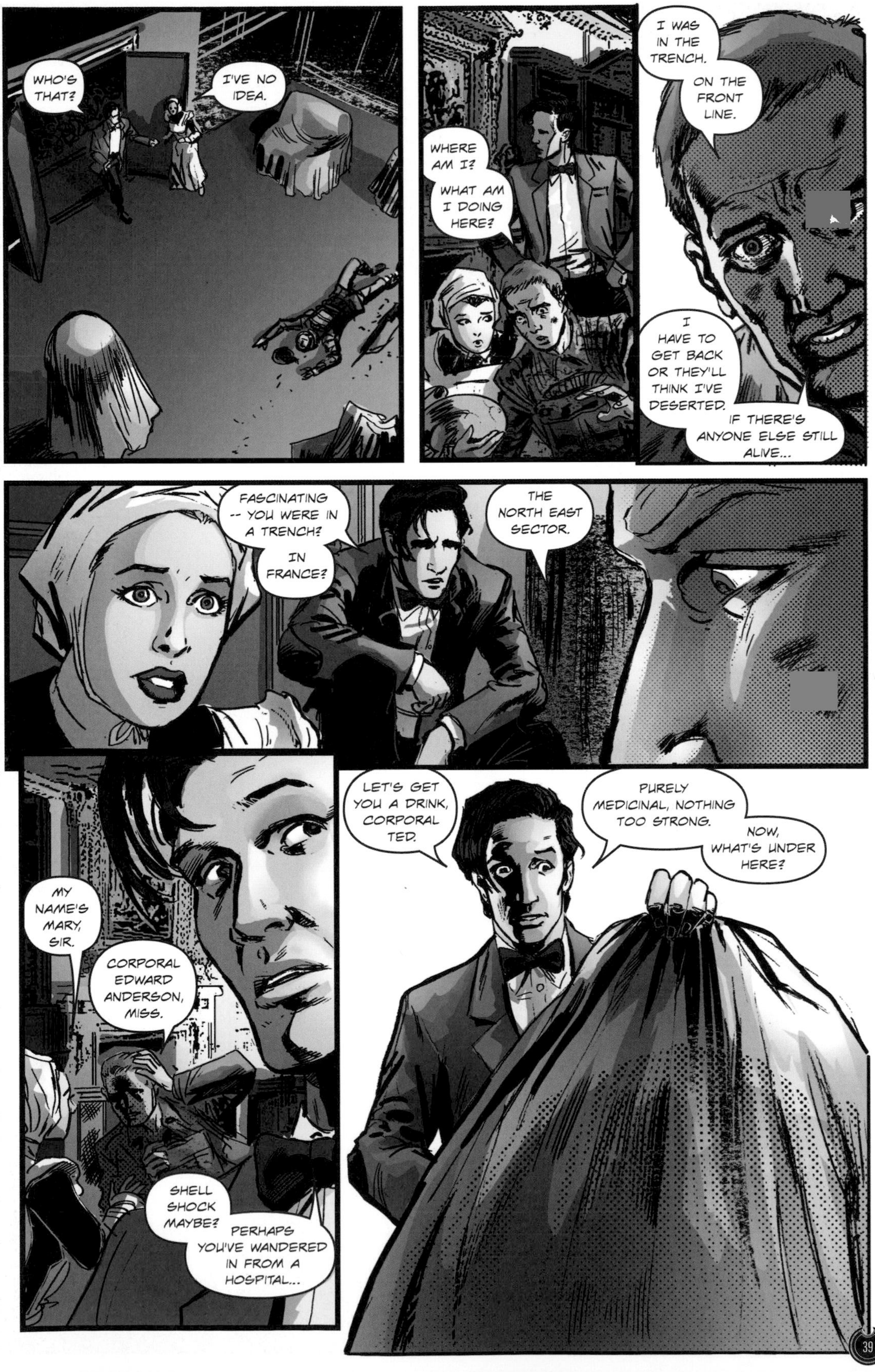
WHO'S THAT?
I'VE NO IDEA.
WHERE AM I?
WHAT AM I DOING HERE?
I WAS IN THE TRENCH.
ON THE FRONT LINE.
I HAVE TO GET BACK OR THEY'LL THINK I'VE DESERTED.
IF THERE'S ANYONE ELSE STILL ALIVE...
FASCINATING -- YOU WERE IN A TRENCH?
IN FRANCE?
THE NORTH EAST SECTOR.
MY NAME'S MARY, SIR.
CORPORAL EDWARD ANDERSON, MISS.
SHELL SHOCK MAYBE?
PERHAPS YOU'VE WANDERED IN FROM A HOSPITAL...
LET'S GET YOU A DRINK, CORPORAL TED.
PURELY MEDICINAL, NOTHING TOO STRONG.
NOW, WHAT'S UNDER HERE?

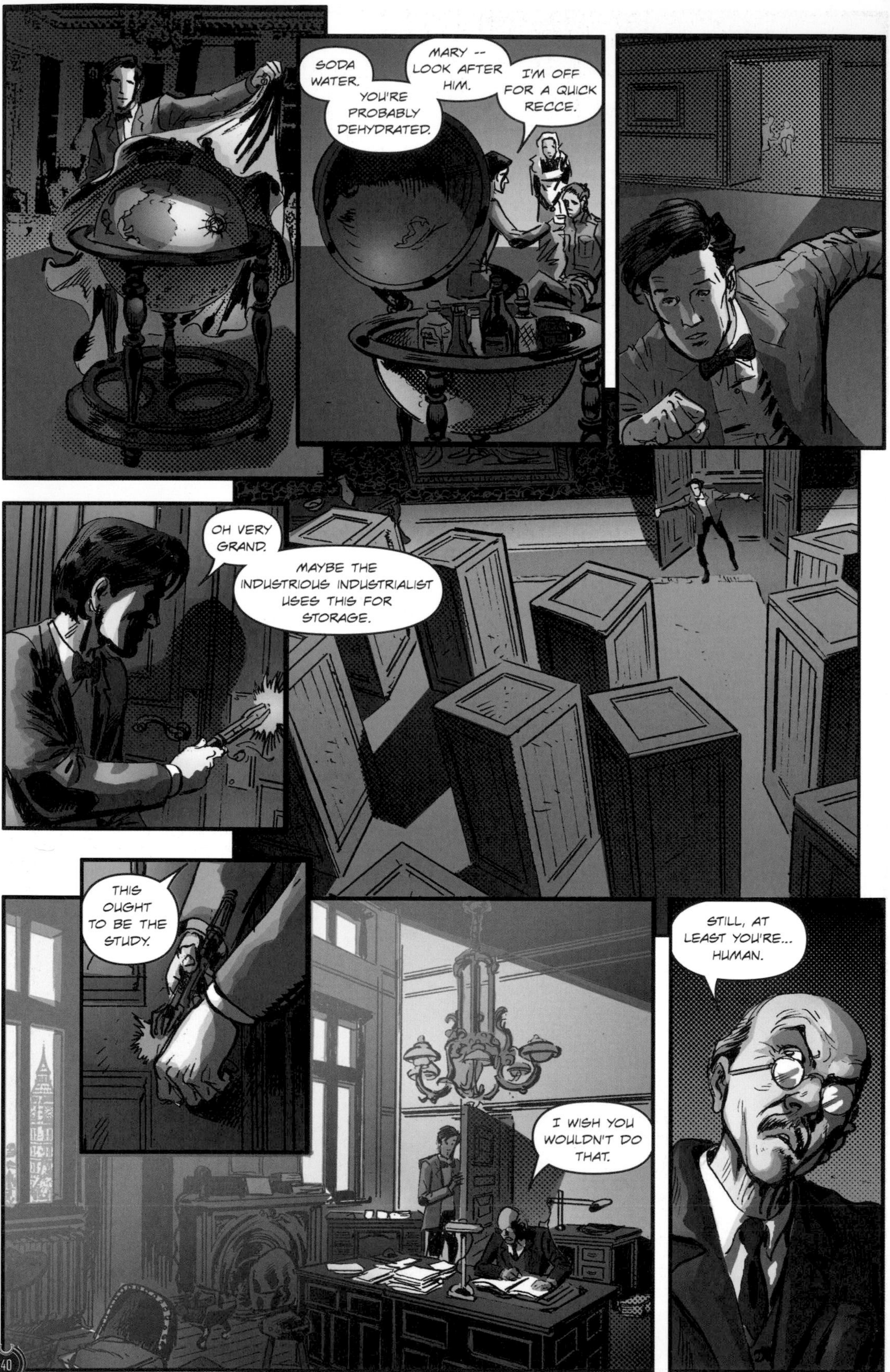
SODA WATER.
YOU'RE PROBABLY DEHYDRATED.
MARY -- LOOK AFTER HIM.
I'M OFF FOR A QUICK RECCE.
OH VERY GRAND.
MAYBE THE INDUSTRIOUS INDUSTRIALIST USES THIS FOR STORAGE.
THIS OUGHT TO BE THE STUDY.
I WISH YOU WOULDN'T DO THAT.
STILL, AT LEAST YOU'RE... HUMAN.

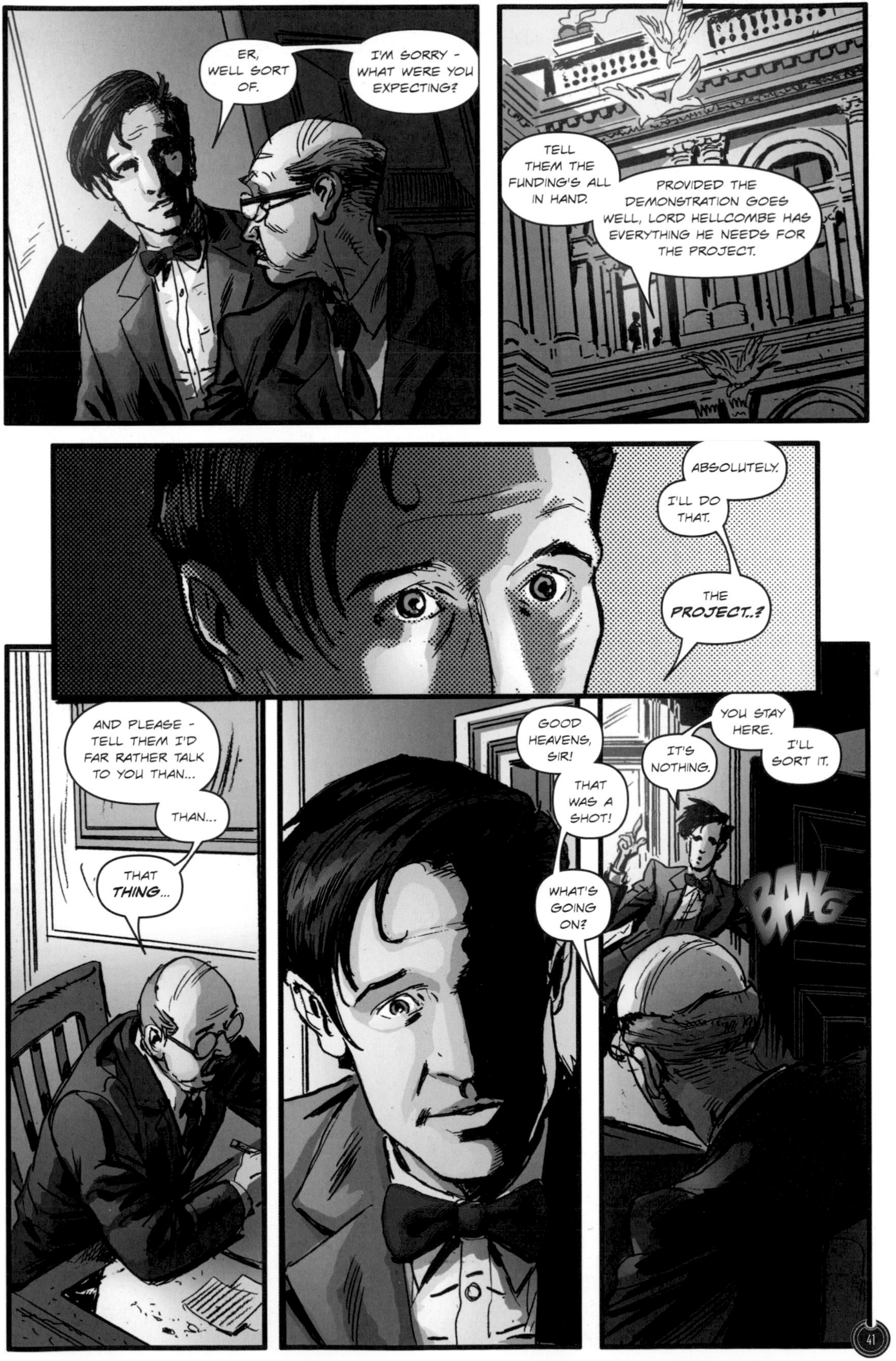
ER, WELL SORT OF.
I'M SORRY - WHAT WERE YOU EXPECTING?
TELL THEM THE FUNDING'S ALL IN HAND.
PROVIDED THE DEMONSTRATION GOES WELL, LORD HELLCOMBE HAS EVERYTHING HE NEEDS FOR THE PROJECT.
ABSOLUTELY.
I'LL DO THAT.
THE *PROJECT..?*
AND PLEASE - TELL THEM I'D FAR RATHER TALK TO YOU THAN...
THAN...
THAT *THING*...
GOOD HEAVENS, SIR!
THAT WAS A SHOT!
WHAT'S GOING ON?
IT'S NOTHING.
YOU STAY HERE.
I'LL SORT IT.
BANG

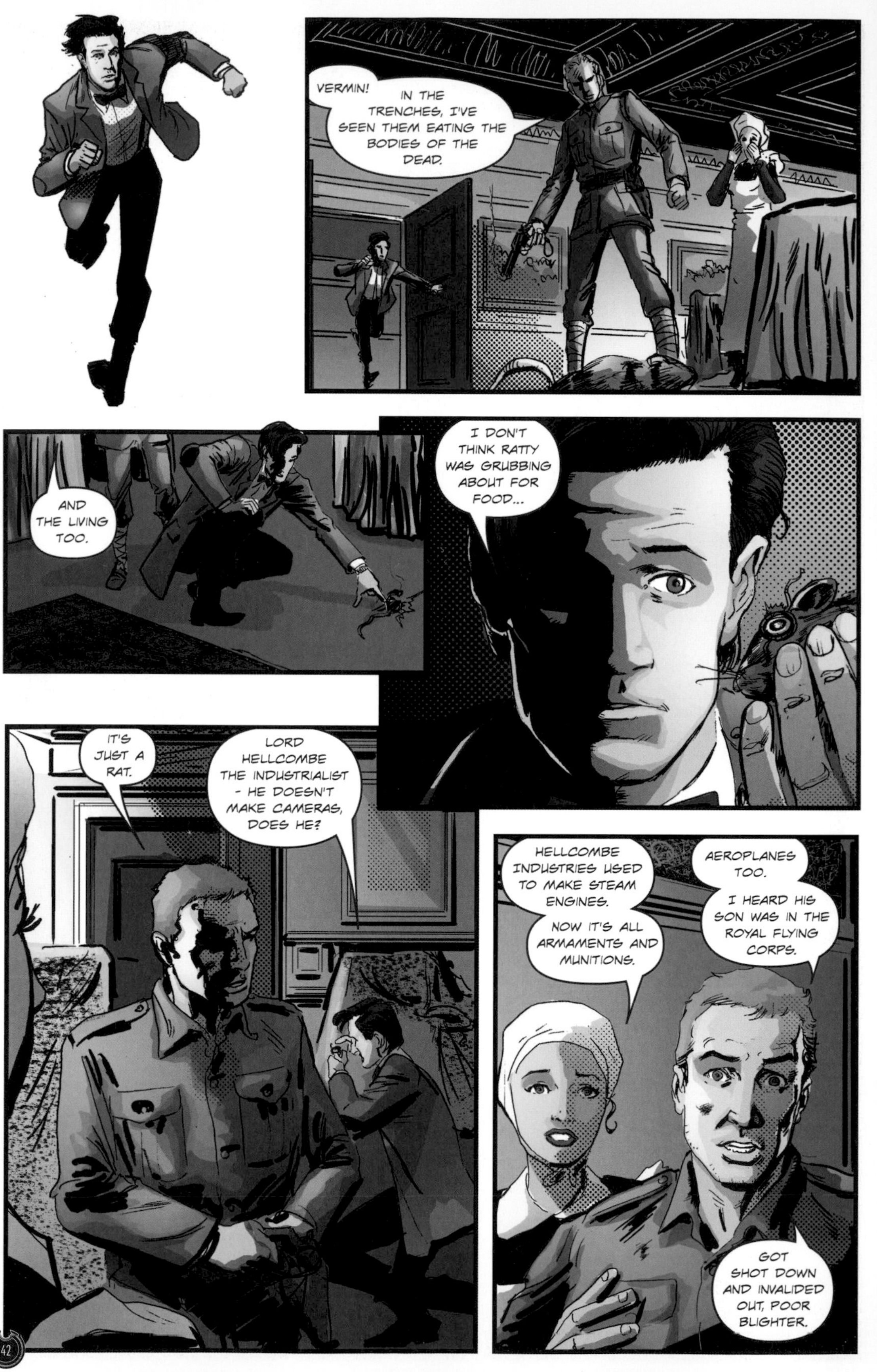
VERMIN!
IN THE TRENCHES, I'VE SEEN THEM EATING THE BODIES OF THE DEAD.
AND THE LIVING TOO.
I DON'T THINK RATTY WAS GRUBBING ABOUT FOR FOOD...
IT'S JUST A RAT.
LORD HELLCOMBE THE INDUSTRIALIST - HE DOESN'T MAKE CAMERAS, DOES HE?
HELLCOMBE INDUSTRIES USED TO MAKE STEAM ENGINES.
NOW IT'S ALL ARMAMENTS AND MUNITIONS.
AEROPLANES TOO.
I HEARD HIS SON WAS IN THE ROYAL FLYING CORPS.
GOT SHOT DOWN AND INVALIDED OUT, POOR BLIGHTER.

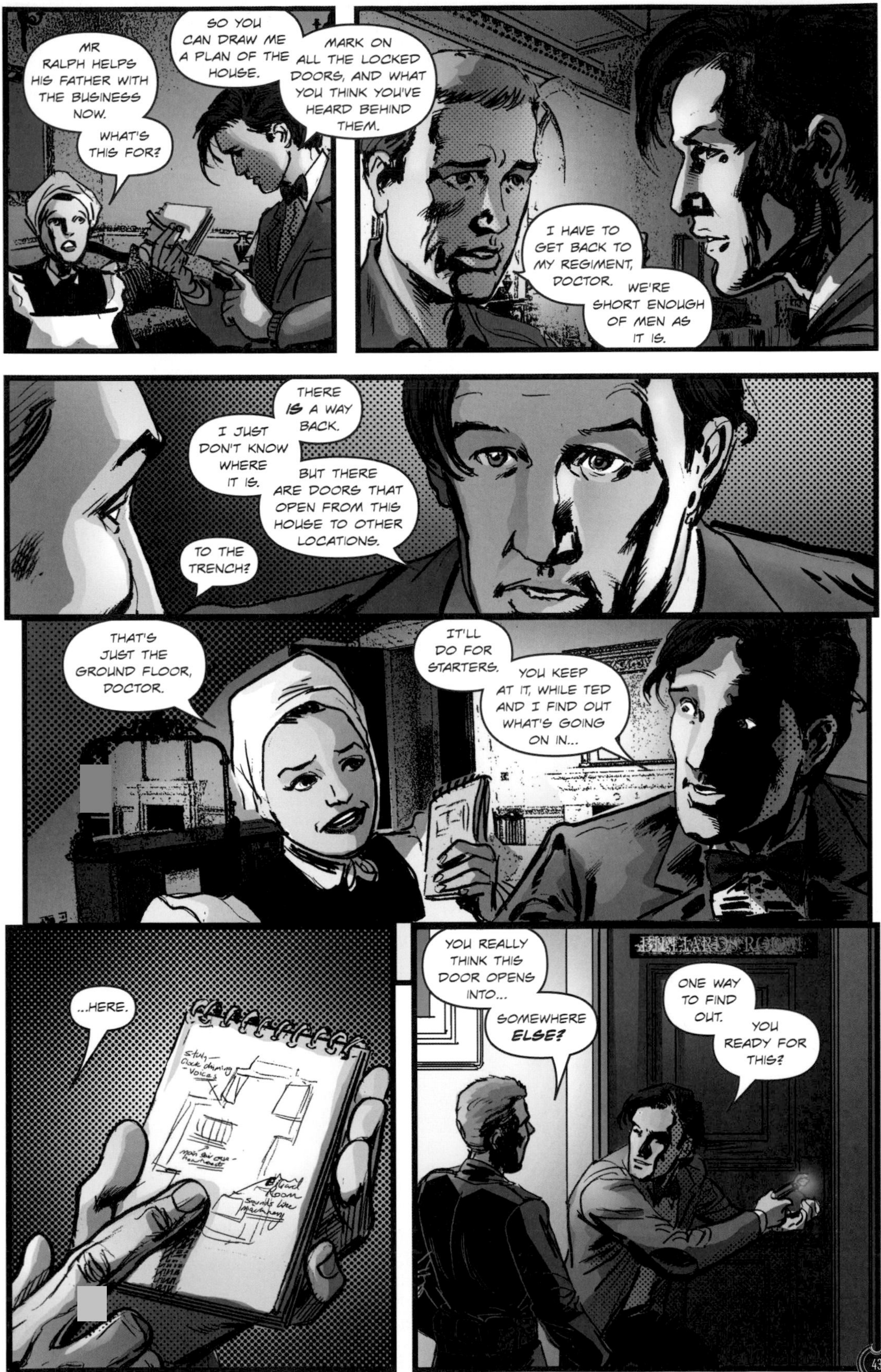
MR RALPH HELPS HIS FATHER WITH THE BUSINESS NOW.
WHAT'S THIS FOR?
SO YOU CAN DRAW ME A PLAN OF THE HOUSE.
MARK ON ALL THE LOCKED DOORS, AND WHAT YOU THINK YOU'VE HEARD BEHIND THEM.
I HAVE TO GET BACK TO MY REGIMENT, DOCTOR.
WE'RE SHORT ENOUGH OF MEN AS IT IS.
THERE ***IS*** A WAY BACK.
I JUST DON'T KNOW WHERE IT IS.
BUT THERE ARE DOORS THAT OPEN FROM THIS HOUSE TO OTHER LOCATIONS.
TO THE TRENCH?
THAT'S JUST THE GROUND FLOOR, DOCTOR.
IT'LL DO FOR STARTERS.
YOU KEEP AT IT, WHILE TED AND I FIND OUT WHAT'S GOING ON IN...
...HERE.
YOU REALLY THINK THIS DOOR OPENS INTO...
SOMEWHERE ***ELSE?***
ONE WAY TO FIND OUT.
YOU READY FOR THIS?

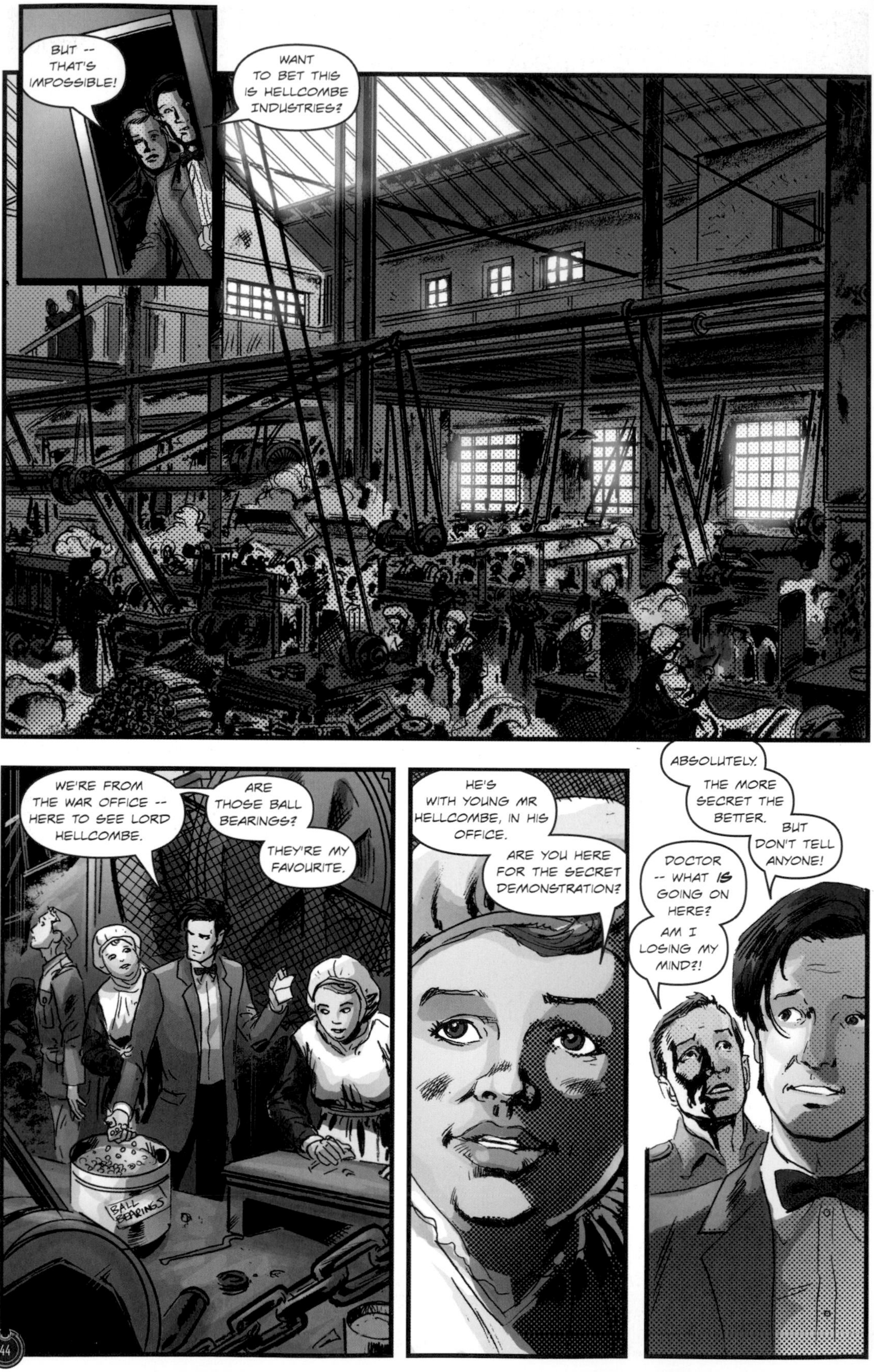
BUT -- THAT'S IMPOSSIBLE!
WANT TO BET THIS IS HELLCOMBE INDUSTRIES?
WE'RE FROM THE WAR OFFICE -- HERE TO SEE LORD HELLCOMBE.
ARE THOSE BALL BEARINGS?
THEY'RE MY FAVOURITE.
BALL BEARINGS
HE'S WITH YOUNG MR HELLCOMBE, IN HIS OFFICE.
ARE YOU HERE FOR THE SECRET DEMONSTRATION?
ABSOLUTELY.
THE MORE SECRET THE BETTER.
BUT DON'T TELL ANYONE!
DOCTOR -- WHAT *IS* GOING ON HERE?
AM I LOSING MY MIND?!

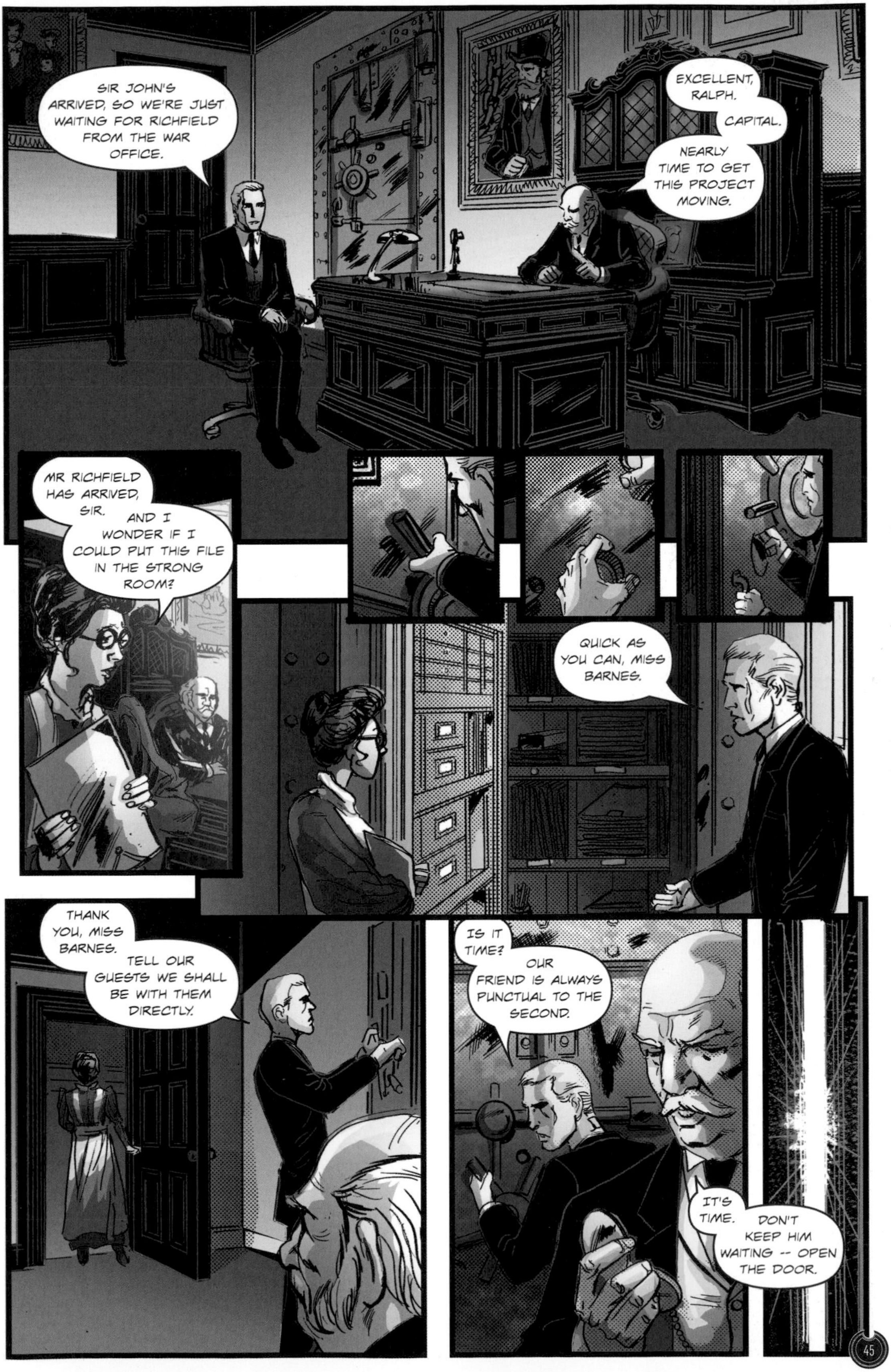
SIR JOHN'S ARRIVED, SO WE'RE JUST WAITING FOR RICHFIELD FROM THE WAR OFFICE.
EXCELLENT, RALPH.
CAPITAL.
NEARLY TIME TO GET THIS PROJECT MOVING.
MR RICHFIELD HAS ARRIVED, SIR.
AND I WONDER IF I COULD PUT THIS FILE IN THE STRONG ROOM?
QUICK AS YOU CAN, MISS BARNES.
THANK YOU, MISS BARNES.
TELL OUR GUESTS WE SHALL BE WITH THEM DIRECTLY.
IS IT TIME?
OUR FRIEND IS ALWAYS PUNCTUAL TO THE SECOND.
IT'S TIME.
DON'T KEEP HIM WAITING -- OPEN THE DOOR.

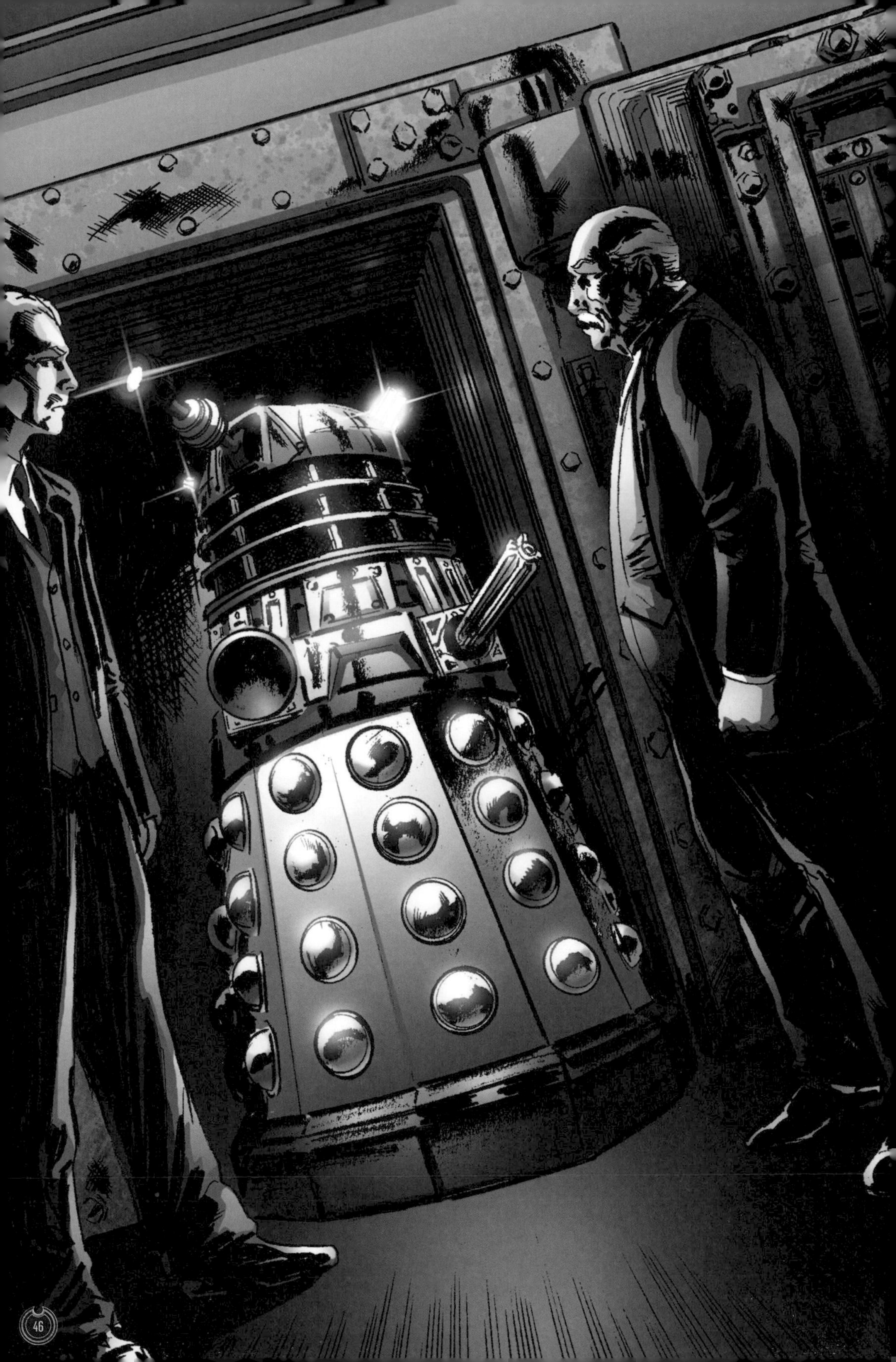

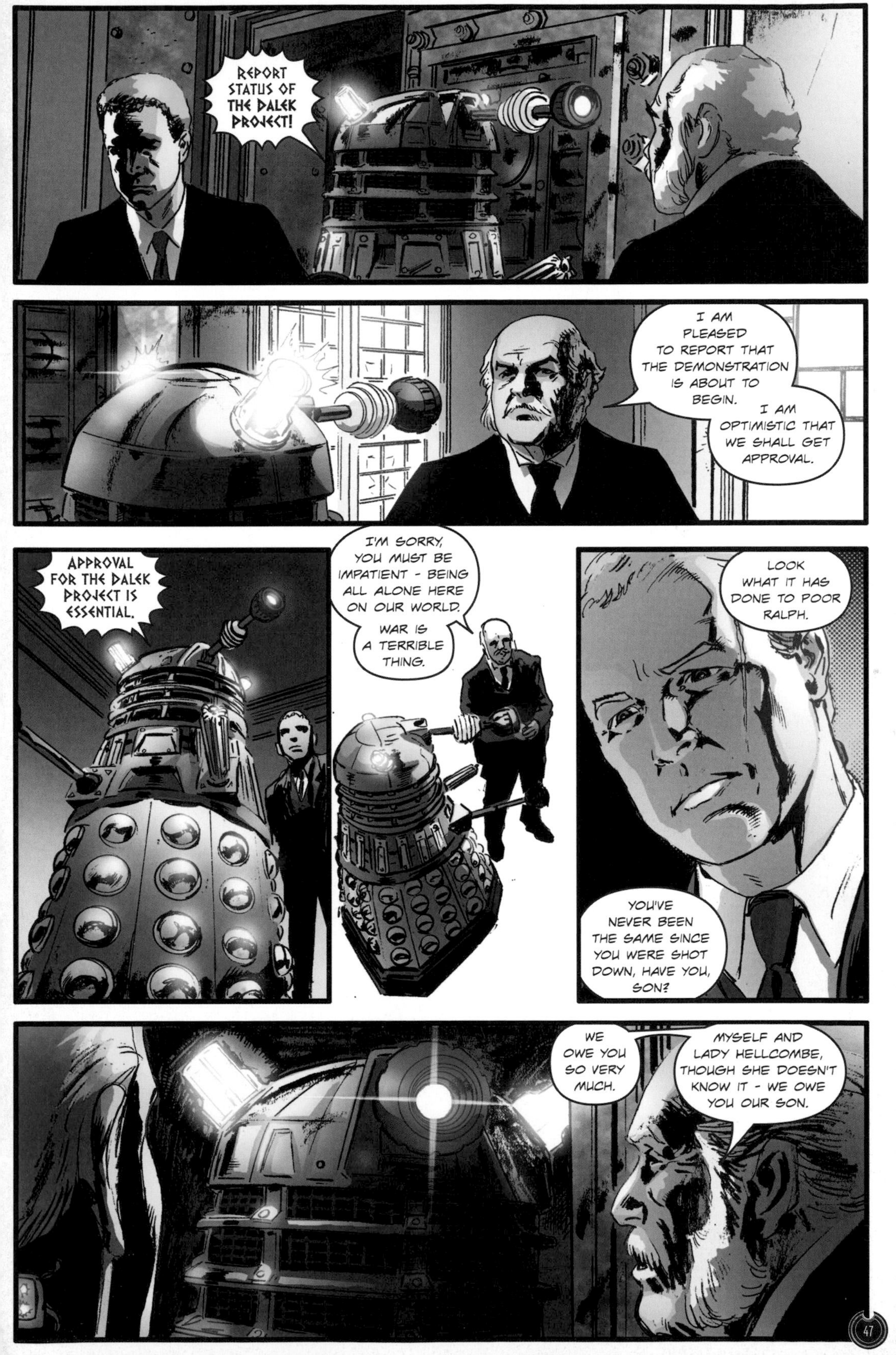
REPORT STATUS OF THE DALEK PROJECT!
I AM PLEASED TO REPORT THAT THE DEMONSTRATION IS ABOUT TO BEGIN.
I AM OPTIMISTIC THAT WE SHALL GET APPROVAL.
APPROVAL FOR THE DALEK PROJECT IS ESSENTIAL.
I'M SORRY, YOU MUST BE IMPATIENT - BEING ALL ALONE HERE ON OUR WORLD.
WAR IS A TERRIBLE THING.
LOOK WHAT IT HAS DONE TO POOR RALPH.
YOU'VE NEVER BEEN THE SAME SINCE YOU WERE SHOT DOWN, HAVE YOU, SON?
WE OWE YOU SO VERY MUCH.
MYSELF AND LADY HELLCOMBE, THOUGH SHE DOESN'T KNOW IT - WE OWE YOU OUR SON.

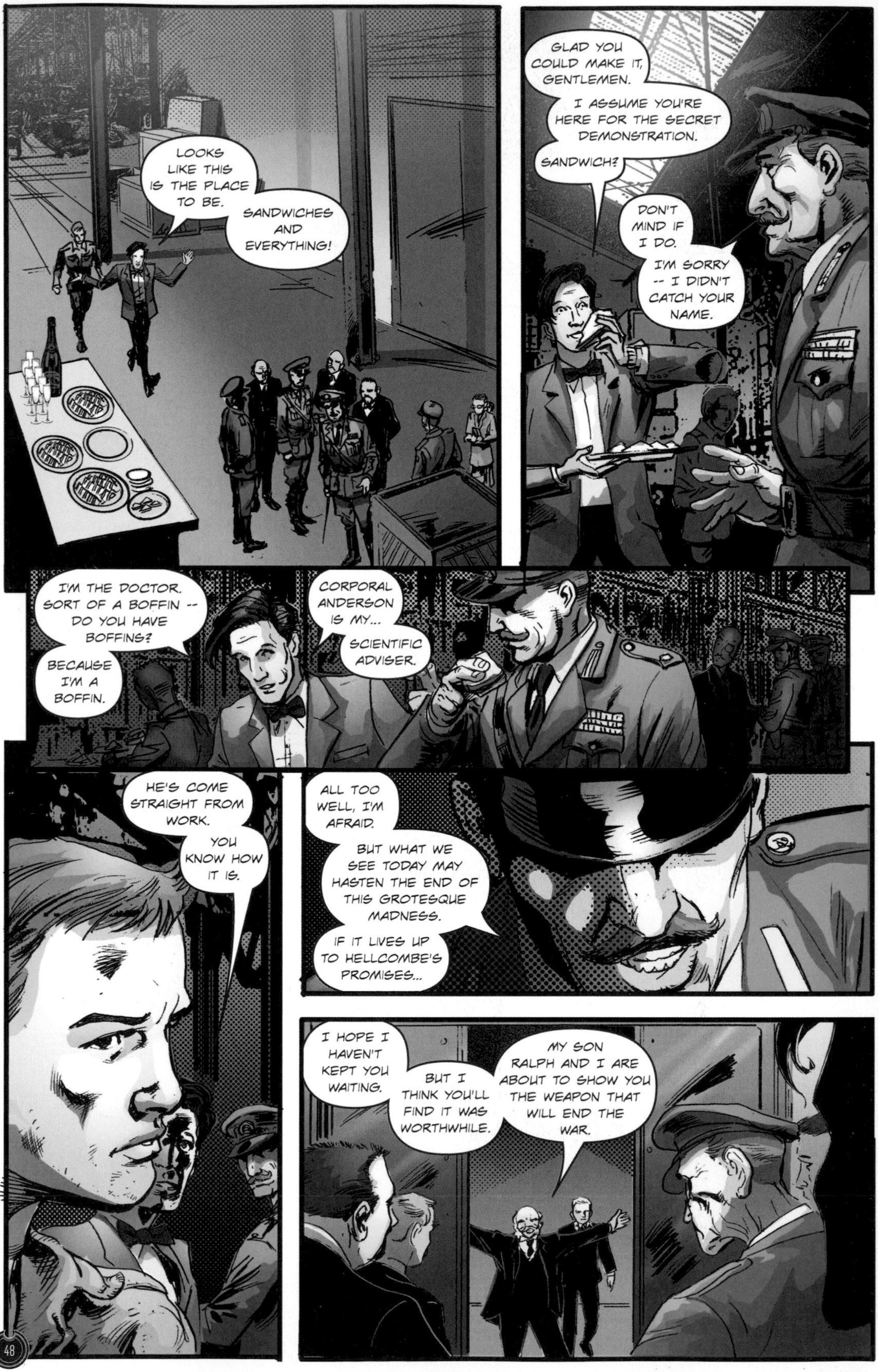
LOOKS LIKE THIS IS THE PLACE TO BE.
SANDWICHES AND EVERYTHING!
GLAD YOU COULD MAKE IT, GENTLEMEN.
I ASSUME YOU'RE HERE FOR THE SECRET DEMONSTRATION.
SANDWICH?
DON'T MIND IF I DO.
I'M SORRY -- I DIDN'T CATCH YOUR NAME.
I'M THE DOCTOR. SORT OF A BOFFIN -- DO YOU HAVE BOFFINS?
BECAUSE I'M A BOFFIN.
CORPORAL ANDERSON IS MY...
SCIENTIFIC ADVISER.
HE'S COME STRAIGHT FROM WORK.
YOU KNOW HOW IT IS.
ALL TOO WELL, I'M AFRAID.
BUT WHAT WE SEE TODAY MAY HASTEN THE END OF THIS GROTESQUE MADNESS.
IF IT LIVES UP TO HELLCOMBE'S PROMISES...
I HOPE I HAVEN'T KEPT YOU WAITING.
BUT I THINK YOU'LL FIND IT WAS WORTHWHILE.
MY SON RALPH AND I ARE ABOUT TO SHOW YOU THE WEAPON THAT WILL END THE WAR.

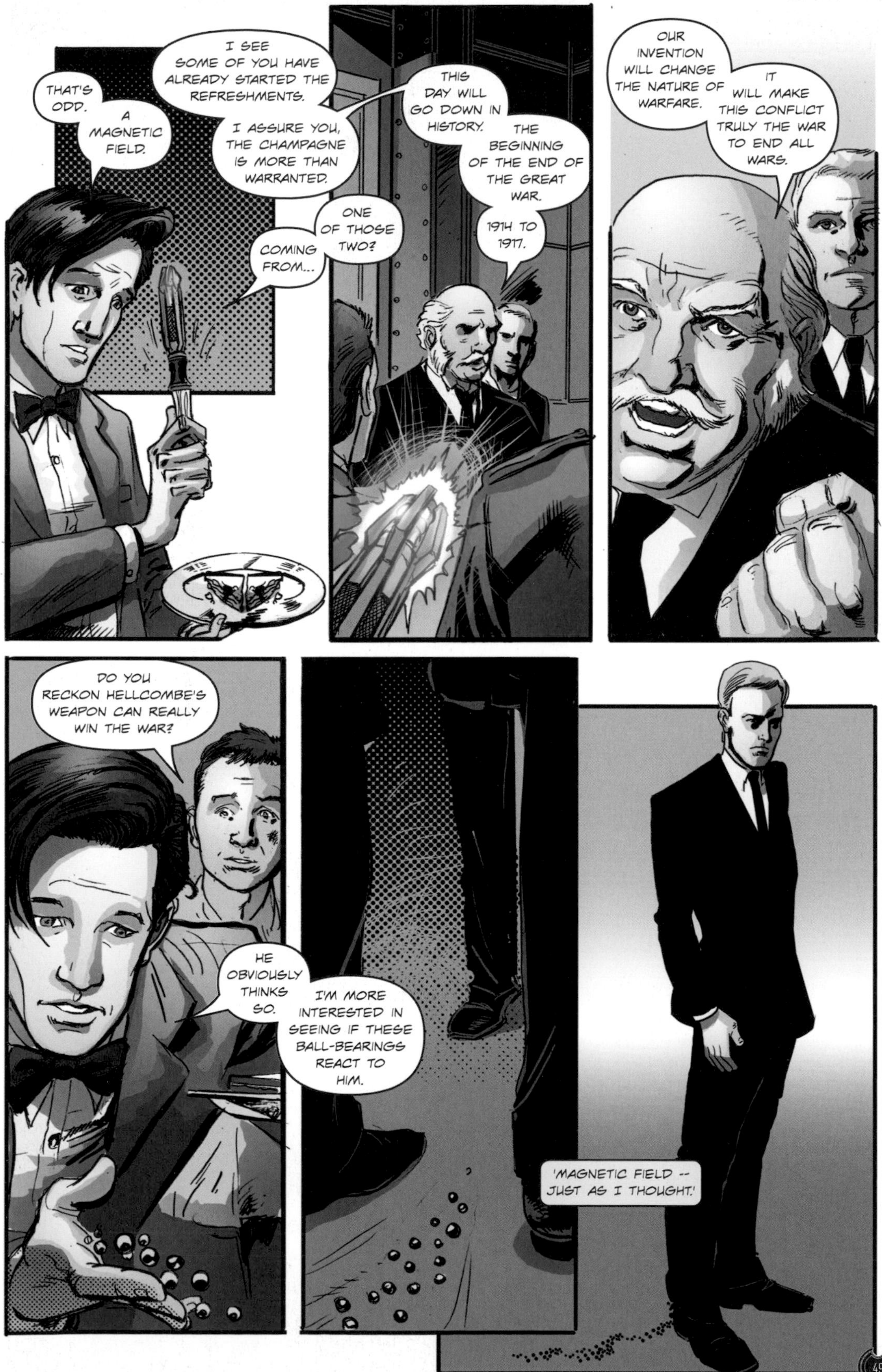
THAT'S ODD.
A MAGNETIC FIELD.
I SEE SOME OF YOU HAVE ALREADY STARTED THE REFRESHMENTS.
I ASSURE YOU, THE CHAMPAGNE IS MORE THAN WARRANTED.
COMING FROM...
ONE OF THOSE TWO?
THIS DAY WILL GO DOWN IN HISTORY.
THE BEGINNING OF THE END OF THE GREAT WAR.
1914 TO 1917.
OUR INVENTION WILL CHANGE THE NATURE OF WARFARE.
IT WILL MAKE THIS CONFLICT TRULY THE WAR TO END ALL WARS.
DO YOU RECKON HELLCOMBE'S WEAPON CAN REALLY WIN THE WAR?
HE OBVIOUSLY THINKS SO.
I'M MORE INTERESTED IN SEEING IF THESE BALL-BEARINGS REACT TO HIM.
'MAGNETIC FIELD -- JUST AS I THOUGHT.'

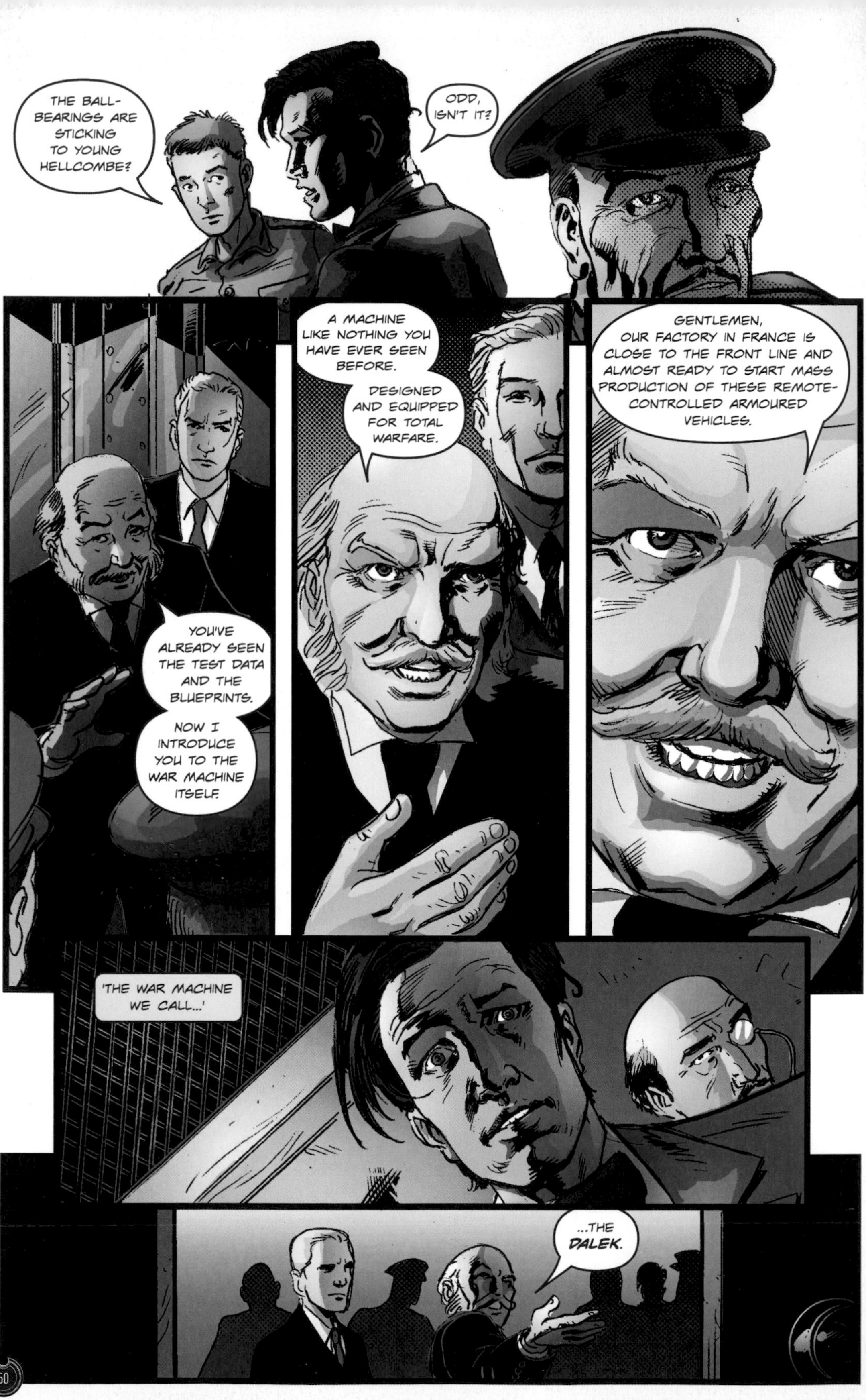
THE BALL-BEARINGS ARE STICKING TO YOUNG HELLCOMBE?
ODD, ISN'T IT?
YOU'VE ALREADY SEEN THE TEST DATA AND THE BLUEPRINTS.
NOW I INTRODUCE YOU TO THE WAR MACHINE ITSELF.
A MACHINE LIKE NOTHING YOU HAVE EVER SEEN BEFORE.
DESIGNED AND EQUIPPED FOR TOTAL WARFARE.
GENTLEMEN, OUR FACTORY IN FRANCE IS CLOSE TO THE FRONT LINE AND ALMOST READY TO START MASS PRODUCTION OF THESE REMOTE-CONTROLLED ARMOURED VEHICLES.
'THE WAR MACHINE WE CALL...'
...THE *DALEK*.

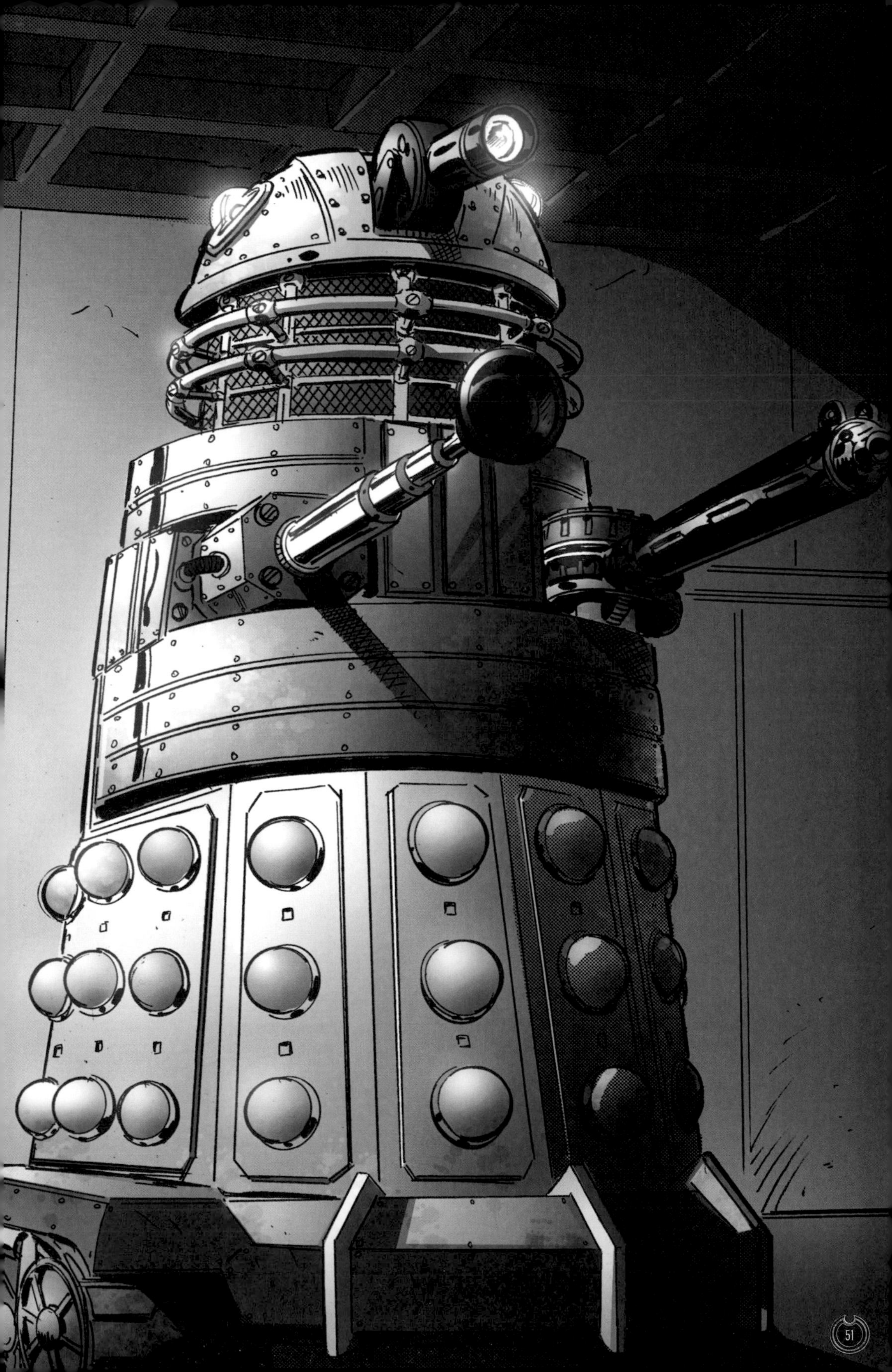

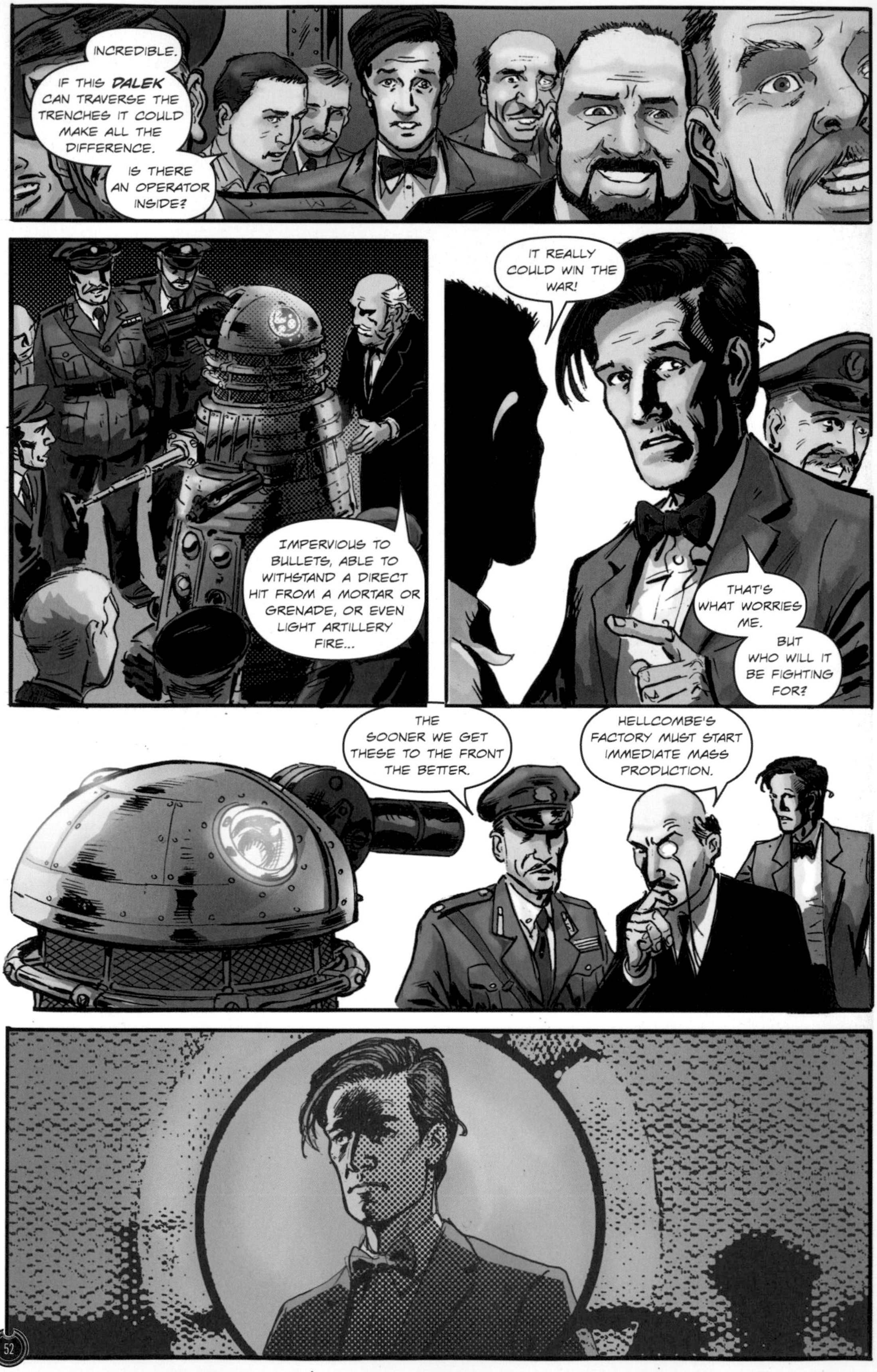
INCREDIBLE.
IF THIS DALEK CAN TRAVERSE THE TRENCHES IT COULD MAKE ALL THE DIFFERENCE.
IS THERE AN OPERATOR INSIDE?
IMPERVIOUS TO BULLETS, ABLE TO WITHSTAND A DIRECT HIT FROM A MORTAR OR GRENADE, OR EVEN LIGHT ARTILLERY FIRE...
IT REALLY COULD WIN THE WAR!
THAT'S WHAT WORRIES ME.
BUT WHO WILL IT BE FIGHTING FOR?
THE SOONER WE GET THESE TO THE FRONT THE BETTER.
HELLCOMBE'S FACTORY MUST START IMMEDIATE MASS PRODUCTION.

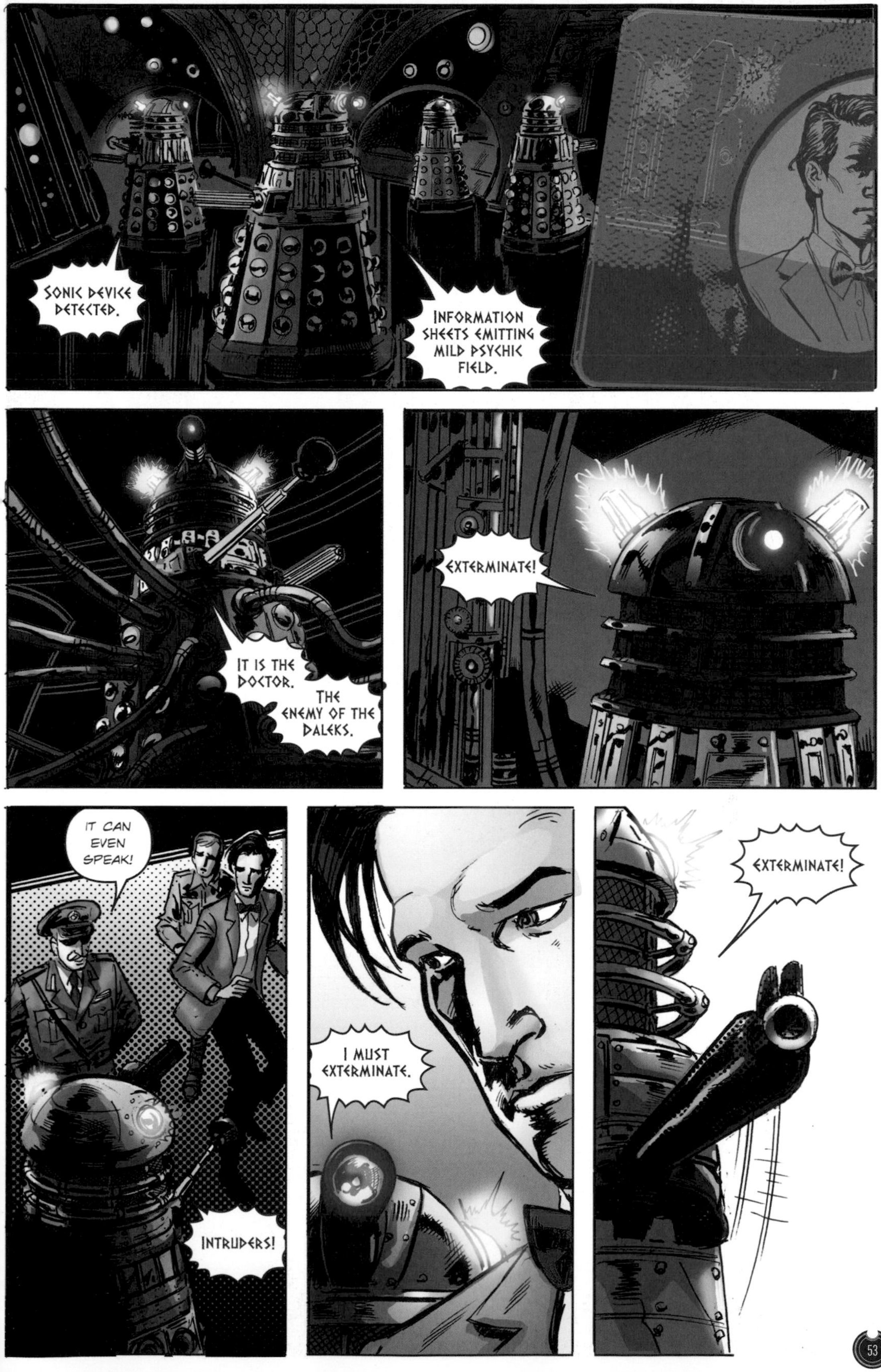
SONIC DEVICE DETECTED.
INFORMATION SHEETS EMITTING MILD PSYCHIC FIELD.
IT IS THE DOCTOR.
THE ENEMY OF THE DALEKS.
EXTERMINATE!
IT CAN EVEN SPEAK!
INTRUDERS!
I MUST EXTERMINATE.
EXTERMINATE!

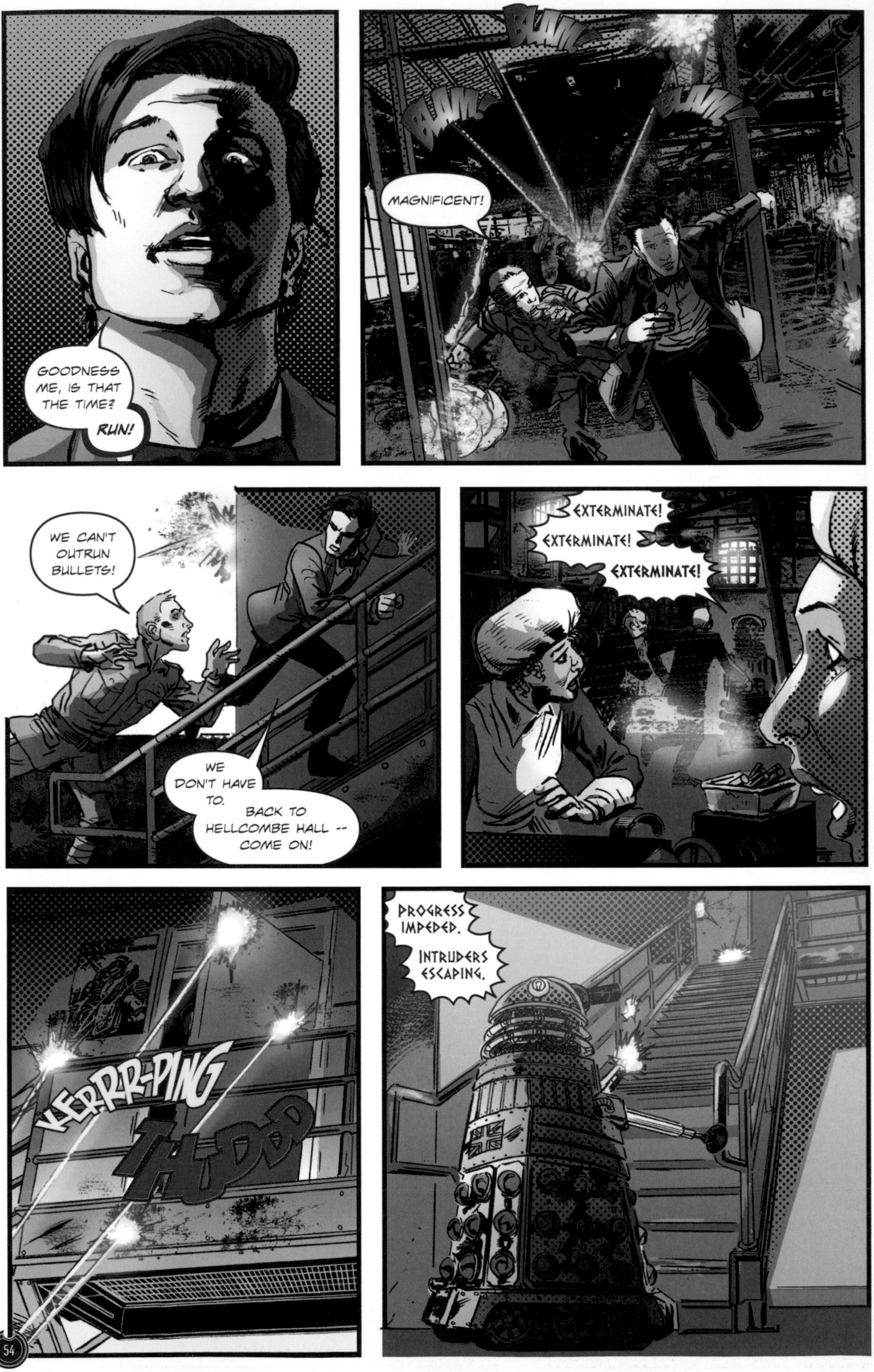
GOODNESS ME, IS THAT THE TIME?
RUN!
BLAM!
BLAM!
BLAM!
MAGNIFICENT!
WE CAN'T OUTRUN BULLETS!
WE DON'T HAVE TO.
BACK TO HELLCOMBE HALL -- COME ON!
EXTERMINATE!
EXTERMINATE!
EXTERMINATE!
KERRR-PING
THUDDD
PROGRESS IMPEDED.
INTRUDERS ESCAPING.

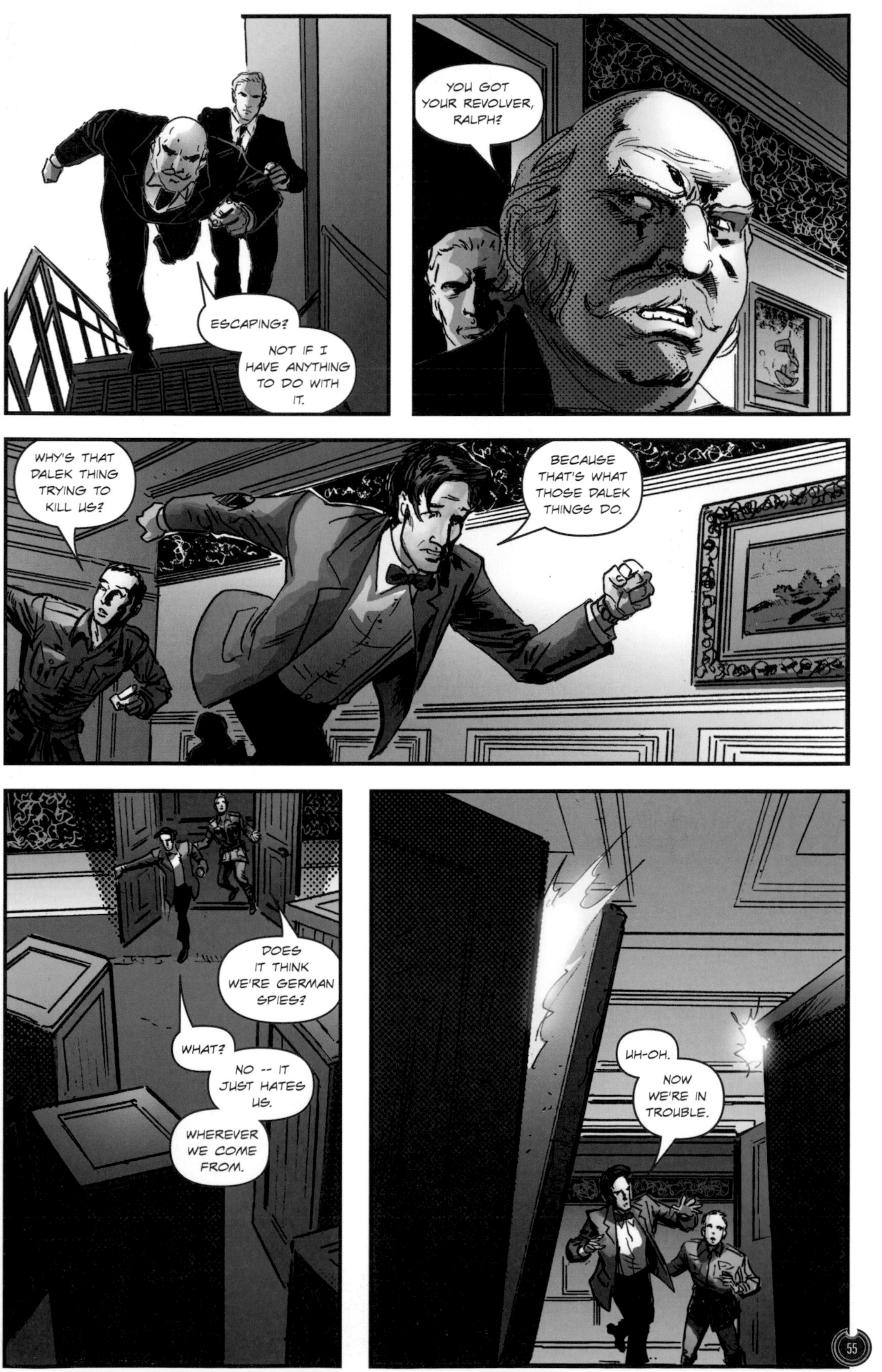
ESCAPING?
NOT IF I HAVE ANYTHING TO DO WITH IT.
YOU GOT YOUR REVOLVER, RALPH?
WHY'S THAT DALEK THING TRYING TO KILL US?
BECAUSE THAT'S WHAT THOSE DALEK THINGS DO.
DOES IT THINK WE'RE GERMAN SPIES?
WHAT?
NO -- IT JUST HATES US.
WHEREVER WE COME FROM.
UH-OH.
NOW WE'RE IN TROUBLE.

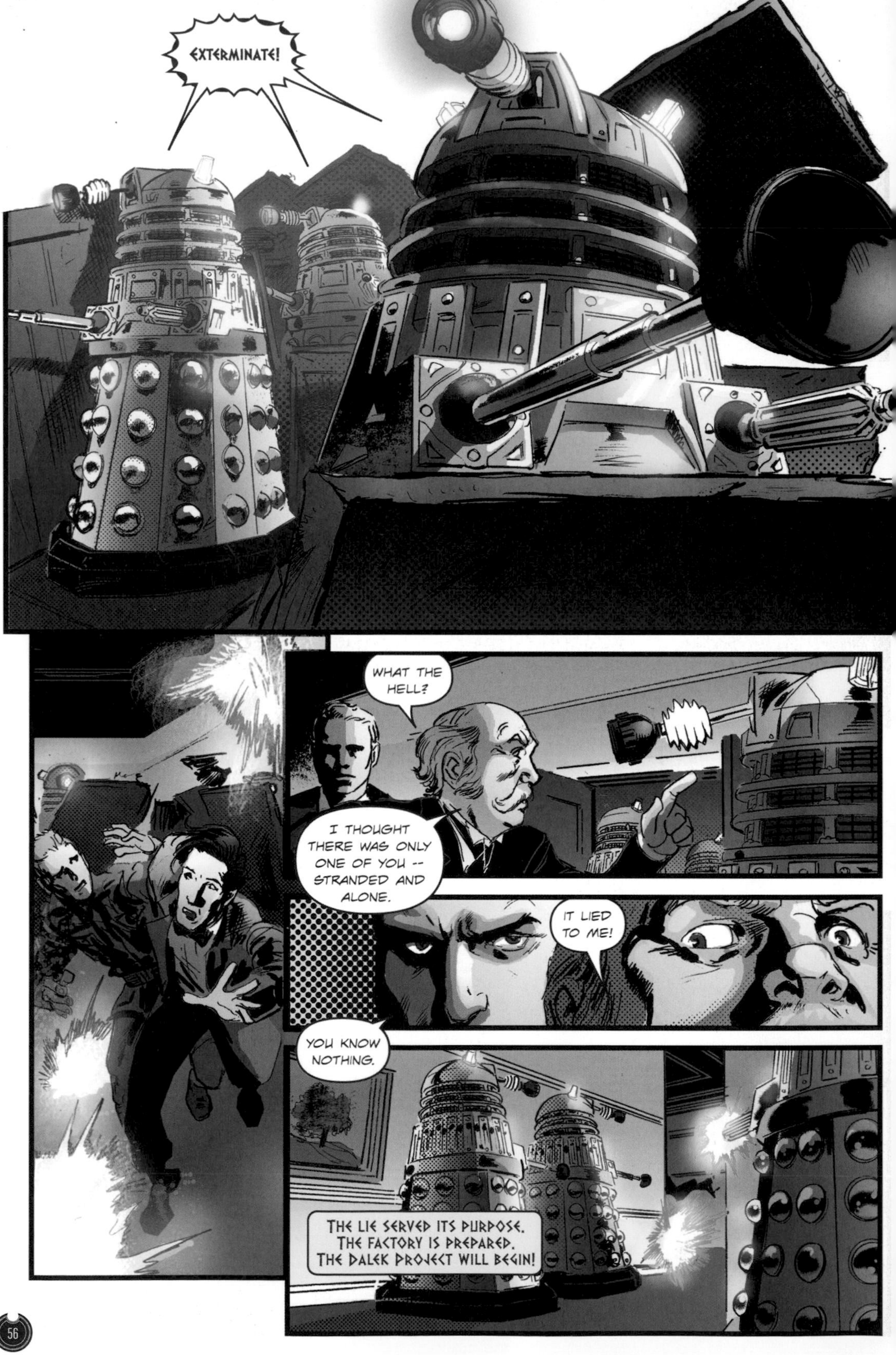
EXTERMINATE!
WHAT THE HELL?
I THOUGHT THERE WAS ONLY ONE OF YOU -- STRANDED AND ALONE.
IT LIED TO ME!
YOU KNOW NOTHING.
THE LIE SERVED ITS PURPOSE. THE FACTORY IS PREPARED. THE DALEK PROJECT WILL BEGIN!

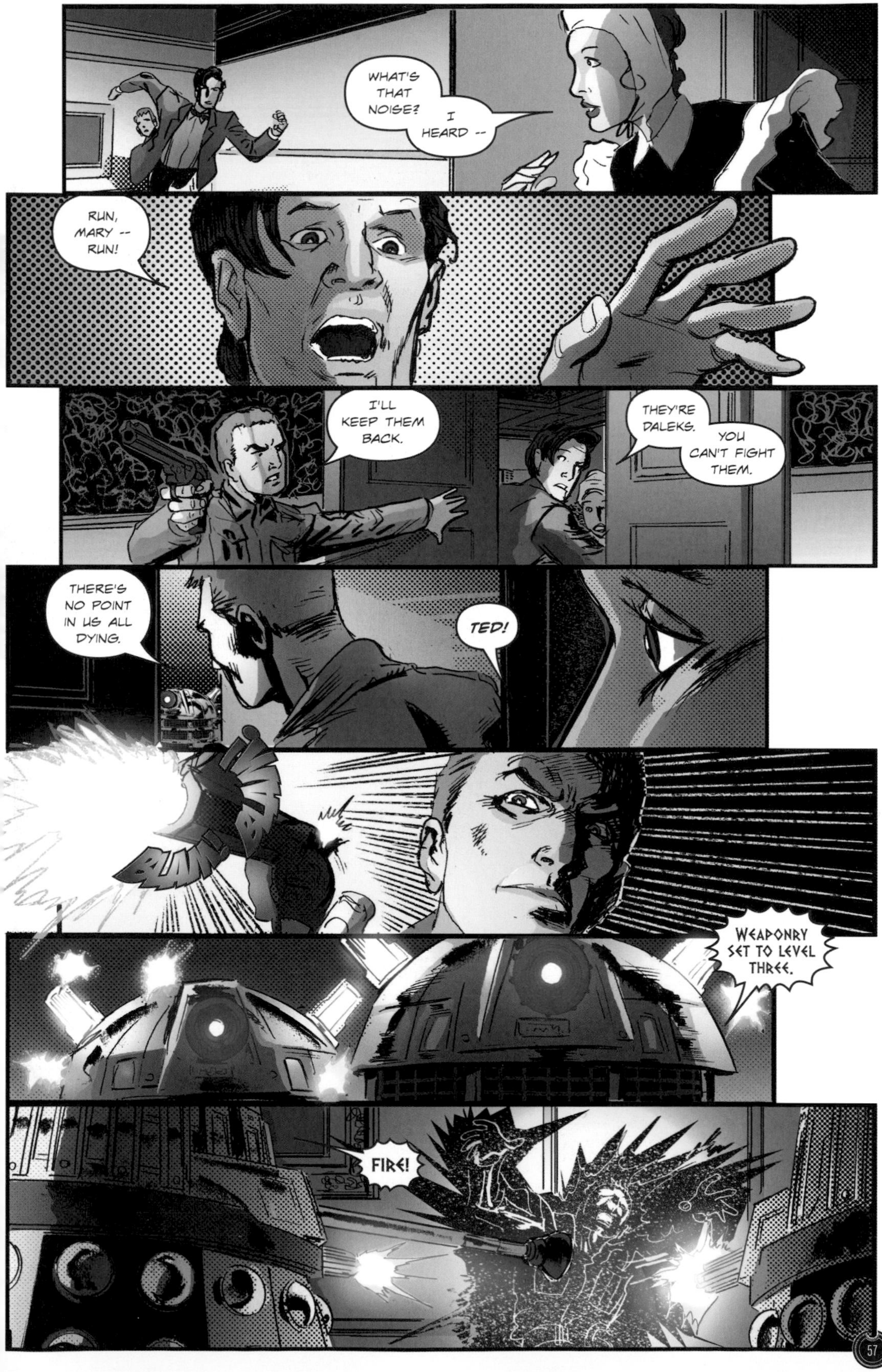

WHAT'S THAT NOISE?
I HEARD --
RUN, MARY -- RUN!
I'LL KEEP THEM BACK.
THEY'RE DALEKS.
YOU CAN'T FIGHT THEM.
THERE'S NO POINT IN US ALL DYING.
TED!
BLAM! BLAM!
WEAPONRY SET TO LEVEL THREE.
FIRE!

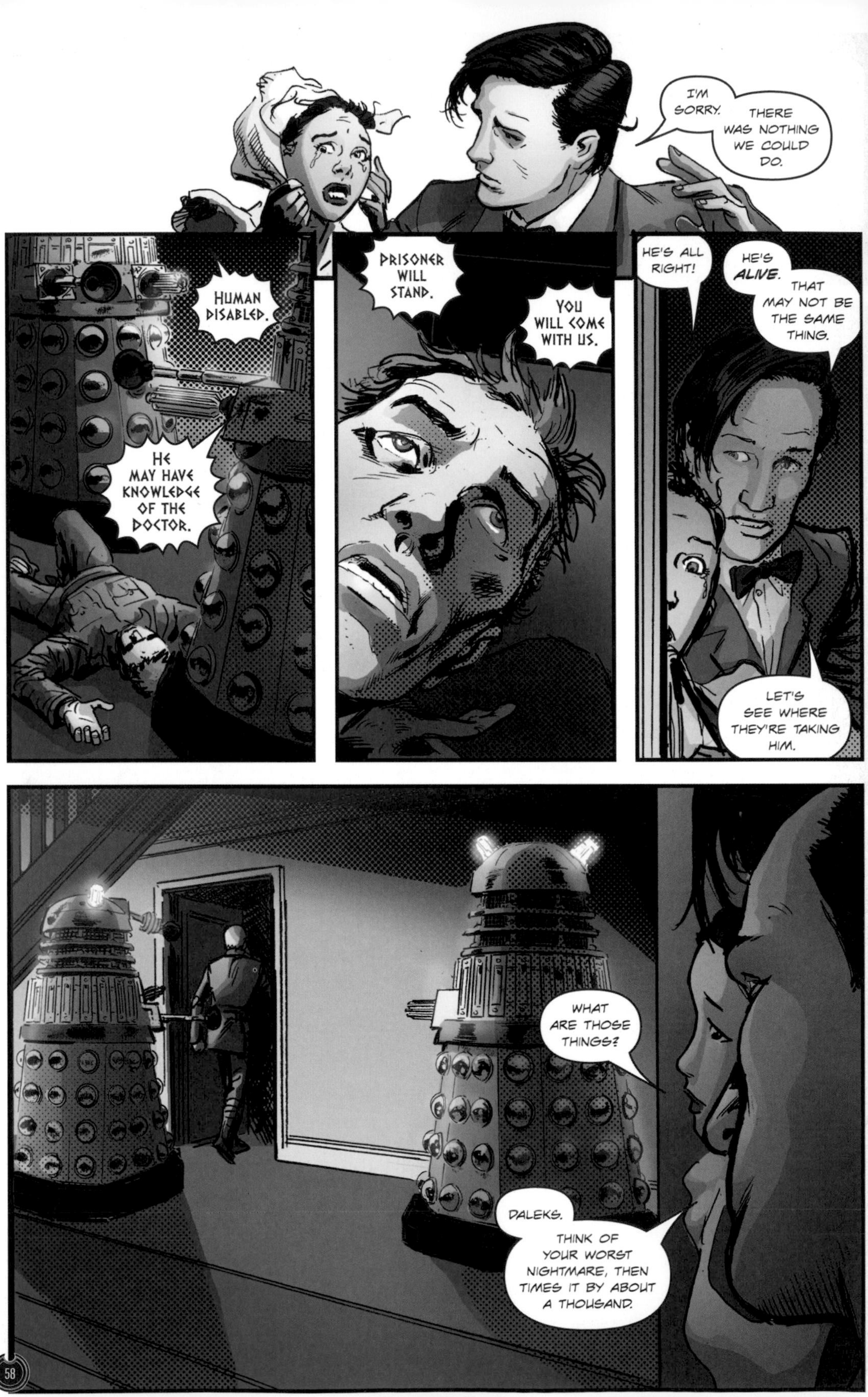
I'M SORRY.
THERE WAS NOTHING WE COULD DO.
HUMAN DISABLED.
HE MAY HAVE KNOWLEDGE OF THE DOCTOR.
PRISONER WILL STAND.
YOU WILL COME WITH US.
HE'S ALL RIGHT!
HE'S ALIVE. THAT MAY NOT BE THE SAME THING.
LET'S SEE WHERE THEY'RE TAKING HIM.
WHAT ARE THOSE THINGS?
DALEKS.
THINK OF YOUR WORST NIGHTMARE, THEN TIMES IT BY ABOUT A THOUSAND.

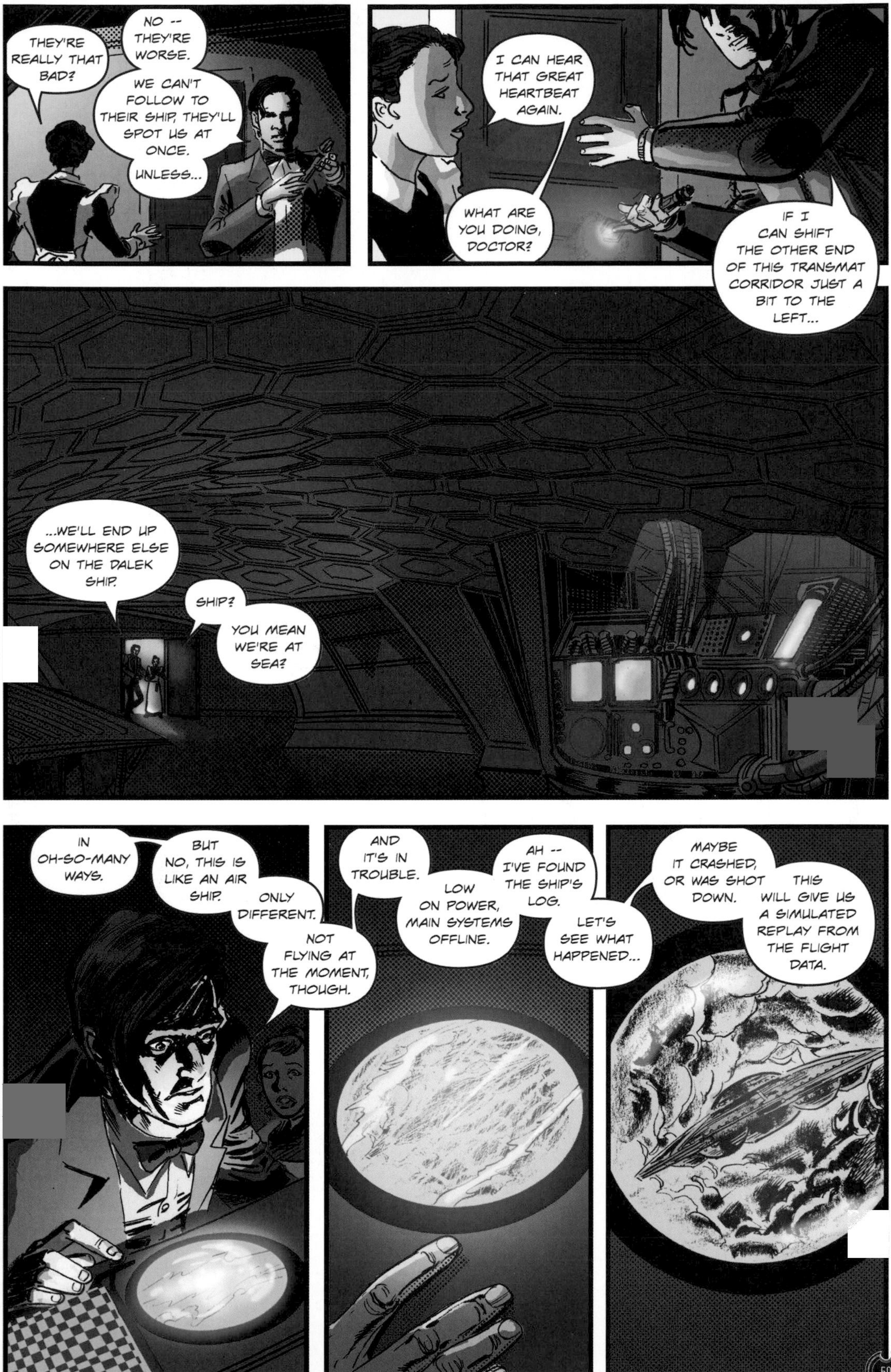
THEY'RE REALLY THAT BAD?
NO -- THEY'RE WORSE.
WE CAN'T FOLLOW TO THEIR SHIP, THEY'LL SPOT US AT ONCE.
UNLESS...
I CAN HEAR THAT GREAT HEARTBEAT AGAIN.
WHAT ARE YOU DOING, DOCTOR?
IF I CAN SHIFT THE OTHER END OF THIS TRANSMAT CORRIDOR JUST A BIT TO THE LEFT...
...WE'LL END UP SOMEWHERE ELSE ON THE DALEK SHIP.
SHIP?
YOU MEAN WE'RE AT SEA?
IN OH-SO-MANY WAYS.
BUT NO, THIS IS LIKE AN AIR SHIP.
ONLY DIFFERENT.
NOT FLYING AT THE MOMENT, THOUGH.
AND IT'S IN TROUBLE.
LOW ON POWER, MAIN SYSTEMS OFFLINE.
AH -- I'VE FOUND THE SHIP'S LOG.
LET'S SEE WHAT HAPPENED...
MAYBE IT CRASHED, OR WAS SHOT DOWN.
THIS WILL GIVE US A SIMULATED REPLAY FROM THE FLIGHT DATA.

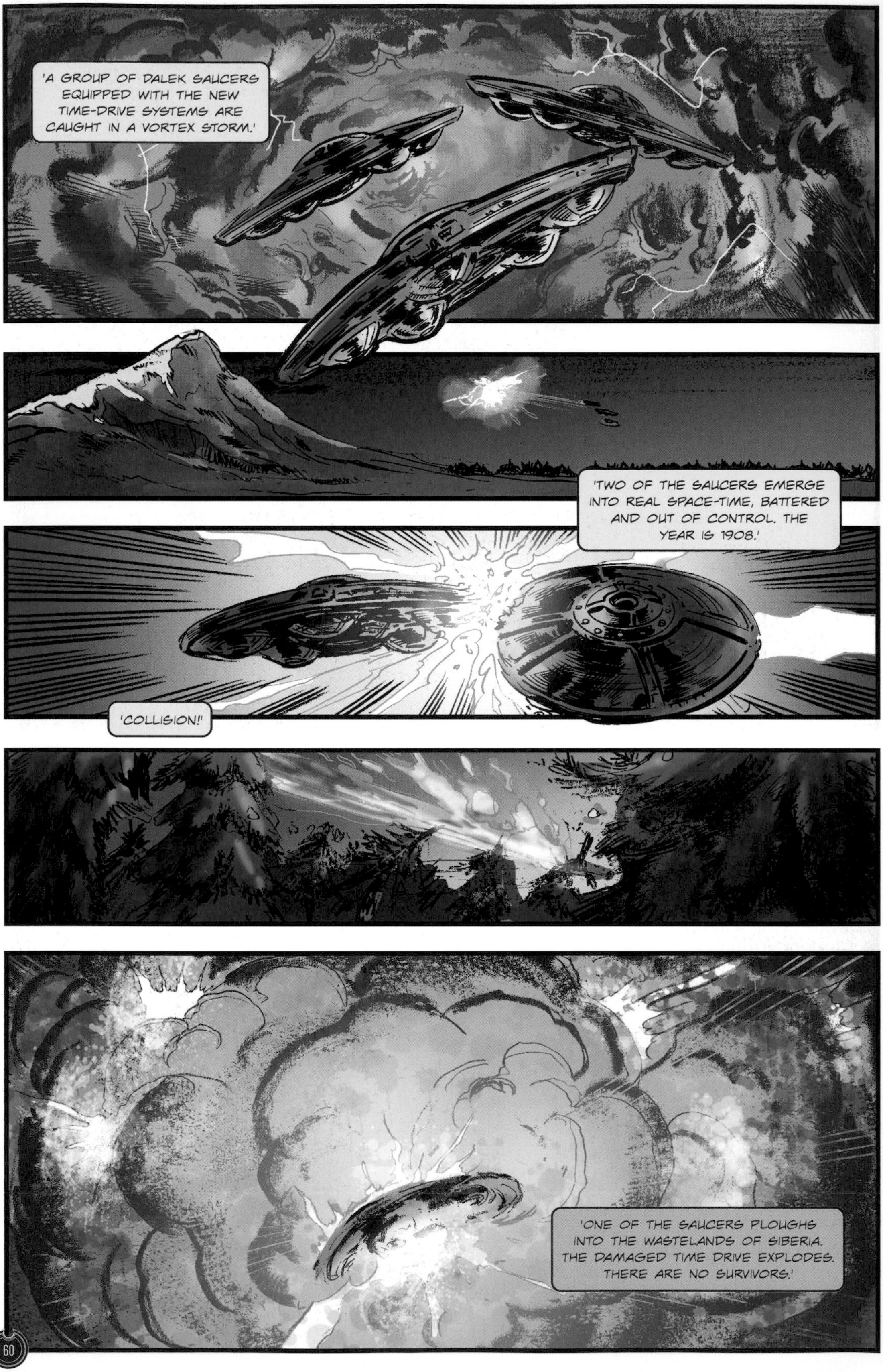
'A GROUP OF DALEK SAUCERS EQUIPPED WITH THE NEW TIME-DRIVE SYSTEMS ARE CAUGHT IN A VORTEX STORM.'
'TWO OF THE SAUCERS EMERGE INTO REAL SPACE-TIME, BATTERED AND OUT OF CONTROL. THE YEAR IS 1908.'
'COLLISION!'
'ONE OF THE SAUCERS PLOUGHS INTO THE WASTELANDS OF SIBERIA. THE DAMAGED TIME DRIVE EXPLODES. THERE ARE NO SURVIVORS.'

'NOTHING HERE ABOUT THE OTHER SAUCER. BUT THE LAST ONE -- THIS ONE -- IS BADLY DAMAGED...'

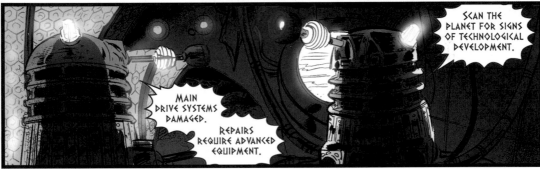

REPORT.

SCAN THE PLANET FOR SIGNS OF TECHNOLOGICAL DEVELOPMENT.

MAIN DRIVE SYSTEMS DAMAGED. REPAIRS REQUIRE ADVANCED EQUIPMENT.

'AND THE SAUCER MAKES A CONTROLLED CRASH-LANDING CLOSE TO THE DALEK OBJECTIVE.'

PRIMITIVE EMISSIONS SUGGEST RESEARCH AND DEVELOPMENT IN PROGRESS AT TARGET LOCATION.

'CLOSE TO: HELLCOMBE HALL. THE DALEKS ARE NOTHING IF NOT PATIENT. THEY WORKED FOR YEARS BEFORE THEY WERE READY TO CONTACT LORD HELLCOMBE.'

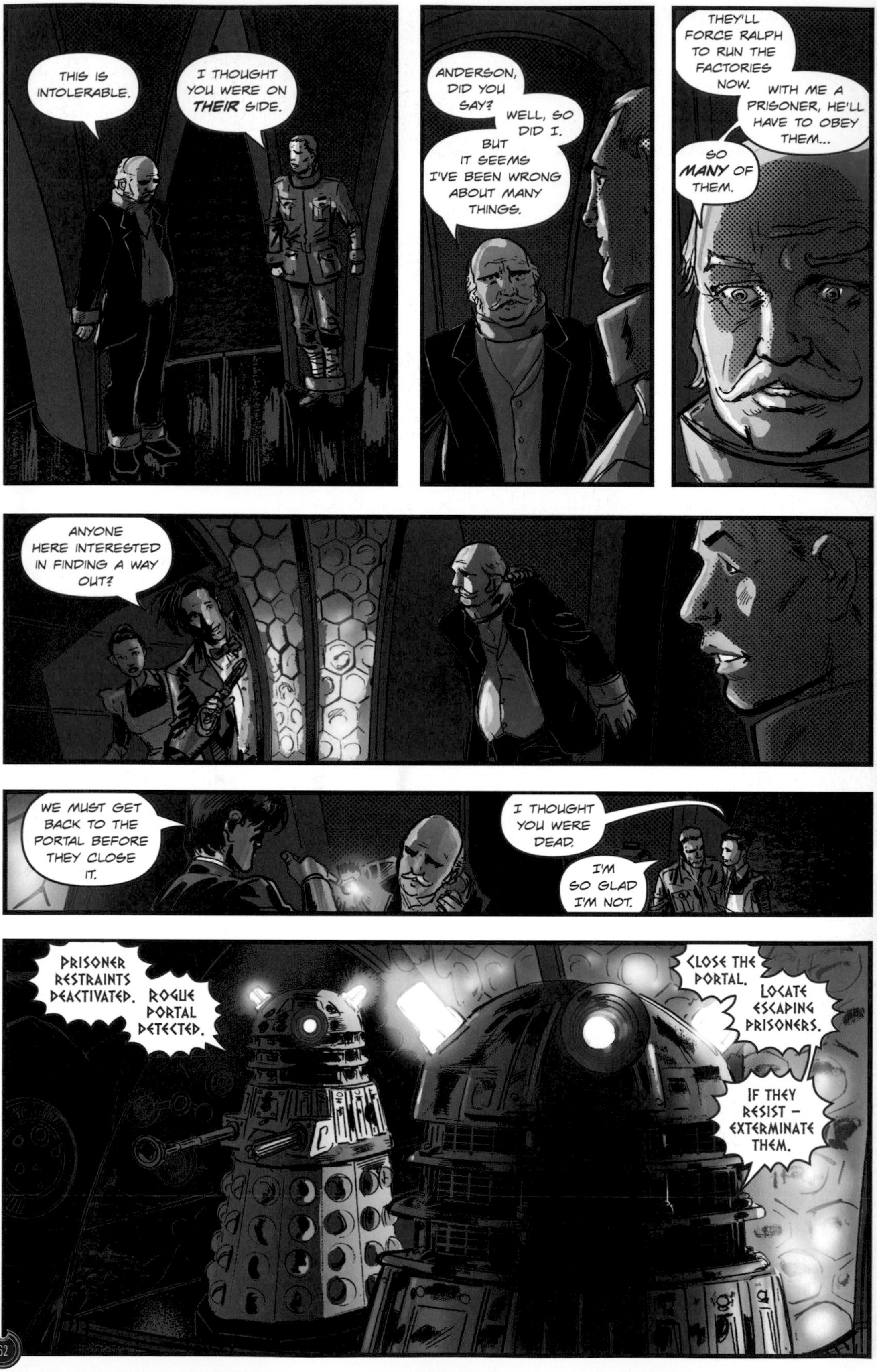

THIS IS INTOLERABLE.
I THOUGHT YOU WERE ON THEIR SIDE.
ANDERSON, DID YOU SAY?
WELL, SO DID I.
BUT IT SEEMS I'VE BEEN WRONG ABOUT MANY THINGS.
THEY'LL FORCE RALPH TO RUN THE FACTORIES NOW.
WITH ME A PRISONER, HE'LL HAVE TO OBEY THEM...
SO MANY OF THEM.
ANYONE HERE INTERESTED IN FINDING A WAY OUT?
WE MUST GET BACK TO THE PORTAL BEFORE THEY CLOSE IT.
I THOUGHT YOU WERE DEAD.
I'M SO GLAD I'M NOT.
PRISONER RESTRAINTS DEACTIVATED.
ROGUE PORTAL DETECTED.
CLOSE THE PORTAL.
LOCATE ESCAPING PRISONERS.
IF THEY RESIST – EXTERMINATE THEM.

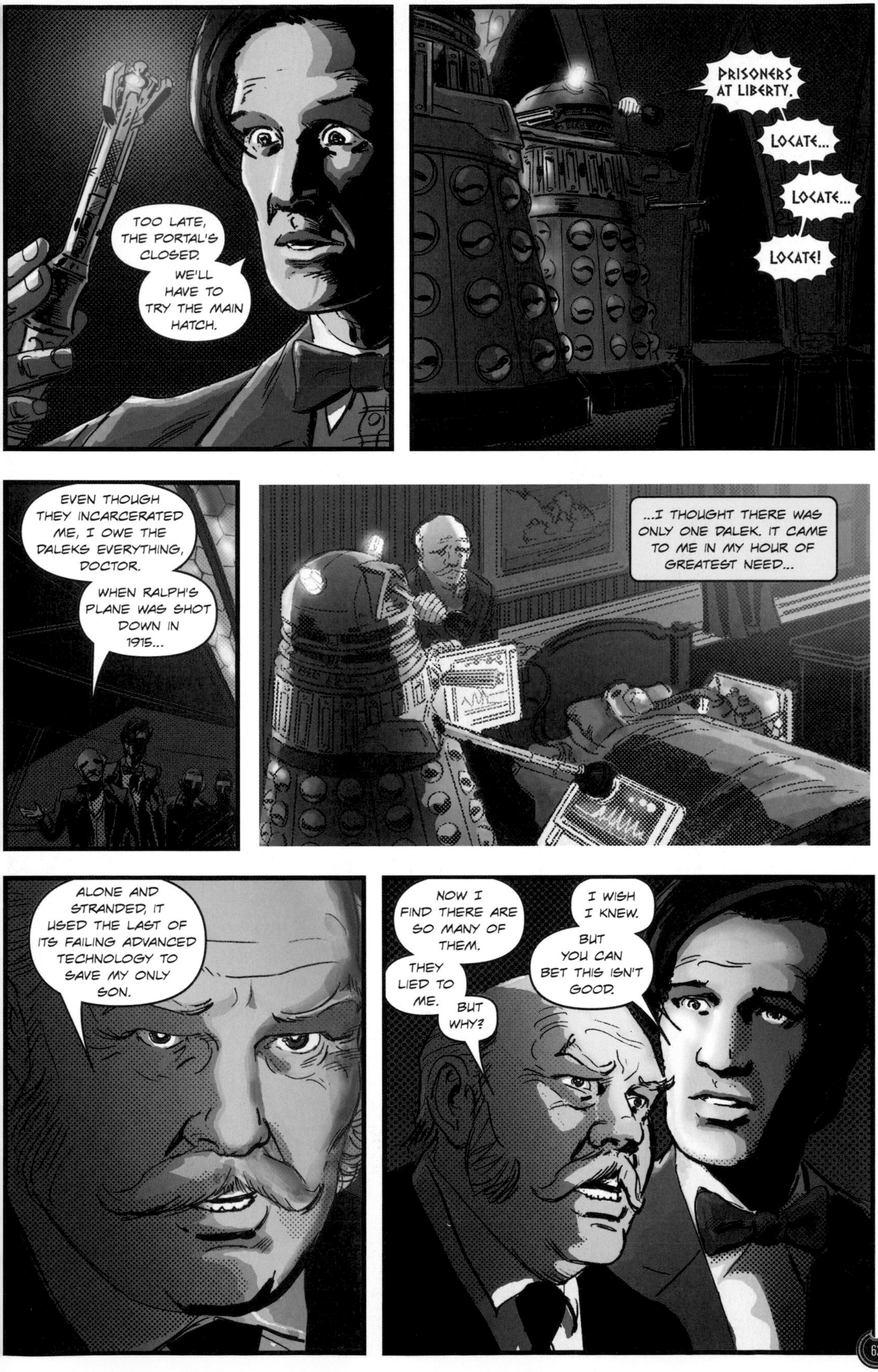
TOO LATE, THE PORTAL'S CLOSED.
WE'LL HAVE TO TRY THE MAIN HATCH.
PRISONERS AT LIBERTY.
LOCATE...
LOCATE...
LOCATE!
EVEN THOUGH THEY INCARCERATED ME, I OWE THE DALEKS EVERYTHING, DOCTOR.
WHEN RALPH'S PLANE WAS SHOT DOWN IN 1915...
...I THOUGHT THERE WAS ONLY ONE DALEK. IT CAME TO ME IN MY HOUR OF GREATEST NEED...
ALONE AND STRANDED, IT USED THE LAST OF ITS FAILING ADVANCED TECHNOLOGY TO SAVE MY ONLY SON.
NOW I FIND THERE ARE SO MANY OF THEM.
THEY LIED TO ME.
BUT WHY?
I WISH I KNEW.
BUT YOU CAN BET THIS ISN'T GOOD.

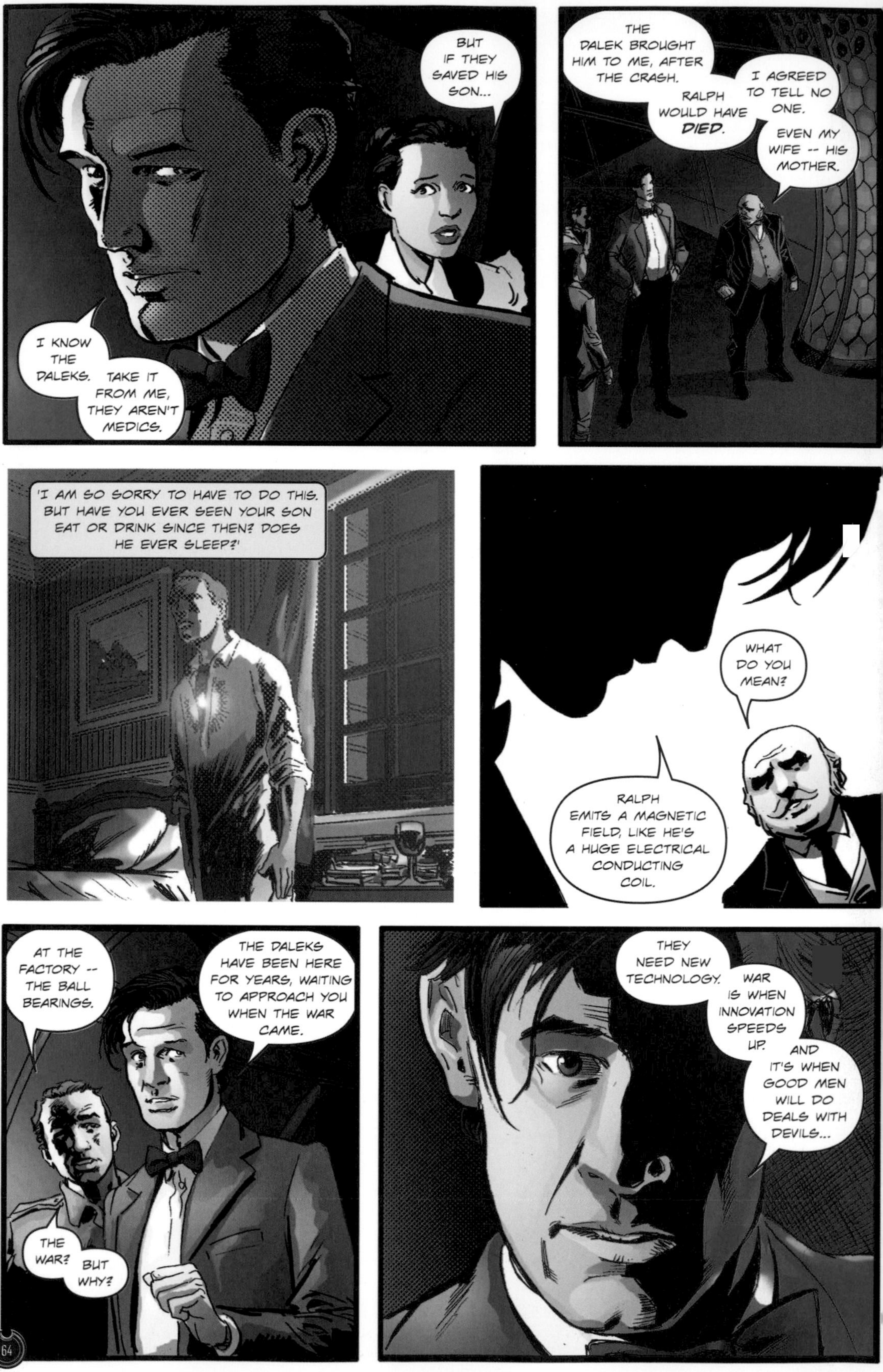
BUT IF THEY SAVED HIS SON...
I KNOW THE DALEKS.
TAKE IT FROM ME, THEY AREN'T MEDICS.
THE DALEK BROUGHT HIM TO ME, AFTER THE CRASH.
RALPH WOULD HAVE ***DIED***.
I AGREED TO TELL NO ONE.
EVEN MY WIFE -- HIS MOTHER.
'I AM SO SORRY TO HAVE TO DO THIS. BUT HAVE YOU EVER SEEN YOUR SON EAT OR DRINK SINCE THEN? DOES HE EVER SLEEP?'
WHAT DO YOU MEAN?
RALPH EMITS A MAGNETIC FIELD, LIKE HE'S A HUGE ELECTRICAL CONDUCTING COIL.
AT THE FACTORY -- THE BALL BEARINGS.
THE DALEKS HAVE BEEN HERE FOR YEARS, WAITING TO APPROACH YOU WHEN THE WAR CAME.
THE WAR?
BUT WHY?
THEY NEED NEW TECHNOLOGY.
WAR IS WHEN INNOVATION SPEEDS UP.
AND IT'S WHEN GOOD MEN WILL DO DEALS WITH DEVILS...

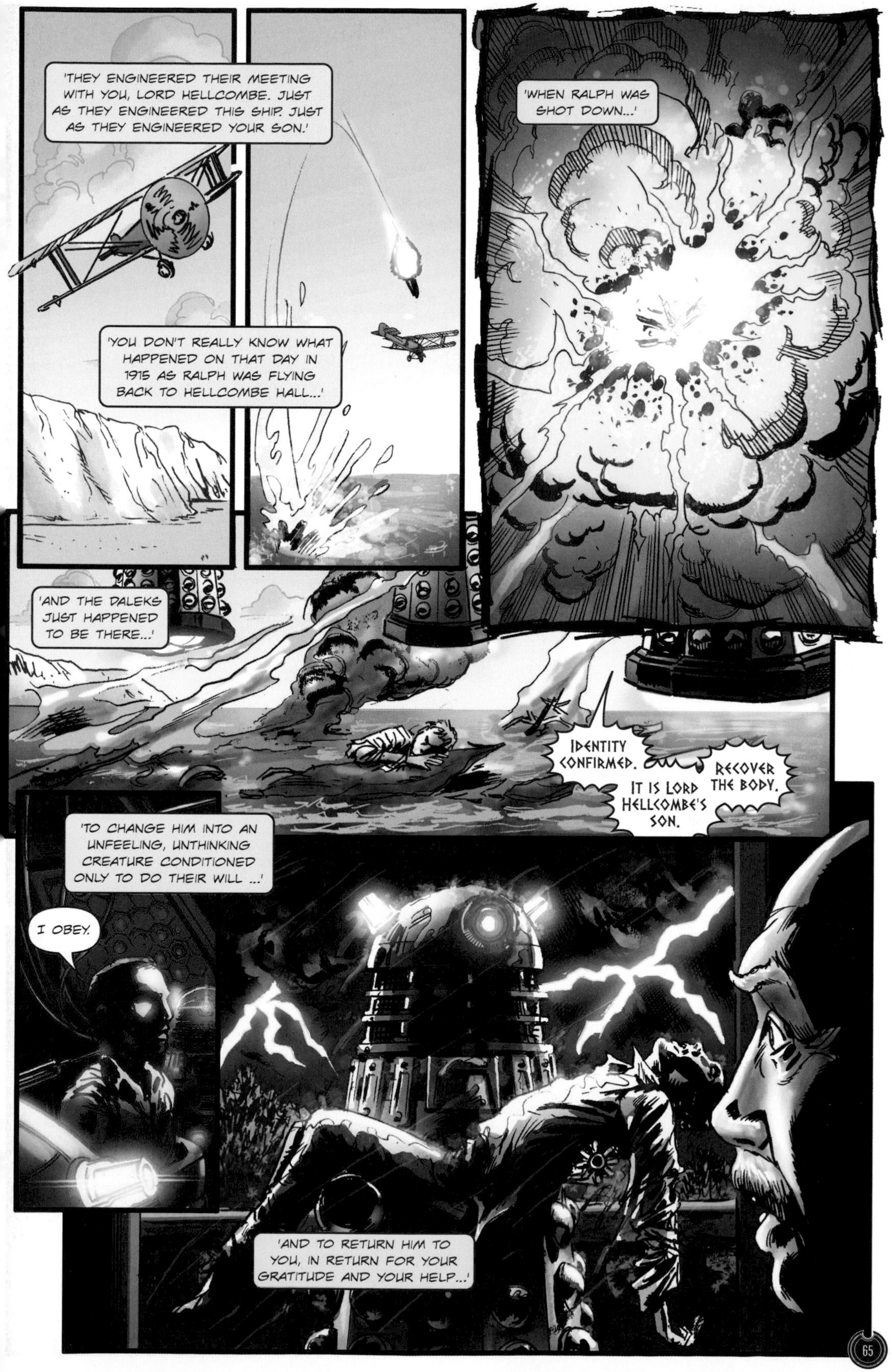
'THEY ENGINEERED THEIR MEETING WITH YOU, LORD HELLCOMBE. JUST AS THEY ENGINEERED THIS SHIP. JUST AS THEY ENGINEERED YOUR SON.'
'YOU DON'T REALLY KNOW WHAT HAPPENED ON THAT DAY IN 1915 AS RALPH WAS FLYING BACK TO HELLCOMBE HALL...'
'WHEN RALPH WAS SHOT DOWN...'
'AND THE DALEKS JUST HAPPENED TO BE THERE...'
IDENTITY CONFIRMED.
IT IS LORD HELLCOMBE'S SON.
RECOVER THE BODY.
'TO CHANGE HIM INTO AN UNFEELING, UNTHINKING CREATURE CONDITIONED ONLY TO DO THEIR WILL ...'
I OBEY.
'AND TO RETURN HIM TO YOU, IN RETURN FOR YOUR GRATITUDE AND YOUR HELP...'

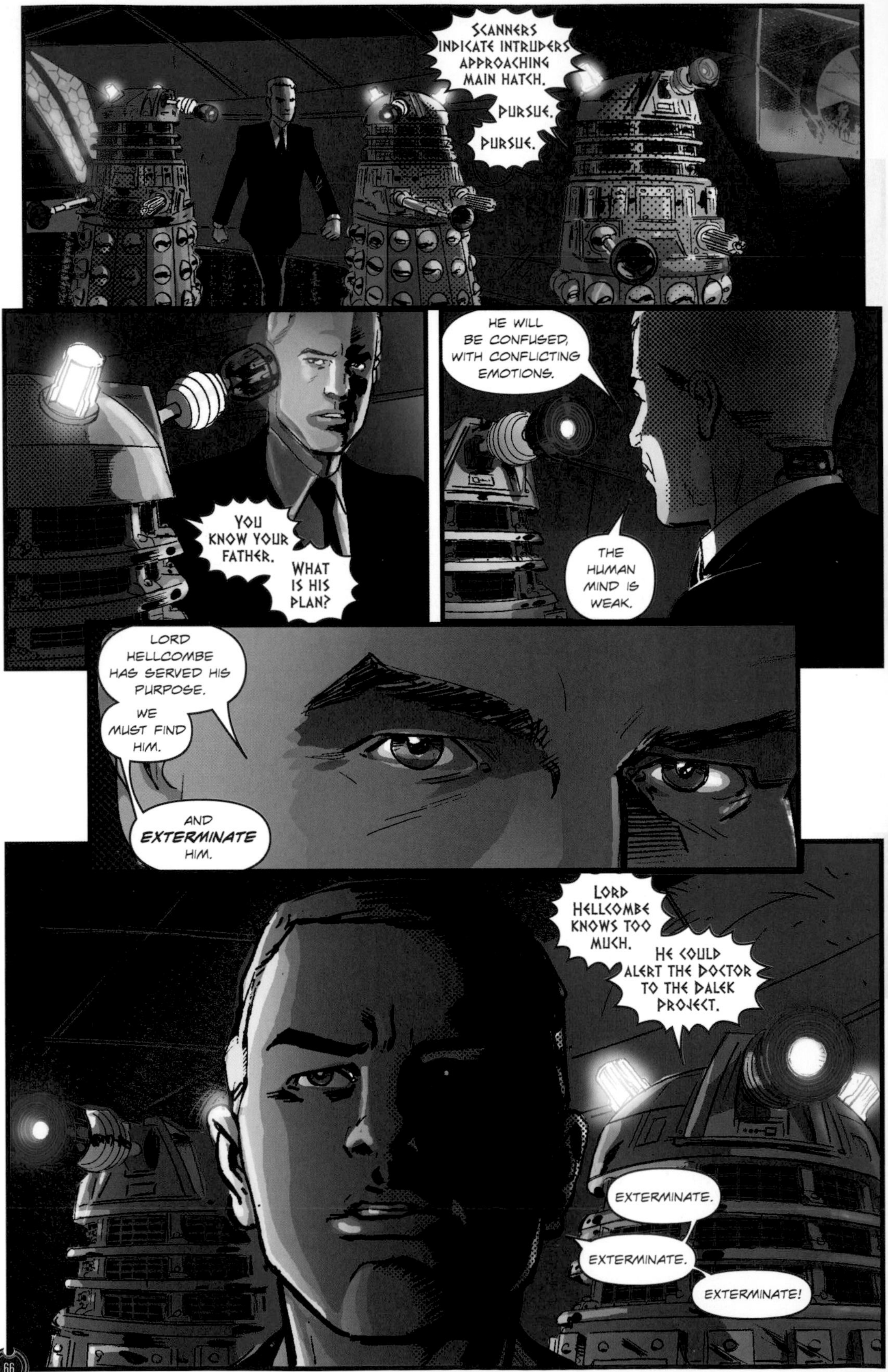
SCANNERS INDICATE INTRUDERS APPROACHING MAIN HATCH.
PURSUE.
PURSUE.
YOU KNOW YOUR FATHER.
WHAT IS HIS PLAN?
HE WILL BE CONFUSED, WITH CONFLICTING EMOTIONS.
THE HUMAN MIND IS WEAK.
LORD HELLCOMBE HAS SERVED HIS PURPOSE.
WE MUST FIND HIM.
AND ***EXTERMINATE*** HIM.
LORD HELLCOMBE KNOWS TOO MUCH.
HE COULD ALERT THE DOCTOR TO THE DALEK PROJECT.
EXTERMINATE.
EXTERMINATE.
EXTERMINATE!

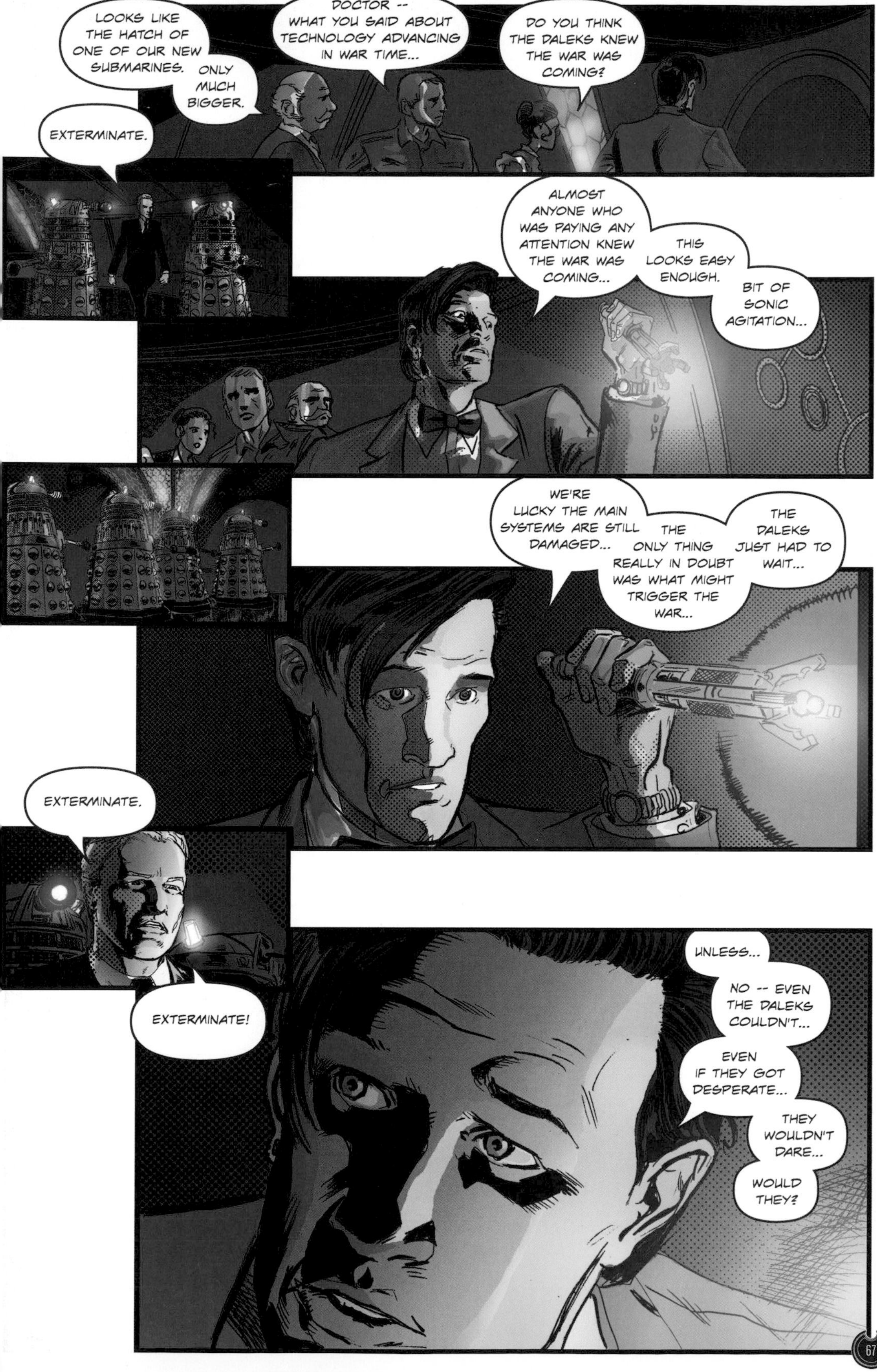
LOOKS LIKE THE HATCH OF ONE OF OUR NEW SUBMARINES.
ONLY MUCH BIGGER.
DOCTOR -- WHAT YOU SAID ABOUT TECHNOLOGY ADVANCING IN WAR TIME...
DO YOU THINK THE DALEKS KNEW THE WAR WAS COMING?
EXTERMINATE.
ALMOST ANYONE WHO WAS PAYING ANY ATTENTION KNEW THE WAR WAS COMING...
THIS LOOKS EASY ENOUGH.
BIT OF SONIC AGITATION...
WE'RE LUCKY THE MAIN SYSTEMS ARE STILL DAMAGED...
THE ONLY THING REALLY IN DOUBT WAS WHAT MIGHT TRIGGER THE WAR...
THE DALEKS JUST HAD TO WAIT...
EXTERMINATE.
EXTERMINATE!
UNLESS...
NO -- EVEN THE DALEKS COULDN'T...
EVEN IF THEY GOT DESPERATE...
THEY WOULDN'T DARE...
WOULD THEY?

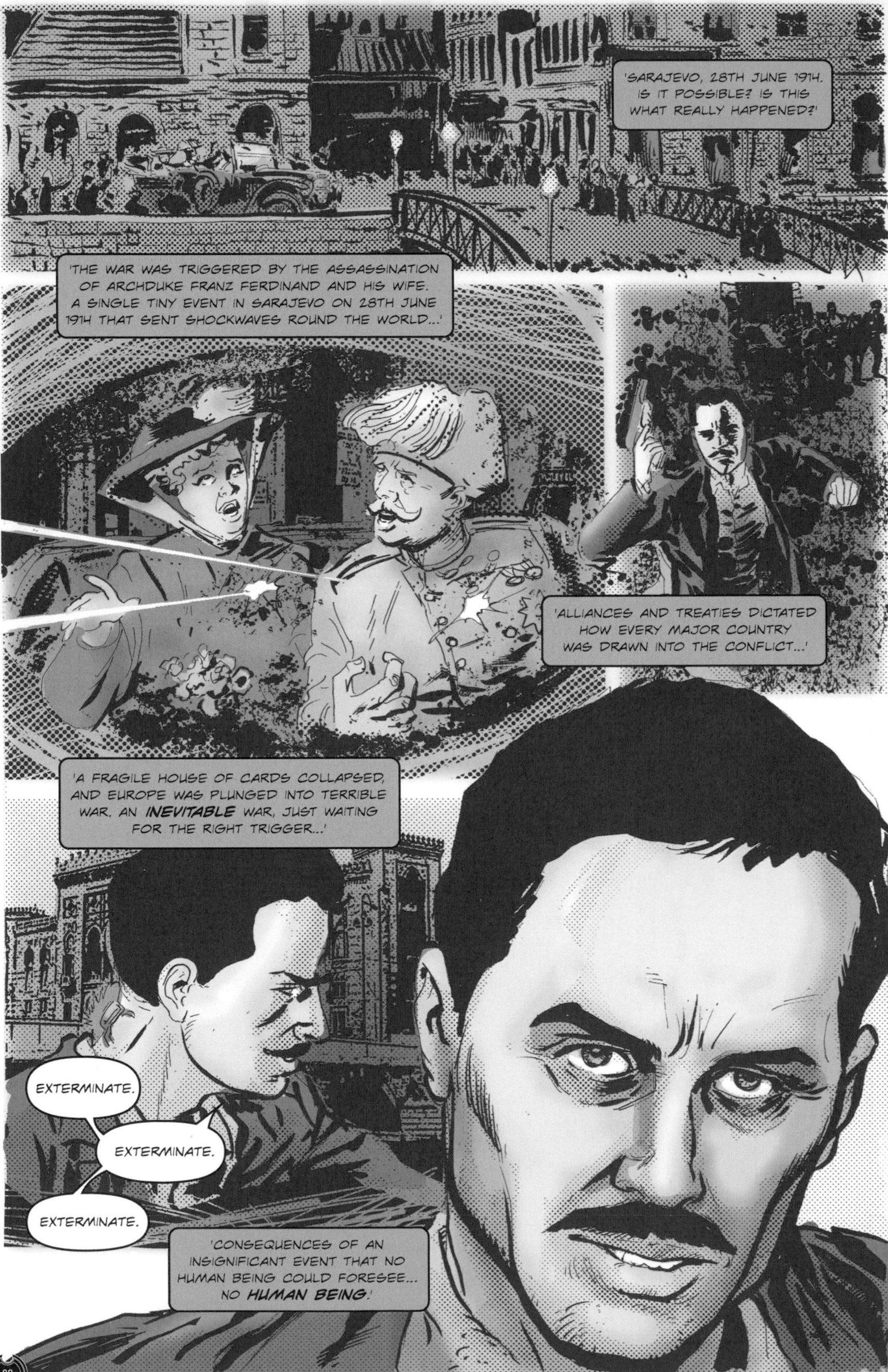
'SARAJEVO, 28TH JUNE 1914. IS IT POSSIBLE? IS THIS WHAT REALLY HAPPENED?'
'THE WAR WAS TRIGGERED BY THE ASSASSINATION OF ARCHDUKE FRANZ FERDINAND AND HIS WIFE. A SINGLE TINY EVENT IN SARAJEVO ON 28TH JUNE 1914 THAT SENT SHOCKWAVES ROUND THE WORLD...'
'ALLIANCES AND TREATIES DICTATED HOW EVERY MAJOR COUNTRY WAS DRAWN INTO THE CONFLICT...'
'A FRAGILE HOUSE OF CARDS COLLAPSED, AND EUROPE WAS PLUNGED INTO TERRIBLE WAR. AN *INEVITABLE* WAR, JUST WAITING FOR THE RIGHT TRIGGER...'
EXTERMINATE.
EXTERMINATE.
EXTERMINATE.
'CONSEQUENCES OF AN INSIGNIFICANT EVENT THAT NO HUMAN BEING COULD FORESEE... NO *HUMAN BEING*.'

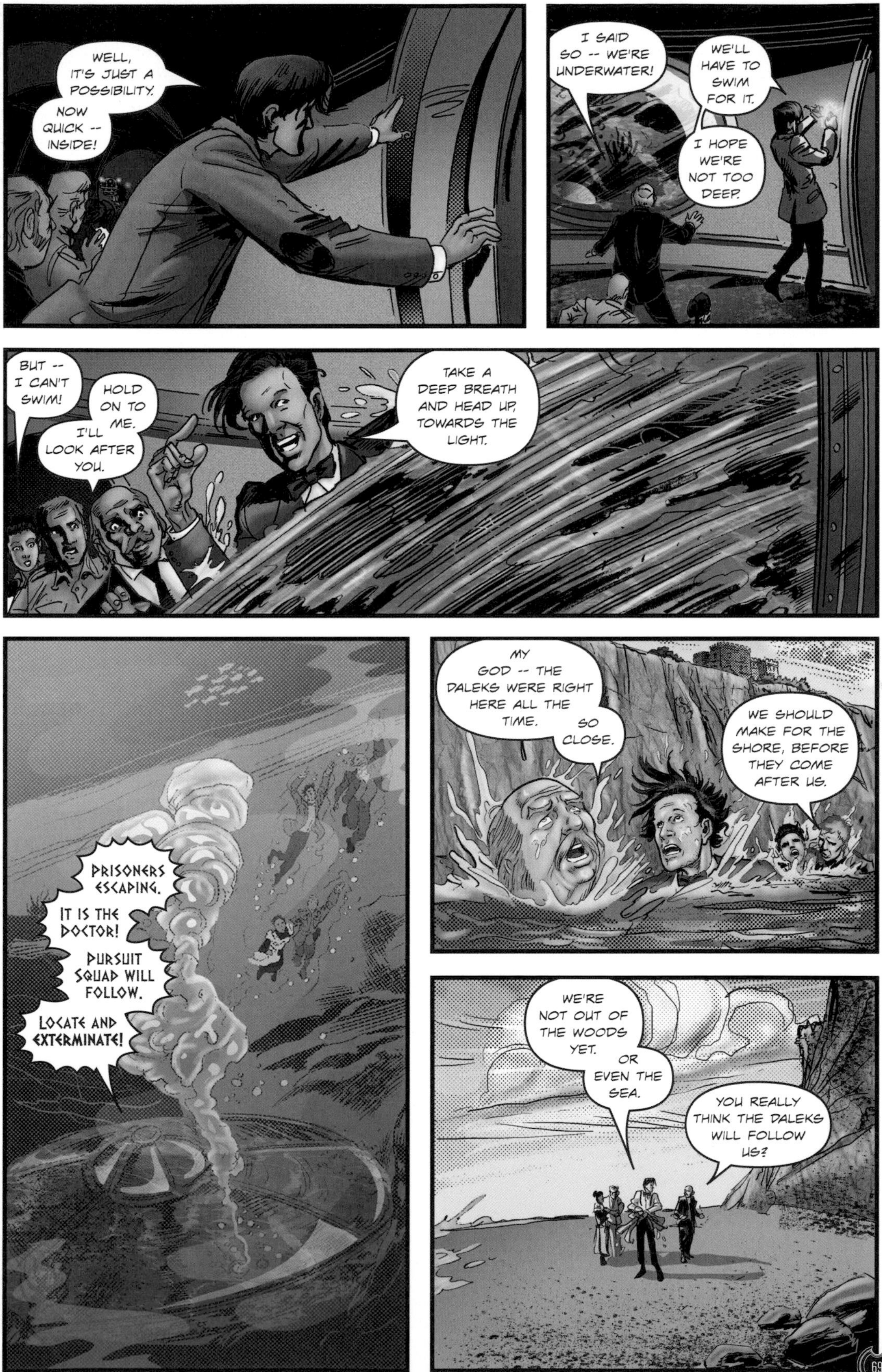
WELL, IT'S JUST A POSSIBILITY.
NOW QUICK -- INSIDE!
I SAID SO -- WE'RE UNDERWATER!
WE'LL HAVE TO SWIM FOR IT.
I HOPE WE'RE NOT TOO DEEP.
BUT -- I CAN'T SWIM!
HOLD ON TO ME.
I'LL LOOK AFTER YOU.
TAKE A DEEP BREATH AND HEAD UP, TOWARDS THE LIGHT.
PRISONERS ESCAPING.
IT IS THE DOCTOR!
PURSUIT SQUAD WILL FOLLOW.
LOCATE AND EXTERMINATE!
MY GOD -- THE DALEKS WERE RIGHT HERE ALL THE TIME.
SO CLOSE.
WE SHOULD MAKE FOR THE SHORE, BEFORE THEY COME AFTER US.
WE'RE NOT OUT OF THE WOODS YET.
OR EVEN THE SEA.
YOU REALLY THINK THE DALEKS WILL FOLLOW US?

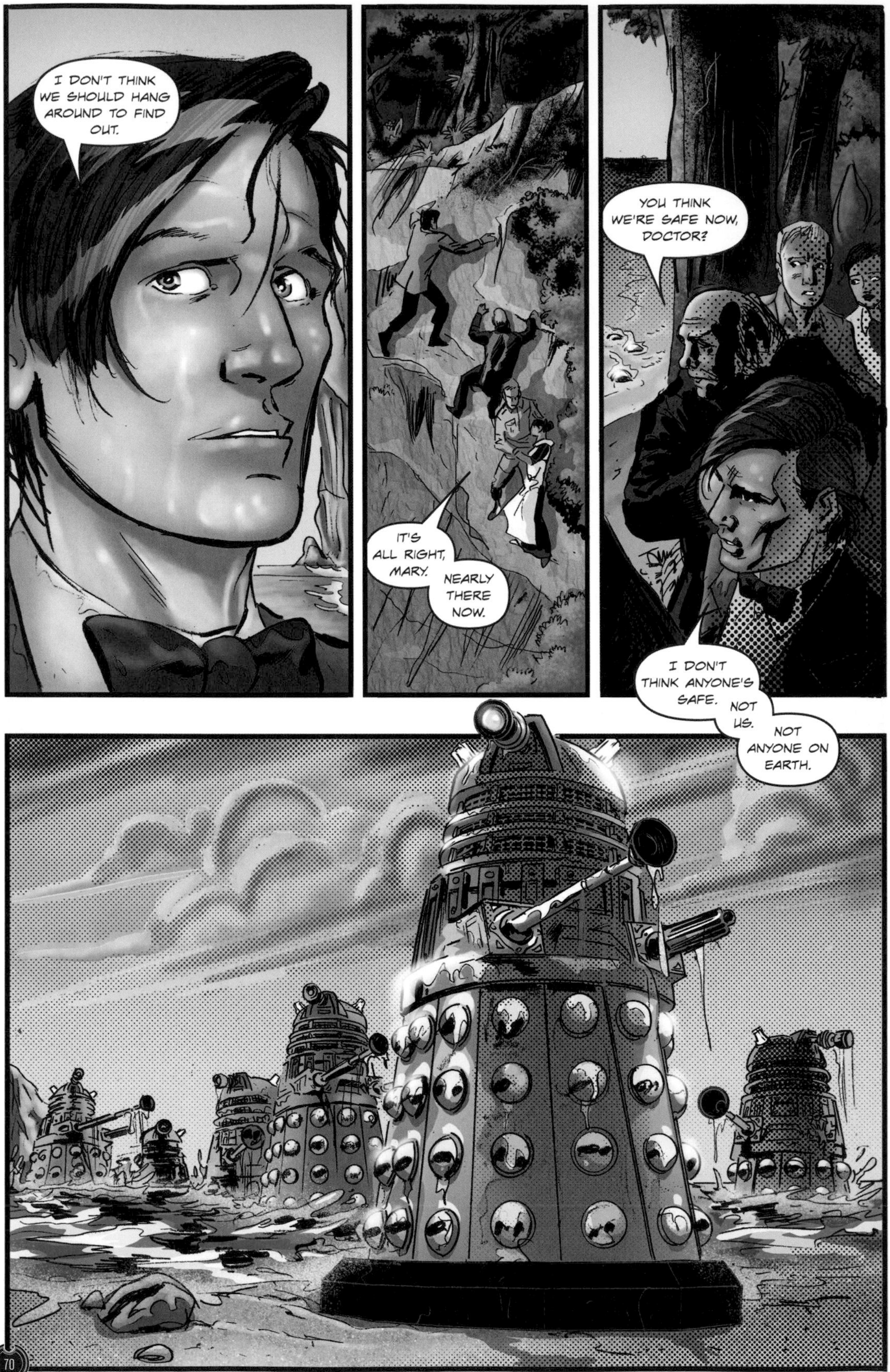
I DON'T THINK WE SHOULD HANG AROUND TO FIND OUT.
IT'S ALL RIGHT, MARY.
NEARLY THERE NOW.
YOU THINK WE'RE SAFE NOW, DOCTOR?
I DON'T THINK ANYONE'S SAFE.
NOT US.
NOT ANYONE ON EARTH.

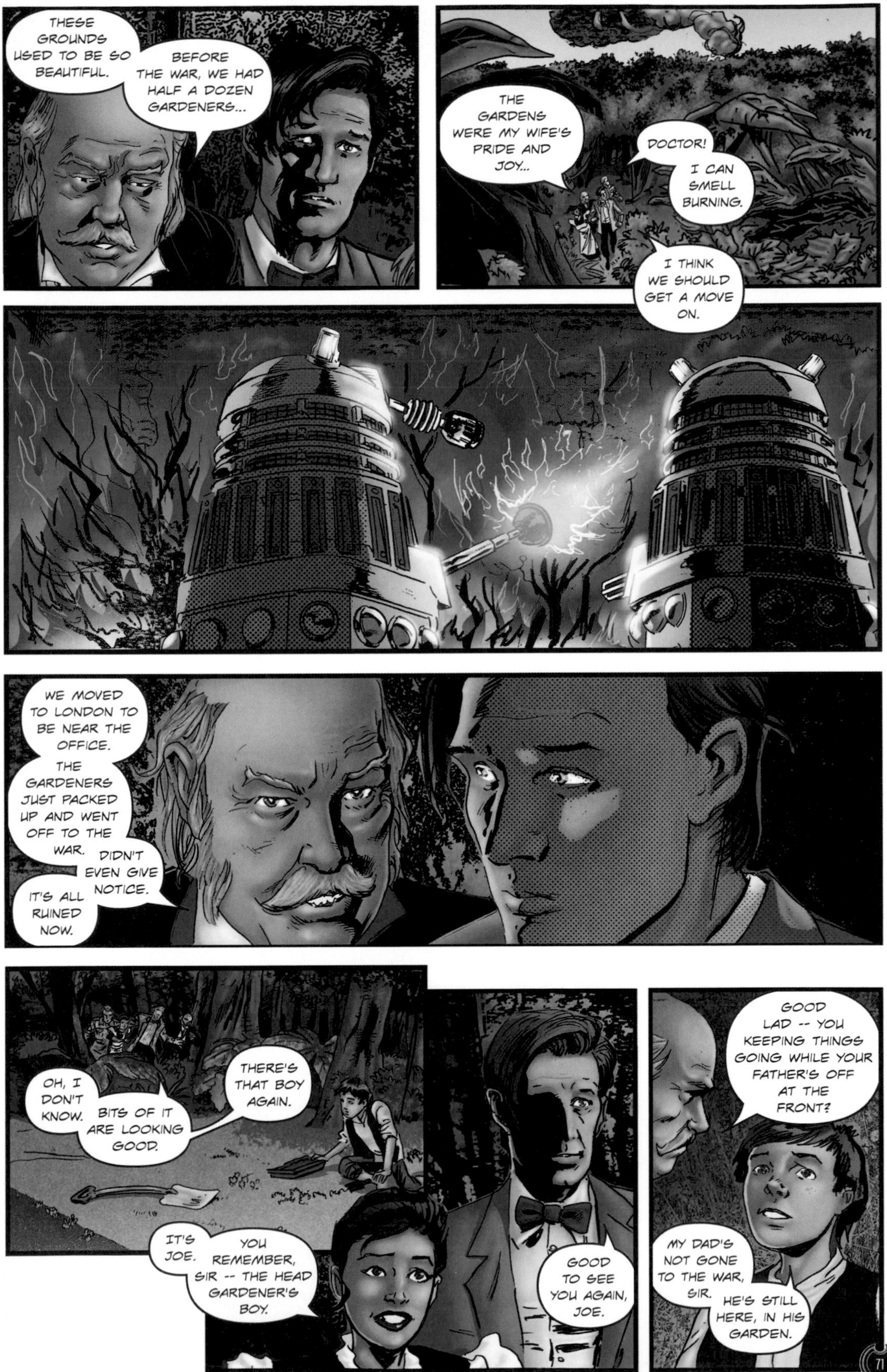
THESE GROUNDS USED TO BE SO BEAUTIFUL.
BEFORE THE WAR, WE HAD HALF A DOZEN GARDENERS...
THE GARDENS WERE MY WIFE'S PRIDE AND JOY...
DOCTOR!
I CAN SMELL BURNING.
I THINK WE SHOULD GET A MOVE ON.
WE MOVED TO LONDON TO BE NEAR THE OFFICE.
THE GARDENERS JUST PACKED UP AND WENT OFF TO THE WAR.
DIDN'T EVEN GIVE NOTICE.
IT'S ALL RUINED NOW.
OH, I DON'T KNOW.
BITS OF IT ARE LOOKING GOOD.
THERE'S THAT BOY AGAIN.
IT'S JOE.
YOU REMEMBER, SIR -- THE HEAD GARDENER'S BOY.
GOOD TO SEE YOU AGAIN, JOE.
GOOD LAD -- YOU KEEPING THINGS GOING WHILE YOUR FATHER'S OFF AT THE FRONT?
MY DAD'S NOT GONE TO THE WAR, SIR.
HE'S STILL HERE, IN HIS GARDEN.

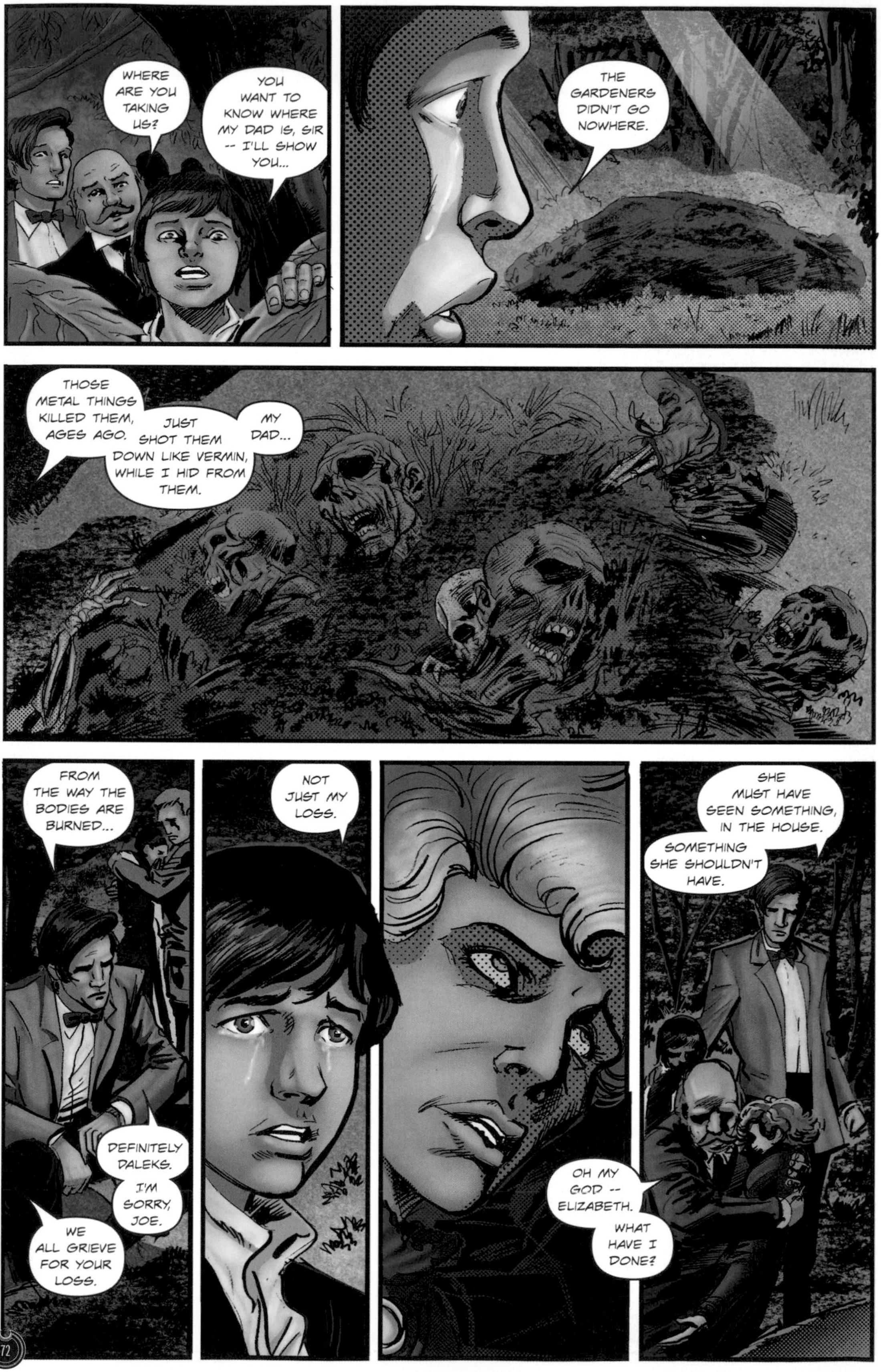
WHERE ARE YOU TAKING US?
YOU WANT TO KNOW WHERE MY DAD IS, SIR -- I'LL SHOW YOU...
THE GARDENERS DIDN'T GO NOWHERE.
THOSE METAL THINGS KILLED THEM, AGES AGO.
JUST SHOT THEM DOWN LIKE VERMIN, WHILE I HID FROM THEM.
MY DAD...
FROM THE WAY THE BODIES ARE BURNED...
DEFINITELY DALEKS.
I'M SORRY, JOE.
WE ALL GRIEVE FOR YOUR LOSS.
NOT JUST MY LOSS.
OH MY GOD -- ELIZABETH.
WHAT HAVE I DONE?
SHE MUST HAVE SEEN SOMETHING, IN THE HOUSE.
SOMETHING SHE SHOULDN'T HAVE.

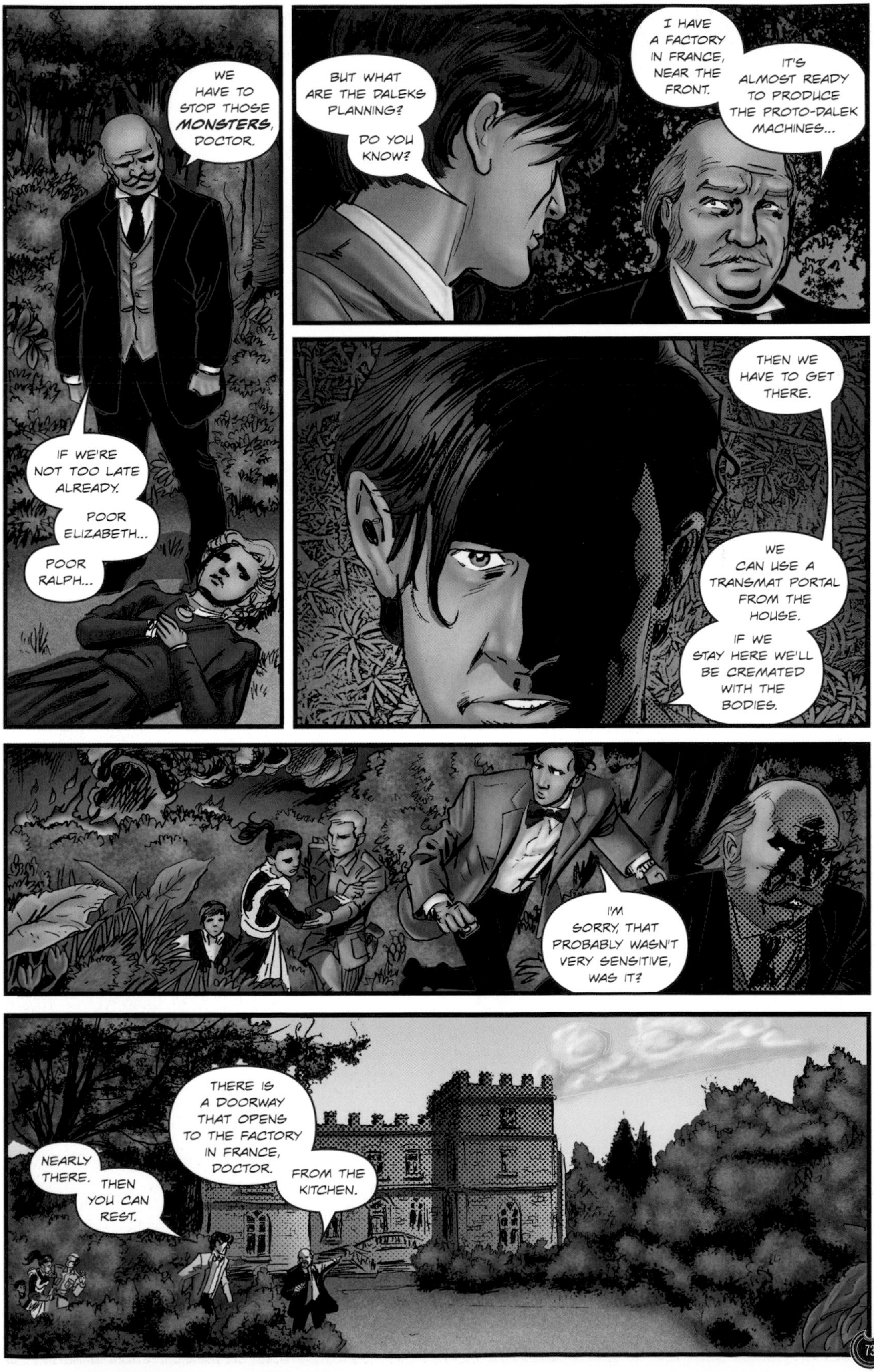
WE HAVE TO STOP THOSE MONSTERS, DOCTOR.
IF WE'RE NOT TOO LATE ALREADY.
POOR ELIZABETH...
POOR RALPH...
BUT WHAT ARE THE DALEKS PLANNING?
DO YOU KNOW?
I HAVE A FACTORY IN FRANCE, NEAR THE FRONT.
IT'S ALMOST READY TO PRODUCE THE PROTO-DALEK MACHINES...
THEN WE HAVE TO GET THERE.
WE CAN USE A TRANSMAT PORTAL FROM THE HOUSE.
IF WE STAY HERE WE'LL BE CREMATED WITH THE BODIES.
I'M SORRY, THAT PROBABLY WASN'T VERY SENSITIVE, WAS IT?
NEARLY THERE.
THEN YOU CAN REST.
THERE IS A DOORWAY THAT OPENS TO THE FACTORY IN FRANCE, DOCTOR.
FROM THE KITCHEN.

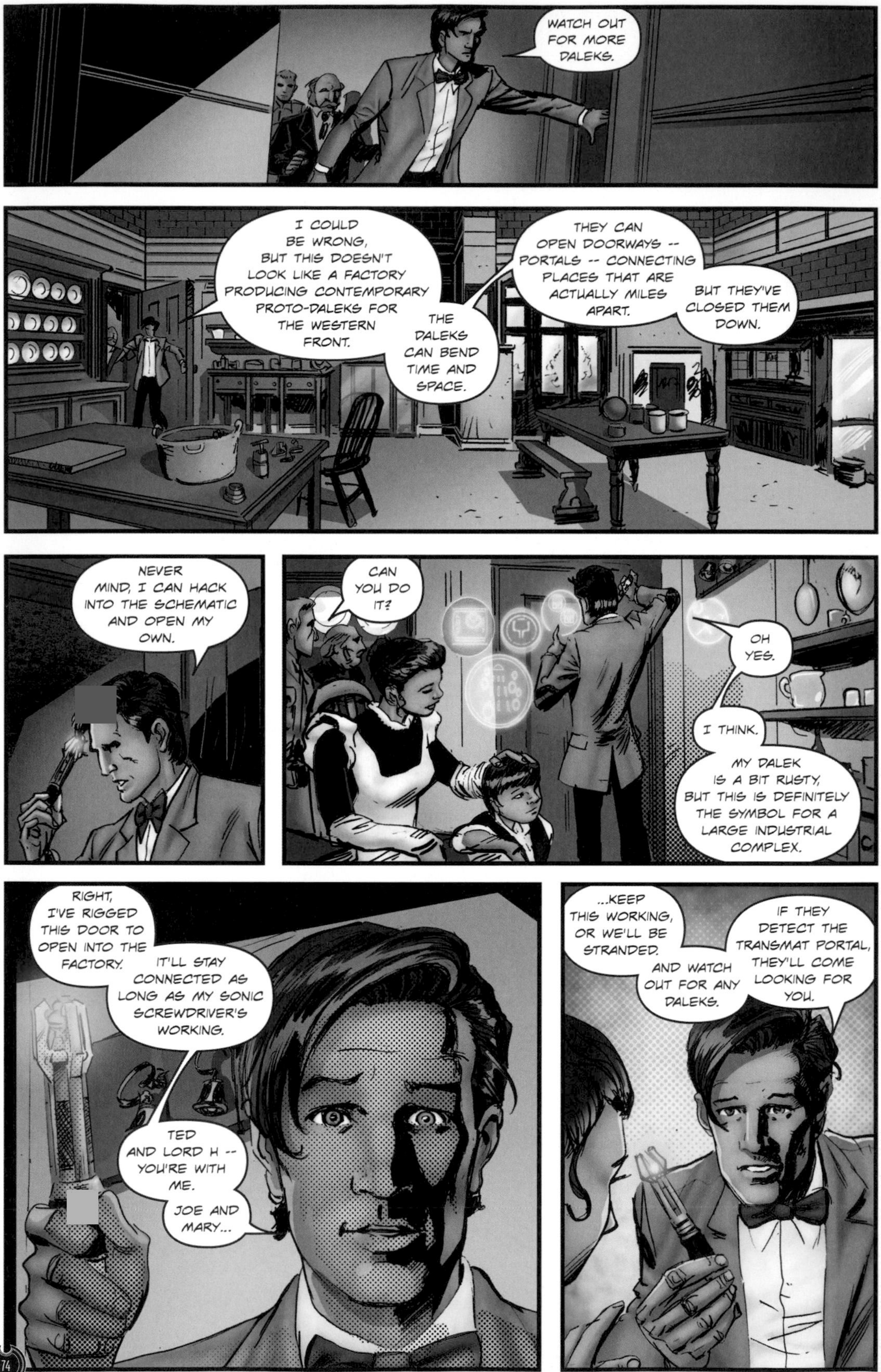
WATCH OUT FOR MORE DALEKS.
I COULD BE WRONG, BUT THIS DOESN'T LOOK LIKE A FACTORY PRODUCING CONTEMPORARY PROTO-DALEKS FOR THE WESTERN FRONT.
THE DALEKS CAN BEND TIME AND SPACE.
THEY CAN OPEN DOORWAYS -- PORTALS -- CONNECTING PLACES THAT ARE ACTUALLY MILES APART.
BUT THEY'VE CLOSED THEM DOWN.
NEVER MIND, I CAN HACK INTO THE SCHEMATIC AND OPEN MY OWN.
CAN YOU DO IT?
OH YES.
I THINK.
MY DALEK IS A BIT RUSTY, BUT THIS IS DEFINITELY THE SYMBOL FOR A LARGE INDUSTRIAL COMPLEX.
RIGHT, I'VE RIGGED THIS DOOR TO OPEN INTO THE FACTORY.
IT'LL STAY CONNECTED AS LONG AS MY SONIC SCREWDRIVER'S WORKING.
TED AND LORD H -- YOU'RE WITH ME.
JOE AND MARY...
...KEEP THIS WORKING, OR WE'LL BE STRANDED.
AND WATCH OUT FOR ANY DALEKS.
IF THEY DETECT THE TRANSMAT PORTAL, THEY'LL COME LOOKING FOR YOU.

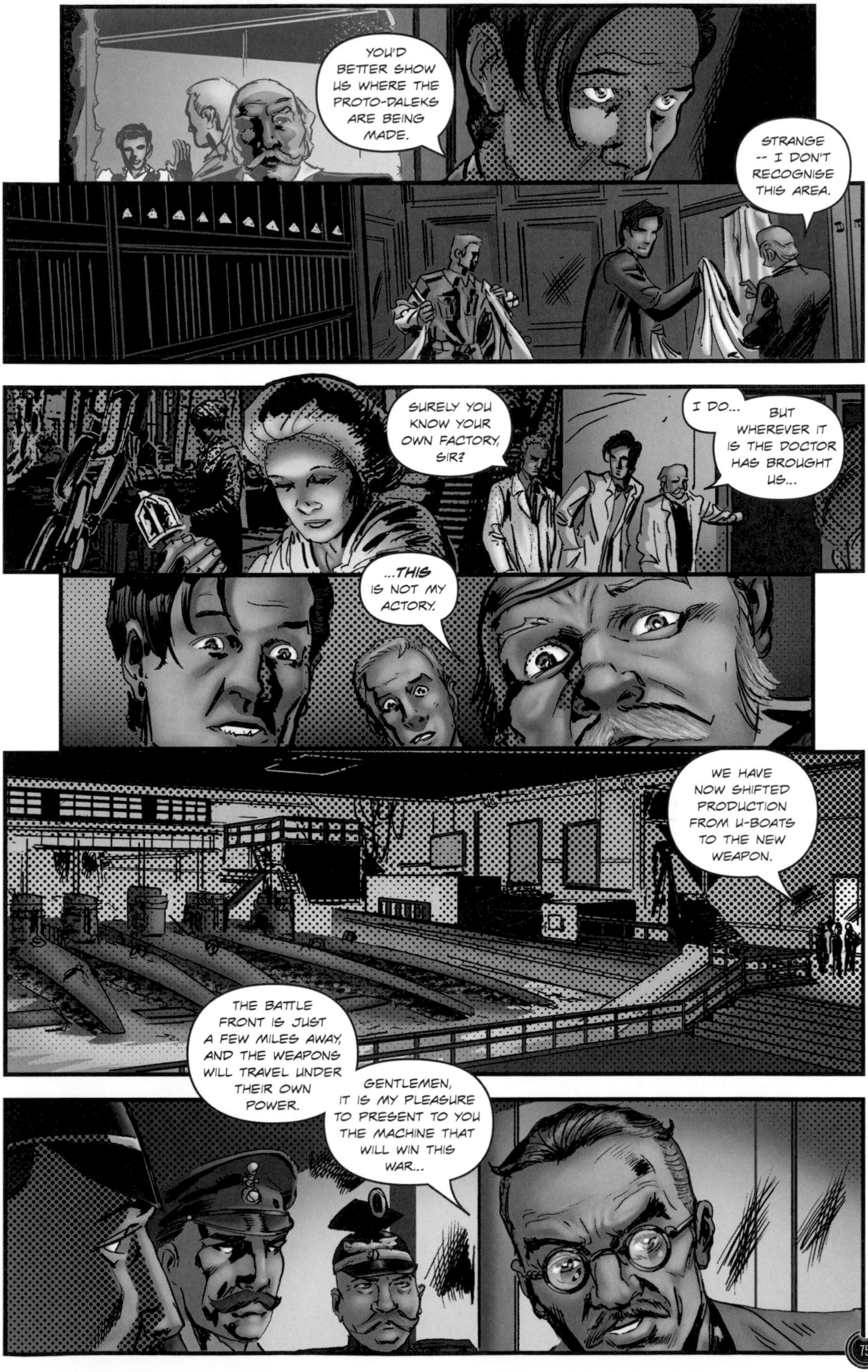
YOU'D BETTER SHOW US WHERE THE PROTO-DALEKS ARE BEING MADE.
STRANGE -- I DON'T RECOGNISE THIS AREA.
SURELY YOU KNOW YOUR OWN FACTORY, SIR?
I DO...
BUT WHEREVER IT IS THE DOCTOR HAS BROUGHT US...
...THIS IS NOT MY ACTORY.
WE HAVE NOW SHIFTED PRODUCTION FROM U-BOATS TO THE NEW WEAPON.
THE BATTLE FRONT IS JUST A FEW MILES AWAY, AND THE WEAPONS WILL TRAVEL UNDER THEIR OWN POWER.
GENTLEMEN, IT IS MY PLEASURE TO PRESENT TO YOU THE MACHINE THAT WILL WIN THIS WAR...

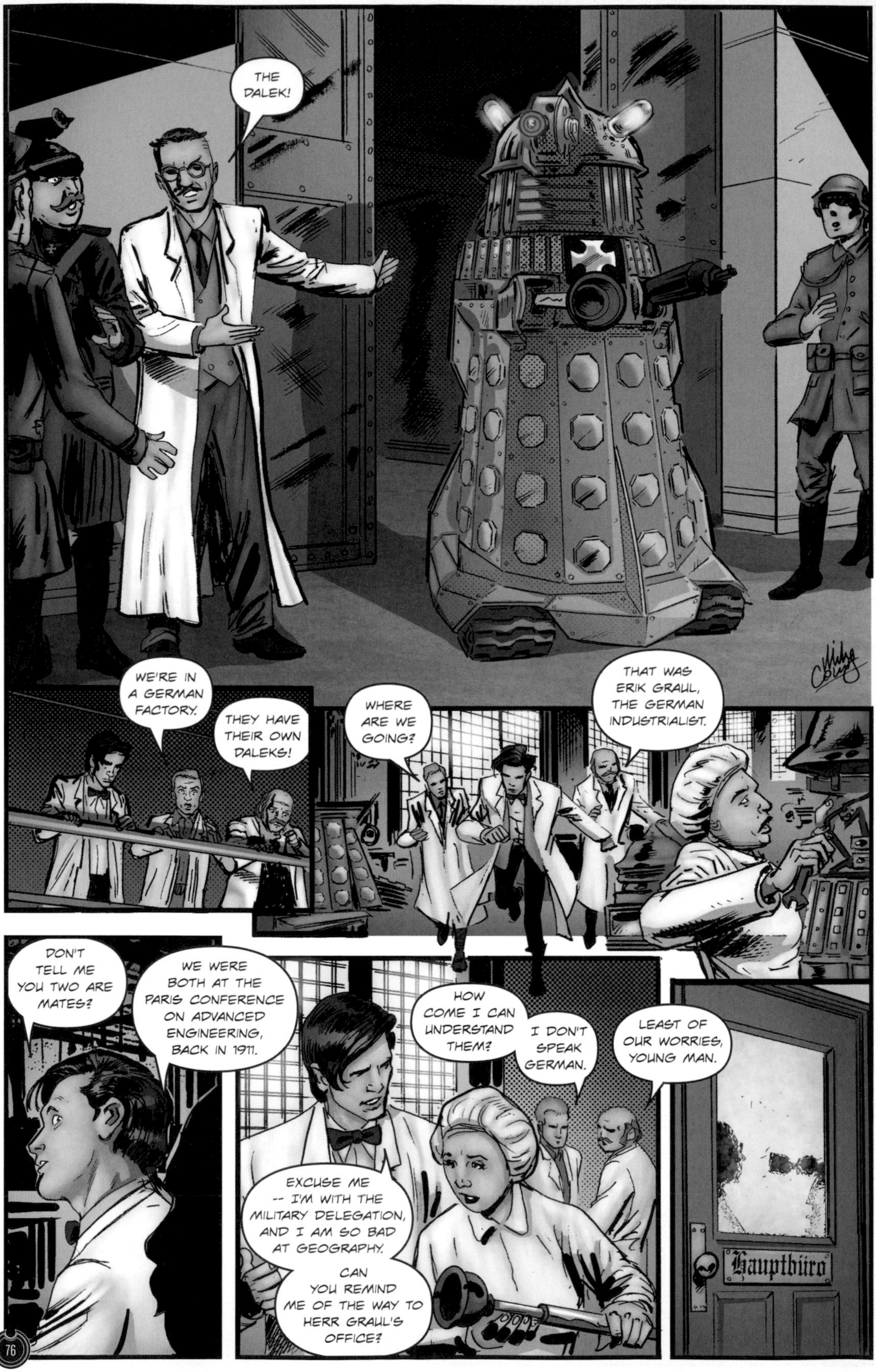
THE DALEK!
WE'RE IN A GERMAN FACTORY.
THEY HAVE THEIR OWN DALEKS!
WHERE ARE WE GOING?
THAT WAS ERIK GRAUL, THE GERMAN INDUSTRIALIST.
DON'T TELL ME YOU TWO ARE MATES?
WE WERE BOTH AT THE PARIS CONFERENCE ON ADVANCED ENGINEERING, BACK IN 1911.
HOW COME I CAN UNDERSTAND THEM?
I DON'T SPEAK GERMAN.
LEAST OF OUR WORRIES, YOUNG MAN.
EXCUSE ME -- I'M WITH THE MILITARY DELEGATION, AND I AM SO BAD AT GEOGRAPHY.
CAN YOU REMIND ME OF THE WAY TO HERR GRAUL'S OFFICE?
Hauptbüro

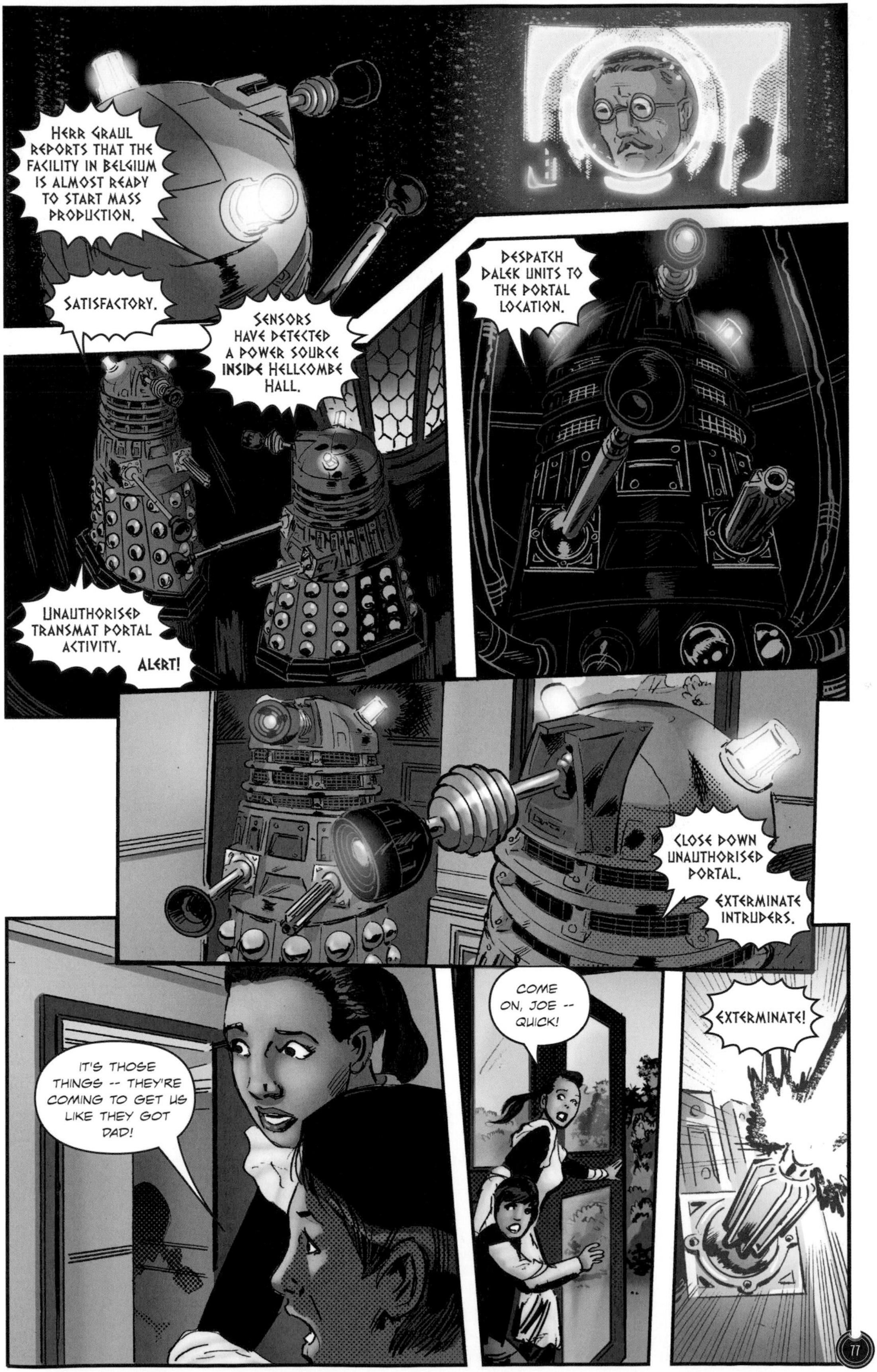
HERR GRAUL REPORTS THAT THE FACILITY IN BELGIUM IS ALMOST READY TO START MASS PRODUCTION.
SATISFACTORY.
SENSORS HAVE DETECTED A POWER SOURCE **INSIDE** HELLCOMBE HALL.
UNAUTHORISED TRANSMAT PORTAL ACTIVITY. **ALERT!**
DESPATCH DALEK UNITS TO THE PORTAL LOCATION.
CLOSE DOWN UNAUTHORISED PORTAL.
EXTERMINATE INTRUDERS.
IT'S THOSE THINGS -- THEY'RE COMING TO GET US LIKE THEY GOT DAD!
COME ON, JOE -- QUICK!
EXTERMINATE!

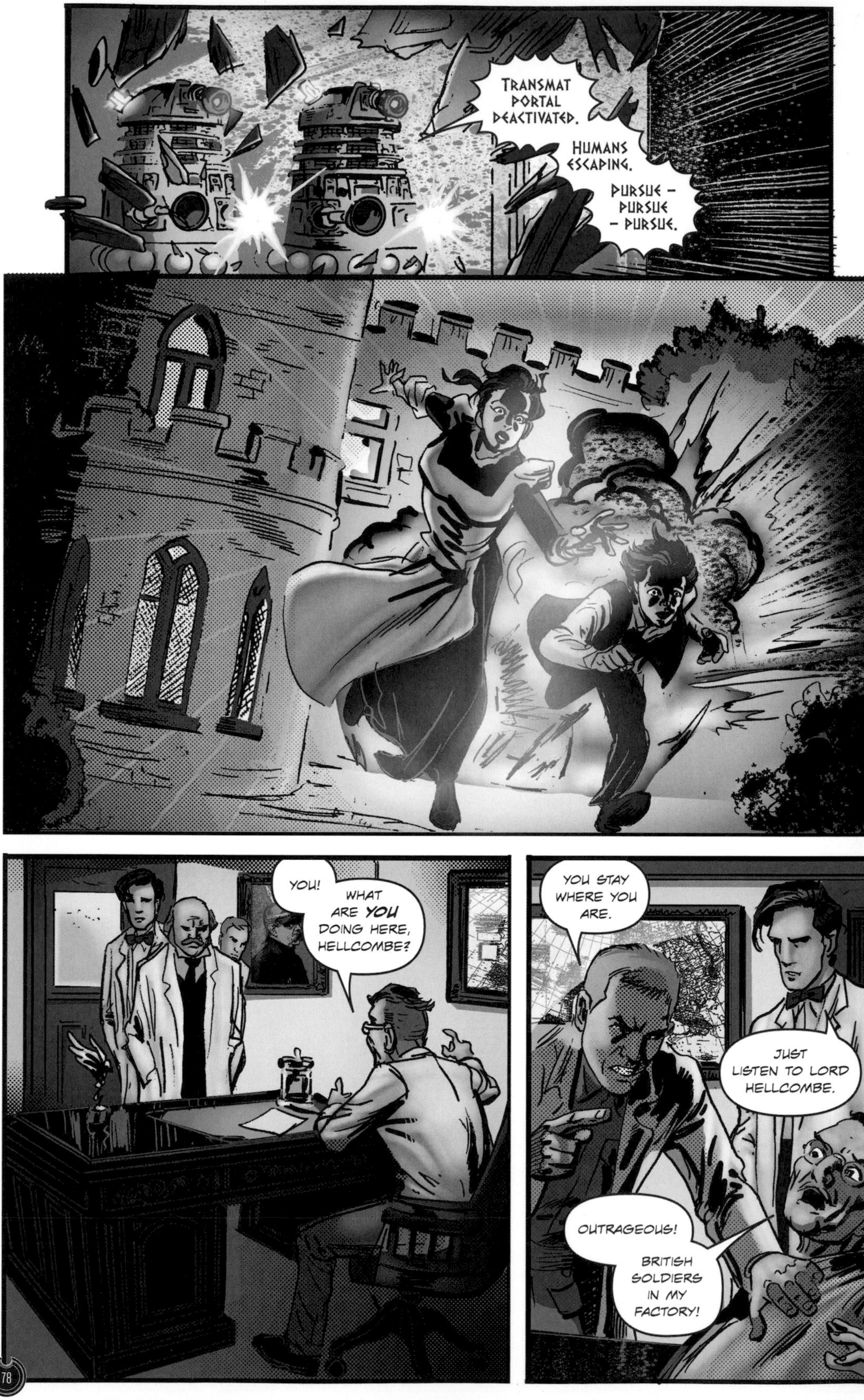
TRANSMAT PORTAL DEACTIVATED.
HUMANS ESCAPING.
PURSUE – PURSUE – PURSUE.
YOU!
WHAT ARE YOU DOING HERE, HELLCOMBE?
YOU STAY WHERE YOU ARE.
JUST LISTEN TO LORD HELLCOMBE.
OUTRAGEOUS!
BRITISH SOLDIERS IN MY FACTORY!

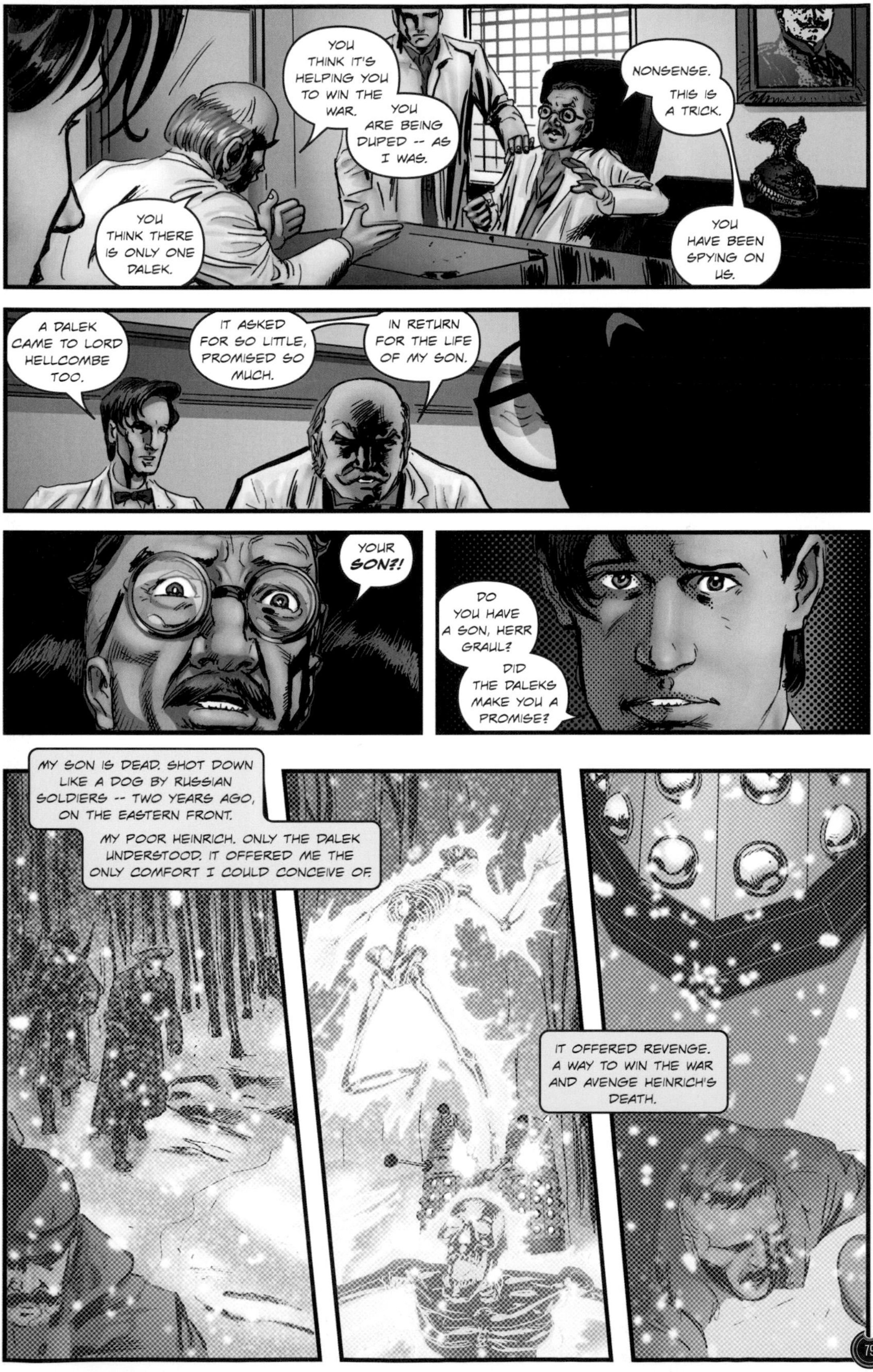
YOU THINK IT'S HELPING YOU TO WIN THE WAR.
YOU ARE BEING DUPED -- AS I WAS.
NONSENSE.
THIS IS A TRICK.
YOU HAVE BEEN SPYING ON US.
YOU THINK THERE IS ONLY ONE DALEK.
A DALEK CAME TO LORD HELLCOMBE TOO.
IT ASKED FOR SO LITTLE, PROMISED SO MUCH.
IN RETURN FOR THE LIFE OF MY SON.
YOUR **SON?!**
DO YOU HAVE A SON, HERR GRAUL?
DID THE DALEKS MAKE YOU A PROMISE?
MY SON IS DEAD. SHOT DOWN LIKE A DOG BY RUSSIAN SOLDIERS -- TWO YEARS AGO, ON THE EASTERN FRONT.
MY POOR HEINRICH. ONLY THE DALEK UNDERSTOOD. IT OFFERED ME THE ONLY COMFORT I COULD CONCEIVE OF.
IT OFFERED REVENGE. A WAY TO WIN THE WAR AND AVENGE HEINRICH'S DEATH.

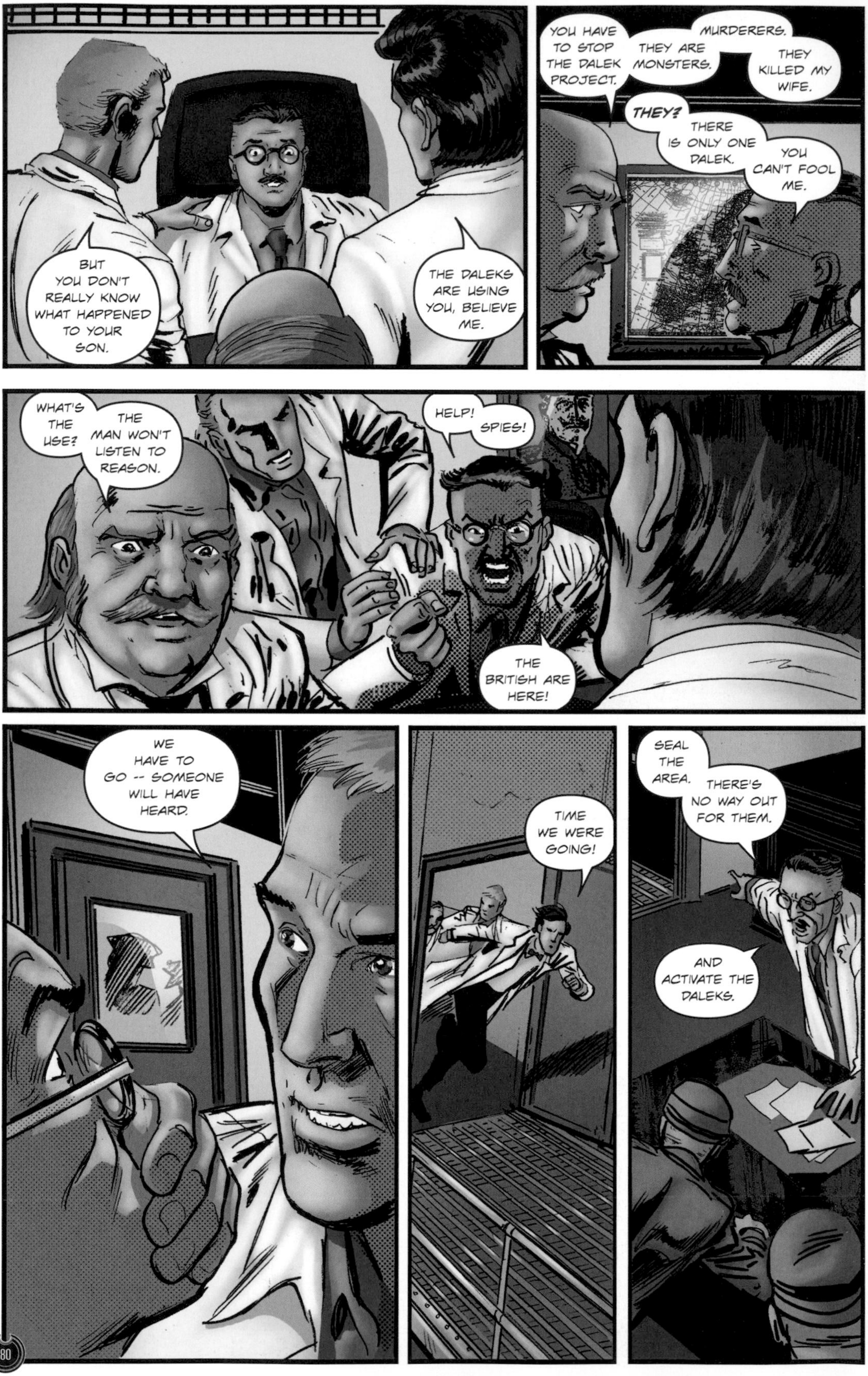
BUT YOU DON'T REALLY KNOW WHAT HAPPENED TO YOUR SON.
THE DALEKS ARE USING YOU, BELIEVE ME.
YOU HAVE TO STOP THE DALEK PROJECT.
THEY ARE MONSTERS.
MURDERERS.
THEY KILLED MY WIFE.
THEY?
THERE IS ONLY ONE DALEK.
YOU CAN'T FOOL ME.
WHAT'S THE USE?
THE MAN WON'T LISTEN TO REASON.
HELP!
SPIES!
THE BRITISH ARE HERE!
WE HAVE TO GO -- SOMEONE WILL HAVE HEARD.
TIME WE WERE GOING!
SEAL THE AREA.
THERE'S NO WAY OUT FOR THEM.
AND ACTIVATE THE DALEKS.

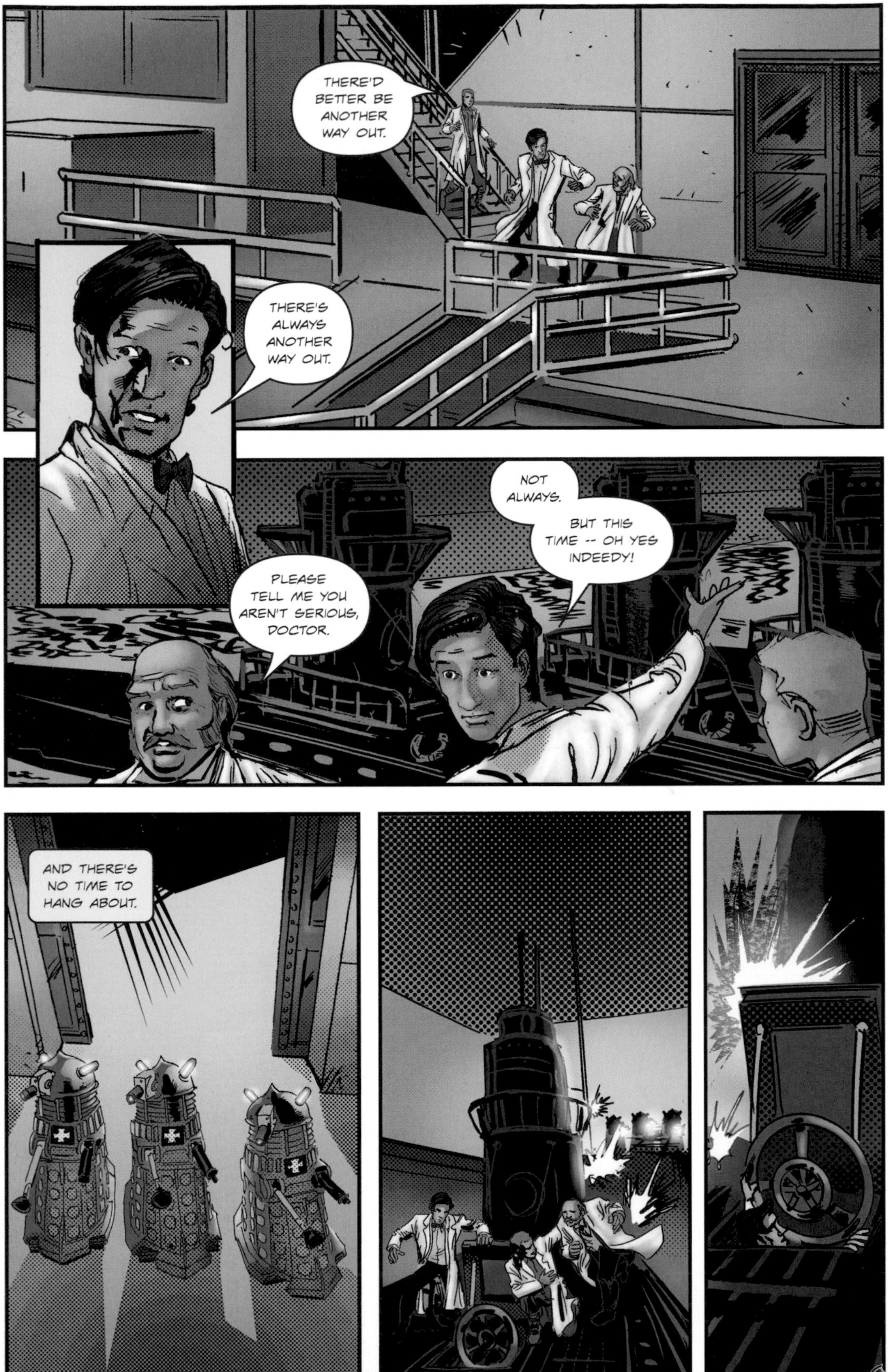
THERE'D BETTER BE ANOTHER WAY OUT.
THERE'S ALWAYS ANOTHER WAY OUT.
NOT ALWAYS.
BUT THIS TIME -- OH YES INDEEDY!
PLEASE TELL ME YOU AREN'T SERIOUS, DOCTOR.
AND THERE'S NO TIME TO HANG ABOUT.

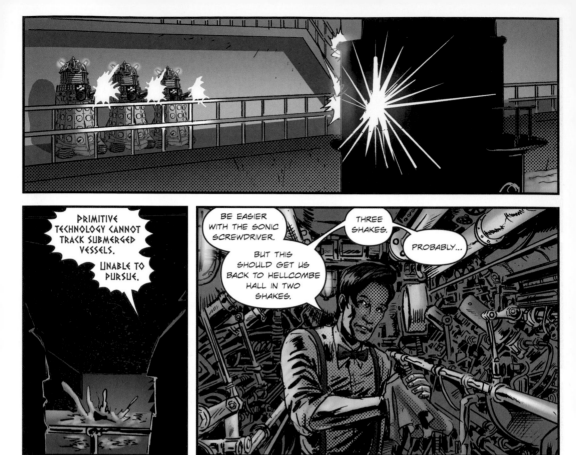

PRIMITIVE TECHNOLOGY CANNOT TRACK SUBMERGED VESSELS.

UNABLE TO PURSUE.

BE EASIER WITH THE SONIC SCREWDRIVER.

BUT THIS SHOULD GET US BACK TO HELLCOMBE HALL IN TWO SHAKES.

THREE SHAKES.

PROBABLY...

'THEY'LL HAVE BEEN WARNED WE'RE COMING. BUT THEY WON'T EXPECT US FOR AGES YET. SO WE SHOULD BE ABLE TO SNEAK UP ON THE DALEK SAUCER. ASSUMING WE CAN FIND KENT...'

SEVERAL HOURS LATER, AS THE U-BOAT DIVES TO SEARCH FOR THE DALEK SHIP...

THERE'S HELLCOMBE HALL, DOCTOR.

SEEMS MY RUSTY NAVIGATION'S STILL UP TO SCRATCH.

WE SHOULD BE IN RANGE NOW.

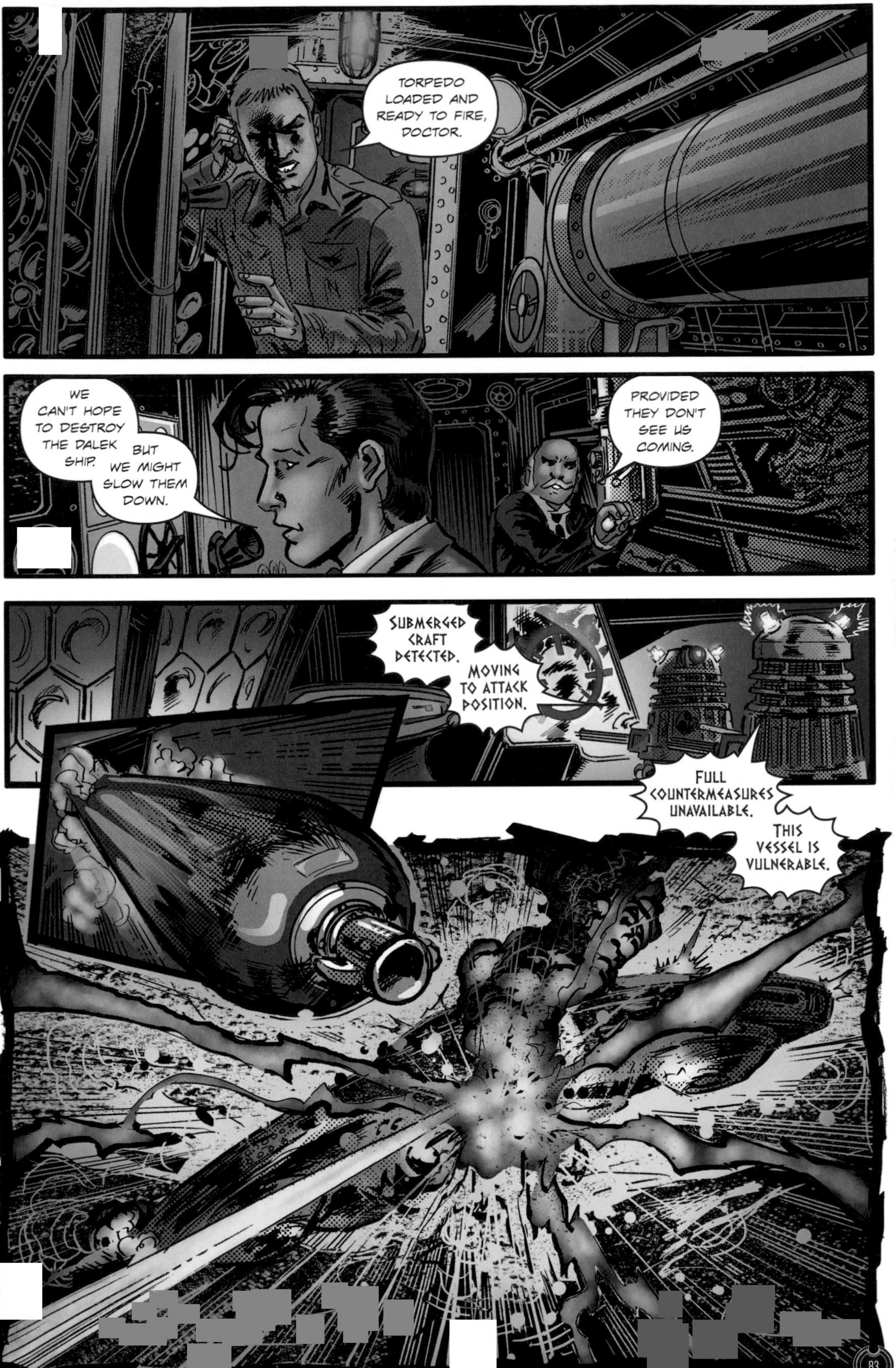
TORPEDO LOADED AND READY TO FIRE, DOCTOR.
WE CAN'T HOPE TO DESTROY THE DALEK SHIP.
BUT WE MIGHT SLOW THEM DOWN.
PROVIDED THEY DON'T SEE US COMING.
SUBMERGED CRAFT DETECTED.
MOVING TO ATTACK POSITION.
FULL COUNTERMEASURES UNAVAILABLE.
THIS VESSEL IS VULNERABLE.

HULL BREACHED.
DRIVE SYSTEMS DAMAGED.
WEAPONRY OFFLINE.
WATER RISING THROUGH ALL SECTIONS.
SEAL ALL AFFECTED SECTIONS.
OPERATE EMERGENCY PUMPS.
REACTIVATE WEAPONS SYSTEMS.
ASSESS DAMAGE AND REPORT.
DEPLOY AQUA-DALEK UNITS TO DESTROY THE ATTACKING VESSEL.
ENEMY VESSEL TARGETED.
EXTERMINATE!

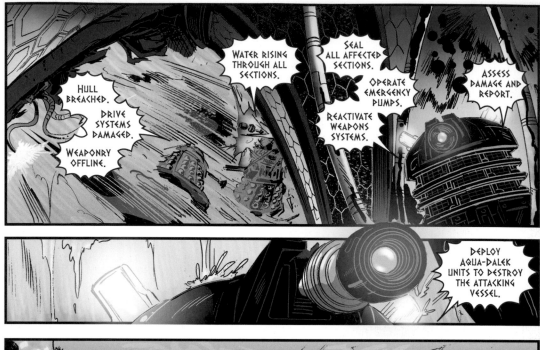

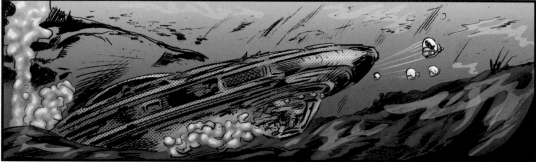

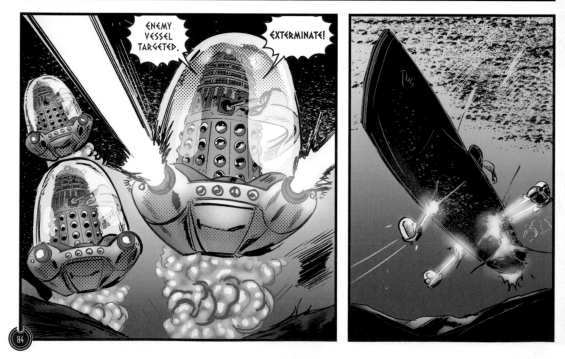

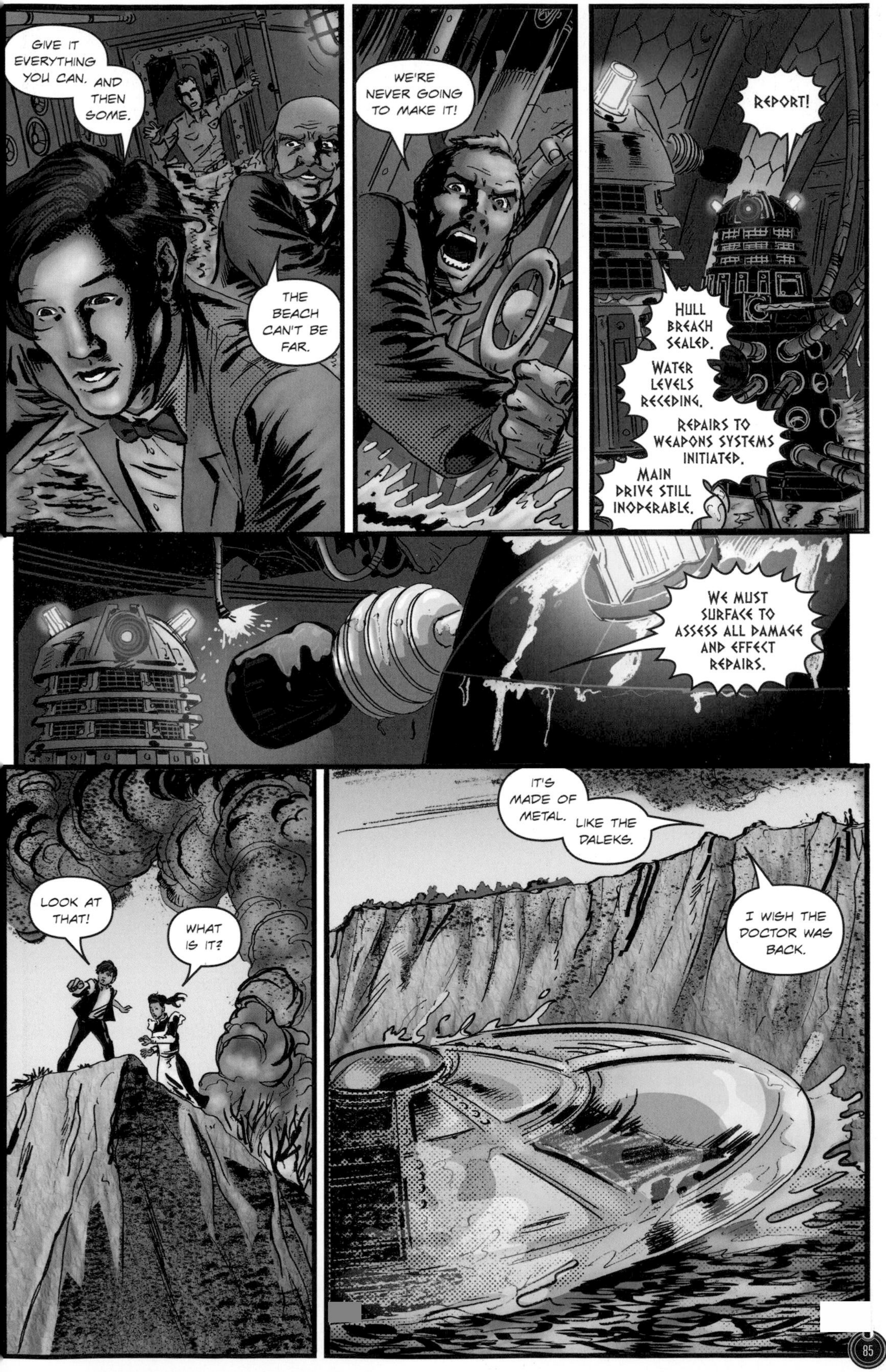
GIVE IT EVERYTHING YOU CAN.
AND THEN SOME.
THE BEACH CAN'T BE FAR.
WE'RE NEVER GOING TO MAKE IT!
REPORT!
HULL BREACH SEALED.
WATER LEVELS RECEDING.
REPAIRS TO WEAPONS SYSTEMS INITIATED.
MAIN DRIVE STILL INOPERABLE.
WE MUST SURFACE TO ASSESS ALL DAMAGE AND EFFECT REPAIRS.
LOOK AT THAT!
WHAT IS IT?
IT'S MADE OF METAL.
LIKE THE DALEKS.
I WISH THE DOCTOR WAS BACK.

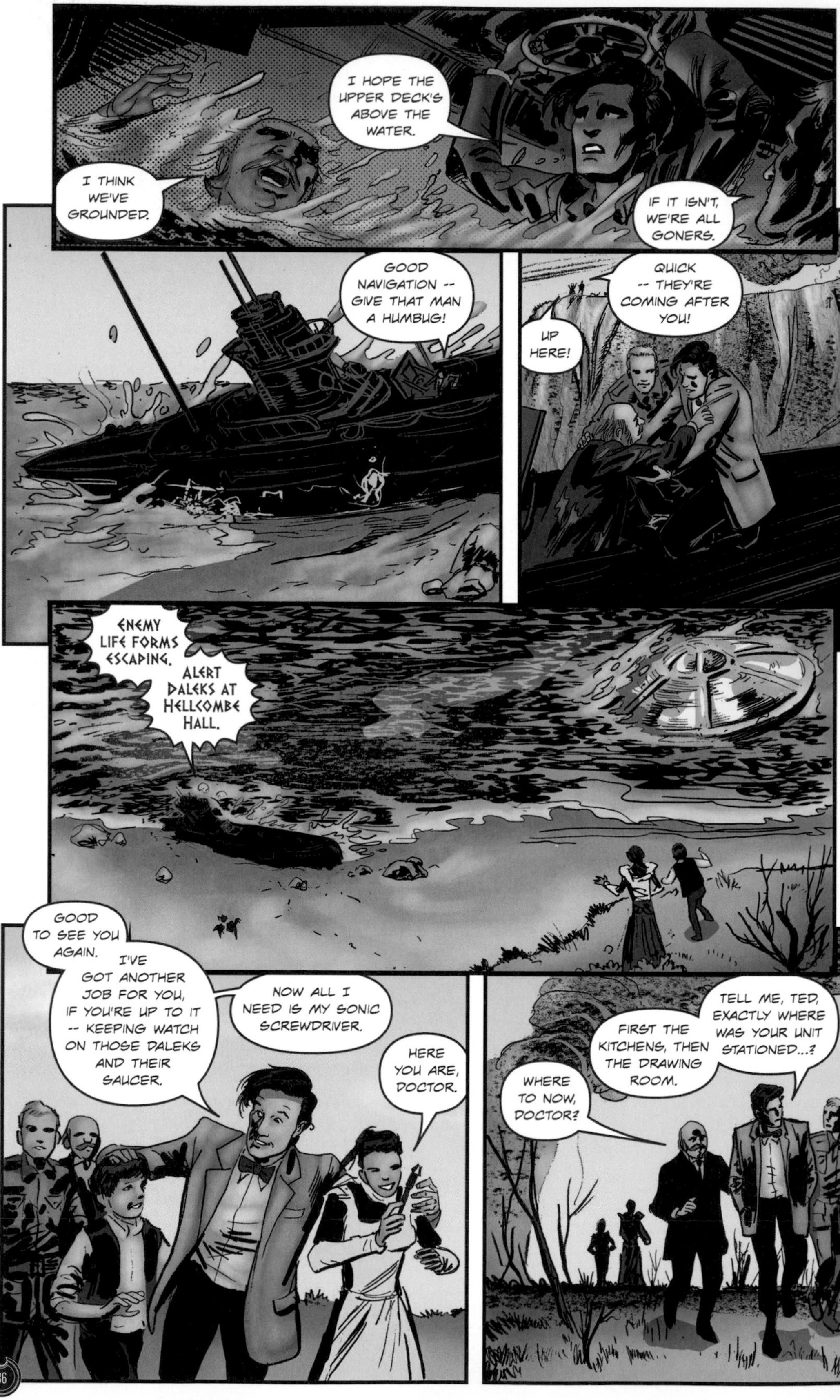
I HOPE THE UPPER DECK'S ABOVE THE WATER.
I THINK WE'VE GROUNDED.
IF IT ISN'T, WE'RE ALL GONERS.
GOOD NAVIGATION -- GIVE THAT MAN A HUMBUG!
QUICK -- THEY'RE COMING AFTER YOU!
UP HERE!
ENEMY LIFE FORMS ESCAPING.
ALERT DALEKS AT HELLCOMBE HALL.
GOOD TO SEE YOU AGAIN.
I'VE GOT ANOTHER JOB FOR YOU, IF YOU'RE UP TO IT -- KEEPING WATCH ON THOSE DALEKS AND THEIR SAUCER.
NOW ALL I NEED IS MY SONIC SCREWDRIVER.
HERE YOU ARE, DOCTOR.
TELL ME, TED, EXACTLY WHERE WAS YOUR UNIT STATIONED...?
FIRST THE KITCHENS, THEN THE DRAWING ROOM.
WHERE TO NOW, DOCTOR?

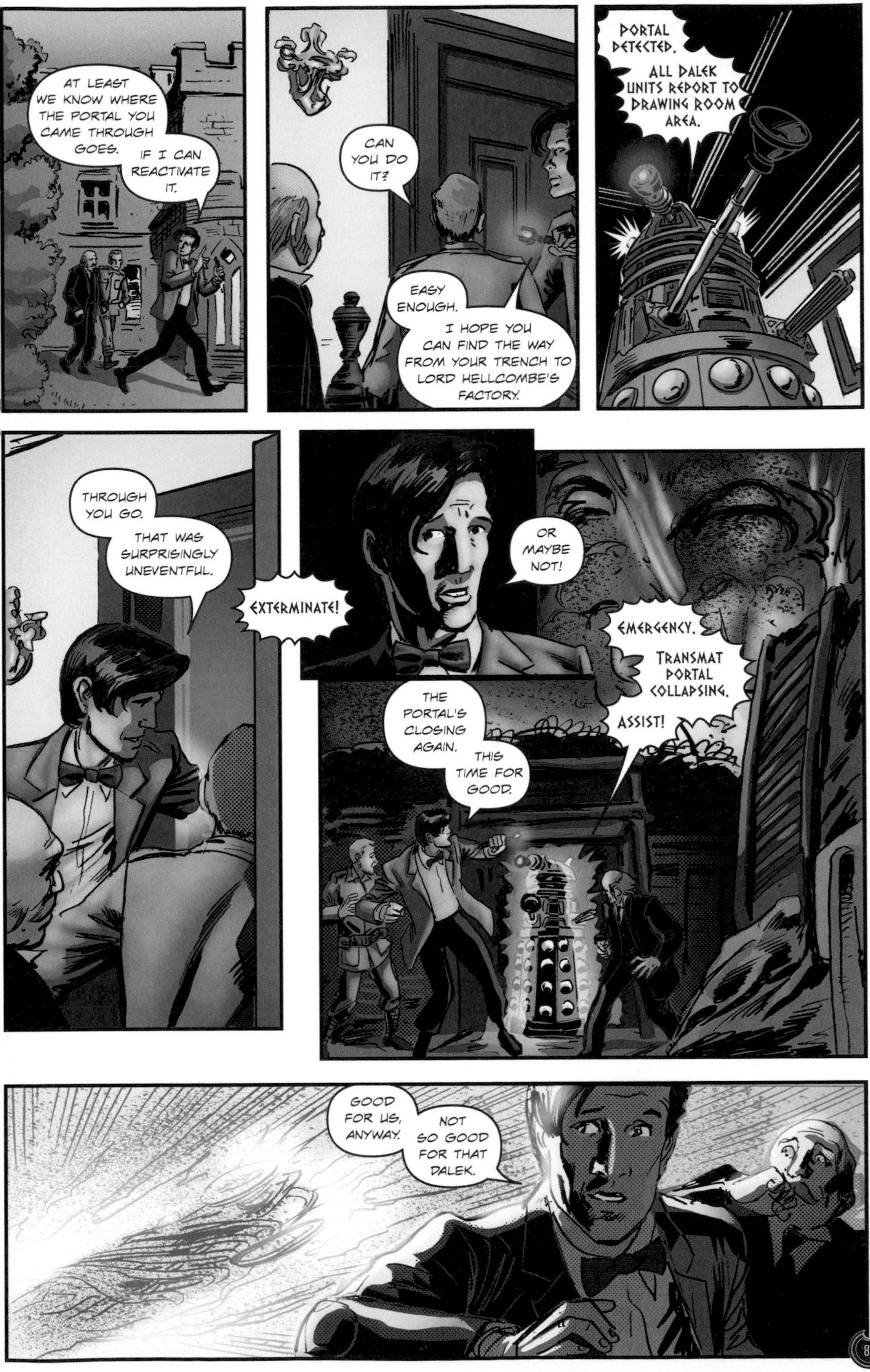
AT LEAST WE KNOW WHERE THE PORTAL YOU CAME THROUGH GOES.
IF I CAN REACTIVATE IT.
CAN YOU DO IT?
EASY ENOUGH.
I HOPE YOU CAN FIND THE WAY FROM YOUR TRENCH TO LORD HELLCOMBE'S FACTORY.
PORTAL DETECTED.
ALL DALEK UNITS REPORT TO DRAWING ROOM AREA.
THROUGH YOU GO.
THAT WAS SURPRISINGLY UNEVENTFUL.
EXTERMINATE!
OR MAYBE NOT!
EMERGENCY.
TRANSMAT PORTAL COLLAPSING.
ASSIST!
THE PORTAL'S CLOSING AGAIN.
THIS TIME FOR GOOD.
GOOD FOR US, ANYWAY.
NOT SO GOOD FOR THAT DALEK.

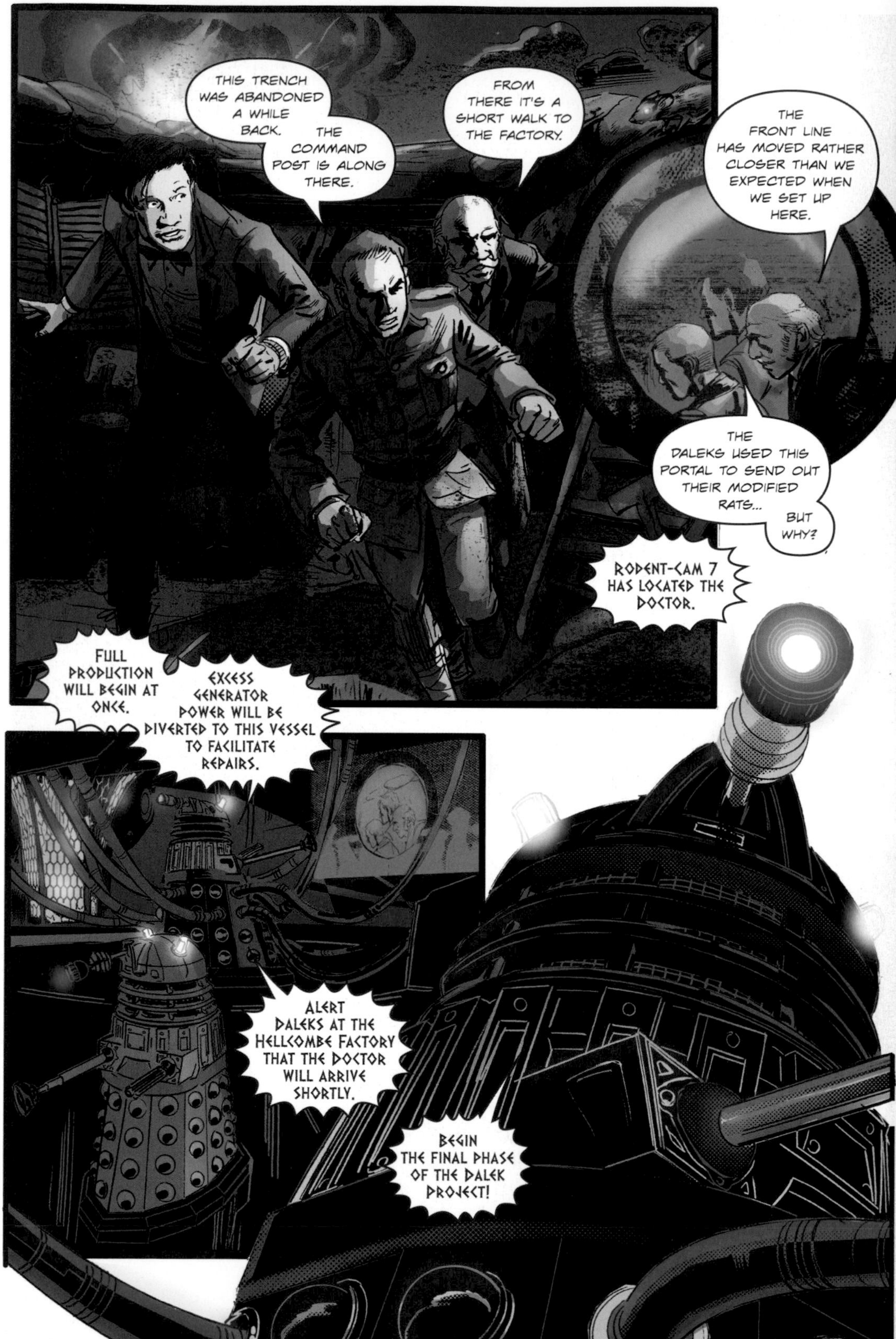
THIS TRENCH WAS ABANDONED A WHILE BACK.
THE COMMAND POST IS ALONG THERE.
FROM THERE IT'S A SHORT WALK TO THE FACTORY.
THE FRONT LINE HAS MOVED RATHER CLOSER THAN WE EXPECTED WHEN WE SET UP HERE.
THE DALEKS USED THIS PORTAL TO SEND OUT THEIR MODIFIED RATS...
BUT WHY?
RODENT-CAM 7 HAS LOCATED THE DOCTOR.
FULL PRODUCTION WILL BEGIN AT ONCE.
EXCESS GENERATOR POWER WILL BE DIVERTED TO THIS VESSEL TO FACILITATE REPAIRS.
ALERT DALEKS AT THE HELLCOMBE FACTORY THAT THE DOCTOR WILL ARRIVE SHORTLY.
BEGIN THE FINAL PHASE OF THE DALEK PROJECT!

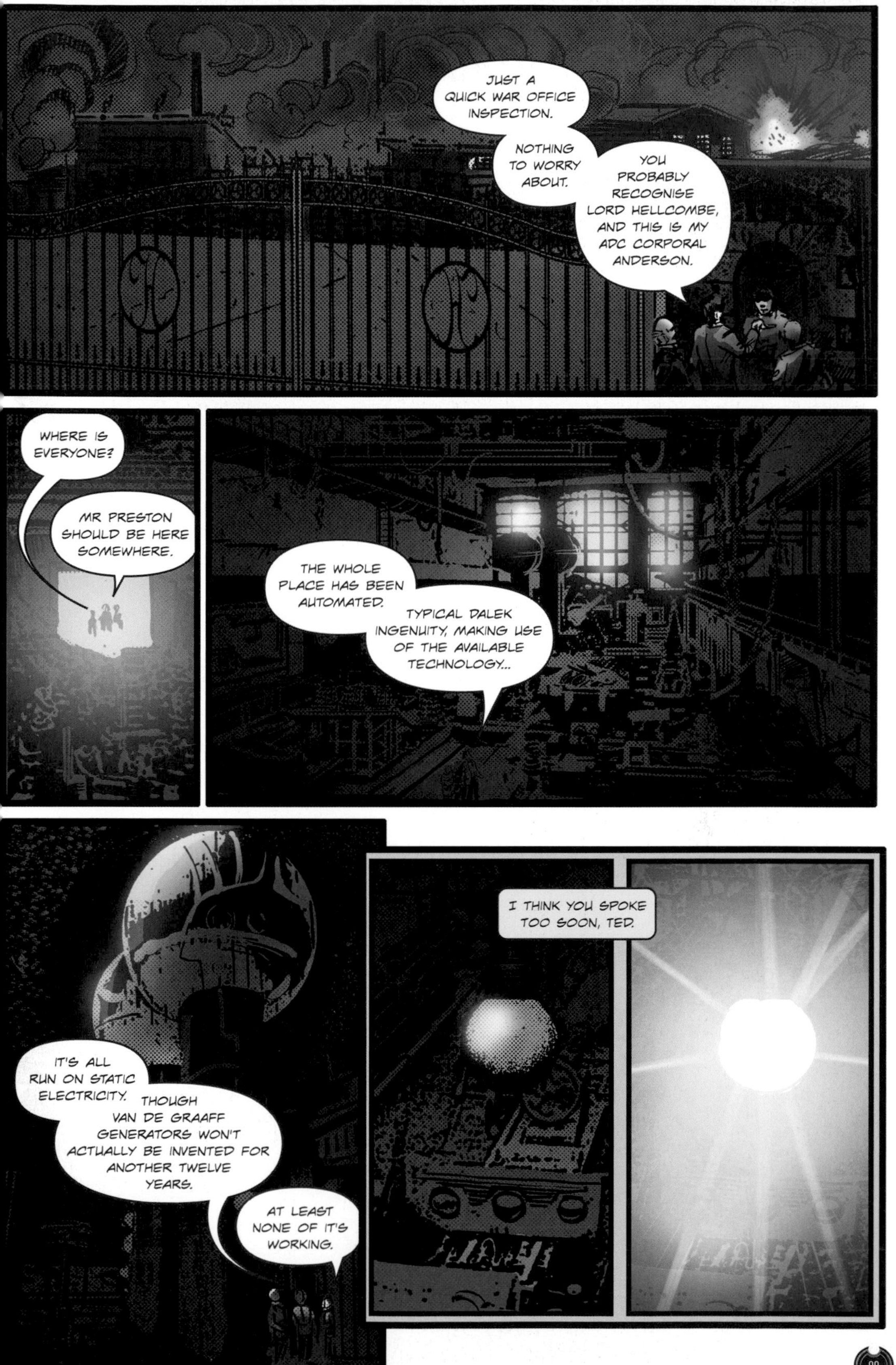

JUST A QUICK WAR OFFICE INSPECTION.
NOTHING TO WORRY ABOUT.
YOU PROBABLY RECOGNISE LORD HELLCOMBE, AND THIS IS MY ADC CORPORAL ANDERSON.
WHERE IS EVERYONE?
MR PRESTON SHOULD BE HERE SOMEWHERE.
THE WHOLE PLACE HAS BEEN AUTOMATED.
TYPICAL DALEK INGENUITY, MAKING USE OF THE AVAILABLE TECHNOLOGY...
IT'S ALL RUN ON STATIC ELECTRICITY.
THOUGH VAN DE GRAAFF GENERATORS WON'T ACTUALLY BE INVENTED FOR ANOTHER TWELVE YEARS.
AT LEAST NONE OF IT'S WORKING.
I THINK YOU SPOKE TOO SOON, TED.

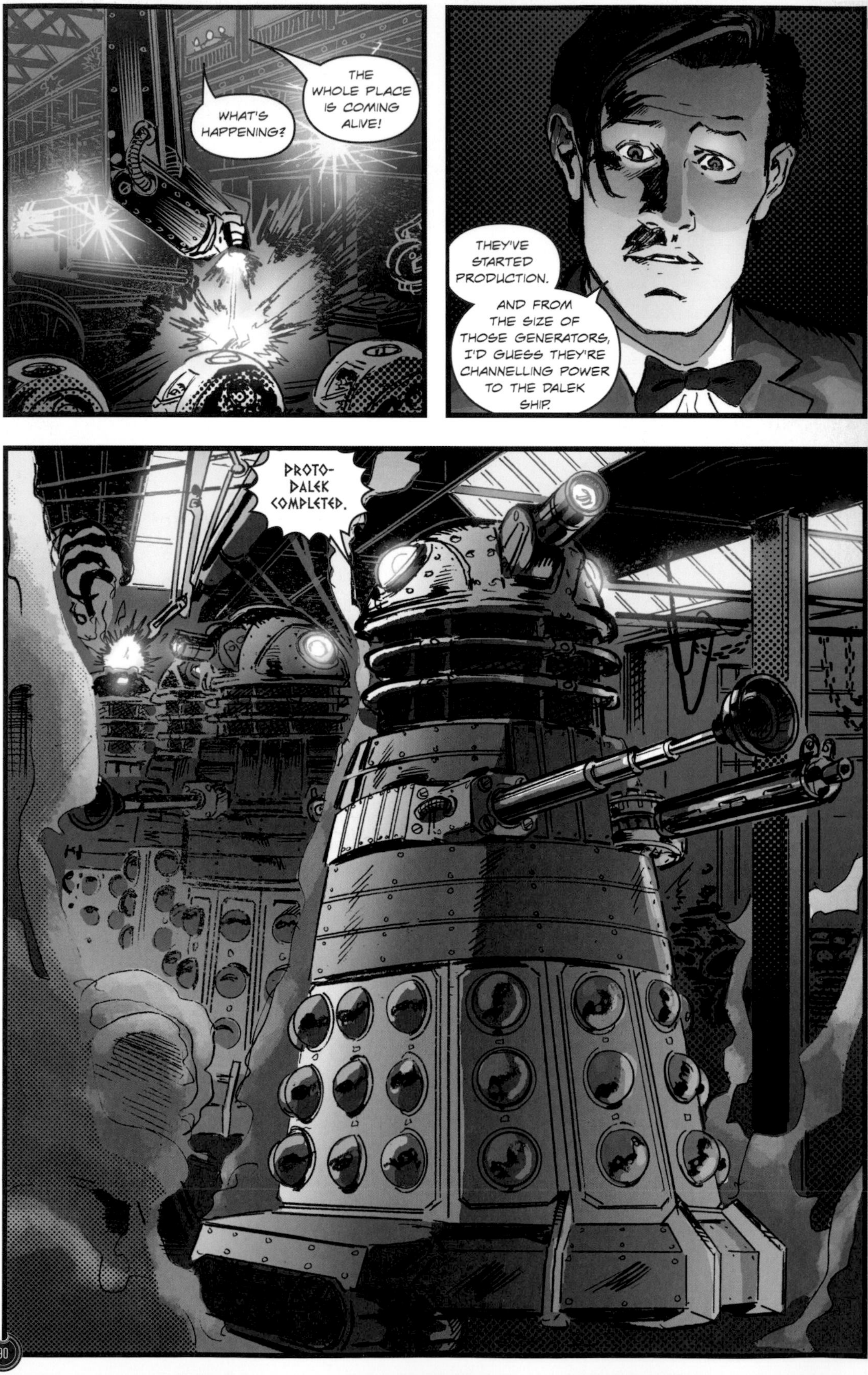

WHAT'S HAPPENING?
THE WHOLE PLACE IS COMING ALIVE!
THEY'VE STARTED PRODUCTION.
AND FROM THE SIZE OF THOSE GENERATORS, I'D GUESS THEY'RE CHANNELLING POWER TO THE DALEK SHIP.
PROTO-DALEK COMPLETED.

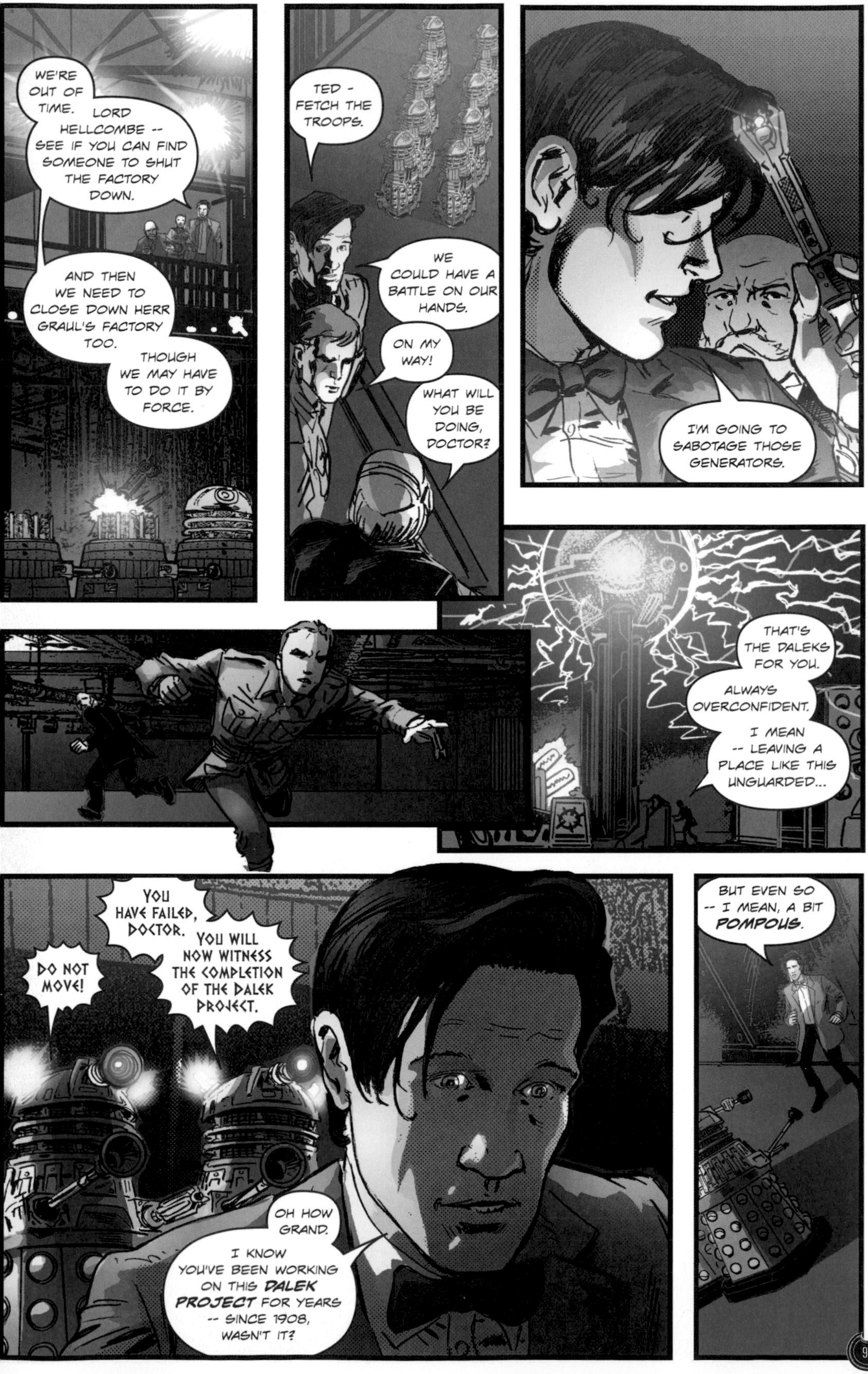
WE'RE OUT OF TIME.
LORD HELLCOMBE -- SEE IF YOU CAN FIND SOMEONE TO SHUT THE FACTORY DOWN.
AND THEN WE NEED TO CLOSE DOWN HERR GRAUL'S FACTORY TOO.
THOUGH WE MAY HAVE TO DO IT BY FORCE.
TED - FETCH THE TROOPS.
WE COULD HAVE A BATTLE ON OUR HANDS.
ON MY WAY!
WHAT WILL YOU BE DOING, DOCTOR?
I'M GOING TO SABOTAGE THOSE GENERATORS.
THAT'S THE DALEKS FOR YOU.
ALWAYS OVERCONFIDENT.
I MEAN -- LEAVING A PLACE LIKE THIS UNGUARDED...
YOU HAVE FAILED, DOCTOR.
YOU WILL NOW WITNESS THE COMPLETION OF THE DALEK PROJECT.
DO NOT MOVE!
OH HOW GRAND.
I KNOW YOU'VE BEEN WORKING ON THIS DALEK PROJECT FOR YEARS -- SINCE 1908, WASN'T IT?
BUT EVEN SO -- I MEAN, A BIT POMPOUS.

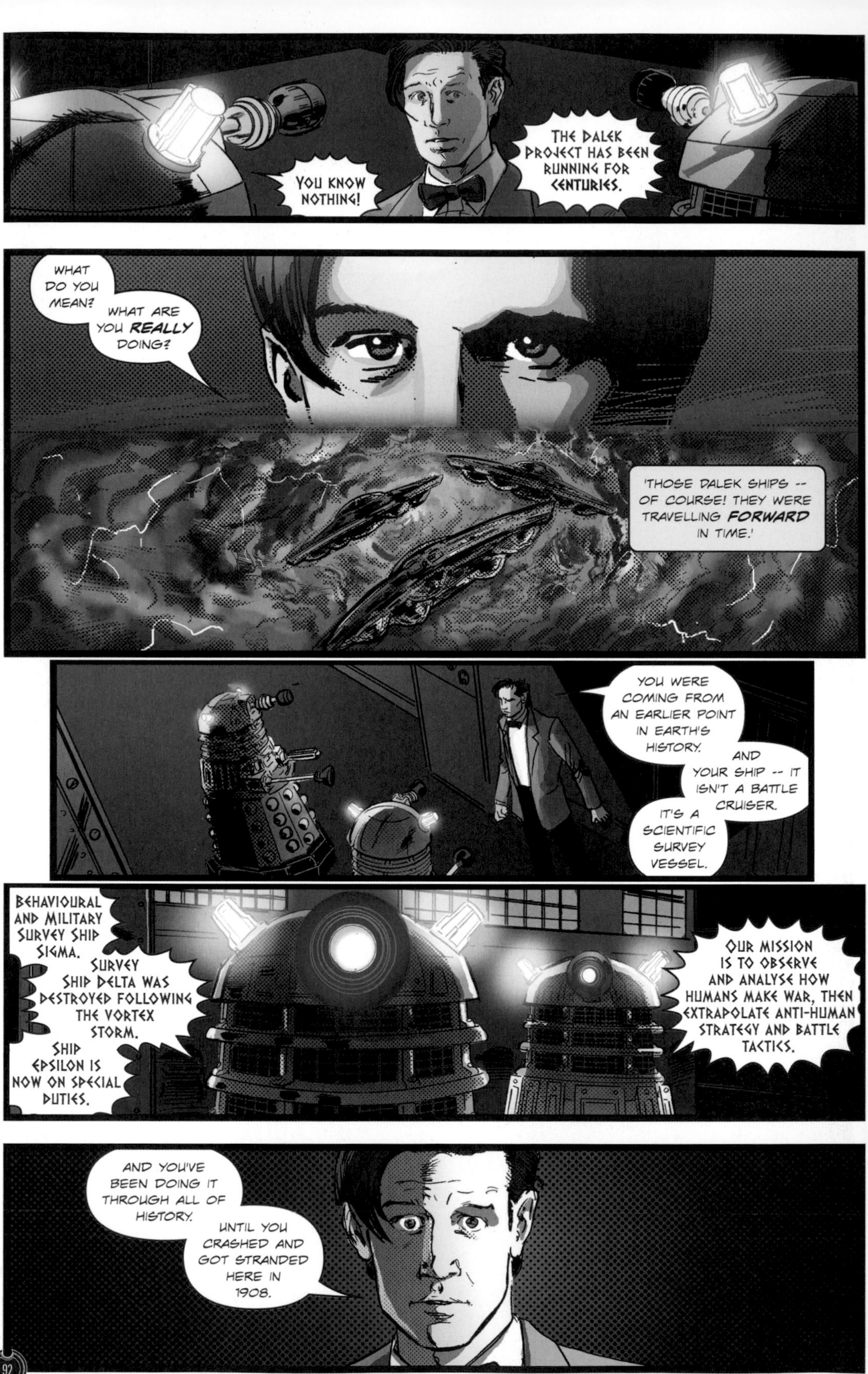
THE DALEK PROJECT HAS BEEN RUNNING FOR CENTURIES.
YOU KNOW NOTHING!
WHAT DO YOU MEAN?
WHAT ARE YOU REALLY DOING?
'THOSE DALEK SHIPS -- OF COURSE! THEY WERE TRAVELLING FORWARD IN TIME.'
YOU WERE COMING FROM AN EARLIER POINT IN EARTH'S HISTORY.
AND YOUR SHIP -- IT ISN'T A BATTLE CRUISER.
IT'S A SCIENTIFIC SURVEY VESSEL.
BEHAVIOURAL AND MILITARY SURVEY SHIP SIGMA.
SURVEY SHIP DELTA WAS DESTROYED FOLLOWING THE VORTEX STORM.
SHIP EPSILON IS NOW ON SPECIAL DUTIES.
OUR MISSION IS TO OBSERVE AND ANALYSE HOW HUMANS MAKE WAR, THEN EXTRAPOLATE ANTI-HUMAN STRATEGY AND BATTLE TACTICS.
AND YOU'VE BEEN DOING IT THROUGH ALL OF HISTORY.
UNTIL YOU CRASHED AND GOT STRANDED HERE IN 1908.

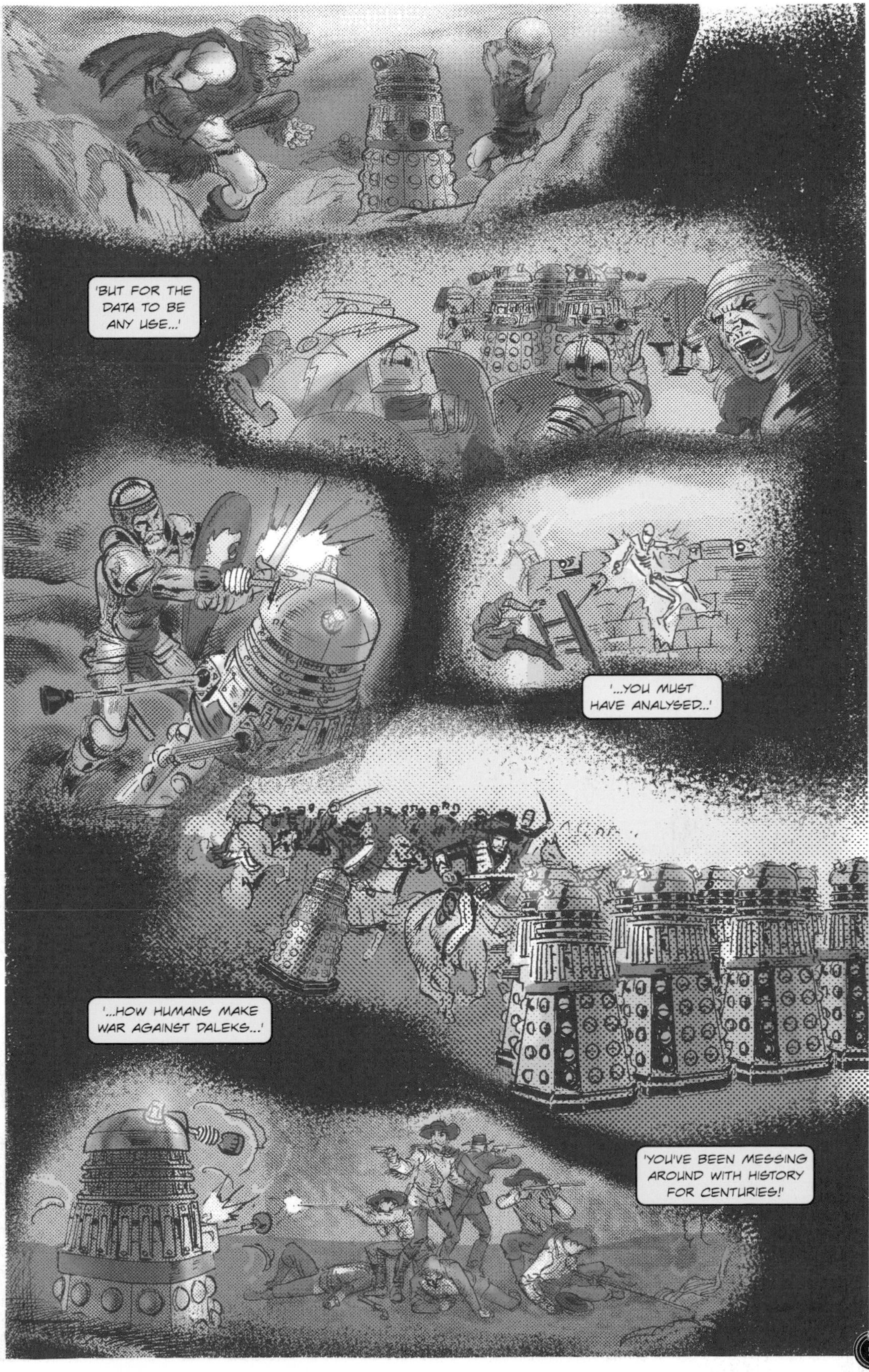
'BUT FOR THE DATA TO BE ANY USE...'
'...YOU MUST HAVE ANALYSED...'
'...HOW HUMANS MAKE WAR AGAINST DALEKS...'
'YOU'VE BEEN MESSING AROUND WITH HISTORY FOR CENTURIES!'

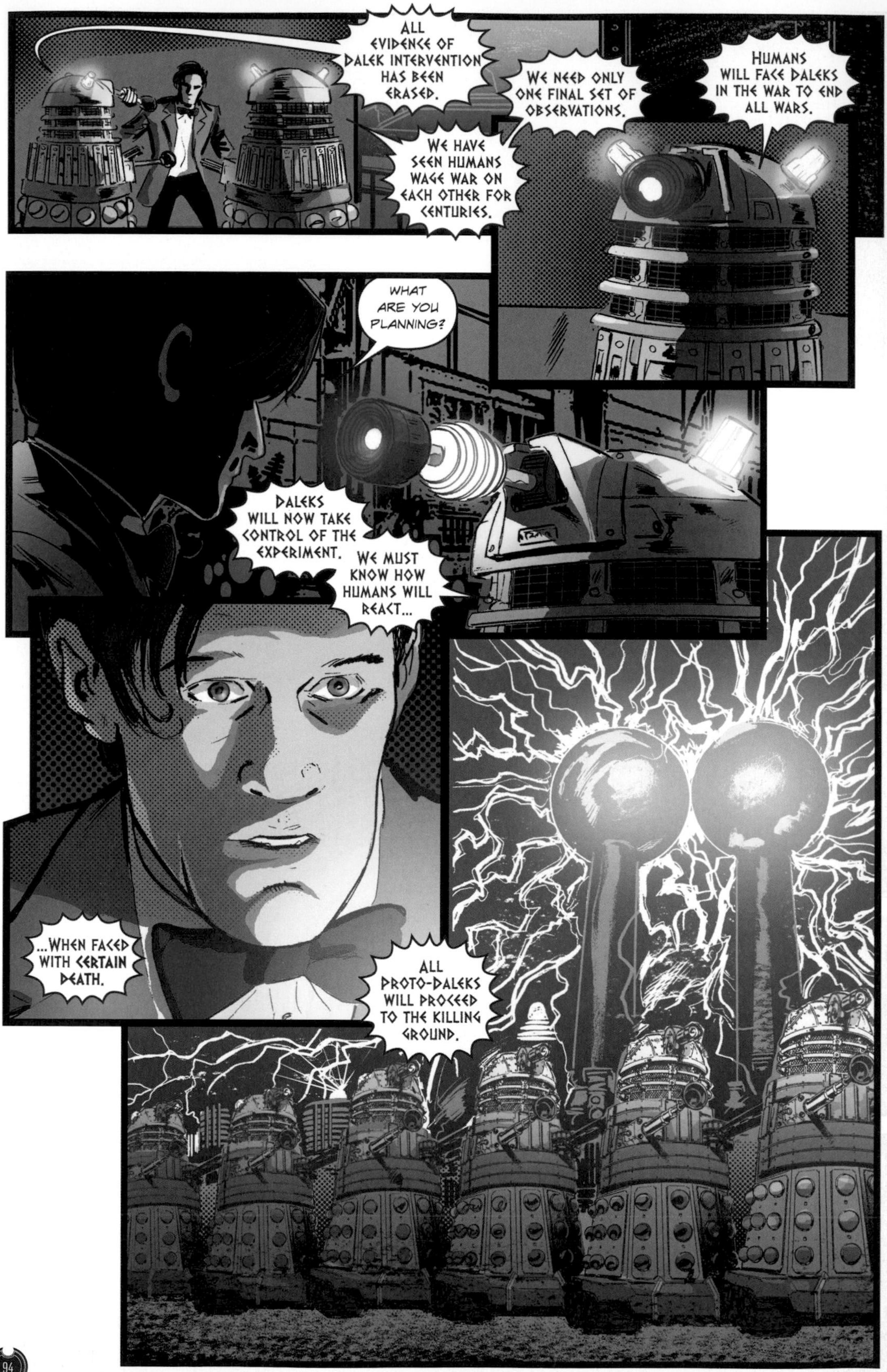
ALL EVIDENCE OF DALEK INTERVENTION HAS BEEN ERASED.
WE HAVE SEEN HUMANS WAGE WAR ON EACH OTHER FOR CENTURIES.
WE NEED ONLY ONE FINAL SET OF OBSERVATIONS.
HUMANS WILL FACE DALEKS IN THE WAR TO END ALL WARS.
WHAT ARE YOU PLANNING?
DALEKS WILL NOW TAKE CONTROL OF THE EXPERIMENT.
WE MUST KNOW HOW HUMANS WILL REACT...
...WHEN FACED WITH CERTAIN DEATH.
ALL PROTO-DALEKS WILL PROCEED TO THE KILLING GROUND.

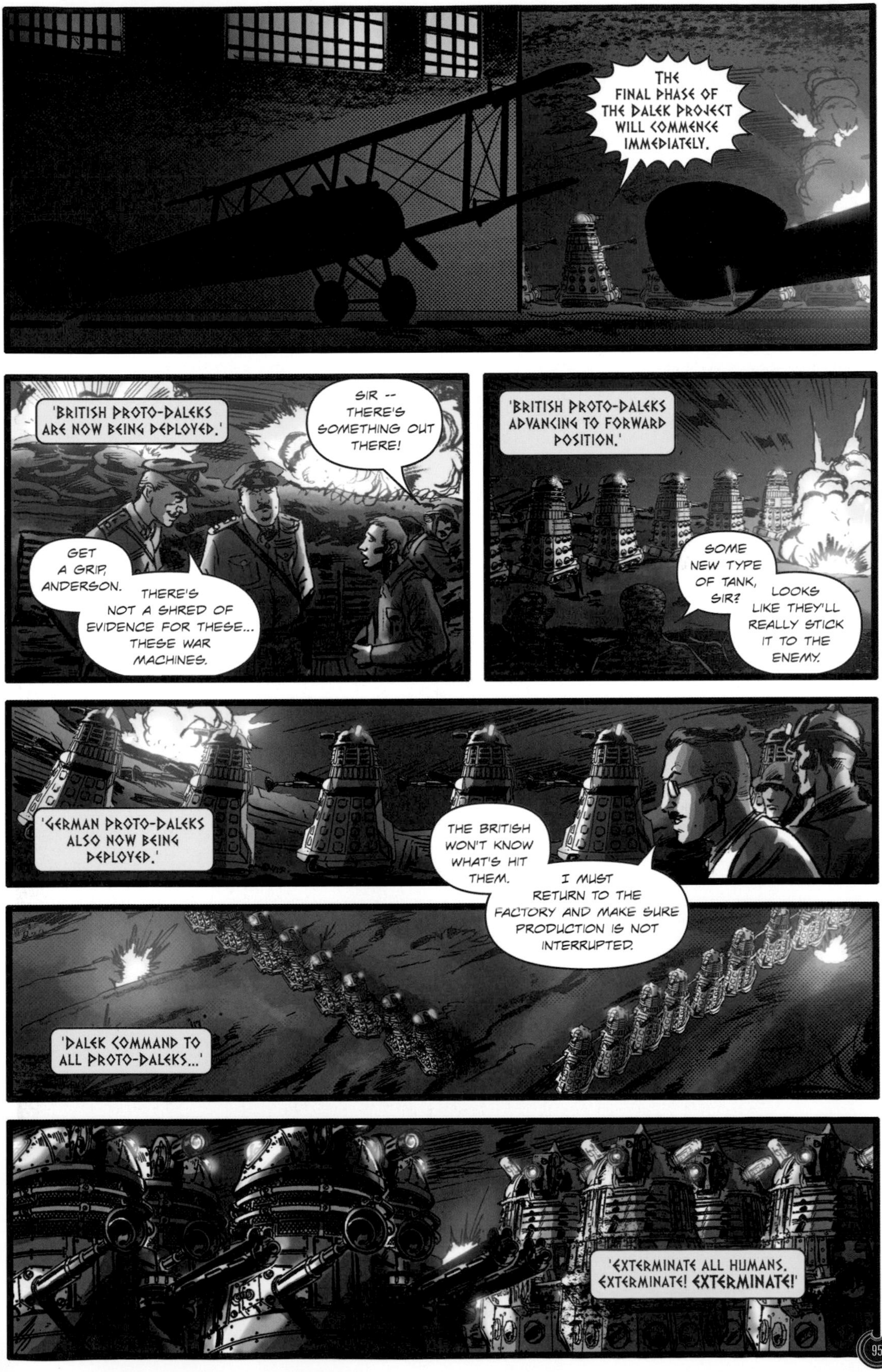
THE FINAL PHASE OF THE DALEK PROJECT WILL COMMENCE IMMEDIATELY.
'BRITISH PROTO-DALEKS ARE NOW BEING DEPLOYED.'
SIR -- THERE'S SOMETHING OUT THERE!
GET A GRIP, ANDERSON.
THERE'S NOT A SHRED OF EVIDENCE FOR THESE... THESE WAR MACHINES.
'BRITISH PROTO-DALEKS ADVANCING TO FORWARD POSITION.'
SOME NEW TYPE OF TANK, SIR?
LOOKS LIKE THEY'LL REALLY STICK IT TO THE ENEMY.
'GERMAN PROTO-DALEKS ALSO NOW BEING DEPLOYED.'
THE BRITISH WON'T KNOW WHAT'S HIT THEM.
I MUST RETURN TO THE FACTORY AND MAKE SURE PRODUCTION IS NOT INTERRUPTED.
'DALEK COMMAND TO ALL PROTO-DALEKS...'
'EXTERMINATE ALL HUMANS. EXTERMINATE! **EXTERMINATE!**'

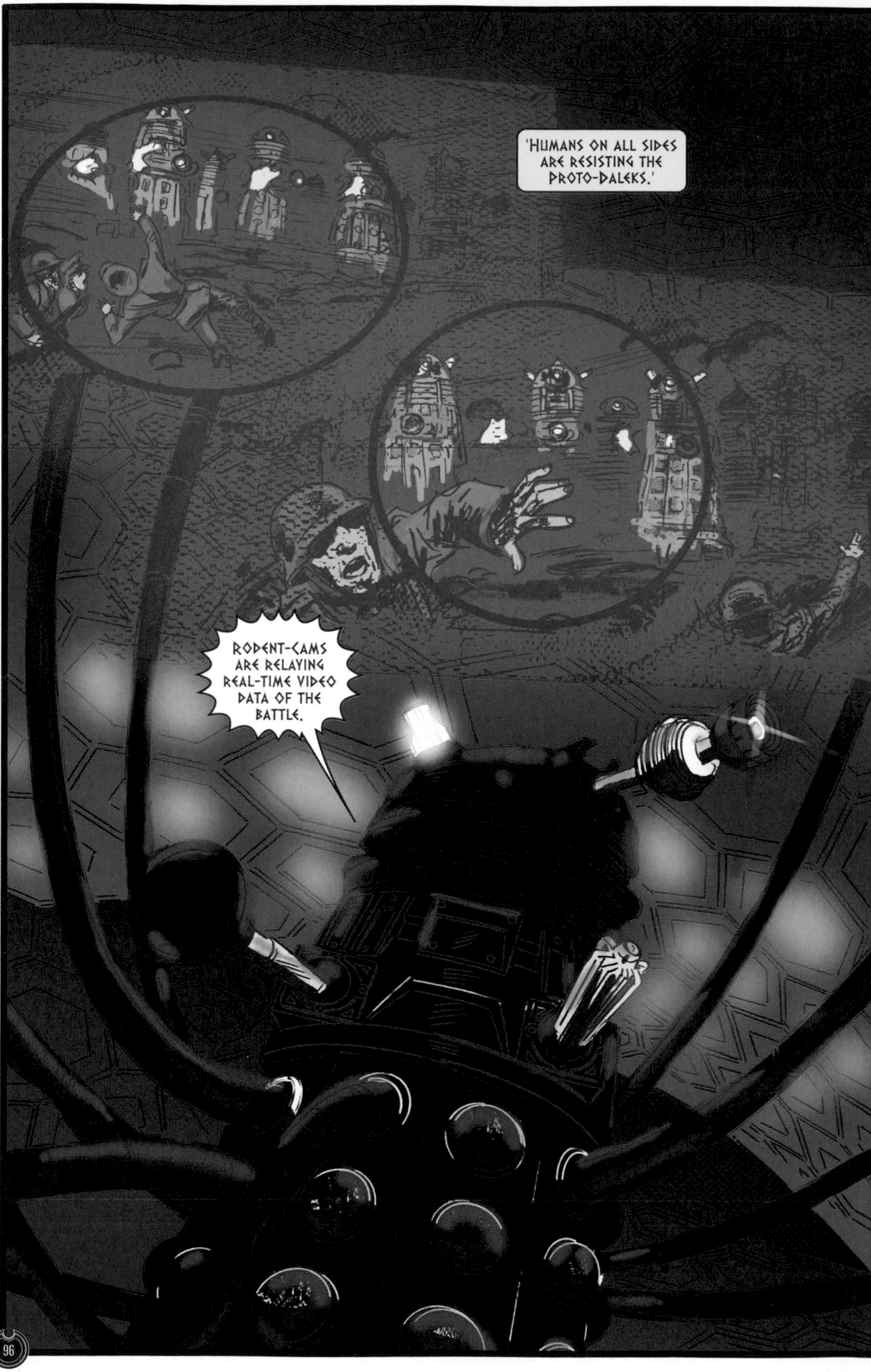
'HUMANS ON ALL SIDES ARE RESISTING THE PROTO-DALEKS.'
RODENT-CAMS ARE RELAYING REAL-TIME VIDEO DATA OF THE BATTLE.

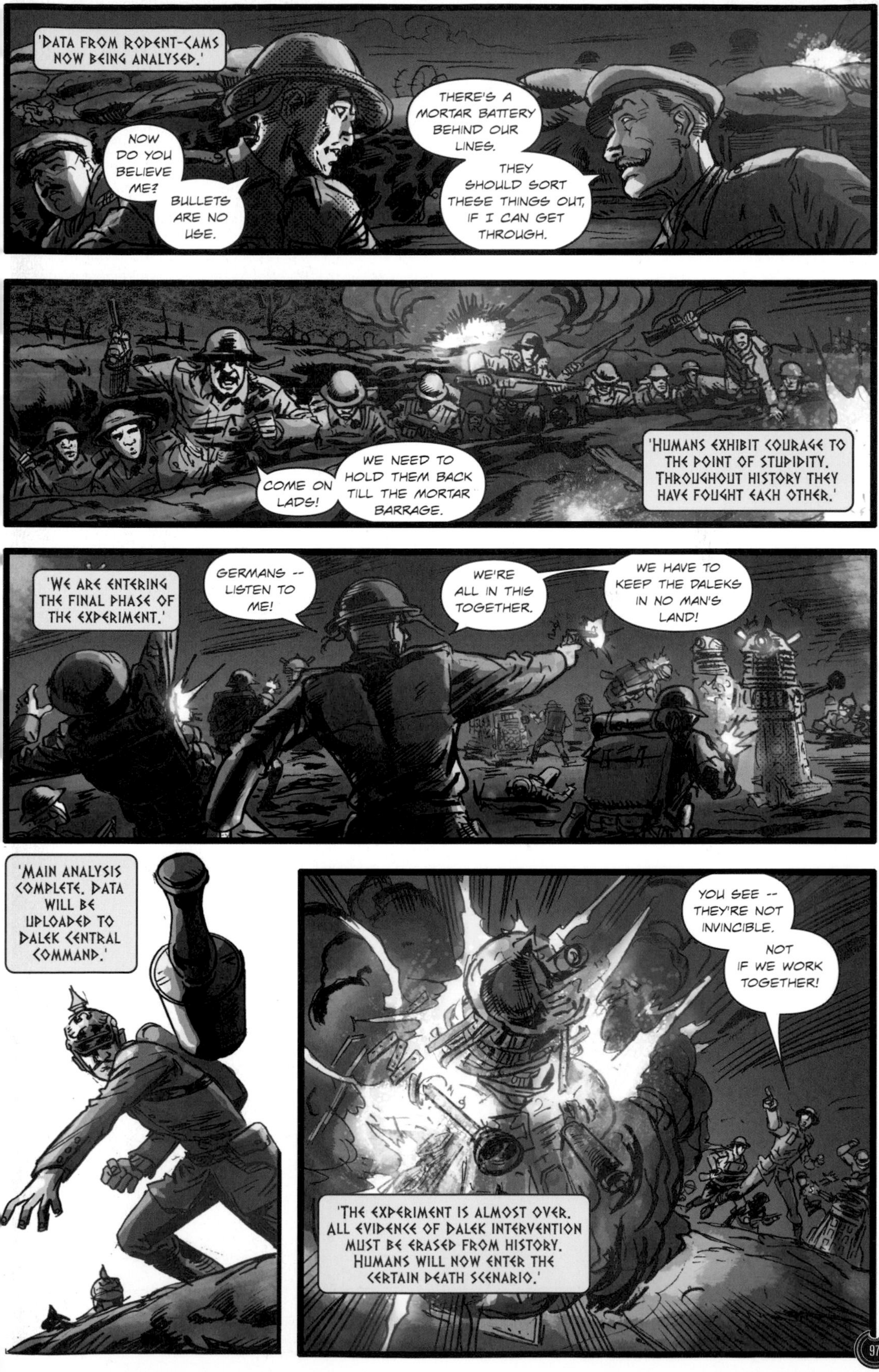
'DATA FROM RODENT-CAMS NOW BEING ANALYSED.'
NOW DO YOU BELIEVE ME?
BULLETS ARE NO USE.
THERE'S A MORTAR BATTERY BEHIND OUR LINES.
THEY SHOULD SORT THESE THINGS OUT, IF I CAN GET THROUGH.
COME ON LADS!
WE NEED TO HOLD THEM BACK TILL THE MORTAR BARRAGE.
'HUMANS EXHIBIT COURAGE TO THE POINT OF STUPIDITY. THROUGHOUT HISTORY THEY HAVE FOUGHT EACH OTHER.'
'WE ARE ENTERING THE FINAL PHASE OF THE EXPERIMENT.'
GERMANS -- LISTEN TO ME!
WE'RE ALL IN THIS TOGETHER.
WE HAVE TO KEEP THE DALEKS IN NO MAN'S LAND!
'MAIN ANALYSIS COMPLETE. DATA WILL BE UPLOADED TO DALEK CENTRAL COMMAND.'
YOU SEE -- THEY'RE NOT INVINCIBLE.
NOT IF WE WORK TOGETHER!
'THE EXPERIMENT IS ALMOST OVER. ALL EVIDENCE OF DALEK INTERVENTION MUST BE ERASED FROM HISTORY. HUMANS WILL NOW ENTER THE CERTAIN DEATH SCENARIO.'

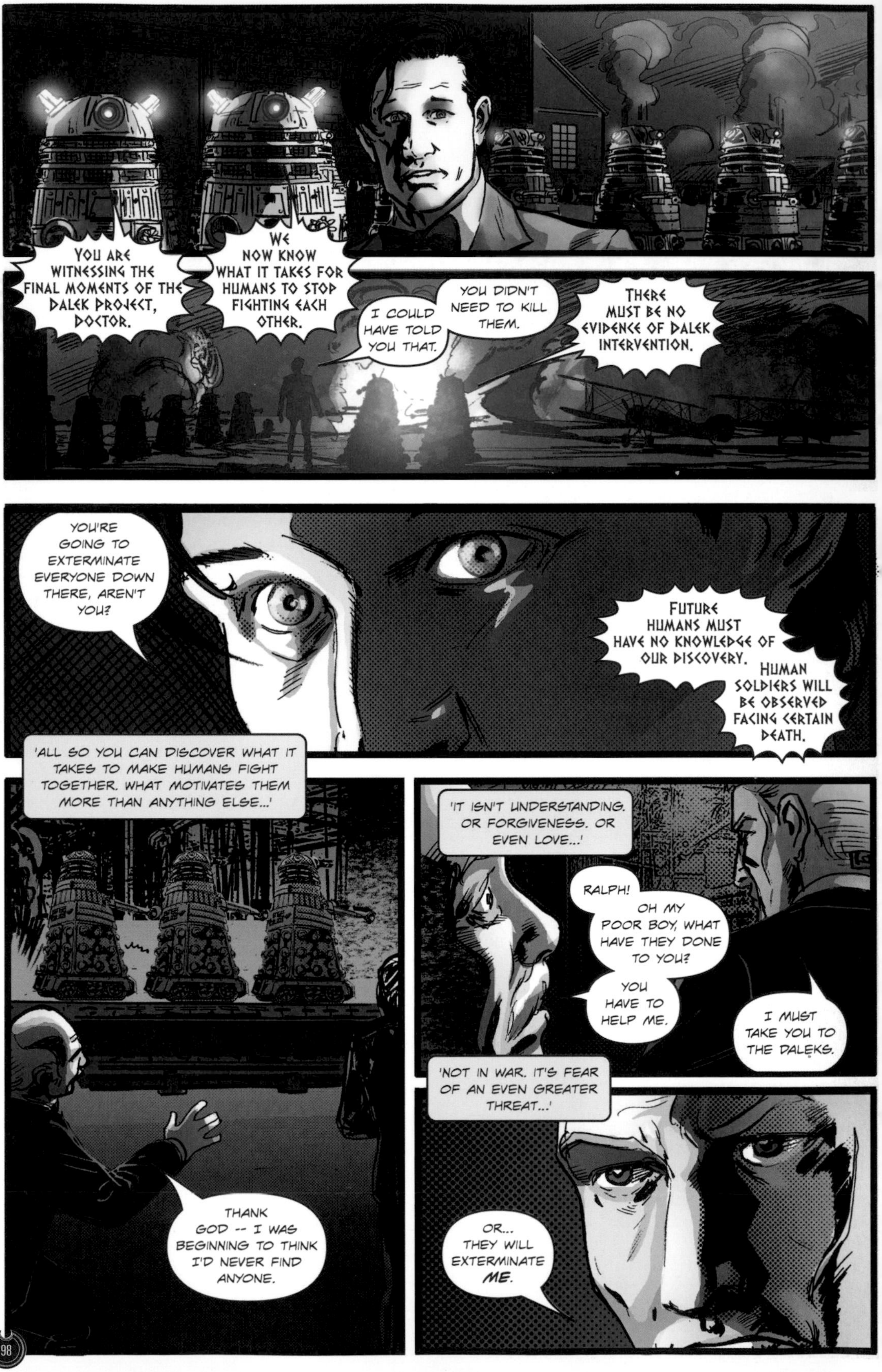
You are witnessing the final moments of the Dalek Project, Doctor.
We now know what it takes for humans to stop fighting each other.
I could have told you that.
You didn't need to kill them.
There must be no evidence of Dalek intervention.
You're going to exterminate everyone down there, aren't you?
Future humans must have no knowledge of our discovery.
Human soldiers will be observed facing certain death.
'All so you can discover what it takes to make humans fight together. What motivates them more than anything else...'
Thank God -- I was beginning to think I'd never find anyone.
'It isn't understanding. Or forgiveness. Or even love...'
Ralph!
Oh my poor boy, what have they done to you?
You have to help me.
I must take you to the Daleks.
'Not in war. It's fear of an even greater threat...'
Or... they will exterminate *me*.

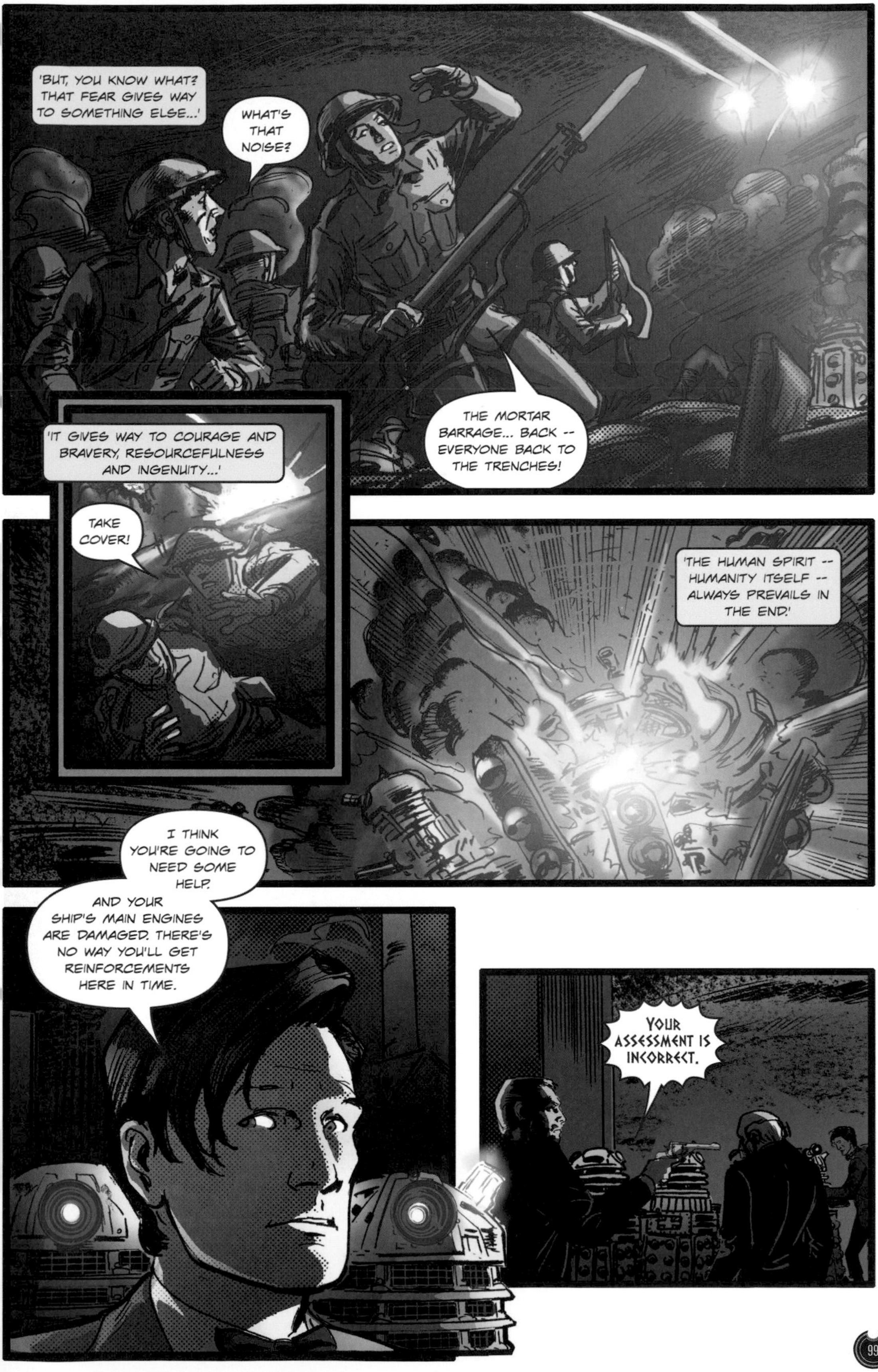
'BUT, YOU KNOW WHAT? THAT FEAR GIVES WAY TO SOMETHING ELSE...'
WHAT'S THAT NOISE?
THE MORTAR BARRAGE... BACK -- EVERYONE BACK TO THE TRENCHES!
'IT GIVES WAY TO COURAGE AND BRAVERY, RESOURCEFULNESS AND INGENUITY...'
TAKE COVER!
'THE HUMAN SPIRIT -- HUMANITY ITSELF -- ALWAYS PREVAILS IN THE END.'
I THINK YOU'RE GOING TO NEED SOME HELP.
AND YOUR SHIP'S MAIN ENGINES ARE DAMAGED. THERE'S NO WAY YOU'LL GET REINFORCEMENTS HERE IN TIME.
YOUR ASSESSMENT IS INCORRECT.

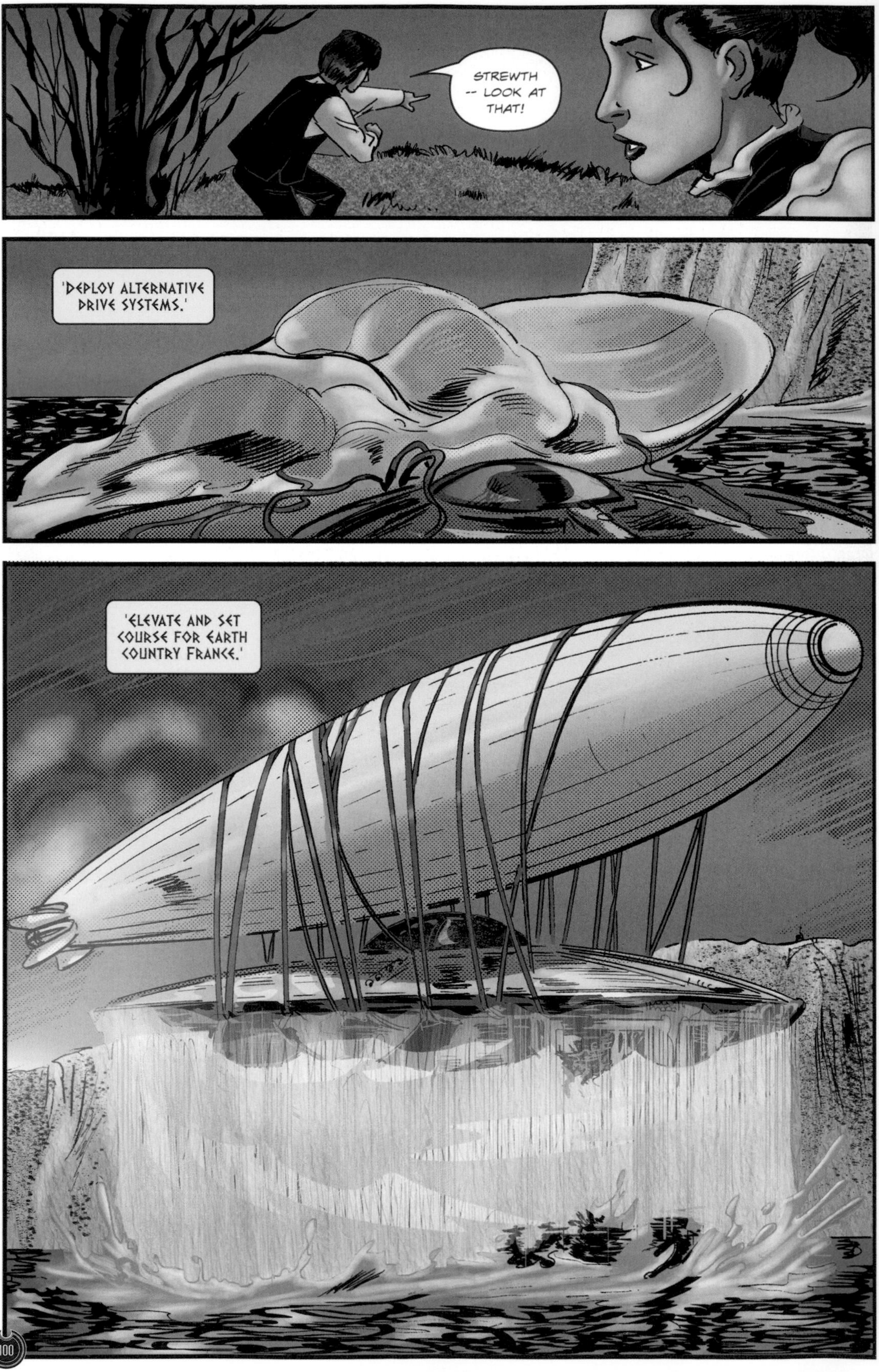
STREWTH -- LOOK AT THAT!
'DEPLOY ALTERNATIVE DRIVE SYSTEMS.'
'ELEVATE AND SET COURSE FOR EARTH COUNTRY FRANCE.'

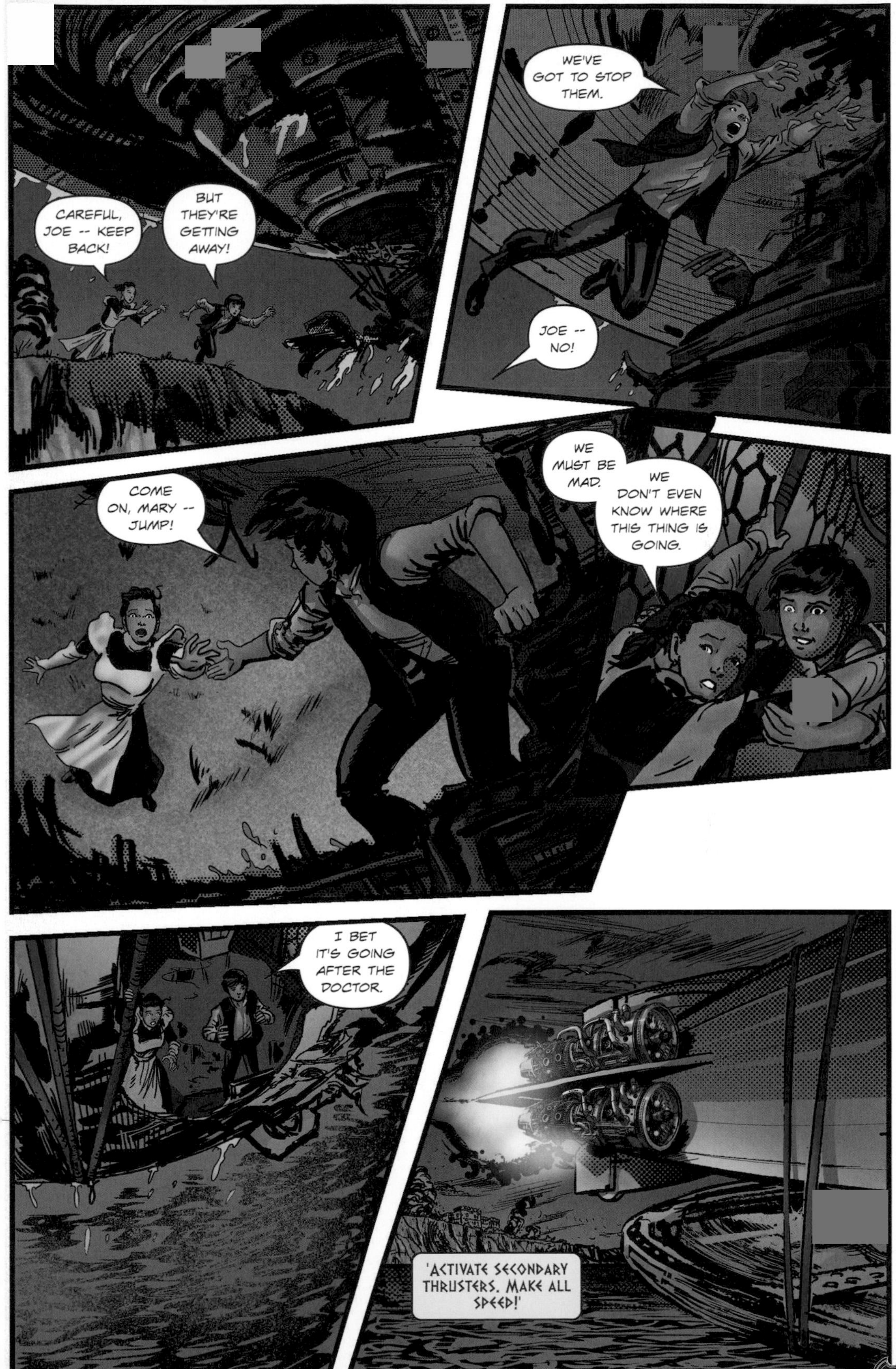
CAREFUL, JOE -- KEEP BACK!
BUT THEY'RE GETTING AWAY!
WE'VE GOT TO STOP THEM.
JOE -- NO!
COME ON, MARY -- JUMP!
WE MUST BE MAD.
WE DON'T EVEN KNOW WHERE THIS THING IS GOING.
I BET IT'S GOING AFTER THE DOCTOR.
'ACTIVATE SECONDARY THRUSTERS. MAKE ALL SPEED!'

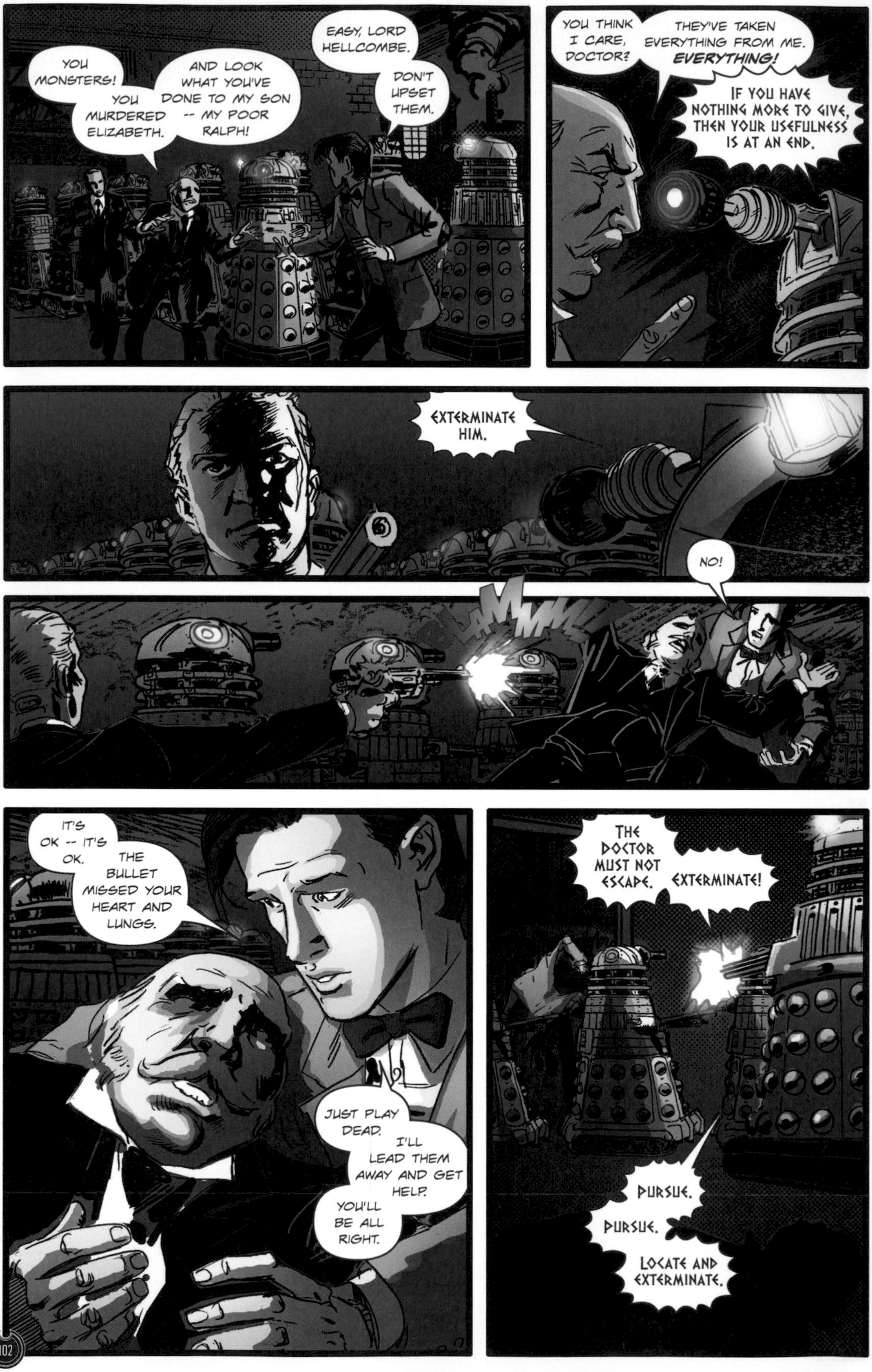
YOU MONSTERS!
YOU MURDERED ELIZABETH.
AND LOOK WHAT YOU'VE DONE TO MY SON -- MY POOR RALPH!
EASY, LORD HELLCOMBE.
DON'T UPSET THEM.
YOU THINK I CARE, DOCTOR?
THEY'VE TAKEN EVERYTHING FROM ME. EVERYTHING!
IF YOU HAVE NOTHING MORE TO GIVE, THEN YOUR USEFULNESS IS AT AN END.
EXTERMINATE HIM.
NO!
IT'S OK -- IT'S OK.
THE BULLET MISSED YOUR HEART AND LUNGS.
JUST PLAY DEAD.
I'LL LEAD THEM AWAY AND GET HELP.
YOU'LL BE ALL RIGHT.
THE DOCTOR MUST NOT ESCAPE.
EXTERMINATE!
PURSUE.
PURSUE.
LOCATE AND EXTERMINATE.

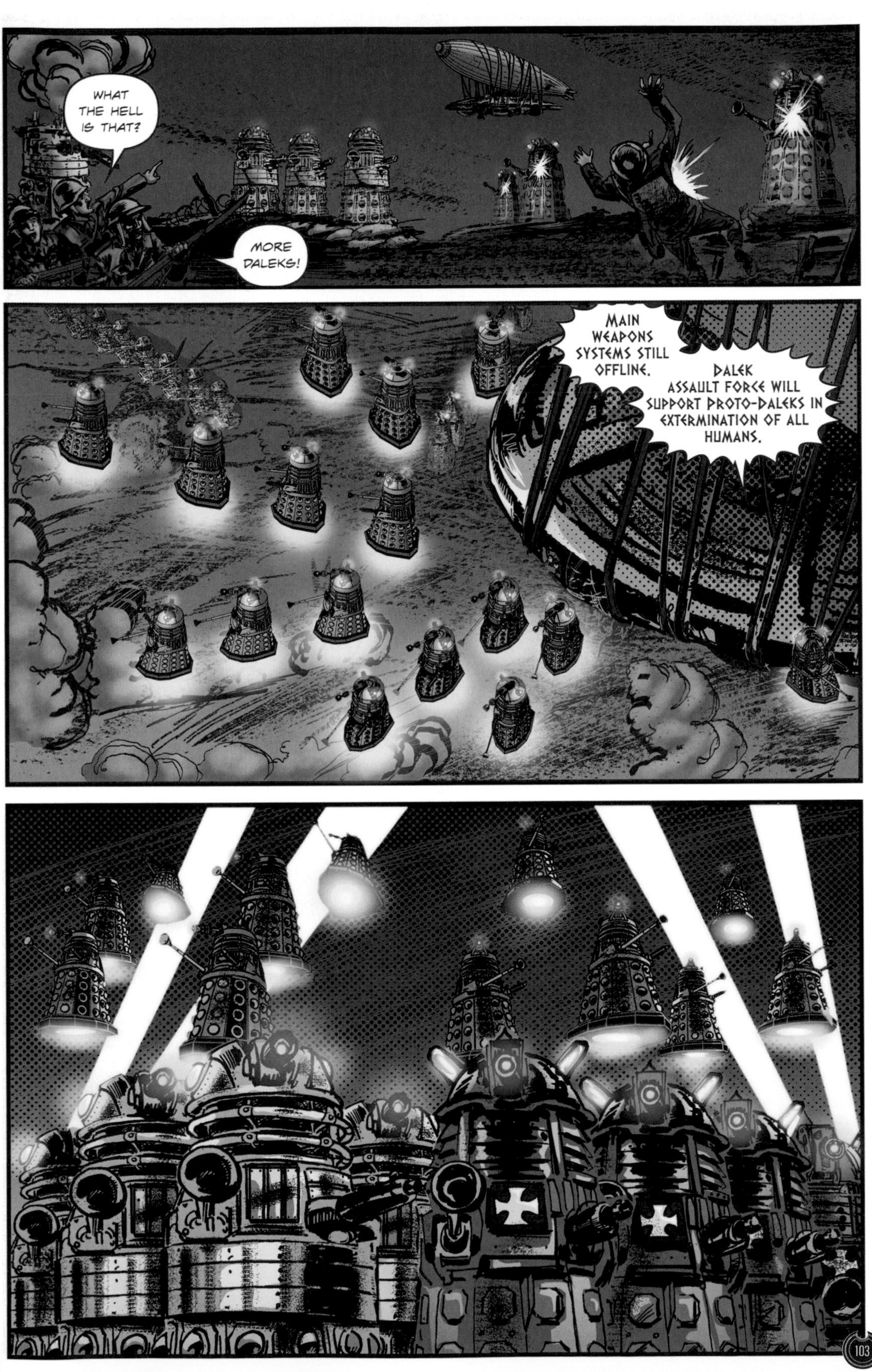
WHAT THE HELL IS THAT?
MORE DALEKS!
MAIN WEAPONS SYSTEMS STILL OFFLINE.
DALEK ASSAULT FORCE WILL SUPPORT PROTO-DALEKS IN EXTERMINATION OF ALL HUMANS.

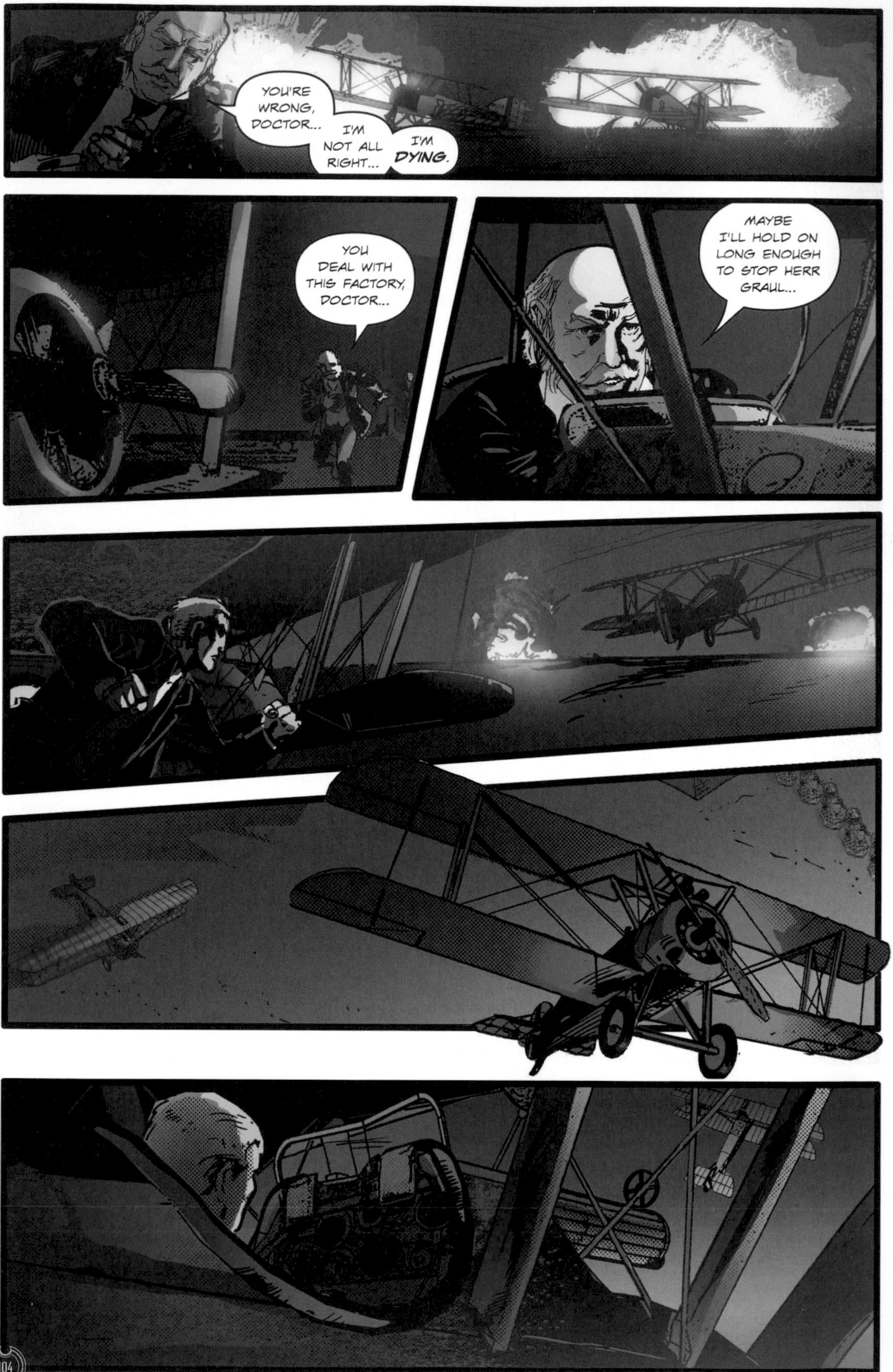
YOU'RE WRONG, DOCTOR...
I'M NOT ALL RIGHT...
I'M DYING.
YOU DEAL WITH THIS FACTORY, DOCTOR...
MAYBE I'LL HOLD ON LONG ENOUGH TO STOP HERR GRAUL...

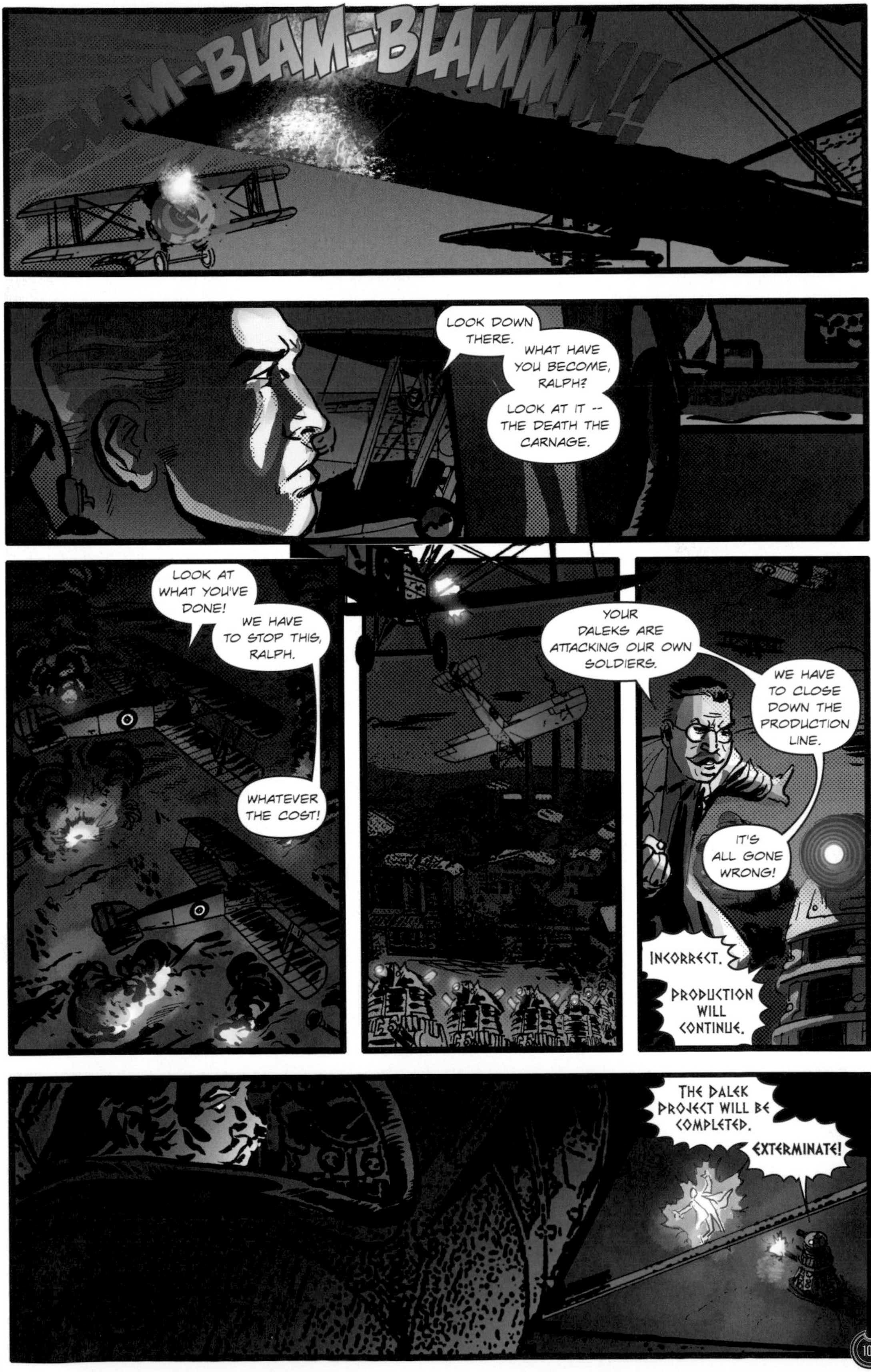
BLAM-BLAM-BLAMMM!!
LOOK DOWN THERE.
WHAT HAVE YOU BECOME, RALPH?
LOOK AT IT -- THE DEATH THE CARNAGE.
LOOK AT WHAT YOU'VE DONE!
WE HAVE TO STOP THIS, RALPH.
WHATEVER THE COST!
YOUR DALEKS ARE ATTACKING OUR OWN SOLDIERS.
WE HAVE TO CLOSE DOWN THE PRODUCTION LINE.
IT'S ALL GONE WRONG!
INCORRECT.
PRODUCTION WILL CONTINUE.
THE DALEK PROJECT WILL BE COMPLETED.
EXTERMINATE!

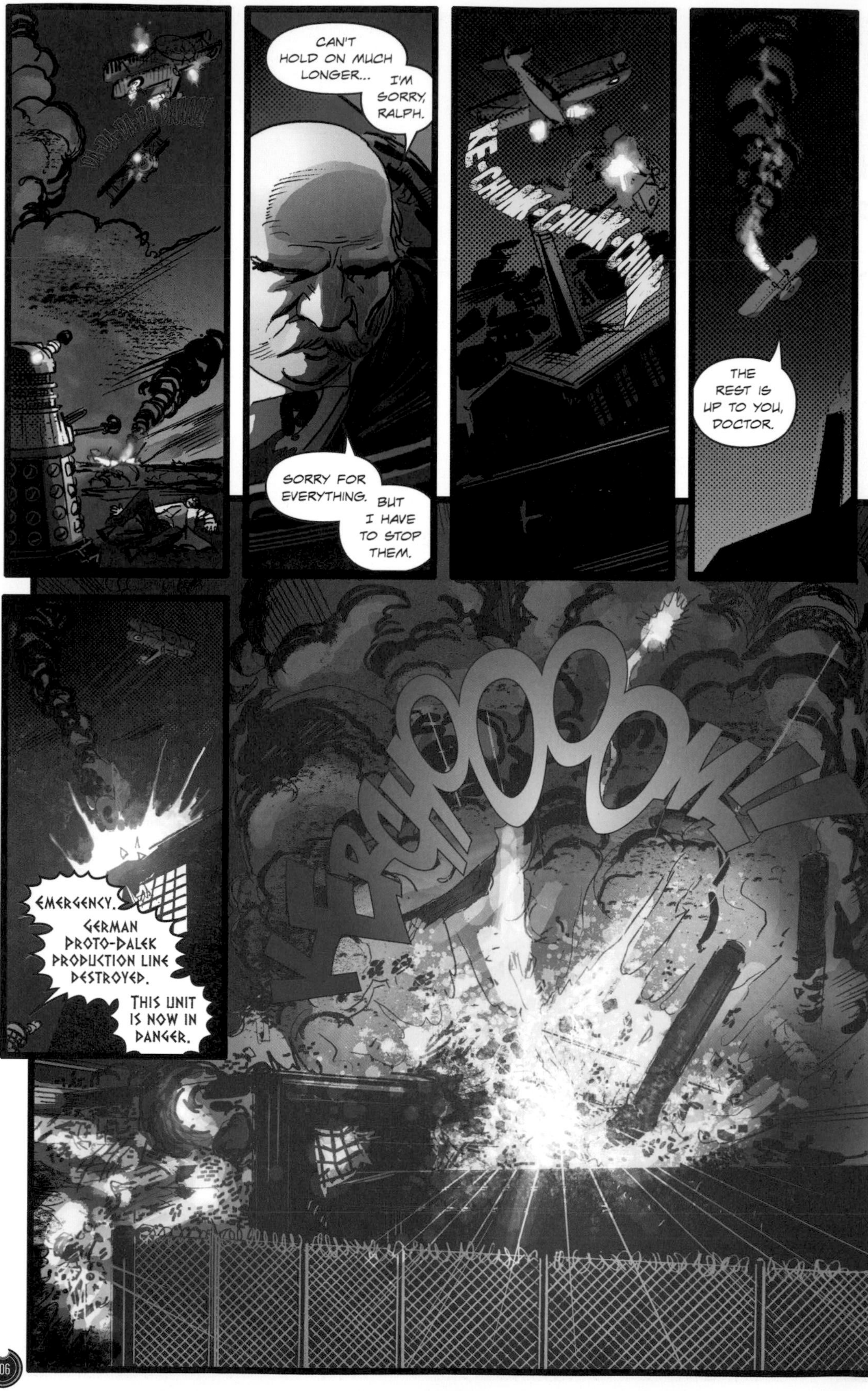
CAN'T HOLD ON MUCH LONGER...
I'M SORRY, RALPH.
SORRY FOR EVERYTHING.
BUT I HAVE TO STOP THEM.
KE-CHUK-CHUK-CHUK
THE REST IS UP TO YOU, DOCTOR.
EMERGENCY.
GERMAN PROTO-DALEK PRODUCTION LINE DESTROYED.
THIS UNIT IS NOW IN DANGER.

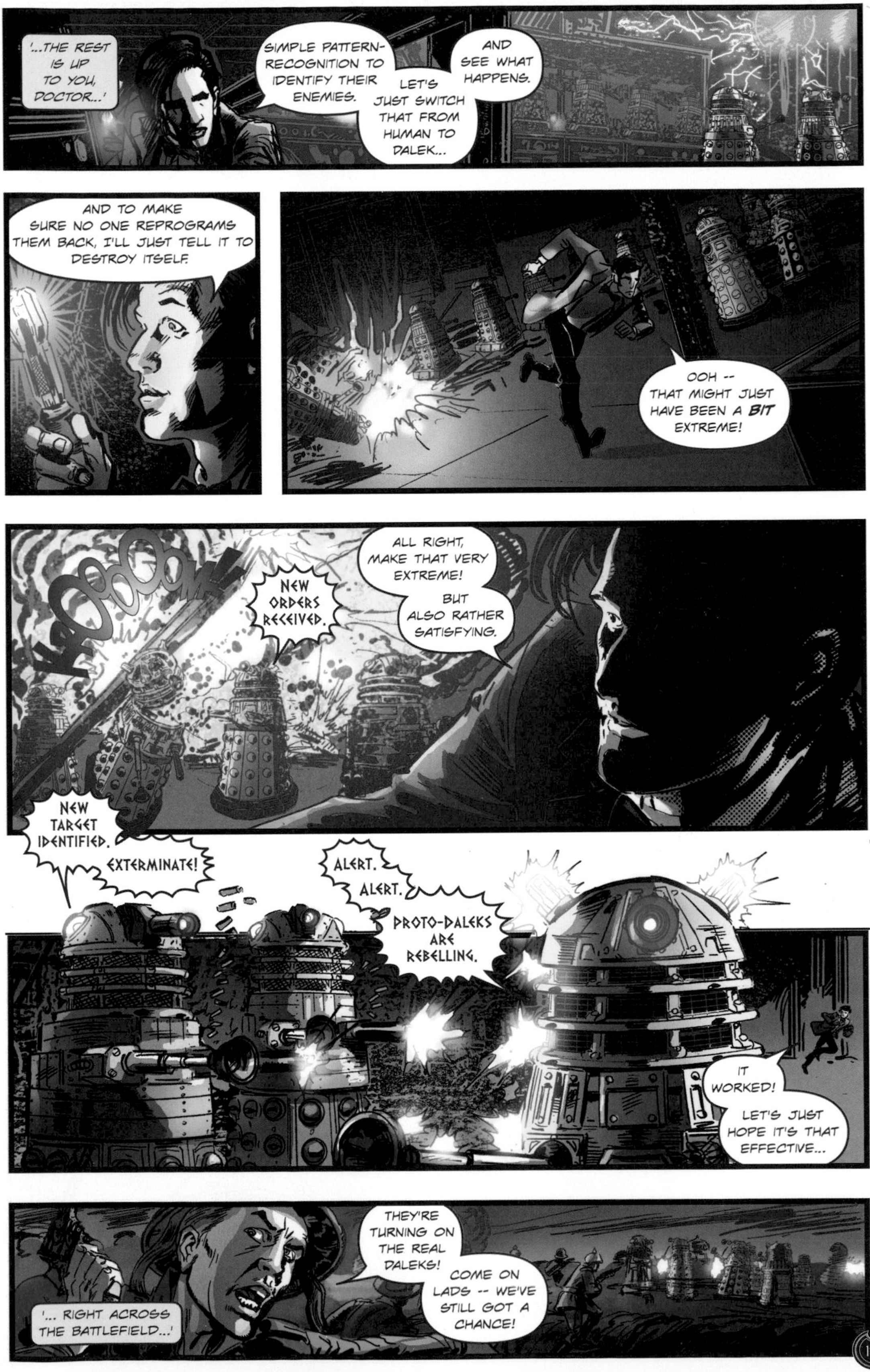
'...THE REST IS UP TO YOU, DOCTOR...'
SIMPLE PATTERN-RECOGNITION TO IDENTIFY THEIR ENEMIES.
LET'S JUST SWITCH THAT FROM HUMAN TO DALEK...
AND SEE WHAT HAPPENS.
AND TO MAKE SURE NO ONE REPROGRAMS THEM BACK, I'LL JUST TELL IT TO DESTROY ITSELF.
OOH -- THAT MIGHT JUST HAVE BEEN A BIT EXTREME!
NEW ORDERS RECEIVED.
ALL RIGHT, MAKE THAT VERY EXTREME!
BUT ALSO RATHER SATISFYING.
NEW TARGET IDENTIFIED.
EXTERMINATE!
ALERT.
ALERT.
PROTO-DALEKS ARE REBELLING.
IT WORKED!
LET'S JUST HOPE IT'S THAT EFFECTIVE...
'... RIGHT ACROSS THE BATTLEFIELD...'
THEY'RE TURNING ON THE REAL DALEKS!
COME ON LADS -- WE'VE STILL GOT A CHANCE!

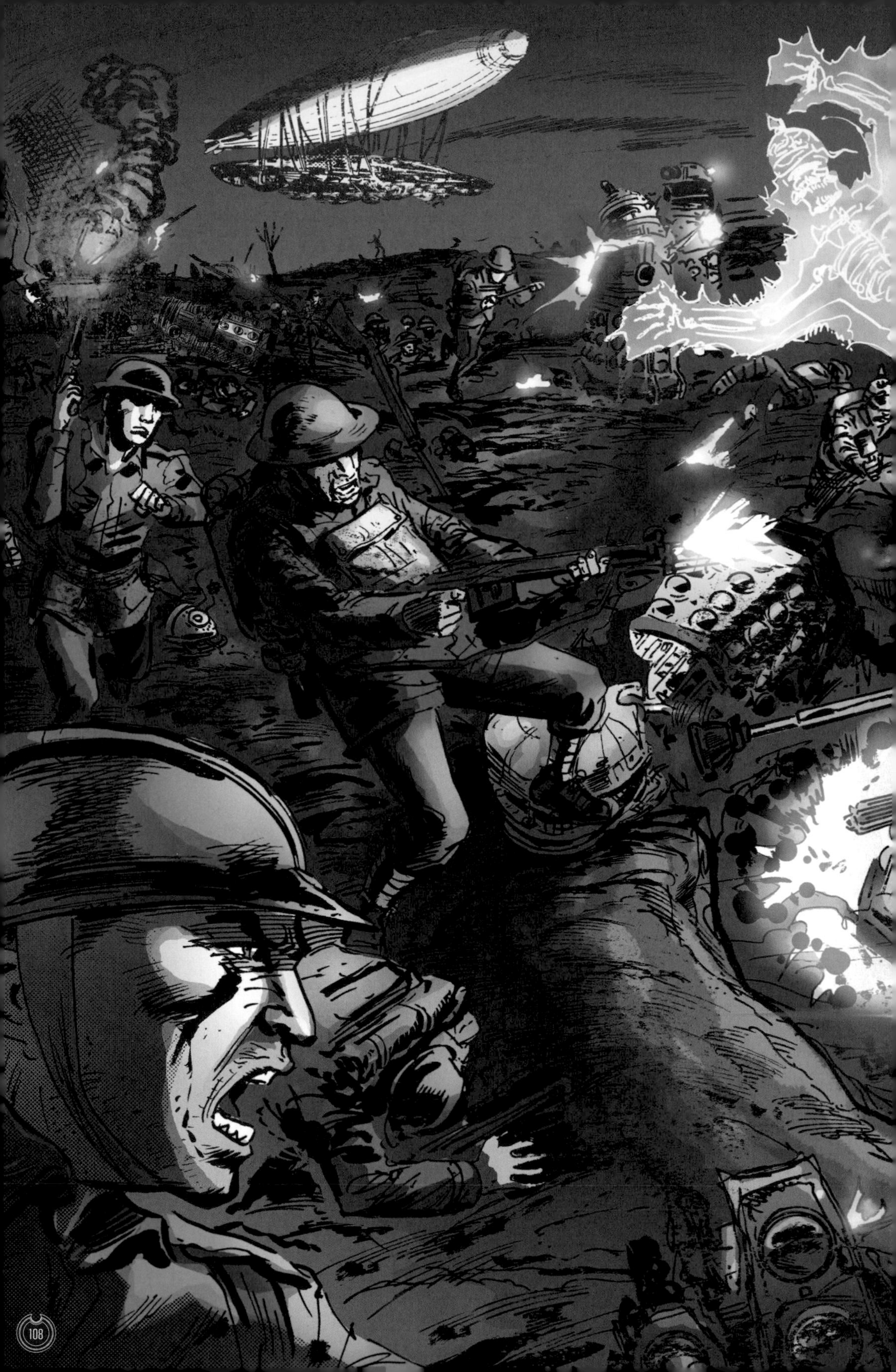

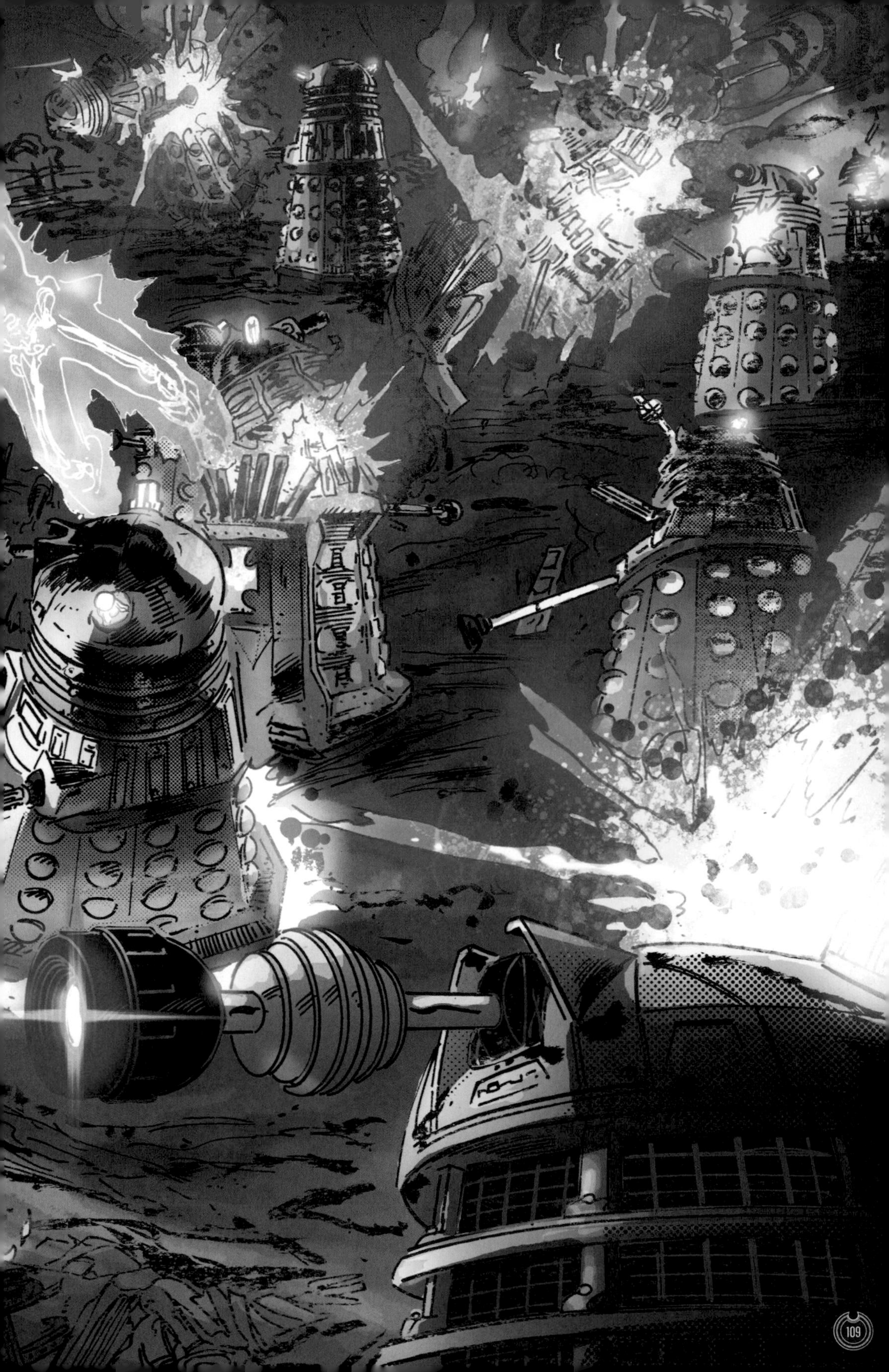

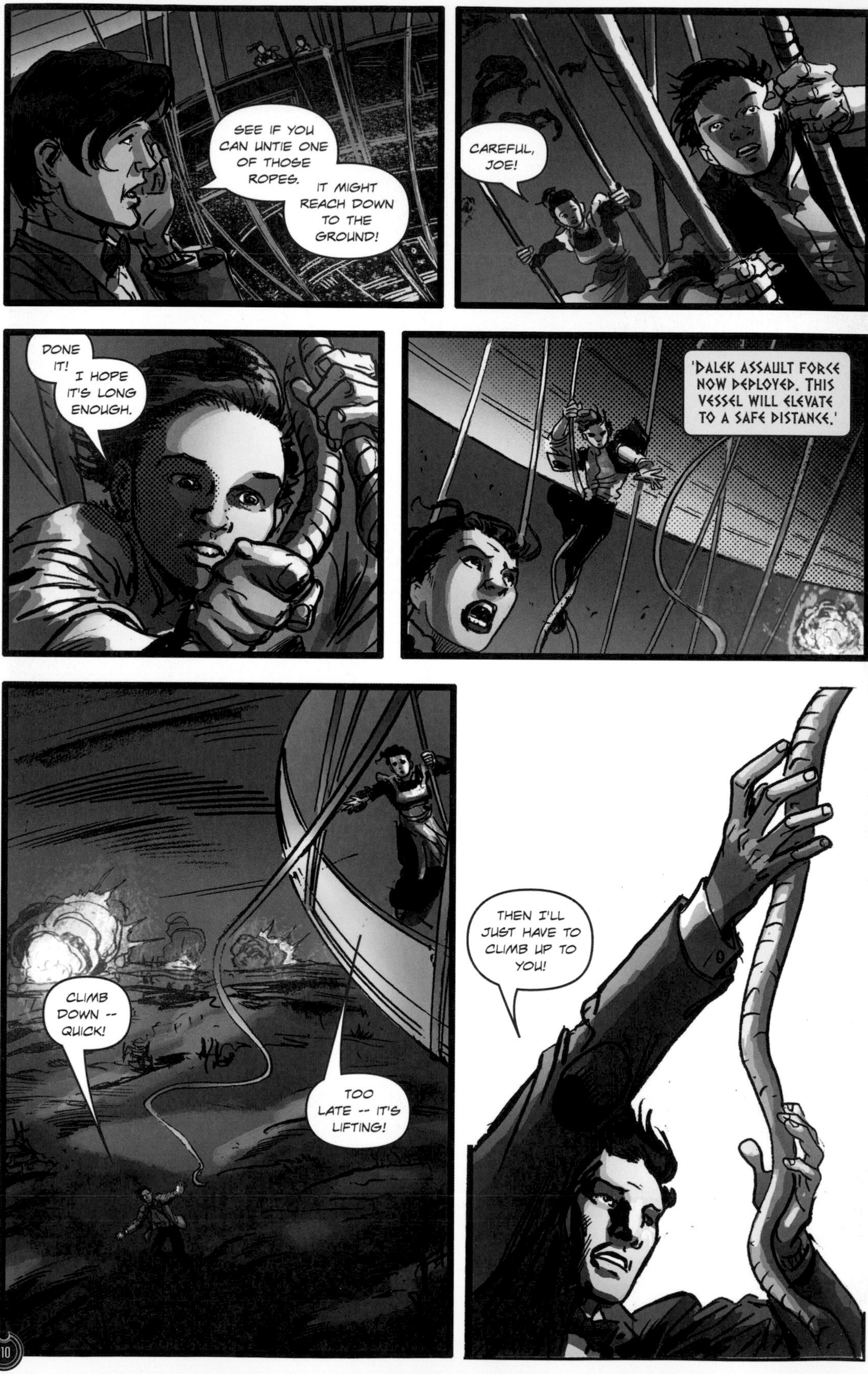
SEE IF YOU CAN UNTIE ONE OF THOSE ROPES.
IT MIGHT REACH DOWN TO THE GROUND!
CAREFUL, JOE!
DONE IT!
I HOPE IT'S LONG ENOUGH.
'DALEK ASSAULT FORCE NOW DEPLOYED. THIS VESSEL WILL ELEVATE TO A SAFE DISTANCE.'
CLIMB DOWN -- QUICK!
TOO LATE -- IT'S LIFTING!
THEN I'LL JUST HAVE TO CLIMB UP TO YOU!

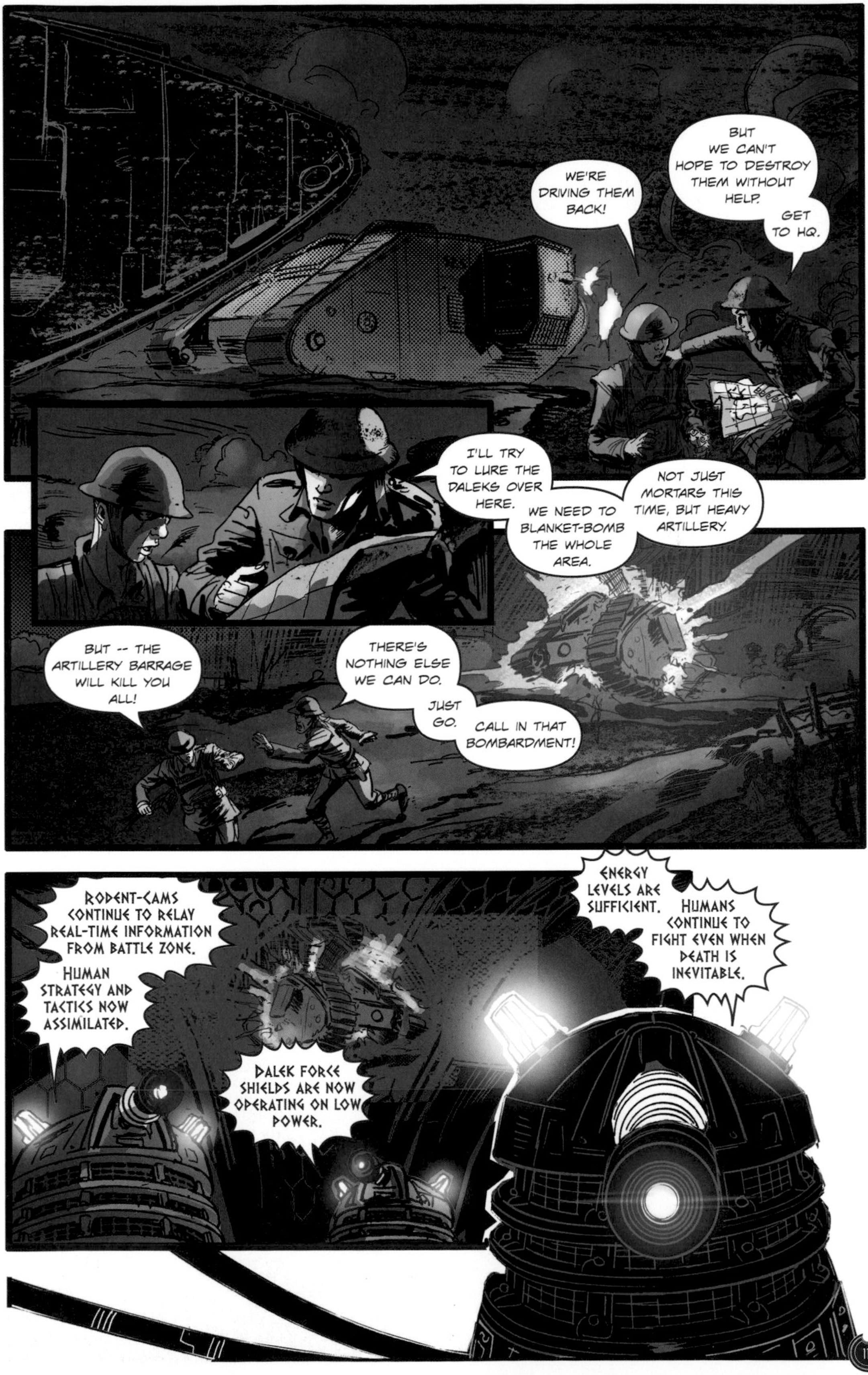
WE'RE DRIVING THEM BACK!
BUT WE CAN'T HOPE TO DESTROY THEM WITHOUT HELP.
GET TO HQ.
I'LL TRY TO LURE THE DALEKS OVER HERE.
WE NEED TO BLANKET-BOMB THE WHOLE AREA.
NOT JUST MORTARS THIS TIME, BUT HEAVY ARTILLERY.
BUT -- THE ARTILLERY BARRAGE WILL KILL YOU ALL!
THERE'S NOTHING ELSE WE CAN DO.
JUST GO.
CALL IN THAT BOMBARDMENT!
RODENT-CAMS CONTINUE TO RELAY REAL-TIME INFORMATION FROM BATTLE ZONE.
HUMAN STRATEGY AND TACTICS NOW ASSIMILATED.
ENERGY LEVELS ARE SUFFICIENT.
HUMANS CONTINUE TO FIGHT EVEN WHEN DEATH IS INEVITABLE.
DALEK FORCE SHIELDS ARE NOW OPERATING ON LOW POWER.

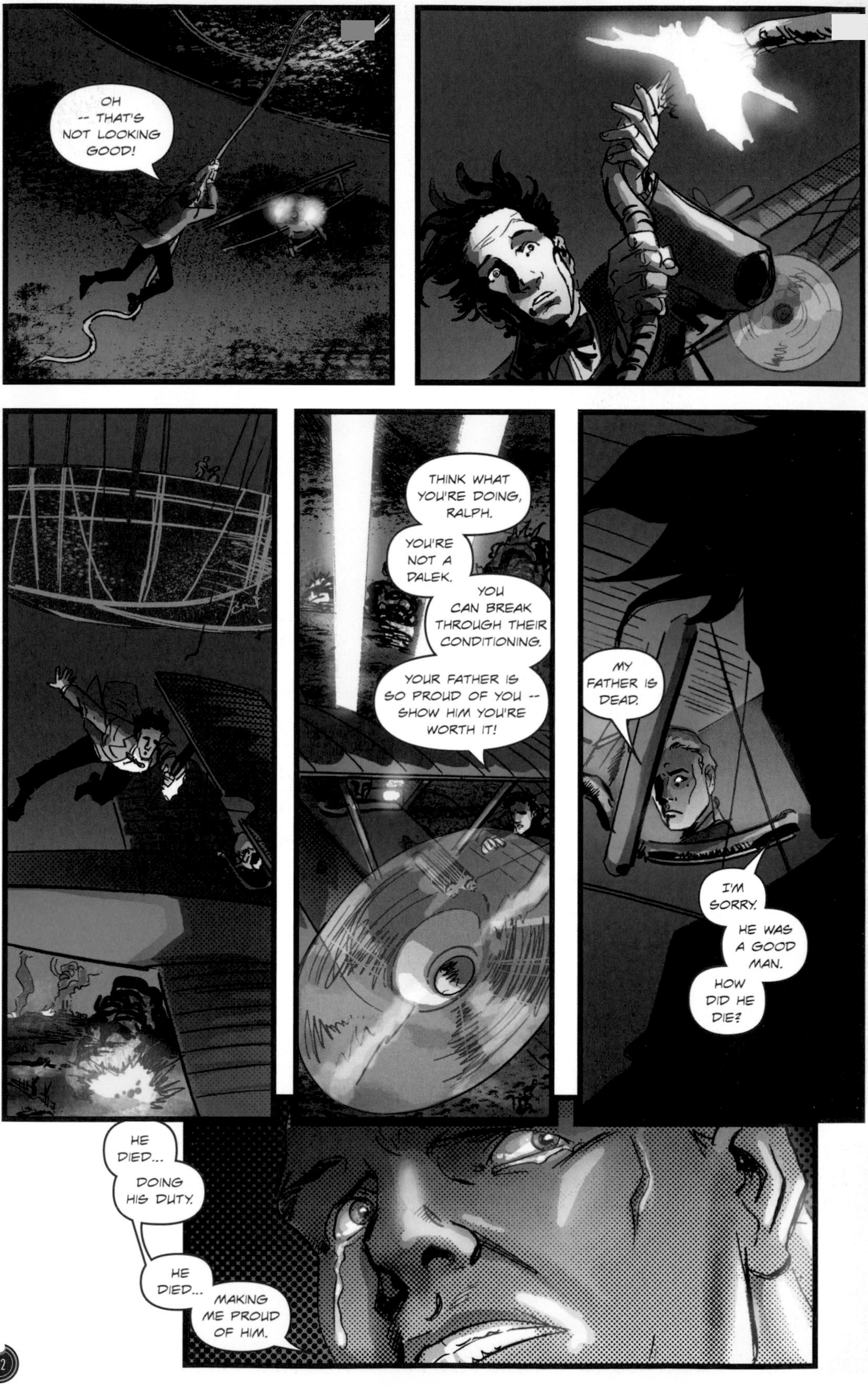
OH -- THAT'S NOT LOOKING GOOD!
THINK WHAT YOU'RE DOING, RALPH.
YOU'RE NOT A DALEK.
YOU CAN BREAK THROUGH THEIR CONDITIONING.
YOUR FATHER IS SO PROUD OF YOU -- SHOW HIM YOU'RE WORTH IT!
MY FATHER IS DEAD.
I'M SORRY.
HE WAS A GOOD MAN.
HOW DID HE DIE?
HE DIED...
DOING HIS DUTY.
HE DIED...
MAKING ME PROUD OF HIM.

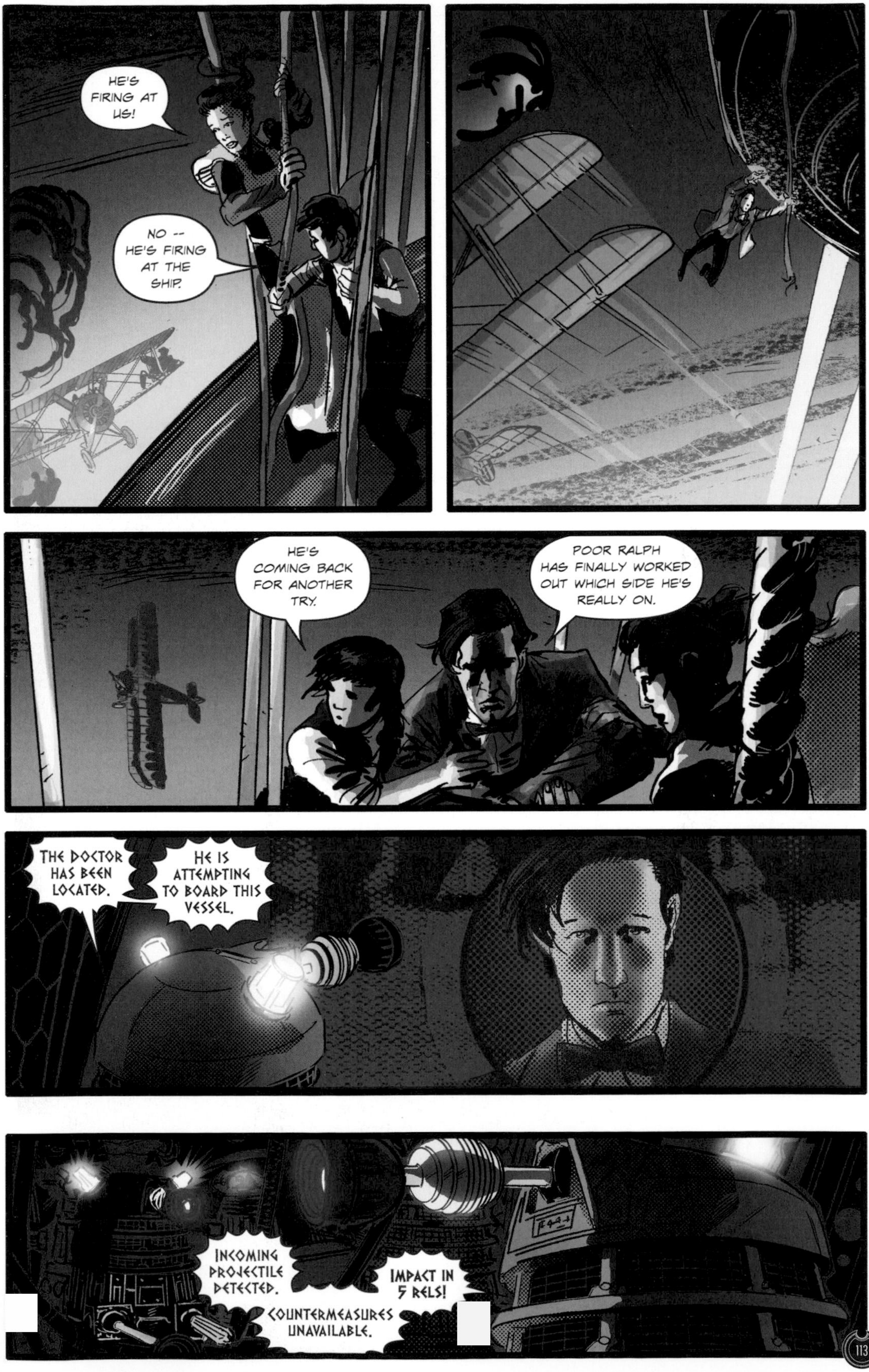
HE'S FIRING AT US!
NO -- HE'S FIRING AT THE SHIP.
HE'S COMING BACK FOR ANOTHER TRY.
POOR RALPH HAS FINALLY WORKED OUT WHICH SIDE HE'S REALLY ON.
THE DOCTOR HAS BEEN LOCATED.
HE IS ATTEMPTING TO BOARD THIS VESSEL.
INCOMING PROJECTILE DETECTED.
IMPACT IN 5 RELS!
COUNTERMEASURES UNAVAILABLE.

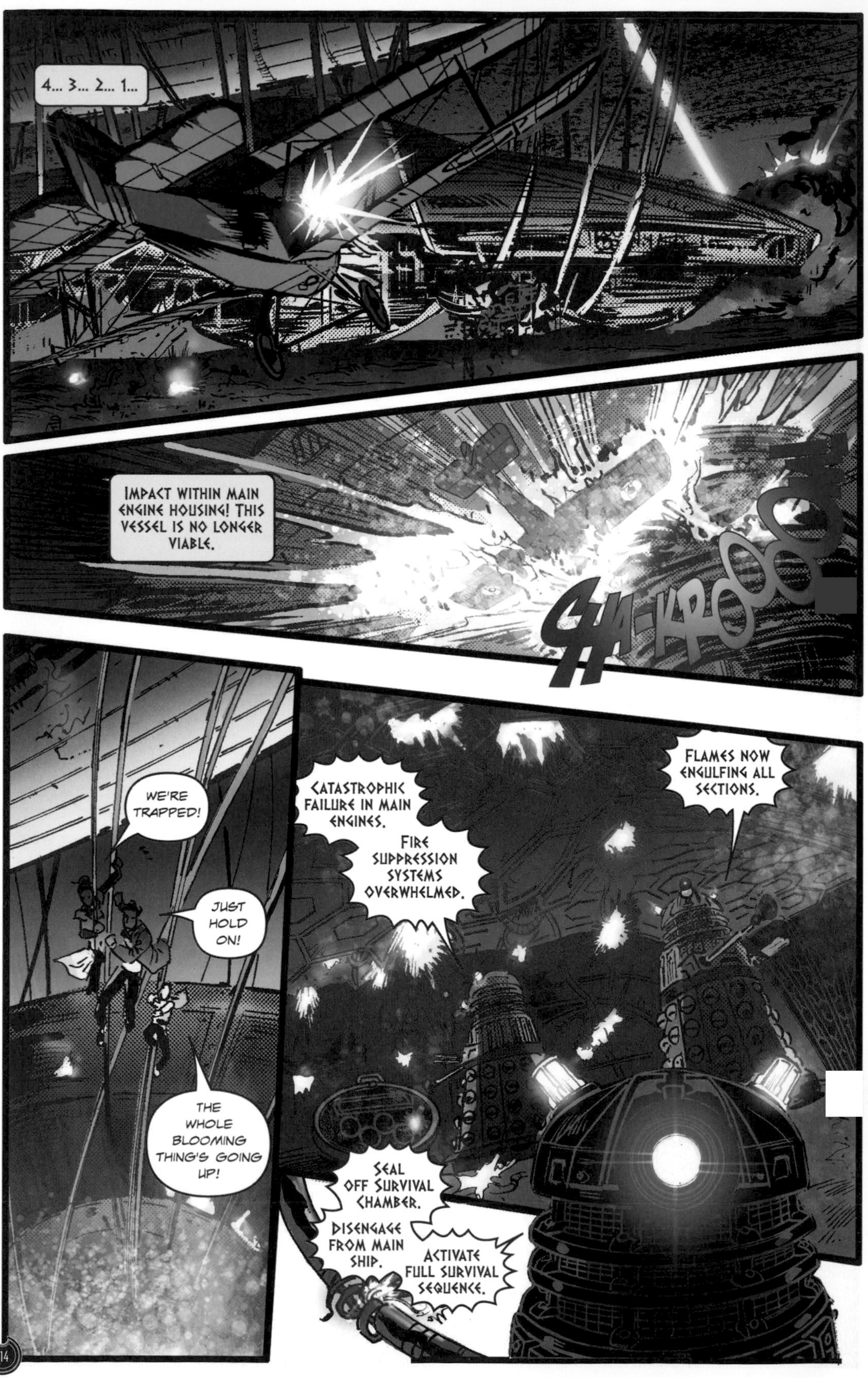

4... 3... 2... 1...
IMPACT WITHIN MAIN ENGINE HOUSING! THIS VESSEL IS NO LONGER VIABLE.
CHA-KROOOOM
WE'RE TRAPPED!
JUST HOLD ON!
THE WHOLE BLOOMING THING'S GOING UP!
CATASTROPHIC FAILURE IN MAIN ENGINES.
FIRE SUPPRESSION SYSTEMS OVERWHELMED.
FLAMES NOW ENGULFING ALL SECTIONS.
SEAL OFF SURVIVAL CHAMBER.
DISENGAGE FROM MAIN SHIP.
ACTIVATE FULL SURVIVAL SEQUENCE.

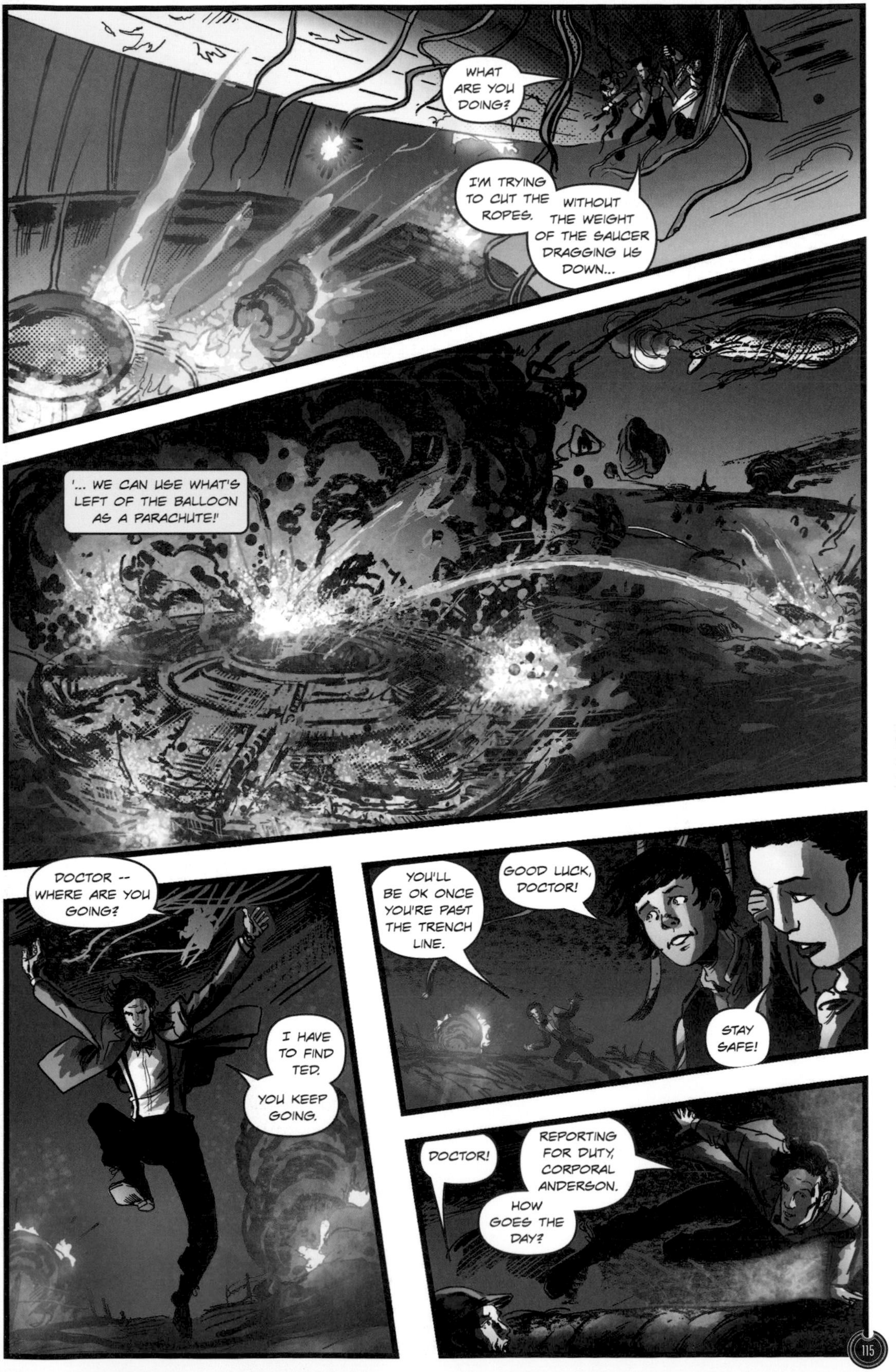
WHAT ARE YOU DOING?
I'M TRYING TO CUT THE ROPES.
WITHOUT THE WEIGHT OF THE SAUCER DRAGGING US DOWN...
'... WE CAN USE WHAT'S LEFT OF THE BALLOON AS A PARACHUTE!'
DOCTOR -- WHERE ARE YOU GOING?
I HAVE TO FIND TED.
YOU KEEP GOING.
YOU'LL BE OK ONCE YOU'RE PAST THE TRENCH LINE.
GOOD LUCK, DOCTOR!
STAY SAFE!
DOCTOR!
REPORTING FOR DUTY, CORPORAL ANDERSON.
HOW GOES THE DAY?

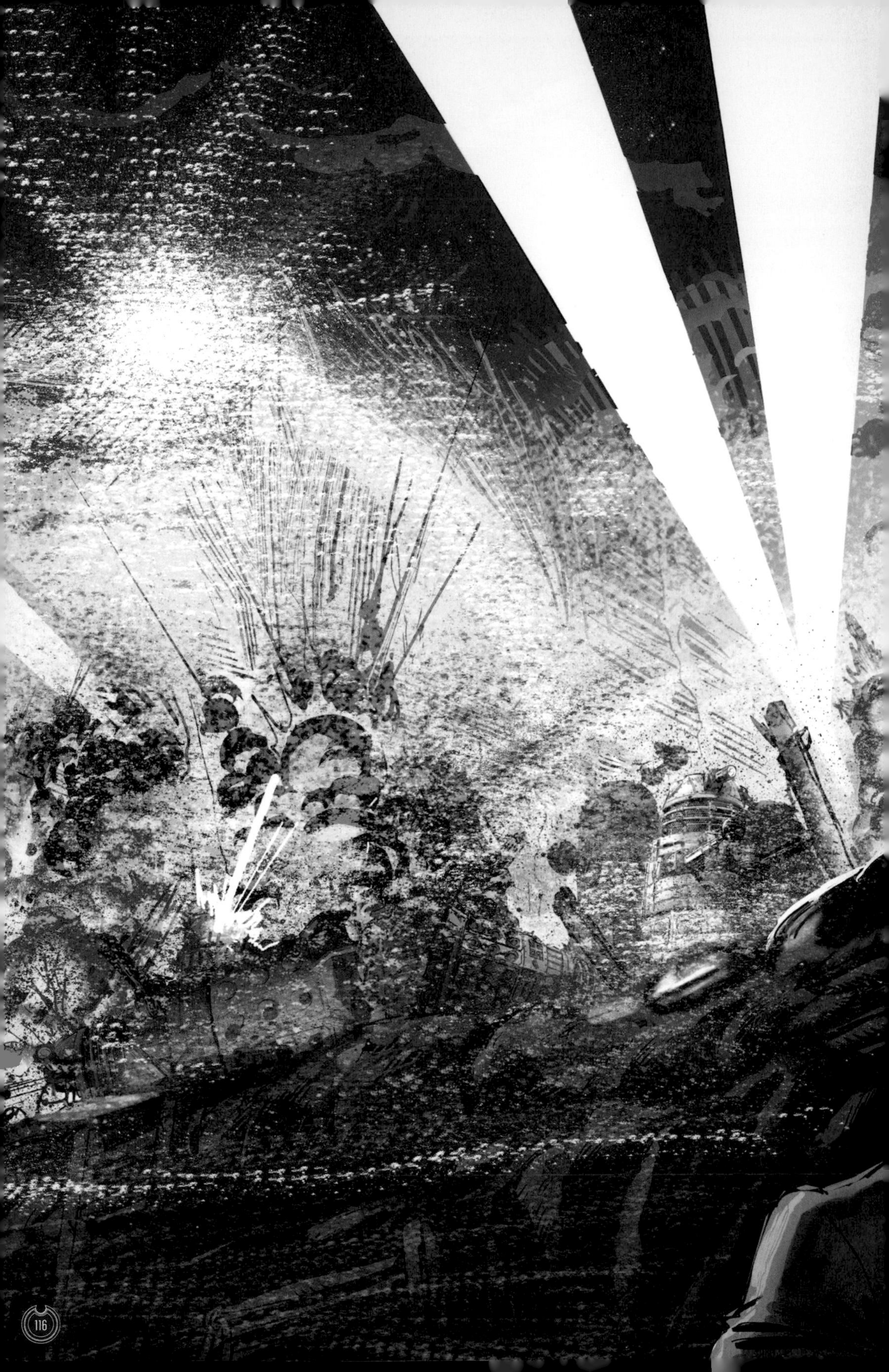

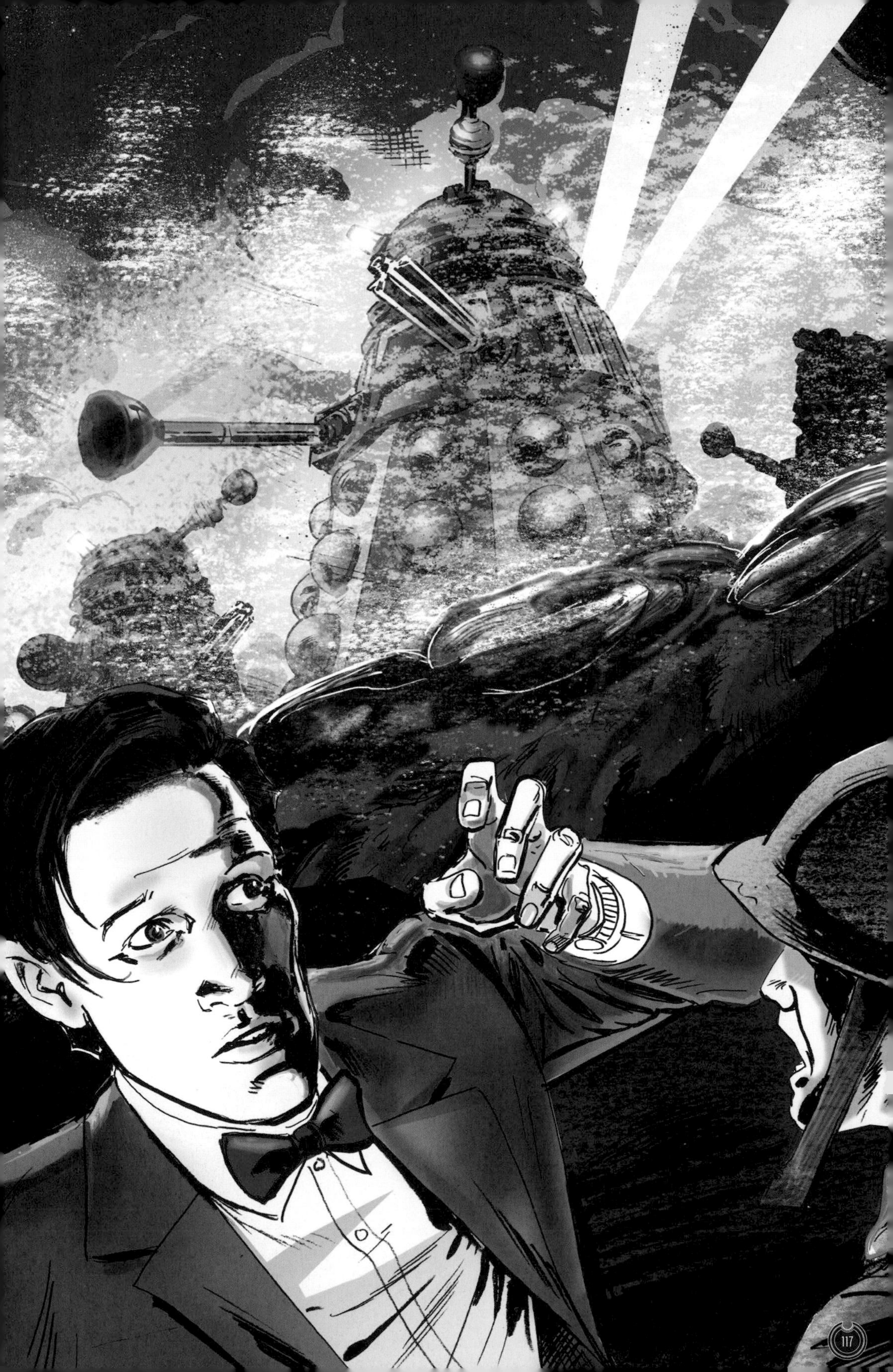

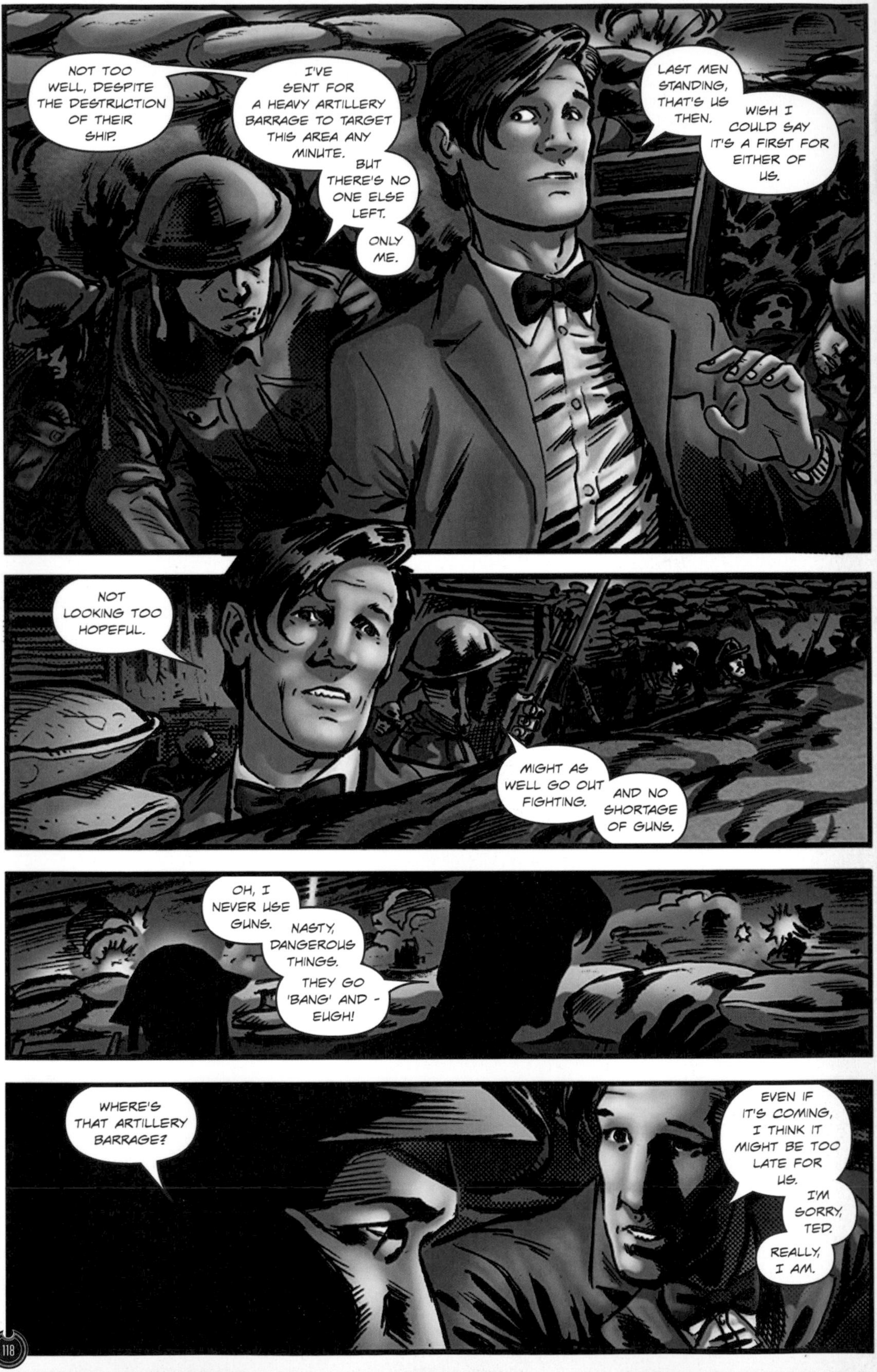
NOT TOO WELL, DESPITE THE DESTRUCTION OF THEIR SHIP.
I'VE SENT FOR A HEAVY ARTILLERY BARRAGE TO TARGET THIS AREA ANY MINUTE.
BUT THERE'S NO ONE ELSE LEFT.
ONLY ME.
LAST MEN STANDING, THAT'S US THEN.
WISH I COULD SAY IT'S A FIRST FOR EITHER OF US.
NOT LOOKING TOO HOPEFUL.
MIGHT AS WELL GO OUT FIGHTING.
AND NO SHORTAGE OF GUNS.
OH, I NEVER USE GUNS.
NASTY, DANGEROUS THINGS.
THEY GO 'BANG' AND - EUGH!
WHERE'S THAT ARTILLERY BARRAGE?
EVEN IF IT'S COMING, I THINK IT MIGHT BE TOO LATE FOR US.
I'M SORRY, TED.
REALLY, I AM.

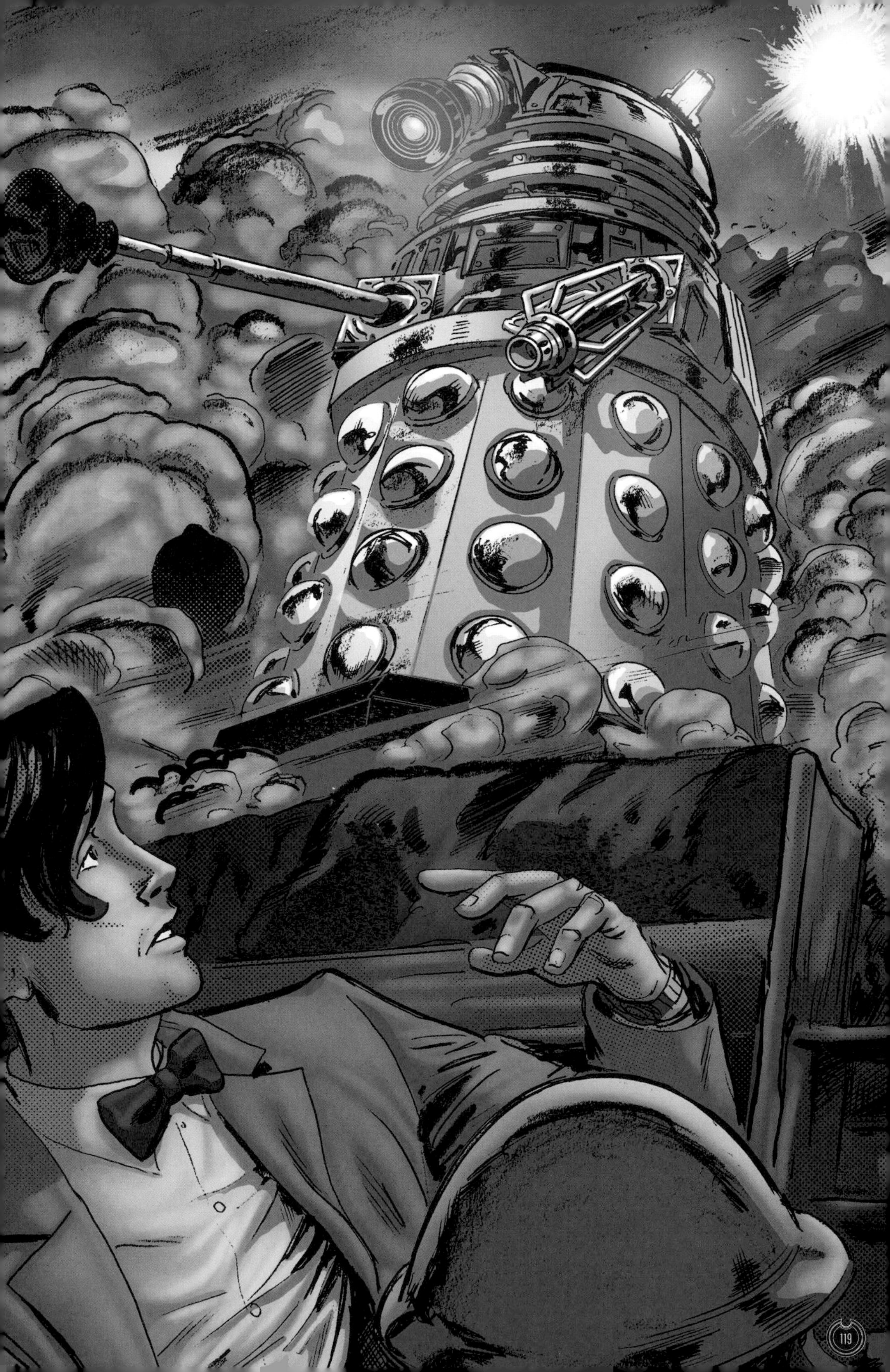

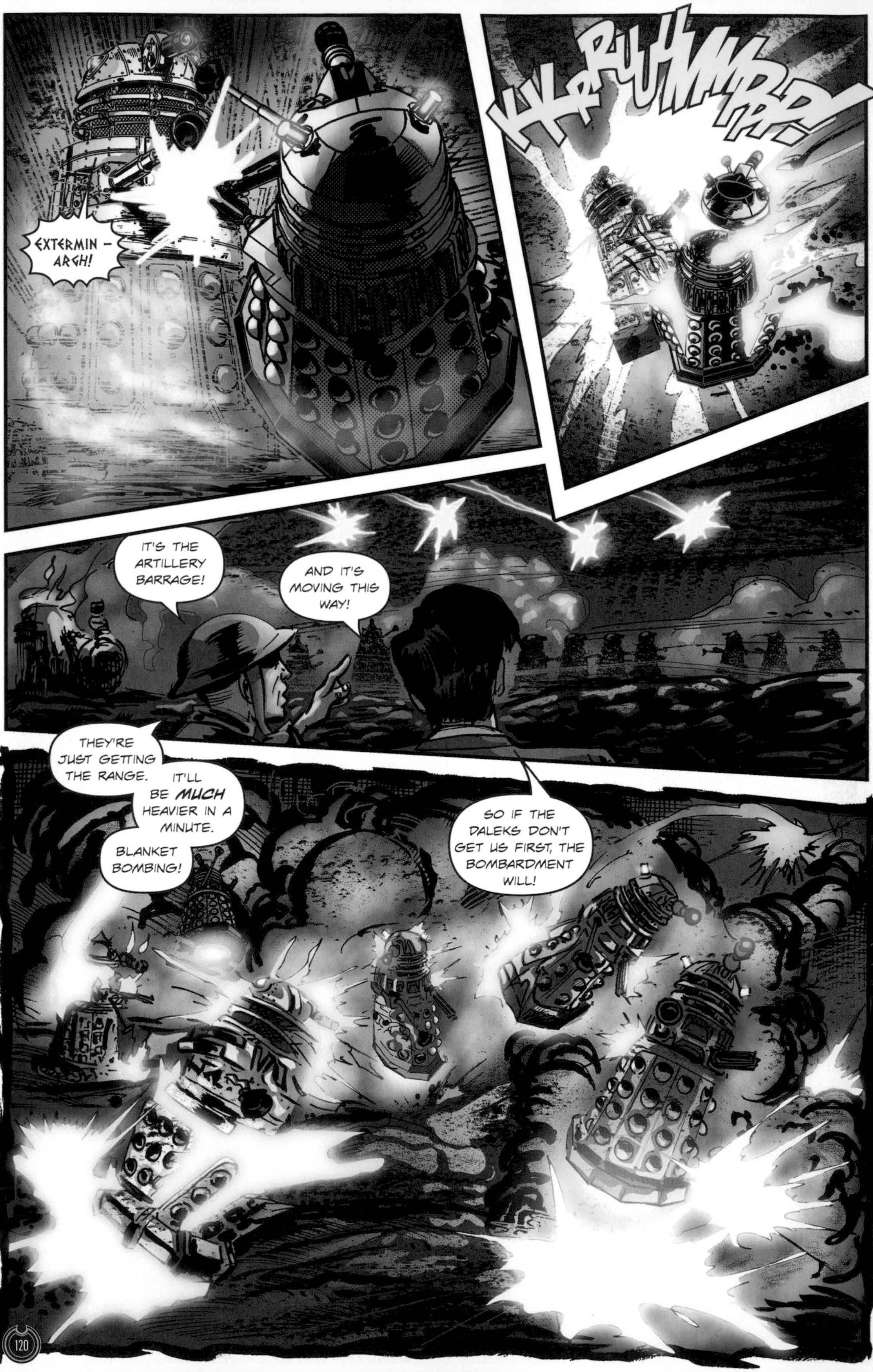
EXTERMIN - ARGH!
KKRUHMMBRP!
IT'S THE ARTILLERY BARRAGE!
AND IT'S MOVING THIS WAY!
THEY'RE JUST GETTING THE RANGE.
IT'LL BE *MUCH* HEAVIER IN A MINUTE.
BLANKET BOMBING!
SO IF THE DALEKS DON'T GET US FIRST, THE BOMBARDMENT WILL!

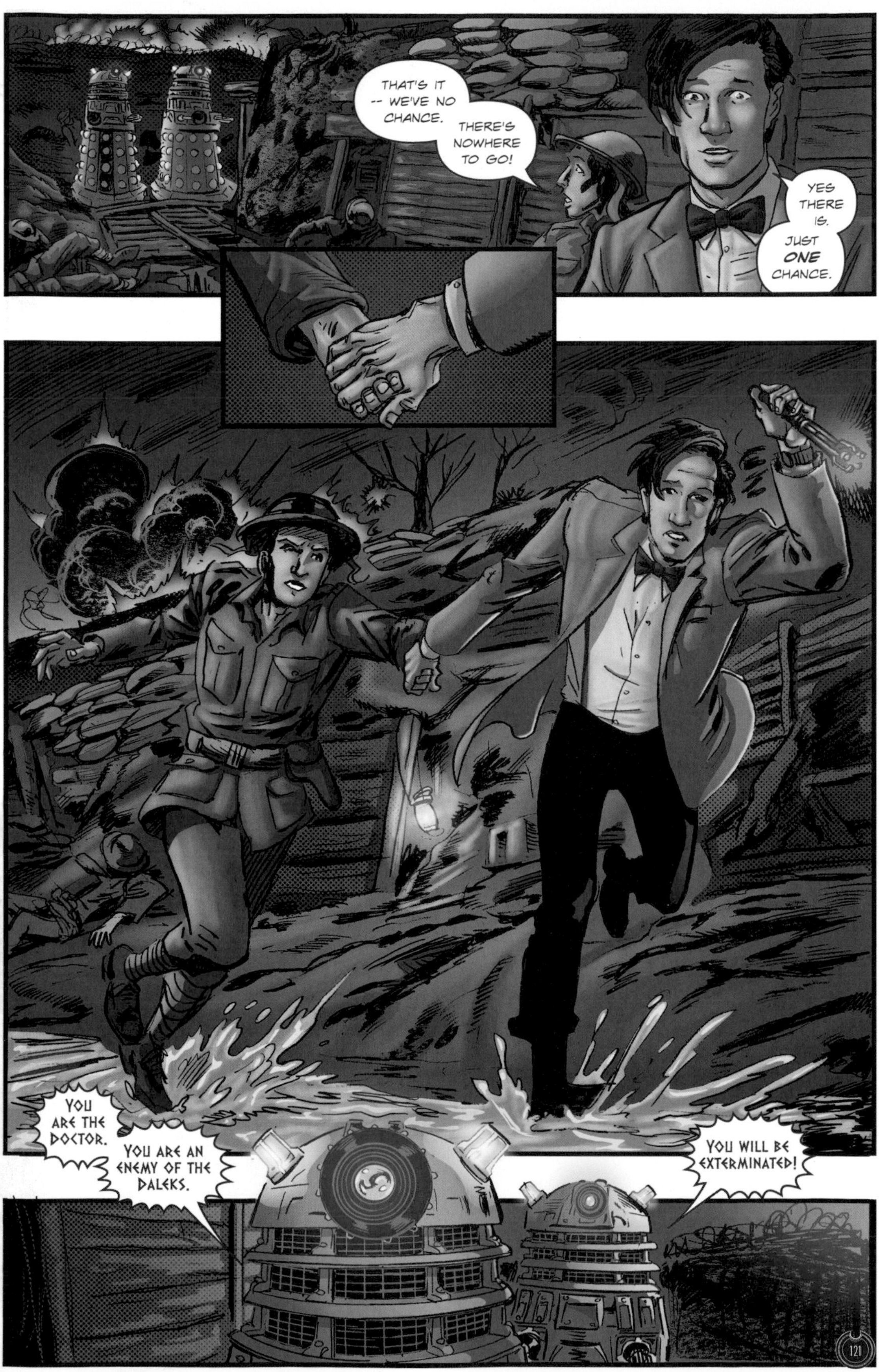
THAT'S IT -- WE'VE NO CHANCE.
THERE'S NOWHERE TO GO!
YES THERE IS. JUST ONE CHANCE.
YOU ARE THE DOCTOR.
YOU ARE AN ENEMY OF THE DALEKS.
YOU WILL BE EXTERMINATED!

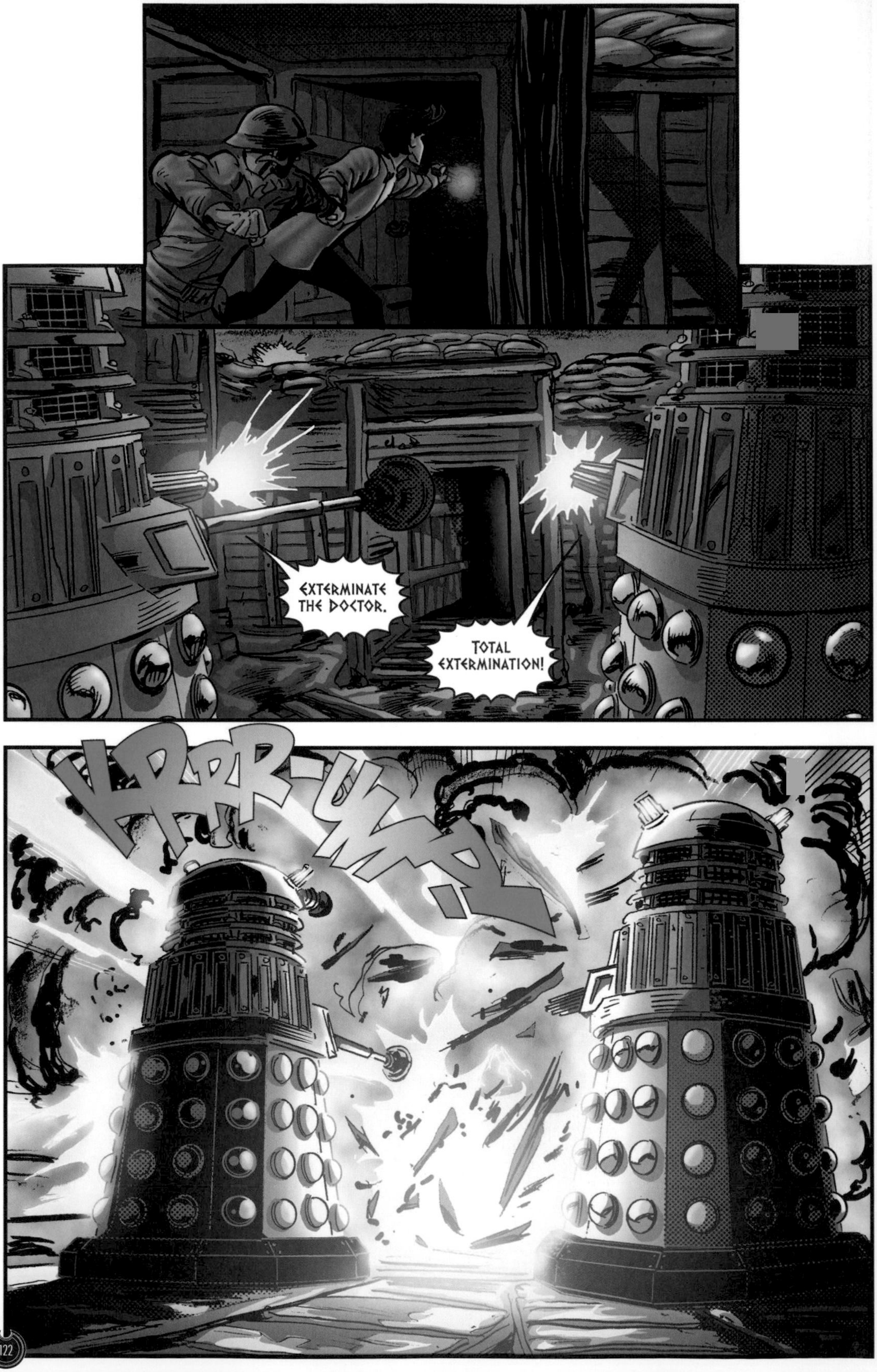
EXTERMINATE THE DOCTOR.
TOTAL EXTERMINATION!
KRR-UMP

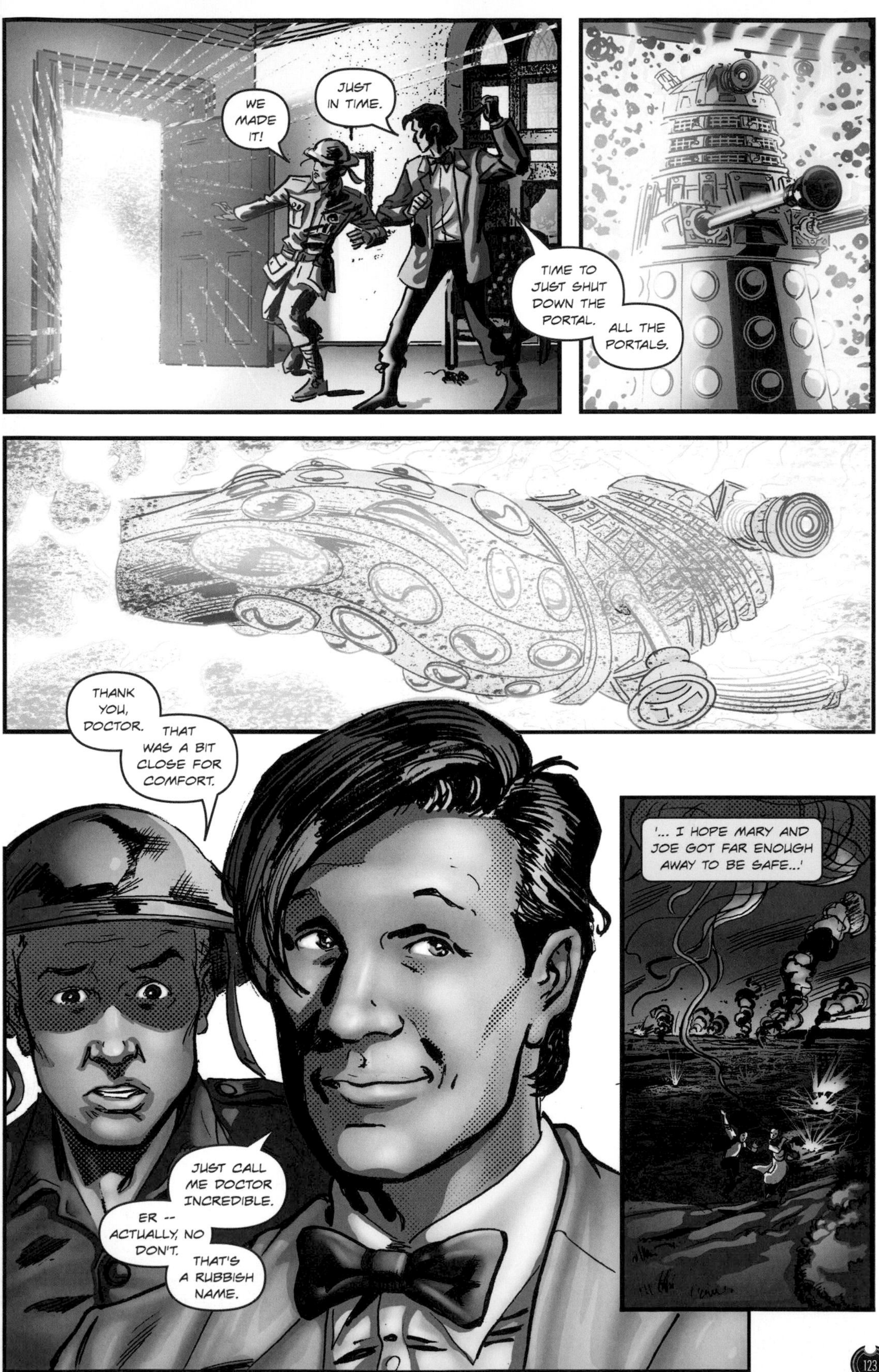
WE MADE IT!
JUST IN TIME.
TIME TO JUST SHUT DOWN THE PORTAL.
ALL THE PORTALS.
THANK YOU, DOCTOR.
THAT WAS A BIT CLOSE FOR COMFORT.
JUST CALL ME DOCTOR INCREDIBLE.
ER -- ACTUALLY, NO DON'T.
THAT'S A RUBBISH NAME.
'... I HOPE MARY AND JOE GOT FAR ENOUGH AWAY TO BE SAFE...'

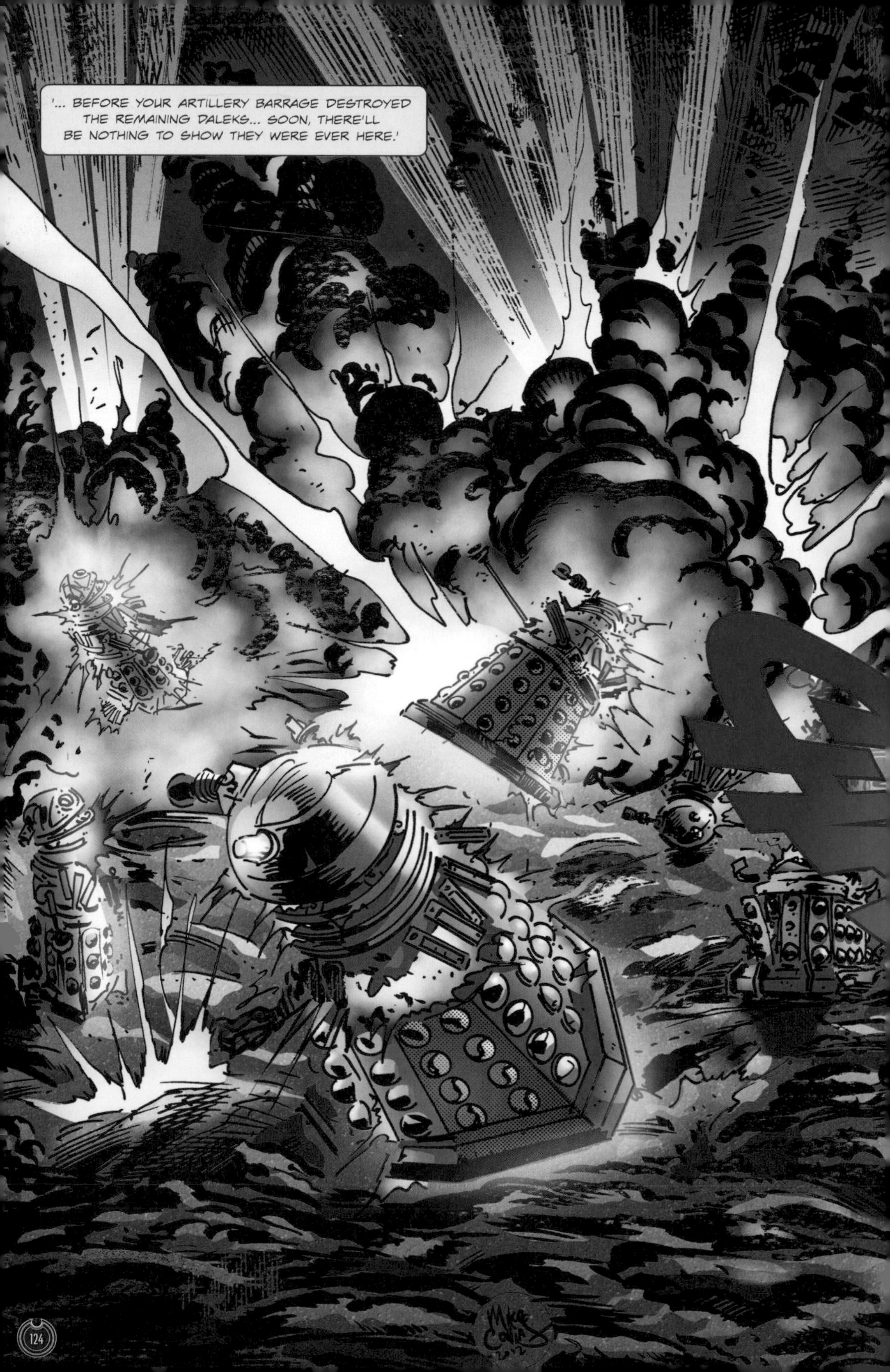
'... BEFORE YOUR ARTILLERY BARRAGE DESTROYED THE REMAINING DALEKS... SOON, THERE'LL BE NOTHING TO SHOW THEY WERE EVER HERE.'

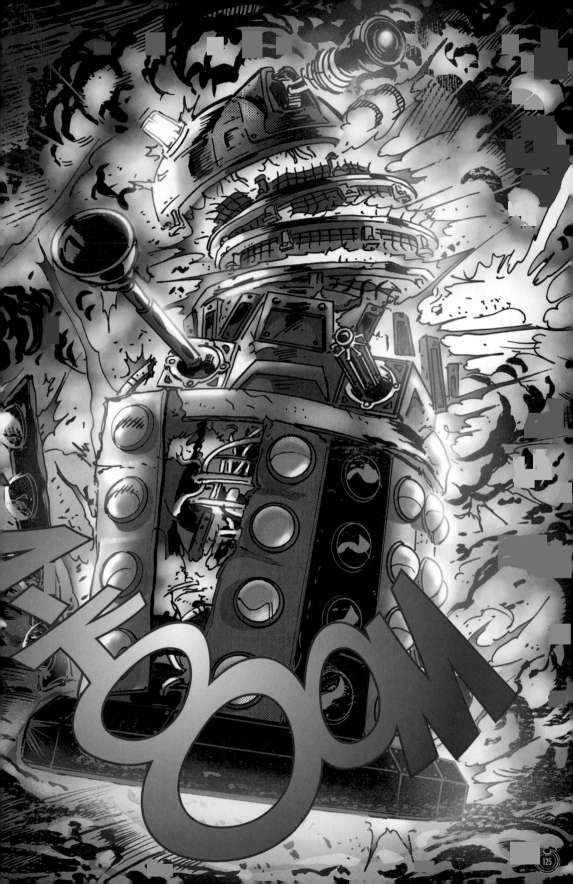

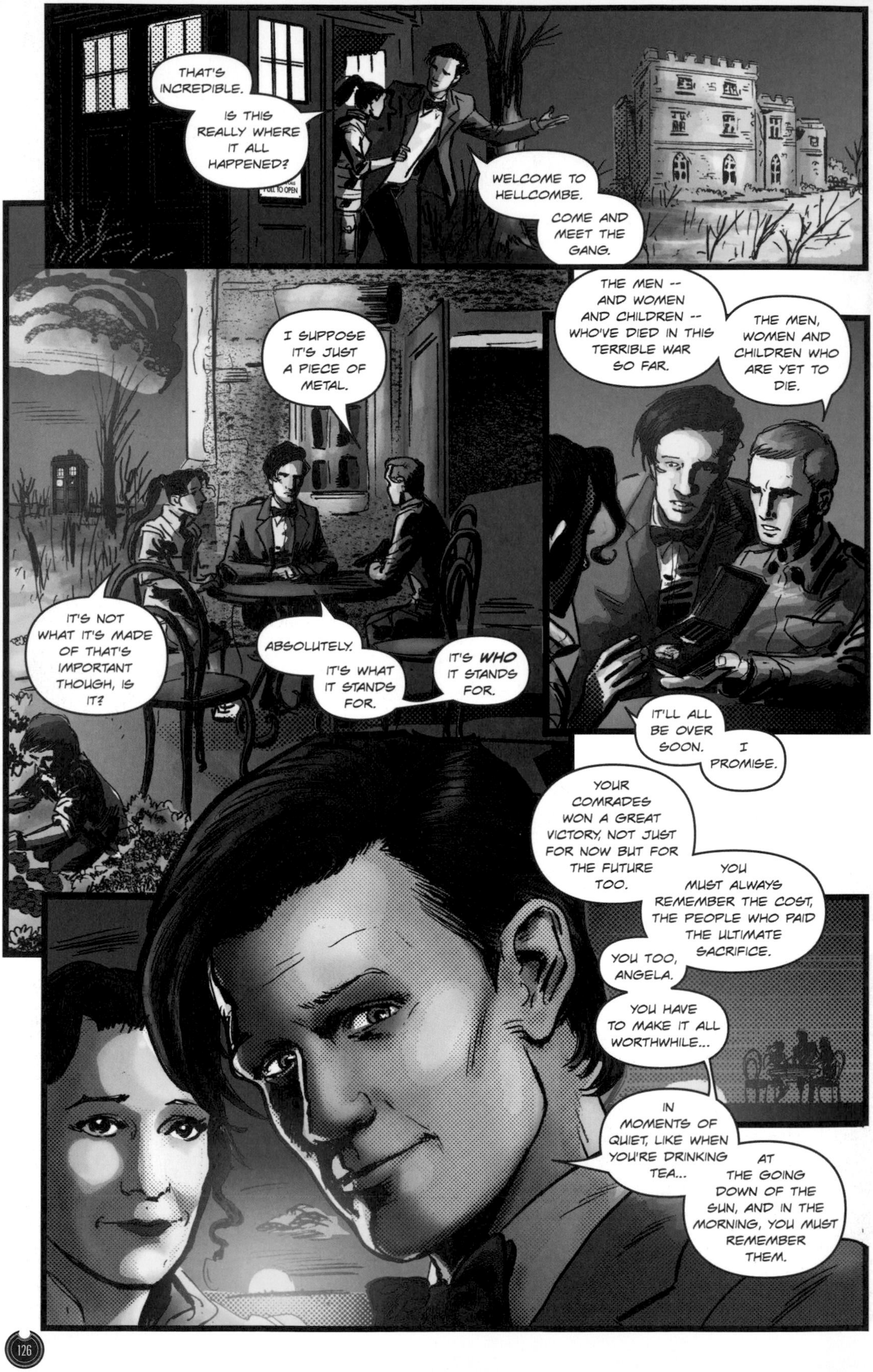
THAT'S INCREDIBLE.
IS THIS REALLY WHERE IT ALL HAPPENED?
WELCOME TO HELLCOMBE.
COME AND MEET THE GANG.
I SUPPOSE IT'S JUST A PIECE OF METAL.
IT'S NOT WHAT IT'S MADE OF THAT'S IMPORTANT THOUGH, IS IT?
ABSOLUTELY.
IT'S WHAT IT STANDS FOR.
IT'S ***WHO*** IT STANDS FOR.
THE MEN -- AND WOMEN AND CHILDREN -- WHO'VE DIED IN THIS TERRIBLE WAR SO FAR.
THE MEN, WOMEN AND CHILDREN WHO ARE YET TO DIE.
IT'LL ALL BE OVER SOON.
I PROMISE.
YOUR COMRADES WON A GREAT VICTORY, NOT JUST FOR NOW BUT FOR THE FUTURE TOO.
YOU MUST ALWAYS REMEMBER THE COST, THE PEOPLE WHO PAID THE ULTIMATE SACRIFICE.
YOU TOO, ANGELA.
YOU HAVE TO MAKE IT ALL WORTHWHILE...
IN MOMENTS OF QUIET, LIKE WHEN YOU'RE DRINKING TEA...
AT THE GOING DOWN OF THE SUN, AND IN THE MORNING, YOU MUST REMEMBER THEM.

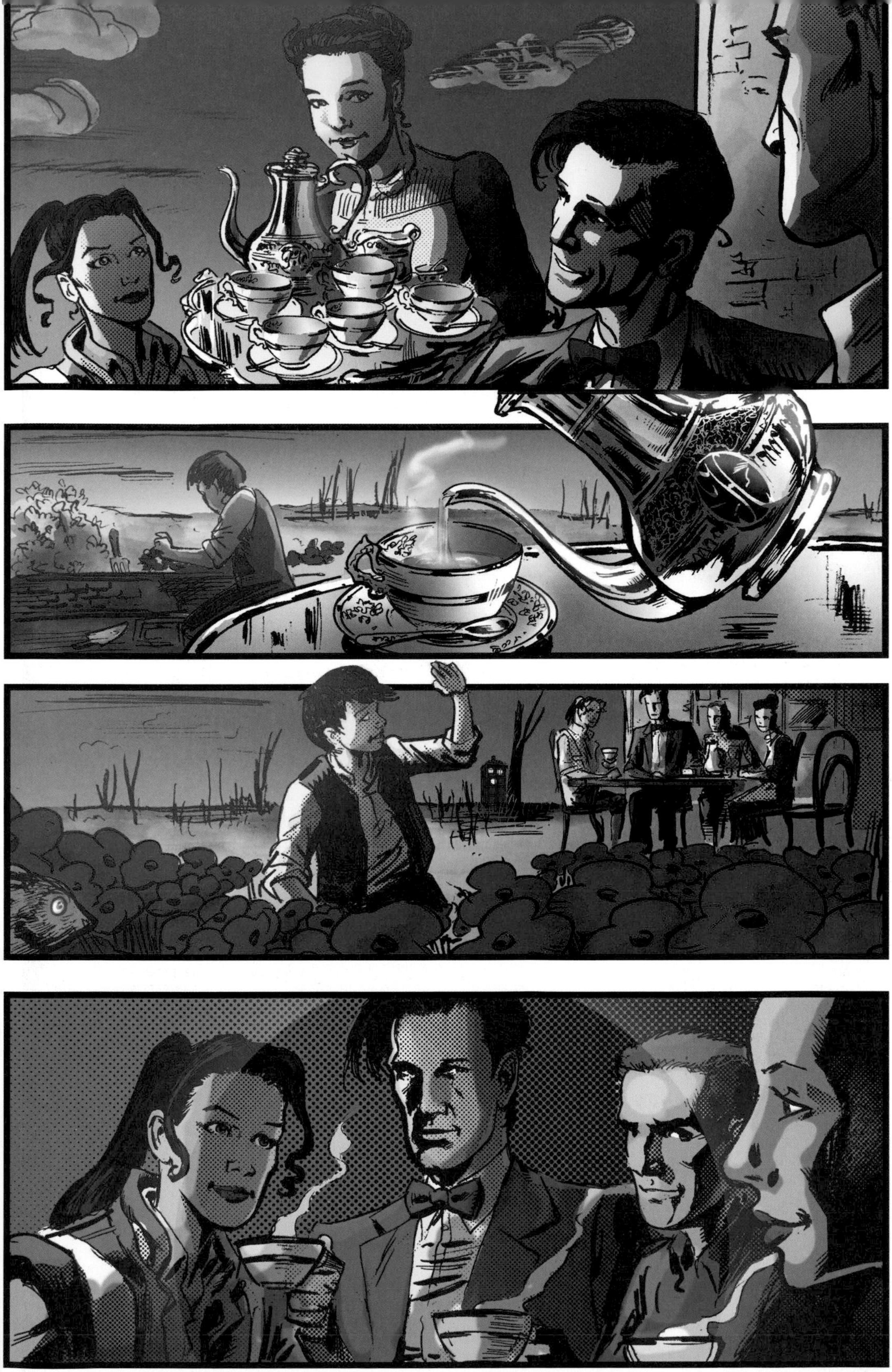

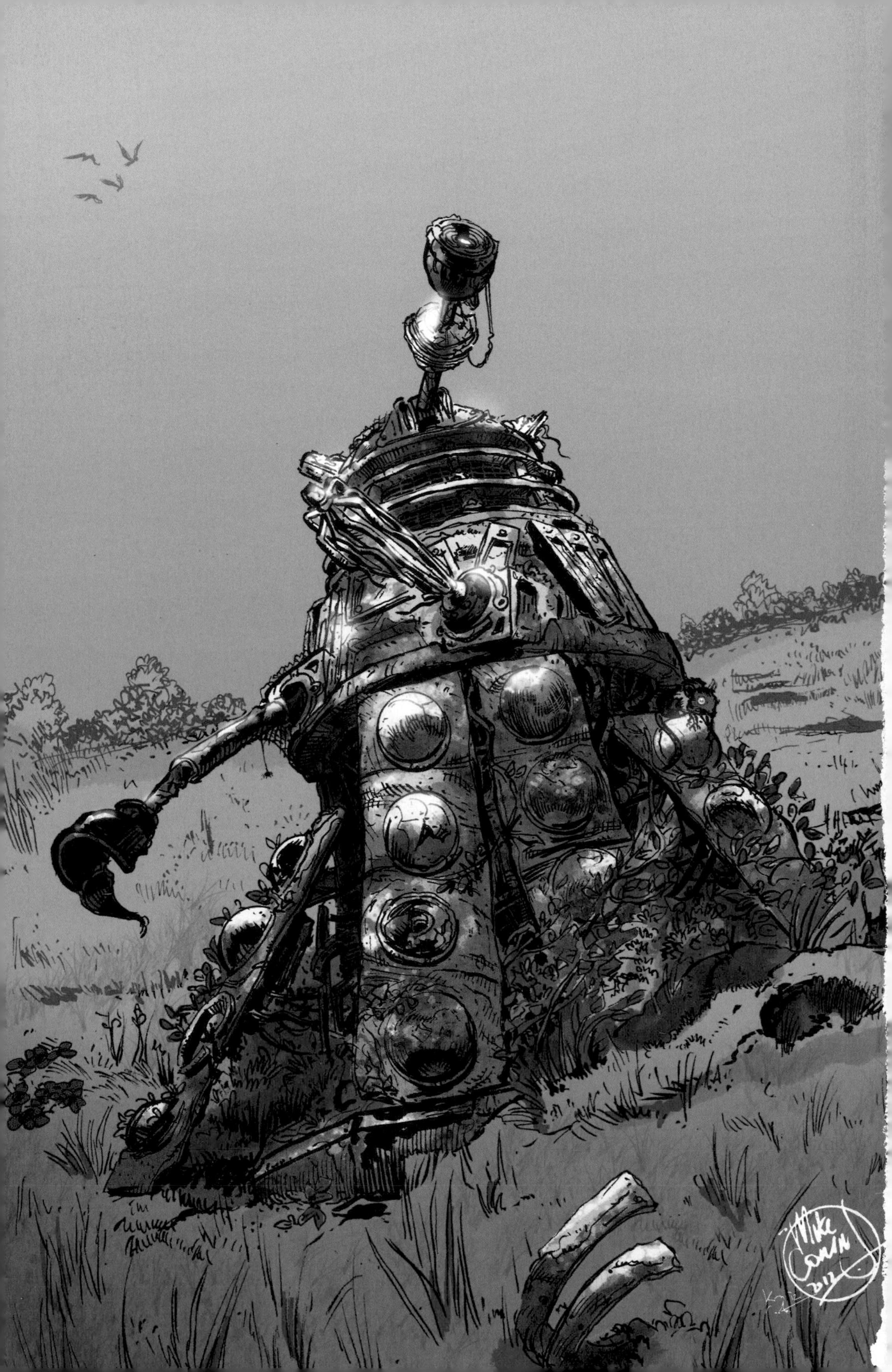